WITHDRAWN FROM FINGAL
COUNTY LIBRARY STOCK

BAD FOR GOOD

WITHDRAWN FROM FINGAL
COUNTY LIBRARY STOCK

'WITHDRAWN FROM FINGAL
COUNTY LIBRARY STOCK

a&b

BAD FOR GOOD

GRAHAM BARTLETT

Allison & Busby Limited
11 Wardour Mews
London W1F 8AN
allisonandbusby.com

First published in Great Britain by Allison & Busby in 2022.

Copyright © 2022 by GRAHAM BARTLETT, SOUTH DOWNS LEADERSHIP AND MANAGEMENT
SERVICES LTD.

The moral right of the author is hereby asserted in accordance with
the Copyright, Designs and Patents Act 1988.

All characters and events in this publication,
other than those clearly in the public domain,
are fictitious and any resemblance to actual persons,
living or dead, is purely coincidental.

All rights reserved. No part of this publication may be reproduced,
stored in a retrieval system, or transmitted, in any form or by
any means without the prior written permission of the publisher,
nor be otherwise circulated in any form of binding or cover
other than that in which it is published and without a similar
condition being imposed on the subsequent buyer.

A CIP catalogue record for this book is available from
the British Library.

First Edition

HB ISBN 978-0-7490-2842-8

TPB ISBN 978-0-7490-2847-3

Typeset in 11.5/16.5 pt Adobe Garamond Pro by
Allison & Busby Ltd

FSC
www.fsc.org
MIX
Paper from
responsible sources
FSC® C171272

Printed and bound by
CPI Group (UK) Ltd., Crowdon, CR0 4YY

For Julie, Conall, Niamh and Deaglan.
You make all my dreams come true xxx

I always tell authors that the story and characters must come first. With that in mind, this is a work of fiction, hence some structures, titles, locations, even some police procedures, have been modified to serve the story and the characters for your enjoyment.

Part One

1

8.30 a.m., Friday 27th April

As the steel baton shattered his right kneecap, Wayne Tanner wished he had broken his golden rule and driven away from trouble this time.

'What the fuck?' he cried, as he concertinaed into the dirt. Writhing and screaming in agony, he barely registered the second swing as it disintegrated his left shoulder.

He'd had ample opportunity to lose the black Audi tailing him out of Brighton city centre, but that was not in his nature. Now, trapped in the remote Ditchling Beacon car park and hemmed in by four truncheon-wielding thugs, there was no way out.

His reluctant yet desperate attempts to clamber away only resulted in his flaccid leg shooting fiery pains through him with every drag. He'd only managed a couple of yards before another flurry of strikes rained down, crippling his other knee and left forearm.

'You're fucking killing me!' he yelled, as he heard his white van cough into life. 'Whatever it is, you've got the wrong bloke.'

'Oh, I don't think so, Wayne,' came the reply from the impassive spectator who then raised his hand, which immediately stopped the beating.

Leabharlanna Fhine Gall

'Who the fuck are you?' Wayne cried.

'Friends of Susie's. Or rather, her dad.' Wayne detected a northern accent but couldn't place it.

'Reg?'

'See, we are on the same wavelength.'

'What are you on about and where's he going with that?' he shouted, as his van disappeared onto the Beacon Road.

'We'll take good care of your motor. Can't say the same for you though,' the man said as he pile-drove his boot on Wayne's shattered leg.

A flock of gulls screeched into flight.

'See, Reg never liked you. Couldn't see what Susie saw in you. So when you put her in hospital, well he wasn't best pleased.'

'But I got nicked for that. I'm on bail and I can't go near her again.'

'Yet even if it gets to court, you'll get a small fine and a smack on the wrist. Reg didn't think that was enough, so asked us to help.'

'But . . .' Tanner pleaded.

The man turned to the others, their batons at the ready. 'Get him in the car.'

Wayne's howls went unheeded as they dragged his crumpled body to the Audi. Pausing to plasticuff his wrists together, they shoved him into the back seat.

As the door slammed behind him, one of his attackers slid in the other side and shoved Wayne's head forward into his lap.

'Where are you taking me?' he groaned, as the car wheel-span out of the car park.

The man fiddled with the satnav, then turned and said, 'Let's just say, you'll soon wish you'd never met Susie Parker.'

2

8.00 a.m., Monday 30th April

Detective Superintendent Joanne Howe had worked harder than most to get where she was. Some kinder souls, unaware of her professional and personal struggles, described her as lucky. Her more vicious rivals attributed her holding the most coveted of detective jobs to positive discrimination.

Her status was the last thing on her mind though, as she scurried between her sleek new kitchen and the bomb site of a lounge where her boys – Ciaran, four, and Liam, three – were spooning Weetabix everywhere but in their mouths while glued to an eternal loop of *SpongeBob SquarePants* on Nickelodeon.

At forty, children and her dream job, the Head of Major Crime, had come late in life and now, as those two frenetic worlds collided, she wondered why on earth she had craved them for so long. Her husband, Darren, was her rock – when he was around. As an investigative journalist for the *Daily Journal,* his habit of zipping off to far-flung cities for days on end was beginning to grate; even if that was how they'd met. At least now that she was in charge, she could work her turn as the duty Senior Investigating Officer – SIO – around his absences. In theory.

The familiar chirp of her work mobile phone snapped her from her domestic chaos.

Eventually locating it nestled under the sheaf of Major Crime Unit performance reports she had been fretting over last night, she tapped 'accept'.

'Jo Howe, can I help you?'

'Morning ma'am, it's the duty inspector at Brighton here. Have you got a moment?'

Jo scurried into the lounge, grabbed the cereal bowls and mouthed, 'Brush your teeth,' to the boys.

'Yes, go ahead.'

'Are you duty SIO today?'

'No, but you've got me now, so what is it?' she replied, battling to keep the irritation out of her voice.

'Oh sorry, I was looking at the wrong on-call sheet. Well, if you're sure. We've had a misper reported. Bloke called Wayne Tanner. He's been missing since Friday morning. I wouldn't normally bother you, but he was last seen when we bailed him from custody for a domestic assault.'

'Woah. Rewind a second. Why are you worried about him? I'm taking it he had a bust-up with his partner?'

'Yes ma'am, he punched his girlfriend. It's just odd. There's no trace of his van, he's not turned up at his usual haunts, no trace of his phone and no activity on his bank. And he only had £3.50 when he was released from custody.'

'OK, I'll have a look at it, but raise it at your own DMM too. Give me an hour, as I have to wait for my childcare to arrive.'

She detected a faint sigh from the other end of the line. She bet the blokes never got that reaction. That was the police for you. If she said she was at the football and would come out at half-time, no one would bat an eyelid. Say, God forbid, that you have kids that need looking after, then the chauvinists got all sniffy. But she always made that point, as part of her crusade to chip away at the stigma that came with being a working mum in the police.

* * *

Monday mornings after his duty weekend sparked Phil Cooke's mischievous side.

Having spent most of his thirty-five years' service at Brighton and Hove Division, at every rank from PC to chief superintendent, he knew at first-hand the carnage his officers would have endured since Friday.

Age had been kind to him. The wrong side of fifty, but his passion for the weekly five-a-side football tournament and a job where meals were a rare luxury stemmed any middle-age spread. His sandy close-cropped hair was holding its own against the creeping grey that afflicted so many of his peers. Only his ruddy complexion hinted that life – or the drink – was taking its toll.

As the divisional commander, he bore a huge responsibility to the City's quarter of a million residents, eight million visitors and the ever-thinning blue line of around four hundred cops. In awe of the brave young men and women who faced violence and misery on a daily basis, he conceded that they worked considerably harder than he and his erstwhile colleagues ever had.

The changing face of policing over the years meant that out of office hours, the fort was held by the response teams and CID. They ran themselves ragged racing from call to call, scraping up the detritus that went hand in hand with a city that never slept.

Come Monday morning, everyone else played furious catch-up, struggling to get their heads around the chaos of the last sixty hours. No one wanted to be exposed at the Daily Management Meeting, or DMM, as lacking grip.

Having kept up to speed over the weekend, what Phil didn't already know wasn't worth knowing. So, exploiting the deferential police culture, he loved to breeze into offices, distracting and stressing his industrious juniors with inane small talk.

Ambling across the ramshackle open-plan Divisional Intelligence Unit – DIU – he nodded to the dozen or so bustling detectives and analysts as he beelined towards his old friend, DI Bob Heaton, who was beavering away in his glazed corner office. Bob's rumpled appearance, tatty red-and-white checked tie, already at half mast, and his creased and smudged striped shirt suggested, to those who didn't know him, that rather than having just arrived at work he'd spent the night traipsing through some gruesome crime scene.

'Morning Bob,' Phil chirped as he entered the poky room. 'How was your weekend?'

'Oh, hello sir. Yes, good thanks. Fairly Q here from what I can see,' replied a harassed Bob, observing the police superstition of never saying the word 'quiet' out loud.

'Really? Those chemist shop burglaries looked interesting. Still, save me the details until DMM.'

'Oh right. Yes, I, er, I haven't got to those yet.'

Phil took a seat, then inwardly smirked as he saw the DI crumble in the recognition he would never get the next ten – or maybe fifteen – minutes of his life back.

'Found yourself a new woman yet?' asked Phil, piling on the agony. They had been DSs together years ago and were a formidable team. Since Bob split from Janet ten years ago, his reclusive lifestyle bothered Phil.

'Ha! No, not yet. How's your lot?'

'Harry's being tipped for a professional contract at the Albion. Got all his footballing skills from me, you know,' he joked. 'Ruth's not so good though. That last lot of chemo completely wiped her out. She's tough but I'm not sure how much more she can take. They're even talking about hospices.'

'Kyle?'

'Oh, yes, he's OK. Still mucking about with his band or something.'

'That's good for the boys but I'm so sorry about Ruth, mate.'

'No worries, we'll get through. Look, I better let you get on. Don't forget about those chemist breaks, now will you?'

'As if,' replied Bob, spotting an unfamiliar sag in his boss's posture as he shuffled out of the door.

* * *

The 'Sussex by the Sea' ringtone blaring from Phil's phone drew flashes of irritation as he made his way out of the DIU.

The caller ID sent his mood plummeting to new depths. Every Monday morning his boss, ACC Stuart Acers, phoned each of the three divisional commanders on his drive to Sussex from his sprawling Surrey pad. Despite having a staff officer, he insisted on hearing any dramas direct from his chief superintendents.

'Morning Stuart,' said Phil, as he ambled up the stairs back to his own office, struggling to mask the contempt in his voice.

'Morning Phil. How's Brighton looking?'

'Fine thanks. Fairly Q weekend. Some chemist breaks that Bob Heaton is all over, the usual drug dealing on the estates, a couple of robberies and half a dozen mispers. One of them was in custody for domestic violence last week but I suspect he's just lying low.'

'Sorry, you broke up a bit there. Must have been driving through a dodgy area. Not as dodgy as your city though.'

Tosser, thought Phil. 'Do you want me to go through it again?'

'No. Don't forget, next week's Neighbourhood Policing Board is your last chance to come up with the twenty per cent efficiencies we need from your division before I find them for you.'

'Look, I've told you, you've already cut me to the bone. Most of my teams haven't had a complete set of rest days off for six months. Any more cuts and I might as well put up the "Closed" sign.'

'Sorry, you broke up again there. Anyway, good luck with those savings proposals.' The abrupt silence told Phil this was not up for debate.

'Knobhead,' Phil muttered as he reached the landing, oblivious to the red-faced young PC scurrying past.

*

No one dared call him Marcus nowadays.

Not even his despairing parents, who were now little more than his hoteliers on his rare trips back to London. Since he had 'gone country' to run the north Brighton drugs supply line, he had no further need for them.

Marco, as he insisted on being called now, found 'food' – heroin and crack cocaine – a cinch to shift. Since the London markets had been flooded, the supply almost exceeding demand, exploiting what others quaintly labelled county lines was child's play. The kingpins in the capital sent up-and-coming gang members to rural towns and cities to open new markets and create new addicts.

All Marco had to do was shift the drugs and return the spoils up the line. He strutted like he owned the patch, which spanned from Preston Park to the city's boundary close to Waterhall, but still he remained vigilant.

His only real fear was if the police confiscated his stash. There were no excuses for that. His debt to the bosses could run into thousands and the consequences of default were brutal. A machete up the arse would render him shitting in a colostomy bag for life.

Soon after being recruited at the relatively late age of fourteen, he quickly worked out who to kowtow to, and who he could crush. He took risks, plugging drugs into orifices that, until then, he presumed had only biological functions, but he instinctively knew when to be cautious. His nous quickly impressed his London-based masters and within two years Marco was assigned his own line.

Too many of his peers had failed and paid the ultimate price, so he knew not to let his guard down, and never to show weakness. His ruthless and public destruction of anyone who showed him even the slightest disrespect or moved to usurp his precarious position was well known; beef with Marco and you'd get the pick of mobility scooters.

Tonight, as usual, he was touring his manor, checking up on his minions. He was beyond handling the food himself – far too risky – but he needed to show who was boss.

He ripped about the streets on a black Mongoose BMX bike – his ped. What it lacked in prestige it more than made up for in dexterity, always outrunning and outsmarting any overly inquisitive cops. It was especially useful after dark, its colour and stealth melting him into the gloom.

He whipped around the corner on to Ladies Mile Parade, jack-knifing the back wheel to a halt, smiling when he saw his runners all present and correct.

'Hey Marco, what's happening?' said Junior, lurking in a charity shop doorway. Fifteen-year-old Junior's career had ground to a halt last Christmas after his sluggish bulk enabled a rival gang member to chase him down. The hospital managed to fix the two stab wounds to his leg, but Marco was less than pleased with the hassle of having to firebomb the other gang leader's grandmother's house to teach respect.

'S'good Junior. How's t'ings?'

Junior flashed five fingers, indicating that he and the three younger hoodies, cowering two paces behind, had collected about £500.

'Not bad. Any calls for me?'

'Nah.'

Marco eyed an approaching, battered bottle-green Toyota Yaris. Sensing his apprehension Junior said, 'He's cool. A regular.'

Marco loathed being so close to a deal, but he knew to hide his unease from his lackeys. He watched intently from the shadows.

A flick of Junior's head sent the smallest of his three acolytes forward. The boy swaggered to the parked car and darted his hand in and out of the open passenger window. Marco nodded. He made a mental note to find out the boy's name. He'd seldom seen such a deft deal.

The Yaris sped away, business done.

'Oi! I know what you're up to,' came a sudden shout from the direction of Patcham High School opposite.

A figure, dressed in a green sweatshirt and blue joggers – clearly thrown on in a hurry – marched from the school across the road.

'I saw that. You just passed something into that car. I've called the police and they're on their way.'

Marco pulled his black-and-red bandana up to cover his nose and mouth, tightened the cords of his blue hood around his face and stepped out to confront the man.

'Eh, beat it Grandad,' he hissed.

'Says who? I've seen your sort before. You come here selling your muck, scaring decent people off the streets. I'm not having it.'

The caretaker was now squaring up to Marco, Junior standing at his boss's shoulder. The three younger boys had dissolved into a doorway.

Marco stepped forward.

'Fuck off back to your little wifey and leave the streets to the big boys.'

'I used to eat scum like you for breakfast,' he replied, puffing himself up to his full five foot seven inches.

Marco didn't want a fight, but people couldn't go round calling him scum; that was disrespectful. With the faintest flick of his neck, Marco's headbutt floored the caretaker.

'In there,' Marco told Junior, pointing to a jet-black alleyway between the shops. Each grabbed an arm and pulled the dazed man out of sight.

When Marco and Junior emerged, blood splattered across their fists and white Nike trainers, they spotted the three youngsters huddled in the doorway. 'Split,' Marco ordered, then tutted when he saw the fresh vomit dribbling down the smallest one's hoodie.

He knew none of them would sleep that night, but they had learnt a valuable lesson, and that made it sweet.

3

7.30 a.m., Tuesday 1st May

The following morning Phil traipsed, bleary-eyed, into Ruth's bedroom, mug of tea in hand, his uniform shirt scarred from the hasty ironing session.

He hated that they now slept apart but she had insisted, especially after chemo. Her nausea, together with the numbness and tingling in her hands and feet, guaranteed sleepless nights. Despite his protests, she insisted that if he was going to look after her and the city he loved, the last thing he needed was being kept awake by her tossing and turning.

'Morning love,' he whispered, careful not to jolt her from a rare but inevitably shallow sleep.

'Morning darling. Oh thanks, I'm parched,' she croaked, shuffling up the bed, her arm outstretched to take the tea.

'Here, let me,' Phil insisted as he rearranged the pillows before passing over the Brighton and Hove Albion FC mug. He perched on the side of the bed. 'Good night?'

'Terrible, since you asked. You?'

'Not too bad, considering. Is it tomorrow the Macmillan nurses are coming round?'

'No, it's . . . Oh God, pass me that bowl, quick.'

Phil grabbed the blue washing-up bowl that never left Ruth's side, holding it under her chin just in time to catch her dry retch. He had seen some awful things in his life, but watching the love of his life – her beautiful hair just wisps now – waste away in such pain was killing him.

When she stopped, he passed her a pink towel from the bedside table. She dabbed her mouth as he deftly wiped away his tears before she noticed.

'Sorry, oh I feel so rough. She's coming on Thursday afternoon I think.'

'OK, I'll take a few hours off.'

'No need. I'll be fine. The boys are around.'

'No, it's my place to be with you. You can't expect them to hear conversations like that.'

Their sons, Kyle and Harry, were the loves of their lives. Just eighteen months between them they arrived, after years of infertility, like London buses. Despite being chalk and cheese – Kyle, the eldest at twenty, a musician, Harry a gifted footballer – they were good mates. Since Ruth fell ill, they were great around the house but had their own lives to lead. Phil vowed to become as involved with Kyle's music as he was Harry's football. Ruth had ribbed him about living his failed soccer dreams through his younger son, once even using the 'f' word – favouritism.

He couldn't believe he'd once nearly thrown it all away.

'Hadn't you better get going? I'll get the lads to help me up.'

'Blimey,' he said, checking his watch, 'I better had, but I'm taking Thursday afternoon off, no arguments.'

'If you say so,' she muttered as he pecked her on the cheek.

'Love you.'

'Love you, too,' she said as he shuffled out of the door, choking back more tears.

*

Phil grabbed his chestnut-leather shoulder bag from beneath the stack of jackets on the newel post. This modish accessory was last year's Father's

Day present from the boys, determined to drag him into the twenty-first century. Apparently, his battered black attaché case no longer cut it.

Picking up his work and personal mobiles from the radiator shelf by the front door, he shouted a general 'bye' back into the house, releasing the three security locks.

As he trudged down the path towards his car, he vowed – not for the first time – that on his next day off, he really would tackle the garden.

The bleep from his key fob flashed the lights on the police-issued white Ford Mondeo parked just outside the front gate. He slung in his bag and settled in the front seat.

As he slammed the car door, his work mobile chirped.

'No rest for the wicked,' he muttered to himself glancing at the screen. 'Jesus,' he exclaimed.

'Have you heard what happened last night?' bellowed ACC Acers.

Fuck you, mouthed Phil.

'Stuart, I've just got into my car, so feel free to enlighten me.'

'I've had Penny Raw, the City Council Chief Executive, on the phone . . .'

'I do know who Penny is,' interrupted Phil.

'She is livid. The caretaker of one of their schools was beaten up last night.'

'I'm very sorry to hear that.'

'So you should be. He called the police reporting drug dealers opposite his house. When he got fed up waiting, he went out to confront them. He's in intensive care for his troubles. Massive internal injuries and he's in an induced coma. What's going on, Phil?'

'I just told you, this is the first I knew of it.'

'I mean with your city, you idiot . . .'

'Now look here . . .' Phil just managed to bite his tongue.

'No, you look. I have had enough of fielding complaints about your inability to provide the most basic service. Get a grip. I want an update by ten o'clock,' he demanded, then the phone went dead.

'Twat,' shouted Phil at the inert phone. It wasn't the poor caretaker Acers was worried about, it was how it looked for him and his career prospects. To Phil, the ACC had already been promoted three ranks above his level of competence.

Reluctantly, he scrolled through his contacts to find the number of his deputy, Superintendent Gary Hedges. He hit 'call' before starting the engine, letting the hands-free kick in, as he squeezed the car on to the carriageway.

Gary answered within two rings.

'Afternoon, old fella. Nice lie-in?' joked Gary in his South Wales lilt.

'Piss off. Some of us have actual lives to lead. Look, Acers has been chewing my ear about some caretaker getting a beating last night. Do you know anything about it?'

'I'm already on it mate. Frank Whitehead, caretaker of Patcham High School. He's in a coma in intensive care. His missus says he went to have it out with some druggies outside their house.'

'Not Marco's lot again?'

'Dunno. Anyway, when he didn't come back, she went out and found him sparko in an alleyway.'

'Holy shit.'

'Yeah, she's distraught but won't leave his bedside. House to house, as ever, revealed fuck all so once again we're at a loss.'

'That's the third one in as many weeks.'

'Fourth.'

'Acers said the victim tried to call us before going out there.'

'Yeah but the control room told him it would be at least two hours before anyone would get to him.'

'Two hours?' asked Phil as he darted across Preston Drove to head along the east side of Preston Park. 'How many did we have on last night?'

'Eight.'

'What, eight cars?'

'No, eight officers – across the whole city. By then all but two were tied up in custody.'

'Jesus,' Phil replied, exasperated. 'So I take it CID are picking this up?'

'In your dreams. If we gave every assault to CID they'd sink.'

'This isn't a black eye after some handbags in the pub, Gary. Sounds like he's touch-and-go. If it is Marco's gang, I want them nicked and soon.'

'You're sounding like Acers now. I'll do what I can but we've got twelve missing people, fourteen overnight burglaries, two rapes, an armed robbery and a couple of protests to deal with.'

'Another day in paradise,' Phil sighed. 'Has that Tanner bloke turned up yet?'

'What, the all-action hero who beat up his girlfriend? No. Jo Howe's had a look at it, as he was in custody before, but she's pinged it back to us. I suspect he'll crawl out from whatever stone he is under when he's ready.'

Phil's heart quickened on hearing Jo's name. 'I hope it crushes him first. Right, crack on Gary, I'll be with you in a bit. White, no sugar for when I get in if you don't mind!'

'Homemade cappuccino?' replied Gary, mimicking a phlegmy hawk from the back of his throat.

'You repulse me,' said Phil, killing the call, his melancholy swamping him again as his mind turned back to Ruth.

*

'Let me out you wankers! I need a doctor!' yelled Tanner as he writhed on the cold stone floor.

'Wind your neck in,' spat a voice next to him. 'This isn't the bloody Hilton.'

'Fuck you. I'm in agony here.'

'Yeah, yeah. Wait till you've been here as long as us. And we're the lucky ones.'

'If I don't see someone soon I'll be crippled for life. With all the shit and piss I'm wallowing in, I'll get fucking gangrene.'

The tiny cell in which he and four others were crammed was literally from the dark ages. It was not so much the lack of light – a crack in the roof threw an occasional blade of sunshine, when the rain wasn't streaming through. It was the stench, the bone-chilling damp, and the unrelenting cold and hunger that drove him crazy.

'It's not just you,' came a second voice from behind. Tanner could only imagine what his room-mates looked like. This one, he decided, was a pasty academic: thinning black hair, fingernails chewed to the quick. His tweed jacket probably reduced to rags.

'I'm the only one I give a shit about. Get me a fucking doctor!' he yelled at the door again.

'You'll need an undertaker if you don't wind your neck in,' came a third voice – gruff, clipped, brash. A military man? Tall, muscular, ramrod no doubt. Tanner made it his business to avoid the sergeant-major – well, as much as you could in a six-by-eight-foot cubicle with one stone bench and a single shit-bucket in the corner.

He shuffled away to the lichen-encrusted wall, his chest heaving with despair.

*

It was six months since Helen Ricks had scooped promotion to chief constable and she was growing impatient with Sussex Police.

Her previous force, London's Metropolitan, had its share of bigots and cliques, but there was an embedded intransigence here. Outwardly she was warmly welcomed, but she'd yet to find anyone she could trust.

In her long experience, she knew it sometimes took a monolithic crisis to jolt the police into change. She had lived through the botched investigation into the racist murder of Stephen Lawrence in South London in 1993 and – somehow – avoided the spotlight during the enquiry into undercover policing.

If only they knew.

She just hoped it wouldn't take something like that for her new force to face the fact that the good times, if they ever existed, were over.

When she first arrived in the force, the contrast between the imposing exterior of the Grade I listed building which housed the diminishing Force Command Team and its utilitarian interior, made her chuckle. All fur coat and no knickers.

Sharing her anodyne, yet functional open-plan office with her deputy and the assistant chief constable, she guessed whoever defined these cosy working arrangements as efficient progress had never worked with Stuart Acers.

She kept her bleached MDF desk obsessively clear. It wasn't that she had no personal life, it was just best kept to herself.

This morning had not got off to a great start. Her boss, the police and crime commissioner, Teresa Sutton, had already balled her out over the epidemic of violence blighting Brighton and Hove, and now ACC Stuart Acers' booming West Country burr was resounding down the passageway.

'Just bloody sort it,' he bellowed, bursting into the office, mobile phone clamped to his ear.

'Morning Stuart.'

'Do you know, this job would be a piece of piss if it wasn't for the staff and the public. They make my life a bloody misery.'

'That is the job though,' said Helen.

'You've got to sort out Phil Cooke,' he said, as he hefted his tall-as-wide frame into the groaning swivel chair. 'He's past it. Can't we get rid of him? He refuses to find the cuts we need, and on top of that his troops don't even answer the bloody calls.'

Helen gave Stuart a wry look. He was too dim to spot the irony in his two bones of contention.

'You bleat about Philip day in and day out. I'm not moving him, not this close to his retirement. He's good for Brighton, the locals love him. Just take some responsibility, will you?'

'It's not bloody difficult. Why can't he just get a grip?'

'Stuart, if it's not "bloody difficult", you help him. Look, he's got a lot going on at the moment. His wife's dying of cancer. Cut him some slack for once and be part of the solution. Get alongside him and come up with another way to skin the cat. Use that creative streak you hide so well.'

*

Few people scared Crush, certainly not physically, but there was a coldness, a brutality, in his immediate boss that terrified him.

His imposing frame, tempered through his obsession with iron-man challenges, quivered – ever so slightly – as he rapped on Doug Robinson's office door.

The summons had left no room for doubt or discussion – he was in the shit and if he knew what was good for him, he would get his sorry arse over to Ocean House, nestled in the shadow of Brighton Railway Station, tout suite.

It could be any number of things that had riled the boss. Demands like this usually sprung from nowhere, so far as Crush could see. Robinson's explosive temper was legendary, often sparked by some minor irritation. He had once sent his secretary home in tears, bawling her out when she brought in his tea and bourbons, because she had forgotten he had given up chocolate biscuits for Lent.

'Come in,' the voice bellowed.

He did as he was told, and was relieved his boss was alone. No audience. It was not unheard of for him to call one of his minions over for a bollocking just so he could show off to a business partner or some prospective client.

Crush stepped over to the smoked-glass desk, from behind which Robinson glared, sweat glistening on his bald pate. Avoiding eye contact, Crush sat down in the black leather chair opposite. That was his one insubordination – whatever the balance of power, he was not going to stand like a naughty schoolboy.

'You wanted to see me, boss,' he said, his Tyneside brogue camouflaging his fear.

'Too right. I'm hearing that shit Tanner you grabbed on Friday put up a bit of a fight.'

'Nothing we couldn't handle.'

'I see,' Robinson replied, resting his chin on his steepled fingers. 'So, it was a standard snatch then. Just what the client asked for, yes?'

'Of course.'

'Then why has he got two broken legs, a broken arm and a shattered fucking shoulder?'

'What does that matter? He just needed softening up, that's all. You've never worried before.'

'Don't take me for an idiot,' yelled Robinson, his laser-blue eyes locked on to Crush's. 'This was a Premium Job, not some scally or paedo we swept up like garbage. The client paid a five-figure sum for a bespoke service. He was very specific, a grab, a mild roughing-up, a few nights in the dungeon, then dumped a couple of hundred miles away with some flesh wounds to remind him not to return.'

'I'm sorry boss, but no one told me that. I just thought it was the standard job.'

'Well it fucking wasn't,' bellowed Robinson, slamming his fist on the desk, his mug dancing in protest. 'When I told him what happened he started to bottle. Talked of going to the police, denying everything.'

'Do you want me to sort him out, boss?'

'God no. I'll deal with him.' He paused, took a deep breath, rubbed both his hands over his head then prodded a menacing finger towards Crush. 'If you ever ignore the brief again or fail to keep those gorillas under control, you're out and we don't pay severance.'

'Yes boss. Sorry.'

'Right.' Robinson moved on, much calmer now. 'I need you and a team in Brighton. A caretaker was beaten half to death by drug dealers in Patcham last night. He's not the first one to be left with tubes sticking out of him and booing relatives at his bedside either. Word is he called the Old Bill and when they didn't turn up, he decided to front them up himself.'

'Stupid twat.'

'Yeah, that's as may be, but we need to sort this lot out once and for all. Get down there and send them a message.'

'So, to be clear, is the old caretaker paying for this? If so, what does he want exactly?'

'No, this one has come from the Boss, so it's part of our community service. You're not necessarily looking for the geezer that beat the old man up, you're just going to send a shockwave through these pipsqueak gangs.'

Crush knew the mere mention of 'the Boss' curtailed any further discussion. He had never met this mythical puller of strings, but had been around long enough to know that the one-off grabs were a paid service: people let down by the police, forking out for their own justice. Orders for the more general snatches, beatings and vanishings came from on high. He presumed one funded the other and what the Boss wanted, the Boss got.

'Just a word of warning, guv. We are getting very short of space at the dungeon. Probably only room for about half a dozen more.'

'You need the lorry?'

'Yeah, tonight or tomorrow I'd say. If we can get rid of around ten that should do us for a week or so.'

'OK, I'll see what I can do. It'll be at least three days. That's if we can get the stoker down here today to get the furnaces up to temperature.'

'Thanks boss.'

'It might be best if Tanner's one of them. He's become a complication and the Boss hates complications.'

'Consider it done,' Crush replied, struggling to conceal his grin until he was well clear of the office.

4

6.10 p.m., Tuesday 1st May

Perhaps if Harry Cooke's head wasn't buzzing with his incredible news, he might have spotted the watcher as he skipped off the number 11 bus.

Perhaps if he had not been so engrossed bragging on Snapchat, he might have noticed him trailing his progress as he strutted across the swarming A23 towards Withdean Park, his shortcut home.

But his head was turning cartwheels as he made the call he was most excited about.

'Honest Dad, I reckon it was between three of us, but when the gaffer called me in, I couldn't believe it.'

'Harry, I'm so proud of you. You've worked so hard. God, I could cry,' said Phil.

'I hope you're on your own. Rough tough cops can't go around bawling you know,' he chuckled.

'It's hay fever,' Phil joked. 'Look, I've got to go but bloody well done. I'll get some beers on the way home.'

'I'm going out with the lads to celebrate. And commiserate with the ones who didn't make it.'

'Well don't be too cocky, will you?'

'*Moi?* As if! See you Dad.'

'Yep, see you and, hey, I love you.'

'Love you, too.'

Harry pictured his dad dashing across the corridor to gush to Superintendent Gary Hedges, who would take the piss, then offer his heartfelt congratulations.

As Harry felt the tree-lined park's soft turf cushion his feet, a lump came to his throat. It was on this very field, aged about three, that he had first dribbled a ball.

*

The watcher was only too aware that unless he kept up, it would be game over. However, fortune was smiling on him. Harry was so distracted that he'd been able to match his pace.

As Harry reached the enclosed Puppy Park, close to the woods, there were fifteen yards, twenty tops, between them. Half a dozen dog walkers were still ambling back to their cars over to the right, so pouncing here was out of the question. Witnesses were a risk and getting caught was not an option.

When they disappeared, the point of no return loomed.

Had he thought this through properly? Probably not, but he had no choice. He'd brought this on himself.

Harry disappeared into the shade of the copse. For the first time, the watcher broke into a jog. The thicket was heavy, but narrow; thirty yards and he would be back out in the open on to Woodland Way, where no doubt some Neighbourhood Watch busybody would be twitching their curtains.

It had to be now. Away from prying eyes.

Now or never.

The watcher's focus adjusted quickly to the gloom.

Harry was still gassing.

'Always in the bag,' he heard him brag.

Well, you are going to be in a very different bag soon, thought the watcher.

Harry said his goodbyes.

This was it.

Pulling the red-and-black bandana over his mouth and nose, he sprung forward. 'Oi,' he hissed.

Harry spun round.

'Oh hell . . . What the f—' Harry blurted, his gaping eyes fixed on the glint of steel, dodging back off the path to buy some distance.

'Shut it.' The watcher mirrored Harry's move.

He saw Harry was about to run, so he lunged. The blade shimmered as he thrust it forwards and up. The brief resistance offered by muscle soon gave way and the razor-sharp blade seared deep between Harry's ribs.

Feeling the hilt snag, the watcher yanked it clear.

Harry gasped and then, holding the gaping wound, he stumbled to the ground, dropping his phone. His eyes silently pleaded for help.

The watcher turned and bolted through the bushes, the branches snagging at his clothes. In his haste he tripped on a tree root, just catching himself before he fell.

He was certain no blood had spattered, but when the cops came anyone who'd seen him flee would remember the running man. He had to get away.

Lie low.

Perhaps for ever.

Perhaps in plain sight?

*

Harry prayed it was only a punch. A hell of a punch – a hammer blow even – but a punch nonetheless. Enough to stun, but nothing too serious.

Please God.

Crumpled among the nettles and brush, hearing the crack of branches and the fading thud of footsteps as the watcher fled, he prayed he was just winded. He was going to be OK.

He grabbed his chest. What was with the wheezing? Where was this stickiness coming from? The metallic smell? It took him back to that nasty clash of heads in the Youth Cup final.

Looking down in horror, he found his hands were dripping, the greenery around him drenched in deep crimson.

He felt faint.

Every breath sapped him.

In his haze, he became strangely irritated by the nettles stinging his neck. Frantically groping the ground, he grabbed the slimy plastic of his iPhone, struggling to grip it in his blood-soaked hand. Instinctively he opened the lock screen, barely discerning the white glow.

One 9. Yes, he could do this. His life, his career, everything hung on just two more numbers.

Two 9s. One more to go.

Oh God, he was really hurting now. Feeling so weak. So alone. Fog shrouding his every sense.

Just one more. Just one more . . .

*

The black Audi cruised to a halt outside Carden Park, the northern outpost of Marco's patch. Probably a customer or some busybody who'd soon get the message and piss off.

Junior swaggered up to the open car window, oozing arrogance.

Marco browsed his phone.

The piercing scream jolted him and he darted for a shadow. Had Junior been bottled? Better to watch – take it all in – than show out and put the whole crew in danger, he decided.

True horror hit him when Junior threw himself to the floor, gripping his reddening but unbroken face.

Acid.

Marco fixed on the unfolding scene; a safe – certainly not cowardly, no – distance away.

All four doors of the Audi flew open. From each sprung a black-clad bruiser, each balaclava'd up and wielding a retractable baton.

Under the orange sodium glow of the sparse street lights, the first made straight for the single gated entrance to the park, menacingly guarding the only remaining escape route.

As Junior battled to hold his melting flesh together, the other three dealers were scurrying round like ducklings separated from their mother.

Two were felled by precise knee strikes, collapsing them where they stood. Marco retched at the ear-splitting snap when metal shattered one of their forearms, offered up in hope of clemency.

The other boy quickly submitted. He and his less fortunate ally lay compliant, yet screaming, as the thugs wrenched their arms behind them and plasticuffed their wrists together. Marco was horrified as the automatic boot lid slowly raised and one of the boys was bundled in, the other manhandled into the back seat.

Marco shook in terror, forgetting his fourth dealer until he heard the desperate screams coming from his right.

He peered round a snuffed-out lamp post to glimpse the last of his gang pinned by the throat against an emerald-coloured 'Dogs to be kept on leads' sign. The hulk holding him produced a hunting knife from the back of his belt. The wails intensified.

He watched in horror as the man shoved the boy to the ground. As he hit the deck, the man dropped his full weight on him, knife thrust towards the boy's pleading face.

From this distance, Marco could just pick out the boy's petrified eyes, flicking between his attacker's own and the knife. Surely he was not about to plunge the blade into the boy's outstretched neck. No way would they leave a body out there in the street. Acid burns and broken bones could just about be explained away to an indifferent police force, but a body? Surely not.

The man deftly spun the lad onto his front, then flipped himself round, crushing the boy. Marco struggled to work out what was happening as the man shimmied down the pinioned body.

Clenching the boy's calf, stopping his writhing – a futile attempt to break free – the man twisted his head round, and hissed something inaudible.

He grabbed the boy's right ankle, stretched it a fraction, then sliced the razor-sharp blade across the taut Achilles tendon, severing it in one swipe. The whip-crack of the boy's other ankle being bisected wasn't quite drowned out by his screams.

The man sprung up and threw himself into the waiting Audi, which spun up Carden Avenue and away.

Marco knew he should get the hell out of there – after all, these boys could be replaced – but the begging cries from his two woefully wounded dealers tore at him. How could he abandon them? What would they do if the roles were reversed? Surely he should get help.

Then he remembered his masters' chilling warning. Only the food mattered. Nothing else. *You'll survive any fuck-ups, but lose the drugs and you'll pay, either in Ps or with your life.*

Sobbing uncontrollably, he powered his ped away, wondering, for the first time, if he was ever going to get out of this alive.

5

7.30 a.m., Wednesday 2nd May

Detective Superintendent Joanne Howe had managed to get to work early for a change. Life was tough while Darren was away, but she still felt guilty asking for help with the boys. Few blokes would have such qualms.

Like every other department head, she had to find savings – cuts in the midst of an unyielding tsunami of violent crime. She'd grabbed a desk at the Crowhurst Road police station, next to the custody block, and pored over spreadsheets and pie charts willing for the answer to appear as if from a Magic Eye picture.

The blast of her Eddy Grant ringtone came almost as a relief.

'Morning ma'am.' She hated 'ma'am'. It was so dated. 'It's the control room. The Brighton duty inspector asked me to give you a call. A runner phoned in about half an hour ago to say she had found a body in Withdean Park woods. We've got officers out there and they're asking for you.'

'Me specifically? Have you tried the on-call SIO? It's DCI Scott Porter this week.'

'Yes, but there's a massive pile-up on the M25. He's got no hope of getting here from Kent much before ten o'clock. You're the nearest I'm afraid.'

Jo cursed. This was happening time and time again. It was bad enough when the Major Crime Unit comprised just Surrey and Sussex, but since they took in Kent and Hampshire, most of her officers were spending at least four hours a day on the road. And when this ate into the Golden Hour – the time during which finding and securing evidence was most crucial – killers were literally getting away with murder.

'Right, tell me what you've got and I'll get there as soon as I can.'

The controller read over everything he knew. Jo then reeled off a list of instructions and made him repeat them back, before grabbing her go-bag and car keys, glad to leave the number-crunching until later.

*

Phil's guilt at leaving Ruth tortured him as he abandoned his car at the back of Brighton Police Station. While neither mentioned it, both knew she was dying. Her determination to do so at home, surrounded by those she loved and memories of happier times, was all that mattered.

There was never a good time to leave for work early but, if Phil was to be with her tomorrow when the Macmillan nurses would doubtless broach 'end of life pathways', he needed to make a dent in the shedload of reports, authorisations and whatever other unread tedium was clogging up his inbox.

If only the boys had woken up to take over when he left. Gone were the days when he could waltz into their rooms and demand they get their act together. Nowadays he risked stumbling on a scene that no dad should see. They were eighteen and twenty, after all. He wanted them at home for as long as possible, so if they brought a girl, or in Kyle's case a boy, back – so what? He'd rather that than force them into dossing in some shitty drug-infested bedsit, as so many of their mates did.

As he swiped his access card across the reader, his phone chirped a text.

This is your early warning system!! The Chief is in your office. Been found out after all these years??!! Lol. Gary.

Shit. Helen Ricks was not a time-waster, but she liked to make the most of her visits to divisions, 'to see the whole coalface'. He would try to fob her off and on to Gary, but knowing that wily git he would have already conjured up some non-existent gold planning meeting or safety advisory group that he couldn't possibly miss.

Plodding up the stairs, frantically trying to plot a credible exit strategy, he nodded and grunted good mornings to the exhausted cops and civilian staff he passed.

The chief constable, he saw, had already made herself at home at his small circular conference table, tapping furiously away at her laptop.

'Oh, morning ma'am,' said Phil, feigning surprise. The steaming cup of coffee next to her made him wonder whether Gary had threatened to gob in hers as well.

'Just a minute, Philip,' she said, waving a hand but not looking up. 'I just need to reply to the PCC. She's on my back again, which is what I want to talk to you about.'

'Sounds ominous,' said Phil, trying to affect nonchalance.

He slipped off his civvy jacket and, as he hung it on the coat stand, he glimpsed Gary in his office opposite, grinning. His pumped biceps jumped as he mocked hanging from a noose.

*

Jo and Crime Scene Manager Dean Gartrell listened as the uniformed sergeant briefed them by the fluttering blue-and-white police tape.

A couple of clarification questions later and they both struggled into their 'one-size-fits-no-one' forensic barrier suits, gloves, masks and overshoes.

Dean held the tape up for Jo to duck under, then they edged their way towards the wood, the grisly tableau emerging into view.

The canopy of trees eclipsed the early morning sun and they inched into its shade, balancing on the steel stepping-plates laid out. On reaching the red-and-white tape that marked the inner cordon, the kernel of the scene, they silently peered at the horror before them.

The blood-soaked corpse lay flat on its back on a bed of ruddied nettles and bracken, eyes still agape in shock. The reek of decomposition had yet to take hold; the only aroma was the perfume of fresh vegetation tainted with the ferrous, slightly sweet, tang of spilt blood.

The chaffinches high in the trees chirped their mockery at the butchery below.

An explosion of red rendered the corpse's Brighton and Hove Albion tracksuit top barely recognisable. The phone resting beside the open left hand would no doubt hold clues but the foliage, the post-mortem and, God willing, witnesses would be the key to this senseless death.

Jo crouched for a closer look. She studied the cadaver, then sprung up.

Something about the boy's features. In death, people looked different – pasty and drawn, all colour and structure stripped away – but she was sure she had seen him before.

'Dean, do you recognise him?'

They squatted together, Dean's hood and mask hiding his furrowed brow.

'I don't think so. It's hard to tell.'

She remained on her haunches, her tilting head in deep thought.

'Look closer.'

Dean studied the body from a different angle. Jo watched him in reverential silence as her worst fears swelled.

Someone shut those bloody birds up.

Jo expected him to stretch back up, with either a name or a blank look but, eerily, he remained rooted to the spot.

'Any clue?'

He stood up slowly. Pensive.

'I didn't notice before.'

A deep foreboding swelled deep in Jo's stomach; the gut feeling that this was surging from tragic to catastrophic.

'Well?'

'I can't be sure, but he looks so familiar and, of course, the tracksuit . . .'

Jo offered up a name, her voice trembling.

'I think so.'

'Think?'

'No, I'm sure.'

Jo nodded, dreading where her next stop must be. He had broken her heart once before, but that was nothing compared to what she was about to do to him.

*

Jo drove to the police station in a blur. She should have been planning how to break the news but instead her thoughts were swamped with headier days.

Was it really fifteen years ago? She was Jo Reed then, young, free and single, but that was no excuse. How often had more worldly-wise women on the force warned her against the charms of the senior men? How often had she promised herself she was not that kind of girl?

She had always been cautious after what had happened to her sister, but common sense gave way to lust that night.

It was supposed to have been a quick overnight stay while her and DI Phil Cooke spent two days debriefing a prisoner in Norwich Prison, all in preparation for taking down a vicious crime family – the Larbies – that had the south coast's drug market all sewn up.

The pre-dinner drinks, the bottle of Greek red with their kleftiko, moussaka and then their nightcaps were no excuse for what happened.

She had always found him charming – a bit rough around the edges – but a true gent to her and the young DCs under his command. Off duty though, she found him beguiling, funny, self-effacing and, above all, truly interested in her. Not all 'me, me, me'.

The peck on the cheek that should have sent them to their separate rooms became a lingering kiss and before long they were naked in each other's arms on the 'sleep guaranteed' king-sized bed. The hotel did not live up to its promises that night.

In the morning, as she watched the rise and fall of his honed chest – damned fit for an older bloke – she wanted to feel guilty. He was married, had young kids for God's sake, but her heart ached for this not to be a one-night stand. She'd always baulked at the notion of love at first sight, and this was not first sight by any stretch of the imagination, but something had happened. It was so wrong but felt so right.

The following morning, Phil stretched the enquiries out a couple more days – 'to follow up on some local leads'. In fairness there were more people to see but, aside from that, they hardly left her bedroom over the next forty-eight hours.

The flame of their six-month affair – and plenty more 'overnight work trips' – with all its secrets, betrayals and passion was ignited in that Best Western anonymity.

*

Nailing the clock above the door was one of Phil's first acts as divisional commander.

That way, with just a flick of his eyes he could gauge when his visitors had outstayed their welcome – provided he could bag the seat opposite.

Unfortunately, Chief Constable Helen Ricks knew his ploy and had got in first, leaving Phil to only guess the time. He had no idea how long she had been droning on, but could see his day spiralling down the drain.

'So you see, Philip, it's all about innovation. We can ill afford to have another attack. Certain people are getting jumpy and it's all coming back to you – and me.'

'But I can't get blood out of a stone, ma'am,' pleaded Phil. 'Of course, we would love to do things the way we used to, but the troops have hardly come on duty before they're swallowed up by the vacuum created by the previous understaffed shift. It's a vicious circle.'

'I know, but you need to work with others. The council, schools, youth groups, private businesses. Anyone. We need to stop crime before it starts.'

'So, can I assume that I can ignore ACC Acers' demands for another pound of flesh?'

'Leave Stuart to me, but try to be positive.'

He was about to argue, but was saved by a sharp rap on the door. Phil looked at the chief and on her assenting nod he said, 'Come in.'

Superintendent Gary Hedges opened the door, but rather than bowling in as was his habit, he hovered in the threshold avoiding eye contact.

'What is it, Gary?' demanded Phil.

'Ma'am, can I have a word please?' he said.

'Say whatever it is in front of me,' Phil chuckled. 'Last time I checked I was still the divisional commander.'

'Ma'am?' pleaded Gary.

Helen Ricks shrugged, stood and walked towards the door. 'I won't be long.'

Fear swamped Phil. Was it Ruth? He checked his phone. No missed calls.

Anger took over. He sprung to his feet. No one kept secrets from him, not on his patch, not even the chief bloody constable.

As he stepped into the corridor, a gentle but firm hand clutched his right arm.

He spun round about to unleash a tirade, catching himself just in time as a familiar but tortured face stared at him. He read the signs straight away. Softly she guided him back through his door, saying nothing.

'Jo, what is it? You're scaring me.'

'Phil, please sit down,' said Jo as she eased the door closed.

He moved round the conference table to his favoured chair, his stomach clenched, eyes searching Jo's face for clues, but at the same time praying he'd read this wrong.

Whenever he was about to destroy a family with the worst news imaginable, they always knew – even before he had opened his mouth.

He knew.

Jo sat opposite, her slender features strained. She reached for his hand, but he snatched it away. He needed to take whatever was coming straight.

'Phil, I don't know if you've been told, but early this morning a runner found a body in Withdean Park.'

'Gary is duty command. Perhaps he knows,' he quaked. *Make this go away.*

Jo faltered. Her gaze dropped.

'What? Jo, what is it?'

'I've been to the scene.'

'Tell me.' She was doing this all wrong. Come straight out with it. Good or bad.

'He has been stabbed.'

'He?'

'Yes Phil, he. Look, when I got there I thought I recognised him. I checked with Dean Gartrell and he confirmed it.'

Jo's eyes flicked to the gallery of family photos lined up on the windowsill. Phil followed her eyes.

'Right?' said Phil, now terrified.

'Phil. I am absolutely certain it's Harry.'

'Harry? My Harry?' said Phil, barely able to utter the words.

'Your Harry. I'm certain.'

Phil started shaking. A chill surged through him.

'B-b-but. It can't be. I mean, how can you be sure? It can't be him. He was out with his friends last night celebrating. He got a full-time contract. He'll be at home. Or with friends. No, it's not Harry. Not my Harry.'

'Phil, I am so sorry. We'll need to confirm it, but I wouldn't be telling you if I had any doubt.' She reached for his hand, and this time he relented.

His whole body convulsed.

Jo moved round and held him. Her tender, strong arms provided none of the comfort they once had, but still he surrendered to her caring embrace.

Minutes passed.

He coughed, wiped his eyes and straightened in the chair.

'I need to see him. I need to be sure. Can I see him? Can I see him now? Just in case, you know.'

'He'll be taken to the mortuary in the next hour or so and then, of course, you can see him.'

'Thank you.'

'I don't want to give you false hope. I am certain it's him.'

'No. You have to be wrong,' he replied, still shaking, his eyes fixed on the middle distance. 'Has anyone told Ruth or Kyle yet?'

'No, you were our first port of call, but we shouldn't leave it. We can only keep this quiet for so long.'

'Oh God. This will kill her. You know she's . . .'

'Yes, I know.' She rested her hand on his shoulder and gave it a squeeze.

'Kyle too. They are so close. Oh God, how am I going to tell them?'

'Would you like me to?'

'No. I'll do it?' As far as he was aware, Ruth knew nothing of his affair with Jo, but he'd heard stories of wives suspecting but never mentioning infidelity. He couldn't risk the two loves of his life meeting and a look, a word, maybe blowing his life apart even further. With the cancer – and where they all knew that was heading – and now this, his indiscretions of fifteen years ago couldn't come out. For all their sakes.

'Are you sure?' Jo seemed to understand. 'Maybe Gary then?'

'No. I'll do it.'

'When?'

'Before I go to the . . . Before I see him,' he choked.

'Let Gary take you. You're in no state to drive.'

'OK, I'll speak to him.'

Phil fell silent – trance-like.

'Can you tell me? Do you know if he suffered?'

'We'll know more after the post-mortem, but we think it was a single stab wound. No defence wounds.'

'Oh my God,' said Phil, sobs muffled into his folded arms on the shaking desk.

Jo's gentle hand rested on his shoulders. 'I'll get Gary.'

*

Gary drove Phil in more or less total silence.

He steered well clear of Withdean Park, which was now completely sealed off. Only irritated dog walkers and a ravenous press corps remained, grilling the scene guards for hints of when the park might reopen and titbits for the lunchtime news.

'You want me to come in?' asked Gary, as he pulled up outside Phil's house.

'Please.'

'Look, I can do this if you want. Don't feel you have to.'

'No. I owe it to them.'

'OK,' Gary conceded with a shrug, 'but I'm here, OK?'

They stepped out of the car and, as they had been conditioned to do when giving death messages to strangers, silently clicked the doors shut.

Phil led the way up the path, keys in hand, glancing up at his CCTV camera as was his habit. Following on, Gary scanned the windows for any clue that Ruth or Kyle might have spotted them.

Phil slid the key in the lock and eased the door open.

Only Ruth's hacking cough broke the stillness. There were no signs of Kyle.

'Ruth, it's only me,' Phil called out.

'Hi love,' came the raspy reply.

Phil climbed the stairs, nodding to Gary to follow.

Reaching the landing, instead of going straight to Ruth, he knocked on Kyle's door.

'Kyle, are you in there?'

'Yeah,' came the reply.

Phil choked back tears. 'Can I come in?'

'One sec. OK, come in.'

Phil pushed the door. Kyle was sitting up in bed, iPad on his lap.

'Can you come to your mum's room? And put a dressing gown on. Gary's with me.'

'What is it?' replied Kyle, searching his dad's face for clues.

'Please.' Phil stepped out and across the landing.

Ruth was also sitting up but, rather than an iPad, a sick bowl rested on her lap.

'Love, I've got something to tell you and Kyle.'

'What is it? Shouldn't we get Harry in here too?' She looked so lost, so pained. 'Phil darling, what is it?'

Kyle stepped in, bewildered, barely acknowledging Gary hovering in the corner.

'Sit down, Kyle,' said Phil. The boy obeyed, perching on the edge of his mum's bed.

As he tried to speak, the words gagged in Phil's throat and he collapsed, gasping like a drowning man, on the opposite side of the bed.

Gary dashed to his boss and put his arm around his shoulder. He took over the dreadful task.

'Ruth, Kyle. I'm afraid we've got some bad news. Harry has been found dead. A jogger found him in some undergrowth in Withdean Park this morning. He'd been stabbed.' *Jo could learn a lot from you*, thought Phil.

A second passed, then Ruth screamed. 'No. No. My baby. No No No.' She grasped at the bed sheets, convulsing, pleading to have misunderstood.

Gary moved towards her but before he reached her, Phil had her in his arms. They sobbed in grief, clinging to each other.

Kyle looked stunned. Confused. His eyes filled, as he murmured, 'Do you know who did it?'

'No, but we will find out. I promise,' said Gary.

'Thanks. I'm sure you will,' the boy whispered before he too clung to his mum and dad. A family shipwrecked.

Gary shifted from foot to foot.

Ruth gasped then coughed, desperately. Her frenzied battle for breath froze the three men.

'Mum. Mum,' yelled Kyle, then to Gary, 'Fucking do something.'

Phil bent her forward. Thumped her back. Nothing.

Gary grabbed his mobile phone.

'Ambulance. Now. My friend's wife can't breathe. She is being treated for breast cancer and her son has just been murdered.' He gave the address and was promised an immediate response. 'No, it's OK, I'm first aid trained, I can do CPR. You don't need to talk me through it.'

He flung the phone on the bed and wrenched Phil and Kyle away.

'Go down and wait for the ambulance, Kyle. Phil, you stay here and help me with the CPR. Two breaths to my thirty compressions,' he ordered, and both got to work, Phil praying he would not be robbed twice in one day.

6

6.00 p.m., Wednesday 2nd May

Jo was no stranger to running on adrenaline when a murder investigation broke. With this one though, racked with personal agony and the intense spotlight of expectation, she had hardly drawn breath.

But now, she forced herself to pause. With the first briefing just ten minutes away, her composure would make or break the tone of the enquiry. If she came across as the emotional and physical wreck she felt right now, she would lose the team before they had barely started.

She needed all her acting skills to convince this lot she had her shit together.

She had to be strong. Calm and organised. But above all, positive. One chink of pessimism would spread like a virus.

For the umpteenth time she scanned the trigger notes scribbled in her investigator's notebook. Bold headings to ensure she left nothing unsaid. She just hoped these hieroglyphics would make sense when it mattered.

Jo winced as she slurped the now tepid hot water her deputy, DCI Scott Porter, had thoughtfully handed her two hours ago. Swearing under her breath as she shoved it away, she glimpsed a figure loitering in the doorway.

'Hello ma'am. Thanks for coming,' Jo mumbled as she struggled to her feet.

'Not at all,' replied the chief constable, waving her to sit back down, as she made herself at home in the seat opposite. 'I thought it was important to come and see how you are all getting on.'

'That's very good of you.'

'I won't get in the way but, given the circumstances . . . well, you know.'

'Of course. We are briefing in ten minutes if you want to come along,' said Jo, hoping the chief would decline.

'I know. I'll be there.'

Of course you know, thought Jo. *You have eyes and ears everywhere.*

'I hear Mrs Cooke was rushed to hospital after Phil told her. You don't happen to know how she is, do you? I've not had a moment to check,' asked Jo, guilty that Phil's second trauma of the day had slipped her mind.

'She'll be OK. I visited her and Philip earlier. They are keeping her in overnight but she's breathing on her own now. Gary saved her life.'

A beat passed between them.

'God, what must they be going through?' mused Jo.

'Have you got all you need?' asked the chief, turning to more practical issues.

'For now. Some evidence and a suspect would be good, but everyone's been superb in giving up staff. This has hit the whole force.'

'We are a big family, Joanne, as you well know.'

'Indeed. Right, are you ready?' said Jo, grabbing her notebook, pen and phone, checking the latter was firmly switched to silent.

*

The packed Major Incident Room hushed as Jo walked in, the chief in tow.

Let the show begin.

'OK, gather round everyone,' Jo bellowed, louder than she intended.

Indexers, researchers, analysts and detectives turned as one to face her, some locking their computer screens, others wheeling their chairs away from cramped desks, showing they were all ears.

She took in all the pointers that a murder hunt was in full swing.

Operation Carbon hung in huge letters above maps, photos, association charts and lists – dozens of lists – which covered every inch of wall space. She felt a pang when her eyes fell on the picture of Harry – N1, as the Home Office Large Major Enquiry System (HOLMES2) – had clinically designated him. His jubilant, ruddy face shone. Sporting his grubby Brighton and Hove Albion kit, he was perched on the shoulders of his ecstatic teammates while holding aloft an enormous gold trophy with blue and white ribbons tied to the handles.

Why did she prefer it when they displayed the deceased's most recent custody photo, rather than one so full of life?

'OK, ladies and gents, phones off or to stun please. The sharper among you will have spotted we have been joined by the chief constable.' God, how long could she keep up this cheery pretence, Jo wondered as she turned to her boss. 'Ma'am, would you like to say anything before we start?'

'Thank you, Joanne.' All eyes fell on the county's top cop. 'None of you will have got up this morning imagining that you would be investigating the brutal murder of a colleague's son. You, like me, will be utterly devastated for Mr Cooke and his family. I have been with them this afternoon and they are, of course, beside themselves with grief. So, we have two options. One, we can wallow in our own shock, distress and rage. Or, we put all that aside, become steely professionals and give every ounce to find who is responsible for this despicable deed and bring them to the most swift and ruthless justice.'

Jo could see that a couple of the DCs, who were less familiar with the chief's forthright manner, had winced. She, on the other hand, knew this down-to-earth rhetoric would chime with most who, more than ever before, wanted to nail this bastard.

Helen Ricks stepped back.

'Thank you, ma'am. So, let's get started.' She kicked off with the usual preamble. Who would be in charge of what, how she expected them all to work together, that there were to be no secrets and that she would crucify anyone who went maverick.

Next, she ran through the discovery of the body, touching on the identification that Phil had struggled through. She outlined what had been given to the press, including that Harry was Phil's son. She demanded that nothing, but nothing, should get out without her specific say-so.

She was getting into her groove.

'So, updates please. Anything from house to house?'

'Not so far,' confirmed an inspector.

'Have we got a time of death yet?' asked a voice at the back of the room.

'Not certain, but sometime yesterday evening. A bus driver remembered dropping a lad of similar description off in London Road just by Withdean Park about six last night,' replied DCI Scott Porter. 'He's being interviewed now.'

'CCTV in the bus?' Jo asked.

Scott shrugged. 'Probably. We'll check.'

'Post-mortem?' said Jo.

'Just finished. Cause of death a single stab wound through the chest, piercing the heart. No signs of other injuries, except old bruising probably from football. No defence wounds. The knife is double-edged, at least twelve centimetres long and about three and a half wide. Samples etcetera will take a while so that's all we know at the moment.'

'Anything on his phone?'

'Loads of calls, WhatsApps, texts for about an hour, then they all stop abruptly at 1807 hours. Last call was to his dad. After that it looks like he was trying to call 999 but only managed the first two nines.'

Shock filled the room as everyone took in how desperate Harry must have been in those final moments.

'OK, settle down,' said Jo. 'We've got loads to do and it's all urgent. Someone must have seen something, heard something, know something. The answer is out there. All we have to do is find it. There will be witnesses, somewhere. We leave no stone unturned. Go and collect your actions from the HOLMES team and get to work. I want this cracked, so send a selfie to remind your loved ones what you look like, 'cos no one's going home anytime soon. To work.'

The chatter crescendoed as everyone grabbed car keys, phones and statement folders, rising with determination to Jo's and the chief's challenge.

Jo turned to head back to her office just as an analyst waved a hand.

'Ma'am, I'm not sure if this is connected, but you may want to have a look at a job that came in this morning.'

She walked over and stood behind him, reading the incident serial over his shoulder. 'Holy shit,' she muttered, hardly noticing the chief scuttle off without a word.

*

Rico, the older of the two, sobbed on the cold hard floor, his hands swollen and numb from the plastic bindings cutting into his wrists. That last kick, to his left kidney, was the message they were past the warning stage. The lad convulsed but seemed to avoid the foetal position to protect his back from another onslaught.

'We can keep going all night, man,' yelled Crush. He nodded to the goon whose steel-toe-capped boots had caused most of the damage. His laser aim to the solar plexus brought a bone-crack and a sickening splutter from the stricken boy.

Rico threw up a cocktail of blood, mucus and the dregs of his stomach contents. He wheezed desperately. Crush raised a hand and the goon stepped back.

'Listen bonny lad,' said Crush, calmer now. 'We know you're just cannon fodder, but we have to start somewhere. Folk are getting mightily pissed off with yous lot's shenanigans. No one minds you selling a bit of dope, even to bairns. But this Marco fella, well, he needs stopping. Pushing smack and crack, hooking the kids in, taking over the streets and putting old men in hospital, we can't have that, now can we?'

Rico coughed a plea of ignorance but the words gagged in his throat.

'Speak up, I can barely hear you. Just tell us where to find him. That's all. It's not much to ask, is it? It's not like you're grassing. You're only a grass if you blab to the polis, and we certainly ain't them lot.' The thug in the corner sniggered, which drew a withering glare from Crush. He turned back to his barely conscious captive. 'Just tell us and you get to swap places with him. If you don't, well your wee pal Benji gets this, and worse.'

Rico spat, heaving in a lungful of air. 'Patcham,' he spat out. 'He's always in Patcham. You missed him when you found us.'

Crush glowered at the boy, then pinioned his neck to the floor with his right boot.

'Is that so laddie? So close, eh? So where can we pay him a house call?'

'Don't know,' he gasped. 'We meet on the street.'

'I'm losing patience here,' Crush sneered, as he shifted his whole weight onto Rico's neck, grinning as the lad shuddered in panic. 'His address. Give me his address.'

'I . . . swear . . . I . . . don't . . . know,' Rico pleaded.

Crush nodded to the waiting thug and turned for the door, disappearing down the corridor to the fading thuds of boot on body and the futile screams of a boy pleading for his life.

7

7.30 p.m., Wednesday 2nd May

Jo Howe had fronted up misogynistic chief constables, shrugged off death threats, even faced down drug-crazed warlords in the jungle, but put her in a hospital and sheer terror clenched her like a vice.

Five years ago, she'd spent a heartbreaking week camped out in this very building, the Royal Sussex County Hospital. It had seemed an eternity, dozing in moulded-plastic chairs, feasting on vending-machine trash food while waiting for her father to fade away from the prostate cancer that had shrivelled him to a shell.

All that was a blur now, but as she stepped off the pavement and into the reception of the crumbling building that pre-dated Florence Nightingale, the first whiff of 'Eau de Hospital', a blend of disinfectant, disease and death, triggered a Pavlovian response.

First the stomach cramps, then the nausea, which quickly segued into feverish sweats. Years ago, she'd researched whether cognitive behavioural therapy might help but, frankly, she had neither the time nor the courage to take it any further.

In any case, no amount of therapy would have covered why today's visit was so bad.

Fifteen years ago, her beautiful, if furtive, blossoming relationship hit the brutal skids, just after someone – most likely one of the Larbies – tried to burn Phil's house down with Ruth, Kyle and Harry inside. Phil's guilt at being away with her, rather than at home, got the better of him.

The arrest of three of the Larbies had already made them both targets for retribution. They'd even yelled their promised revenge to them and their families when sentenced, but the prospect of losing Ruth and the boys 'brought him to his senses', or at least that's how he put it in his spineless voicemail.

He had tried to explain on the few occasions she couldn't avoid him, but Jo didn't want to hear it. There was no excuse for such a cowardly dumping.

Thankfully, Jo's shame remained private, as no one knew they'd been an item. More than once she'd been tempted to reveal all to Ruth, but her dignity and not wanting to crush an innocent woman stopped her.

However, resignation had crossed Jo's mind. Her self-confidence crumbled while she was forced to watch from the sidelines as Phil's career skyrocketed.

She pretended it was the threats and the arson attack that sparked her thoughts of a career change, but her mum brought her to her senses when she reminded her why she had joined up in the first place.

Her sister's treatment by the criminal justice system had been scandalous. In 1992, when she was barely twelve years old, she had revealed that a family 'friend', who also happened to be a prominent councillor, had been sexually abusing her for years. Jo watched in disbelief as the tables were callously turned on her sibling, with allegations in open court that the 'pillar of the community had been seduced by this Lolita'. The abuser's acquittal and her sister's subsequent breakdown and suicide attempts drove Jo's dogged determination to fix the injustices from within. Her mother's sharp words reignited that fire. She owed it to her sister to hold on to her resolve.

She opted for some time away, working for the United Nations, building and developing policing in Liberia. Having endured weeks of what they called 'acclimatisation training', which seemed more to do with shooting straight and unarmed combat than cultural awareness, nothing prepared her for the horrors she was about to face.

She was rocked by the locals' casual acceptance that rape and spaced-out child soldiers wielding AK-47s were legitimate weapons of war. But she soon found her niche and became proud of the part she played in helping to turn the country round.

One unintended outcome was finding true love in the shape of Darren Howe, an investigative journalist probing the West's role in the widespread corruption that still raged. They married soon after she returned to the UK, snuffing any candle she might have been tempted to hold for Phil, and she'd avoided him – and certainly Ruth – as much as she could ever since.

But now, here Jo was nauseously making her way along the drab corridors – medics bustling and neglected phones squawking away in abandoned offices – towards the lift that would haul her up to Phil, Ruth and Kyle.

Stopping by the side-ward door, Jo took a deep breath. *Pull yourself together*, she berated herself. *You are the senior investigating officer into Harry's death, for God's sake. Just do your job.*

She tapped lightly, then pushed the door open.

*

As Jo stepped in Phil spun round and, for a beat too long, their eyes locked.

The moment was broken by the screech of alarms as Ruth was racked by a wheezing fit. Phil grabbed the oxygen mask and pinned it over Ruth's mouth and nose, muttering reassurance as her breaths began to deepen and slow.

'If this is a bad time I'll come back later,' muttered Jo.

Ruth pulled the mask from her face and gasped, 'There will never be a good time.'

'Mum,' pleaded Kyle, who had yet to look at Jo. 'Put the oxygen back on.'

Phil touched his son's arm, then turned and gave Jo a wan smile. She just wanted this over.

'Have you got an update?' Phil asked.

'Not much I'm afraid.'

'But something?' asked Ruth, flicking her gaze between Jo and Phil.

Jo struggled to keep her expression neutral, as she took them through what little they had uncovered so far.

Ruth's tears made Jo so glad she hadn't robbed her of her husband before, and seeing her like this, she was even more determined to deliver the justice she deserved.

Phil adopted his familiar air, the one he used at work: steely, inquisitive and focused, but now also glassy-eyed. Kyle's shoulders shook as his mum comforted him.

'So, what about intelligence?' Phil asked.

'We're working on that. Last night, a dog walker found two lads by Carden Park, not far from the scene. One had acid burns and the other had both his Achilles tendons sliced.'

Phil winced. 'What, a gang feud?'

'We don't know yet. They were rushed here but are flatly refusing to talk. Some neighbours thought they heard screaming and a car speeding off but didn't bother to call us.'

'What's this got to do with Harry's murder though?' asked Phil.

'I'm not sure yet. Maybe nothing, but if it was gang-related then maybe whoever did it attacked Harry.'

'Harry wasn't in a gang,' said Ruth.

'Oh, I know. But it could be mistaken identity or he may have stumbled across something. Anyway, we are going to look into it. Just in case.'

Ruth pulled her oxygen mask back to her face and rested back.

'OK, just keep us updated please,' said Phil.

'I will. I'll have a family liaison officer appointed for you by the morning,' she added, almost as an afterthought.

'Don't worry about that. I'll just come through you,' said Phil.

Jo glared at him. *Don't push it.*

'Phil, you know the score. You need an FLO.' She did not mention it was stretching the bounds of impartiality to be even running this case. An FLO would at least be a buffer.

He glanced briefly at his wife and son. 'Yes, you're probably right,' he conceded.

'I'll go now,' Jo said, with barely concealed relief. 'I'll call you tomorrow, or before if there are any updates. I'm so sorry for your loss. We will catch whoever did this. I promise.'

Jo turned and left the room, only then noticing the splitting headache that would now cripple her for hours.

As she left the ward and reached the main corridor, Phil called her name.

She turned around and felt the warmth of his breath. Her heart juddered. 'Was there something else?'

'Thank you so much, Jo. I wouldn't want anyone but you on this.' She just managed to stop his hand caressing her cheek.

'No, Phil. Someone might see. This is work and it has to stay that way.' She nodded back to Ruth's room. 'For all of our sakes.'

'I was just wondering,' Phil said, taking the hint. 'Have you looked at the Larbies?'

'The Larbies?'

'You remember, that lot we locked up when . . . well, you know?'

'I know who they are, but why would I look at them? That was over a decade ago.'

'But they must be out by now and don't forget, it wasn't just me they threatened, they tried to kill my family.'

'That's a long shot. Why would they suddenly go after Harry now?'

'To get at me, of course?'

'But why now? Have you had any more threats? Any attacks?'

'Just look at it, please Jo. It may be nothing but if I'm right, then that puts Ruth and Kyle at risk too.'

Jo squeezed his arm. 'I'll put it in the mix, but please, let me follow the evidence first, and try to not worry. I will catch them.'

'I hope so. I really hope so,' muttered Phil as Jo walked away.

*

Despite its doused lights, Crush could just make out the articulated lorry as it chugged down the road towards him.

They needed to load it quickly, so it would be away before it got caught up in the traffic from the next cross-channel ferry arrival, and could ditch its cargo long before dawn.

It had been a frantic evening. First the chosen prisoners were rounded up from the cells. Crush had taken the personal responsibility of checking them off. Robinson had made it clear that Wayne Tanner had to be on the list. The others were either those who had been there too long or had otherwise outstayed their welcome.

As he corralled them into the old officers' mess, Crush told them they'd soon be leaving. This triggered the desired effect of relief, putting them off their guard. One by one, they were escorted to the disused kitchens on the ruse that they could shower and be provided with fresh clothing.

The first moment they would know something was up was when the guards seized them tighter and an unseen slaughterer pressed the muzzle of an abattoir gun against their temple. The body would then be dragged to what was once a cold store to await butchering. Once clear, the next unfortunate would be brought down.

The bodies had to be dismembered into small enough pieces to fit into narrow cuboid coffins, as only they would fit into the furnaces.

Wayne Tanner had immediately fought when his guard's grip tightened, and the gunman initially missed, causing a flesh wound. Tanner's scream was enough to telegraph to the others waiting that this was no free-pass home. Panic and mayhem ensued and the remaining prisoners were hastily executed in the mess. Crush was livid, as the moving of the bodies and clean-up operation had seriously delayed the whole thing. Someone would pay for that.

He was not squeamish, but the scream of the bandsaws as the butcher chunked up the bodies was something he could live without, so he busied himself supervising the packing of the limbs, torsos and heads, ensuring any remaining jewellery – he couldn't believe what some people had pierced these days – was removed.

As the lorry swung in through the gates, the forklifts scurried into place. The driver nodded to Crush and he copied; the sign both were ready to go. Within ninety seconds all the sides of the trailer had been raised and, in no time, it was packed with its gruesome load.

Crush checked his watch as the trailer was resealed. Fifteen minutes. Not bad. He breathed a sigh of relief, grateful that somewhere in the north of the city, several thousand residents would soon be obliviously inhaling the smoky remains of those who had caused them such misery.

8

8.00 a.m., Thursday 3rd May

Jo took in the shattered faces around the tiny table. She wondered, from their raw eyes and washed-out tones, whether any of her management team had managed even a moment's sleep in the last twenty-four hours.

She certainly hadn't.

No one would mention it though, let alone whinge. It was not that exhaustion was a sign of weakness. It was just that they were all in the same boat, and each knew if they had any chance of catching Harry's killer it would be now.

Memories quickly fade, evidence degrades and killers flee; they had to make the most of these Golden Hours.

She massaged her pounding temples, aching from the hundreds of statements and officers' reports she'd spent the night poring over. She felt like a wreck; in desperate need of a hot bath, a glass of Pinot Grigio and Adele on repeat.

Despite being the boss, hers was a nomadic lifestyle; no office to call her own unless she was actually running a murder enquiry. On those increasingly frequent occasions, she could lay temporary claim to one of the compact yet functional SIO offices for as long as her presence was required. The way things were going on Op Carbon, it looked like she would be setting up home here for the foreseeable future.

These tired, converted bedrooms in the old training wing of police headquarters that now housed the Major Incident Suite, sapped her will to live. Despite their recent spruce-up, the draughty windows and seizure-inducing fluorescent lights strobing every room were a disgrace.

When the bacon-and-egg sandwiches had arrived in her office, the irresistible aroma had coaxed her management team away from their HOLMES2 computers to the first meeting of the day. Over the years she had learnt that the sure-fire way of luring busy detectives to these crucial powwows was to provide cholesterol-enriched fast food.

Once they had all grabbed their share, she called the meeting to order.

'Right, let's have your overnight updates.'

'We're still at the scene,' said Crime Scene Manager Dean Gartrell. 'The weather's been kind but we've put up canopies over where the body was, just in case. The whole park is sealed off but we can't protect it all from the elements. Hopefully we'll be finished by midday tomorrow.'

'OK. What about Harry's bedroom?'

'Nothing. We've taken the usual stuff, laptop, tablet, paperwork, but unless they throw anything up I don't think the answer is there.'

'Assume nothing,' mumbled DCI Scott Porter.

Dean scowled. The frosty relationship of these two harked back to a time when Scott had ordered Dean's SOCOs back to re-examine the room where a woman had been beaten to death. During the DCI's 'signing off' visit – normally a formality where a senior detective approves the release of the scene back to the occupiers – he spotted a SIM card wedged between two floorboards. Furious, he insisted Dean start the whole examination again.

'Right, moving on,' said Jo, keen not to allow this ridiculous feud to re-ignite. 'House to house?'

'Nothing,' confirmed the inspector in charge of that function. 'But I reckon we'll be there for a few days yet. If anyone knows anything, ma'am, we'll find them.'

'Thanks. Intel?' she asked, turning to DI Bob Heaton.

'It's too early to expect much from the sources but, as we know, two drug dealers were attacked not far from the scene on Tuesday evening,' said Bob. A simultaneous wince went round the room when he described their injuries, a couple even abandoning their stringy bacon sandwiches. 'Looks gang-related.'

'How is that relevant to us?' asked Scott Porter.

'It may not be, boss, but Harry's murder looks so random that it could be mistaken identity. He could easily have been thought to be a gang member,' replied Bob.

Scott shook his head.

Jo thought about Phil's theory of a revenge attack. She kept it to herself for now. After all, there was nothing that even hinted the Larbies were behind this.

Jo raced round the others. Nothing from the search teams. The phone data and CCTV footage were being scoured but all were drawing a blank so far.

'What about press?' Jo asked, turning to Clarissa Heard, the media liaison officer.

'No surprise, they are all over it. We've had Sky News trucks blocking up Old Court Close at the back of the woods and we've created a press pen in Peacock Lane.'

'What's their angle?'

'"Promising young footballer just breaking into the big time", "Top cop's son slain", "Broken Brighton". It's a gift for them. Whichever way you look at it, this has just about everything to outrage your average tabloid reader. You don't need me to tell you that the longer it goes on without an arrest, the brighter the spotlight on us . . .'

'On me,' interjected Jo. 'OK, we need to keep them fed, don't give them a vacuum to fill with their own version of the truth.'

'Perhaps if you gave an update from the scene? Usual stuff, tragic senseless killing, thoughts with the family, yada yada yada, then a witness appeal.'

'Sure.'

'Maybe a reconstruction if we haven't got anyone by next Tuesday.'

'We will,' scoffed Scott Porter.

'Well, let's plan anyway,' said Jo.

'How about a joint press conference with you and Mr Cooke?'

Jo pondered that. How would Phil fare? He tended to be fiery in front of the media. Would they provoke him? On the other hand, it was only right that the public see the grieving family.

'OK, let's think about it. I'm not ruling it in or out, but if he agrees he has to stick to the script.'

'Righto,' said Clarissa, scribbling in her notebook.

Jo checked her watch.

'OK folks, time for the main briefing. Just a word of warning though. I'm cancelling all rest days for the foreseeable, so that means no bank holiday off for anyone. Clear?'

'Clear,' came the collective groan. All had expected it, but none were looking forward to breaking the news to their loved ones.

10.00 a.m., Friday 4th May

Phil needed fresh air and proper food.

Having spent the last two days cooped up in Ruth's hospital room, he'd survived on lumps of pastry and gristle masquerading as sausage rolls. His stomach rumbled at the thought of Mac's café, down the road.

Kyle was dog-tired and starving too, but Phil couldn't persuade him to come along; instead he insisted on napping in the chair next to Ruth, whose machines and monitors flickered and bleeped unabated. Phil promised him a sausage sandwich on his return. His heart ached for the boy he would need to get to know better; perhaps he could even go to some of his gigs.

God forbid.

The events of the last few days churned in his mind as he walked down the hill. How had his life fallen apart so completely, and did he really mean he was pleased Jo was SIO?

His mind kept flitting back to those nights in her arms, then how his life jack-knifed when the Larbies, he was sure it was them, tried to burn his house down, taking his family with it. He had to dump Jo after that – the guilt was too much – but he still loved her.

Those scum had something to do with this, he just knew it. He hoped Jo would find out for sure; then they'd throw away the key.

Phil's mouth watered as he gazed at the oasis of the café opposite. Impatiently, he jaywalked towards it, pushing the door open. The tinkle of a bell announced his arrival and the scent of frying bacon wafted to his nostrils. He scanned the clientele. Today, of all days, he yearned for anonymity, his NYC blue baseball cap a perfunctory disguise. He needn't have bothered. No one gave him a second glance.

'Yes my love,' the chirpy, cook-cum-waitress said as he perused the menu board above the counter, though he knew exactly what he was going to order.

'I'll have a Mac's Special and mug of tea, please.'

'That'll be £6.45, please.'

He handed over a ten-pound note.

'Take a seat love, I'll bring your change over with your tea.'

'Righto,' he mumbled, shuffling away towards an empty table, far from anyone else.

As he plonked his exhausted body in one of the red-cushioned metal-framed chairs, he shoved copies of *The Sun* and *The Mirror*, which were strewn over the Formica table, out of his eyeline. The headlines theorising over 'Who Killed Harry?' were the last thing he needed to see, especially as the copy below would no doubt amount to little more than some novice journalist sensationalising his beautiful boy's death.

Instinctively, he pulled his phone out of his trouser pocket. He flinched at the wallpaper, tears pricking his eyes. Harry had been ecstatic that day. Brighton and Hove Albion had beaten Southampton Academy to win the FA Under 18 Cup. This photo of him, on his teammate's shoulders, laughing as he held the cup aloft, summed up his elation.

'Here's your tea and change, my love. Your breakfast's just coming,' chirped the happy lady as she placed the white ceramic mug by Phil's arm. He wondered if she had a care in the world. Of course she did.

'Thanks,' he said, moving the mug a fraction and putting all but £2 of the change in his pocket.

Phil picked his phone back up and soon found himself Googling the Larbies, trying to pin down their release date. Nothing recent, other than a Sunday tabloid article a few years ago heralding Sam Larbie's spiritual rebirth in prison.

'What bollocks,' he muttered, then went to 'recent calls', knowing that Gary's number would be close to the top.

He touched his pal's name. Gary answered before it rang.

'Hi mate. How's things?' Phil flinched at how the usual question sounded so hollow now. His friend's voice cracked a little. 'I— Well, how's Ruth?'

'As good as it can be. I've just popped out for some food at Mac's. Shit Gary, what am I going to do?'

A couple of furtive glances were thrown his way.

'Want me to come down?'

'No, no, I just need some time.'

'If you're sure.'

'Much going on?' asked Phil flatly, as his breakfast was delivered.

'It's fine mate. Don't you worry. Just concentrate on Ruth, Kyle and yourself.'

'This might seem odd, but have the Larbies crossed your radar recently?'

'The who?'

'Never mind,' said Phil, realising all that was long before Gary transferred to Sussex from South Wales Police. His phone beeped with an incoming call. He pulled it away from his ear and saw 'Unknown Caller'.

'Gary, can I call you back? I've got a call waiting. It might be the hospital.'

'Sure, speak later,' Gary replied.

Phil tapped the green icon.

'Phil Cooke,' he said with trepidation.

'Mr Cooke, my sincere condolences for the loss of your son,' the Geordie voice said.

'Who is this?'

'Later. I have a proposition for you.'

'Are you the fucking press?' Phil became aware he was drawing more curious stares. 'Just a minute,' he said, quieter. He pushed his chair back and made for the door. Once outside he said, 'Who are you?'

'I understand your anger, Mr Cooke. That's why I'm calling. I'll cut to the chase. I can find out who killed your boy.'

'What the f . . . ? Look, if you've got information, tell the police.'

'That's not how we work, Mr Cooke,' the Geordie replied. Icy calm. 'You know what I do for a living, I take it?'

'Of course, and you're in a unique position to understand that even if Superintendent Howe does get a lucky break and stumbles across the killer, they'll be out in ten years. We offer a more permanent closure.'

'Look, whoever you are, I'm a cop and if this is some attempt to blackmail me or some scam, I will hunt you down and rip your fucking throat out. If you know something, tell the police, if not then piss off.'

'Is Mrs Howe even allowed to investigate? I mean, there must be some rules about conflict of interest.'

Phil's heart pounded on his ribs. 'What the hell's that supposed to mean?'

'I think we both know the answer to that, don't we?'

'Whoever you are . . .'

'Think about it, Mr Cooke. If there are no arrests in the next couple of days – and there won't be – I'll call back.'

The call went dead. Phil stared at the mute handset, scenarios colliding in his head.

What the hell was that? What was this offer? What did they know? He had no idea, but something told him that wasn't the last he'd hear from them.

* * *

Jo's head pounded as she swung her car into the driveway of her three-bedroomed semi. Just the thought of the amount of work needed to spruce up its dilapidated exterior crushed her.

When she and Darren bought the Benett Drive house eight years ago, it was to be their forever home. They knew, after four years renting, a mortgage would cripple them, so they plumped for a run-down house in a good area. Hove Park was respectable by any standards, but their subsequent neglect had recently attracted some snide comments about dragging the neighbourhood down.

Sneaking home before the 6 p.m. briefing was the boss's privilege, she told herself. She was desperate to reacquaint herself with the boys and, rather belatedly, welcome Darren back from New York. Pinching her waistline, she wished she could squeeze in a run too, but that would have to wait.

Killing the car engine, she grabbed her phone from its cradle and her shoulder bag from the passenger seat, and stepped on to the gravel driveway. She breathed deeply – not another bloody bonfire – and girded herself for the onslaught of noise and revelry that awaited her.

'Mummy's home,' she called, as she opened the door.

Screams of delight heralded the boys scampering then hurling themselves at her legs, almost rugby-tackling her to the floor.

'Steady, steady,' she chuckled, throwing an arm each around Ciaran and Liam, then bending down to hug them properly.

She looked up as Darren sauntered into the hallway, his eyes tired, but wearing that trademark loving smile.

'Hello, handsome,' she said as she stood up, throwing her arms around his neck, while the boys gripped her legs. She kissed him warmly. 'Nice holiday?'

'Cheeky mare,' Darren replied, still smiling. He took her hand and led her into the lounge. The boys demanded to be picked up, still beyond excitement at the rarity of all four of them being in the same room together. She let go of Darren's hand and hoisted Ciaran onto her hip while Darren did the same with Liam.

'Wine?' ask Darren.

'I wish. Hot water would be lovely,' she replied as she collapsed on the settee, still hugging Ciaran.

Darren plonked Liam on Jo's other knee and left her to the mercies of both boys' slobbering kisses, while he disappeared to the kitchen. A few minutes later he returned with two steaming mugs, placing them on the table, then squeezed in next to her.

'Thanks darling. How was your trip?' Jo asked.

'Yes, so so,' Darren replied. 'But what about you? How are you coping? Poor Harry Cooke.'

Typical sweet Darren, Jo thought. Most people would want the juicy details, but he instinctively knew that no one else would have checked in on her.

'Yes, I'm OK. I don't think I'll ever forget telling Phil though. I've given some death messages in my time, but that was the hardest.'

'Poor you. Any progress?'

She looked at him with mock suspicion. 'Which hat are you wearing? Husband or hack?'

He grinned back. 'Husband, for now.' It was a charade they often went through, ever since the scandal in London where a number of senior cops were caught cosying up to prominent journalists.

'No, nothing really. Just some titbits here and there, but no suspects. We're going to try a press conference and reconstruction but, as it's been plastered over the media for the last two days, I'm not sure it's worth it.'

'Well, you never know.'

The boys, now bored by the grown-up talk, had relocated to within three feet of the television, flicking through ubiquitous cartoons.

'How's Phil and Ruth?'

'Not good. Ruth was rushed to hospital when Phil told her.' Jo's phone chirped into life. 'Talk of the devil. I've got to take this,' she said, hitting the 'accept' button. Darren nodded and shuffled down to the floor to join the boys.

'Hi Phil, how are you?' Jo said, walking to the kitchen, the Dora the Explorer theme tune fading into the background.

'Jo, how close are you to making an arrest?' he asked.

She was taken aback. He knew how these things worked. He would be told about any progress when the time was right. She had all but guaranteed him that he would be trusted with more information than most grieving fathers. She also knew not to bullshit him.

'Phil, I promise I'll tell you when I have something. Is everything OK?'

'How many people have you got on the team? What are your main lines of enquiry? Did you check out the Larbies, like I suggested?'

'Whoa. Phil, trust me it's fine. We haven't got much at the moment, but we will catch who did this. And when we do, you'll be the first to know, I swear.'

'I need him locked up before they come after Kyle or Ruth. I need you to pull out all the stops.' She could hear his voice wobble. Drink, maybe? 'Do whatever it takes and let me know if you need me to have a word in anyone's ear.'

She stared at the phone. Incredulous.

'Has something happened?'

'One more thing, have you ever told anyone about us?'

'No, of course not,' she whispered. 'Look, what is this?'

'Nothing. Just keep me informed.' He ended the call.

She stood motionless. What had come over him? Of course he was upset, desperate even, but he seemed to have lost all perspective. Where was his faith? He practically trained her, for God's sake. And what was that about them?

She walked back into the lounge, deep in thought. Darren looked round and tried to read her. 'Everything OK?'

'I'm not sure,' she replied pensively. 'Look, I'd better go back in.' She glided over and kissed Darren and the boys on their heads, muttering, 'Love you. Don't wait up,' as she headed for her car – wondering if she might be missing something.

9

5.00 p.m., Friday 4th May

Jo turned into the police HQ entrance and waved her access card at the electronic reader. As the barrier rose, she turned right and headed towards the two-storey car park. For once she had her pick of the bays. Five o'clock on the Friday of a bank holiday weekend meant HQ's ESSOs – Every Saturday and Sunday Off – had long since gone home.

She lurched to a halt in the bay closest to the stairwell, jumped out of the car and paced up the concrete steps, zapping the car locked as she did so.

She strode into the Major Incident Room, relieved to find it a hive of activity.

'Anyone seen Mr Porter?' Jo called to no one in particular.

'Over here,' said Scott, looking particularly frazzled behind the teetering piles of statements vying for his attention.

'Have you got a minute?' said Jo, nodding towards her office.

'Not especially,' the DCI replied, but stood and followed her anyway.

They sat at the small, cluttered conference table. Jo closed the door.

'Have you spoken to Phil Cooke today?'

'Funny you should ask. I've just had him on the phone. He was moaning that we are not keeping him up to speed.'

'Interesting. I had a similar call and, to be honest, he's bang out of order

70

phoning you after he's tried me. How did you find him?'

'Well, he seemed a bit needy but it's hard to gauge. What's he usually like?'

'Not that,' said Jo.

'Well, for a bloke who walks on water like all you Sussex lot reckon, he needs to wind his neck in. He's demanding chapter and verse and won't believe me when I tell him there are no developments.'

'He has just lost a son.'

'Look, I know there's no manual on how to react after your child has been killed but, in my experience, for someone who knows the score, he's acting really weirdly.'

'OK. Keep an eye on it and let me know if it gets too much. Thanks,' said Jo, signalling the meeting was over.

Porter took the hint and left, tapping at his phone as he did so.

*

The following morning, Jo's anxiety was knotting her up. Normally, three days into an enquiry, something would have emerged from the fog. A promising witness, an informant or at least some forensics. But tumbleweed was blowing through this, her highest-profile job to date.

If only one of the 573 investigative actions her team were working through would bear fruit, or a buoyant scientist would call from the lab announcing a DNA hit. At least then she could give some much-needed good news to Phil, especially after his rant last night. But, in reality, all she had left was to clutch at straws with a reconstruction and press conference.

'Scott,' she called across the corridor on seeing her deputy dart into the incident room.

Jo saw Porter's shoulders drop. 'Don't get settled. We're off to see Phil Cooke.'

'Do we have to? Can't you go on your own?'

'No. I need you there. Are you free to come with me? Forgive me if that sounded like a question.'

* * *

71

Porter scraped the wheel against the kerb as he pulled up outside Phil's house.

'I didn't hear that,' said Jo. 'I'm sure it's not the first scratch this rust bucket has suffered.'

'Whatever.'

Jo led the way as they walked towards Phil's front gate, Porter slouching behind. After what seemed like half a dozen locks being turned, which clearly irritated Scott, the door opened.

'Morning Phil,' Jo said, noting his moth-eaten red tracksuit bottoms and grubby blue-and-green 'Superdry' T-shirt.

'Morning. Come in,' he grumbled, as they stepped over the threshold.

They followed him up the narrow hallway, Jo spotting pictures of Harry on the radiator cabinet to her right. Something of a shrine already.

Phil led them into the ramshackle lounge, which told Jo housework had given way to other priorities over recent months. A faint smell of curry lingered; perhaps a snatched takeaway for Phil and Kyle on the way back from the hospital last night.

The two officers sat side by side on one of the sofas, silently taking in their sad surroundings, neither mentioning Phil forgetting to offer drinks.

'Got news?' he asked. No small talk then.

'How's Ruth?'

'Getting there. She seems to be over the initial shock, but we are seeing someone from the Martlets Hospice later today. They think she's best in there and, to be honest, I'm starting to agree.'

Jo could see the despair in Phil's moist eyes.

'Anyway, that's not why you are here. What have you got for me?'

'No real news I'm afraid. We've got nearly six hundred actions ongoing, a ton of exhibits at the lab and the usual informant taskings.'

'Right. Anything on the Larbies?'

Scott threw Jo a look.

'Haven't you briefed your deputy?' said Phil.

'There's nothing to say,' said Jo. 'Scott, fifteen years ago someone tried to set fire to Phil's house with Ruth and the boys at home. Phil was, er, elsewhere. It was probably down to a gang we locked up and then they made some more threats when they were sentenced, but nothing's happened since.'

'Except those threats, like the arson, were to my family and Jo seems to have it in her head that they're not worth looking at for this. Which means Kyle or Ruth could be next.'

Jo's eyes pleaded with him. 'That's a bit of a stretch, Phil. As far as we know they're still in prison. Anyway, we need to clear the ground under our feet first.'

'Make sure she checks,' said Phil to Scott.

'How do you feel about doing a press conference?' said Jo, changing the subject.

'Eh? You'll have every fruitcake coming out of the woodwork. You'll be swamped.'

'I know, but at this stage I'll try anything.'

'Your call. I'll do it if you want, but it sounds a bit desperate.'

'Humour me. We also want to try a reconstruction if we have nothing by Tuesday.'

'You're kidding.'

'It might help jog some memories. It can't hurt. We wondered if Kyle would consider playing Harry.'

'I don't know,' replied Phil. 'We can ask him. He's upstairs. I'll call him down but go easy on him. He and Harry had such a bond. He's taken all this really badly, turned in on himself – even more than normal.'

'We don't have to ask him now,' said Scott. 'We can leave it to you if you like.'

'No, let's see what he says,' Phil insisted. He pulled himself up from the sofa and strode to the door.

'Kyle,' he shouted up the stairs. 'Can you come down?'

Floorboards creaked above them, then trudging footsteps.

If Phil was dishevelled, Kyle looked positively vagrant. His mousy, matted hair twisted in all directions, while his crumpled and stained grey 'Rag'n'Bone Man' T-shirt and green pyjama trousers hung precariously from him.

'Yeah,' he murmured, glancing at Jo, then nodding to Scott.

'Kyle, sit down a mo,' said Phil. He stood at the doorway, defiantly. 'Jo and Scott want to ask you something.'

Kyle fidgeted and looked to his dad for a clue.

'Kyle, unfortunately we haven't found Harry's killer, so we wondered if you could help us,' said Scott.

'Me? How can I help?' His fidgets became worse.

'Well, we want to run a reconstruction of Harry's last movements. To see if we can jog anyone's memory. This Tuesday evening, a week after he died.'

'I know when he was murdered.'

'Please just listen,' said Phil.

'Thanks,' Scott continued. 'We want someone to play Harry. Walk the route he took. Do the things he did. There would be plenty of people to support you, your dad'll be there too.'

Kyle looked incredulously at each of them in turn.

'Me? You want me to do it? Is this some kind of sick fucking joke? You want me to play my dead brother?' he shouted.

'Mate,' said Phil, stepping over to pacify his son. 'It's quite normal. You can say no if you want.' He tried to put his arm around Kyle's shoulder but it was angrily shrugged off.

'How dare you even think it,' he hissed. 'Have you no respect, no feelings? Of course it's a fucking no. I don't think I can ever go to that park again, let alone pretend to be Harry. You're taking the piss.'

He slammed the lounge door, then ran upstairs, footsteps thundering through the house.

At the banging of an upstairs door, Jo and Scott looked to Phil for the next step. But his pragmatic I-can-handle-this demeanour had vanished.

* * *

Two days after the awkward outburst, Jo and Phil were lost in their own thoughts as Clarissa Heard, red-framed glasses perched on the end of her nose, ran through the final briefing for the press conference.

Unlike most operational police stations, given this was a Bank Holiday Monday, police headquarters had the feel of Western Ghost Town. Even so, the anteroom, next to the conference hall where the press could be heard fretting impatiently about live broadcast slots and looming deadlines, hardly steadied their nerves. Its conversion from stationery cupboard to hot-desk office had been half-hearted. Grubby, cramped and airless, it did little to relax them as they prepared for the baying they knew awaited them on the other side of the door.

'Jo, stick to those three key messages,' Clarissa reminded her, counting them out on her fingers. 'Shocking motiveless killing. All the more tragic on the most exciting day of Harry's life, then finish up with the witness appeal. That's what we want ringing in people's ears.'

Jo nodded politely as she tucked her hair behind her ears. She knew all this. She had, after all, approved the press statement in the first place, but Clarissa was just doing her job.

'And Phil,' Clarissa continued, 'you are here as the father, not the divisional commander. Please stick to your grief and loss.'

'Actually,' Jo interjected, 'why are you in uniform, Phil? Won't that confuse the press and the viewers?' She looked to Clarissa for back-up but she was conveniently distracted by her phone.

'I just feel more comfortable like this. Is that a problem?'

Jo raised her hands in supplication. 'No, I'm sure it's fine.'

'Right, time to go,' announced Clarissa, glad to break the rising tension.

As the three of them trooped in, the mumbling gave way to a din of clicking cameras and a wall of strobing flashlights. A good turnout for a bank holiday. The TV cameras standing sentinel on their Martian tripods on the right side of the room put Jo on edge.

She freed the button of her dark grey blazer as they all settled in their designated places, a pad of paper and glass of water behind each speaker's nameplate on the spotless blue baize-covered table. The familiar roll-up banner behind them, bearing both the Sussex Police and Crimestoppers crests and phone numbers, reminded the press and public how to provide information, either on or off the record.

Jo shot Clarissa a searing stare as she saw that Phil's nameplate read 'Chief Superintendent Phil Cooke', rather than just plain 'Mr', as they had agreed. Clarissa's barely perceptible shrug suggested she had been outranked on that one.

Clarissa raised a hand, bringing the room to order. 'Ladies and gentlemen, can I have your attention for a moment please?' An expectant hush descended. 'As it says in your press packs, Detective Superintendent Howe on my right will update you on Harry Cooke's tragic murder, where we are in terms of the investigation, followed by making an appeal.

'Mr Cooke on my left will then speak on behalf of the family. There will then be a short time for questions which I would ask you to allow me to control. You should all get the time you need. Afterwards, Mrs Howe will be available for one-to-one interviews but Mr Cooke won't be.' Phil glared at Clarissa, but she continued. 'Mr Cooke is grieving from a loss that none of us can imagine, so I ask you to respect his privacy.' She then gently touched Jo's sleeve, the prearranged signal for her to start.

Jo's statement was brisk and to the point. As she had been trained, she imagined connecting with just one person, her mum, as she stared down the camera lenses. She dared not think of the millions of others staring back. There was no point admitting they were clueless as to who had killed Harry. The assembled journalists were battle hardened; they would read between the lines anyway.

'In conclusion, I repeat, if anyone knows anything – anything at all – about why or how Harry Cooke was attacked so callously, or if you were in the Withdean Park area between 5 p.m. and 10 p.m. last Tuesday evening, please contact us at the incident room or call Crimestoppers anonymously on 0800 555 111.'

Phil took his silent cue.

'My wife Ruth, Harry's brother Kyle and I are completely devastated by Harry's senseless and tragic murder. Many of you know, the day he died he was offered a professional contract with Brighton and Hove Albion. His dreams had come true. Then some scum took it all from him, and him from us.'

Jo and Clarissa exchanged worried looks as Phil put his notes to one side. 'Detective Superintendent Howe is a fine detective and I have no doubt that with the people she has, she is doing the best she can, but in this day and age the police need your help more than ever. We have let society sink to the level where lowlifes can wander, unchecked, armed with knives, and murder whoever they like. Well, now they have taken on the wrong family.'

Jo stared at Phil, aghast.

Phil shook off Clarissa's mollifying hand, as all the cameras locked on to him.

'I am ripped apart by what happened, but I am equally anxious that no other parent has to sit here pleading with you to help the diminishing police force find their child's killer. Please help.'

The second he drew breath, the uproar was deafening.

'Do you blame the cuts for your son's death, Mr Cooke?'

'Is Superintendent Howe up to the job, Phil?'

'Is this another example of broken Britain?'

'Couldn't you stop this happening in your own city, Chief Superintendent?'

Jo hissed in Clarissa's ear. 'Bloody stop them. And shut him up too,' she added, jabbing at Phil.

Clarissa's boomed plea for silence went unheeded. They had smelt blood and moved in for the kill.

Only when Phil raised his hand did order return.

'Many of you know I only ever speak the truth and, yes, I wear my heart on my sleeve. But my world has ended and it's only right I say why. First of all, this city has been stripped of over two hundred cops in the last five years. We no longer have police community support officers. We share just about every service with our neighbouring forces. The few officers who are left are spread so thinly they can barely function. This government has decided that you no longer need a police force that does anything but pick up the pieces. We don't even pretend to prevent crime or work with communities any more. Harry's death is a reminder of the human cost of a broken police force. And it won't be the last.'

He sipped his water, trying to see who was asking which question from the dozens shouted.

Jo and Clarissa just gazed ahead.

In a lull, one voice echoed.

'Mr Cooke, in your experience, I ask again, is Detective Superintendent Howe up to the job?'

Jo swung round, her eyes pleading him to silence.

'Of course she is, but . . .'

'But?' came an anonymous voice from the floor.

'No, Phil,' hissed Clarissa.

'But,' he continued, 'a murder of this type takes people to investigate. She won't say this but her inquiry is being run on a shoestring, and even she will admit she's unable to follow up all lines of enquiry. No one should expect their child's murder to be investigated by so few – however good their leader.'

Jo was appalled, but Phil continued. 'She has half the people she needs, and those she has come from across the south-east. The hunt for Harry's killer needs more detectives. Detectives who actually understand this city and the cauldron of violence and depravity we have allowed it to become.'

The barrage of questions and clattering camera shutters exploded again, along with the dazzling flashlights.

'Thank you. This is over,' shouted Clarissa. 'There will be no more questions and no interviews.'

She and Jo sprung to their feet, grabbing their papers as they darted towards the door.

'Get out,' Jo hissed as she barged passed Phil's still-seated frame.

Reluctantly, he rose and followed them from the room, leaving the continuing pleas for headlines unanswered in his wake.

Once in the anteroom, Phil looked shocked at his own outburst. Jo was pacing up and down, her rage undisguised.

'What the fuck was that?' she bellowed, her manicured finger prodding at Phil. 'You played right into their hands. This will be all about the cuts now, nothing about my appeal for people to help catch your son's killer.'

Not giving him a chance to answer, she stormed out, shrugging off Clarissa with an angry flick of her hand.

Phil felt his silenced phone vibrate. He took it from his pocket and glanced at the screen.

The name it displayed told him he had probably just thrown away the one thing he had left.

10

9.30 a.m., Monday 7th May

Phil felt like he was walking the green mile of death row as he trudged across the car park to Malling House. He nodded to a group of officers sneaking a crafty smoke, sensing their discomfort.

ACC Acers had wasted no time in summoning him, despite not having the balls to actually be at the press conference, opting instead to watch it from the safety of his office. He would have hated the heart-wrenching condolences and, worse still, being held accountable for the mess the force was in.

The carved plate on the closed door pronounced it the domain of the chief officers. Phil paused, then knocked. Rather than the usual gruff, 'Come in,' he was ordered to 'Wait.'

He recognised the tactic as one of his own. Let the condemned stew in their own anxiety on the hard seats outside before deigning to grant them entry to face the inevitable.

None of the secretaries and staff officers were in – not on a bank holiday – so he couldn't get the nod on what his obnoxious boss had planned.

He gazed at the frames opposite. Each celebrated a bygone era when policing was a proud profession. The catching of the Brighton Bomber, Patrick Magee, who came within a whisker of assassinating Prime Minister

Margaret Thatcher and her government. The eventual conviction of Russell Bishop for murdering two girls in the 1980s. The horror of the Shoreham Air Disaster which took eleven lives one sunny August lunchtime. He had been involved in the last two, one way or another, over his thirty-five years' service.

All his instincts told him that was all about to end.

A lump came to his throat as the office door was flung open to the brusque command, 'Come in.'

The wooden visitors' chair faced Acers, who sat behind the desk wearing his bloody police tunic.

Tosser.

Phil didn't wait for the invite to sit.

'Right, Phil. I know what you're going through and I am truly sorry for that, but that performance,' he nodded to the TV, 'no, that debacle was a step too far. I know we've not seen eye to eye and, frankly, it's felt like you've spent the last year undermining me and going your own sweet way, but this can't continue. The police and crime commissioner watched it live and was straight on the phone demanding your dismissal. Of course, that can't happen, but you need a break so I'm transferring you to a lower-profile role. Unless you remain on compassionate leave, you will now report directly to me, overseeing the Corporate Fiscal Efficiencies Programme. In essence you are in charge of the cuts. Someone else will take over at Brighton. Now go home and the next time you report for duty, it will be here, working for me.'

'But . . .'

'Goodbye, Phil.'

*

Phil was gutted. He had always thought his career would end on his terms. He had planned to retire soon, just not yet.

He still loved his job – or rather the job that had now been ripped away from him. He'd had no intention of leaving until the buzz he felt whenever

81

he walked into Brighton Police Station faded. Now coming to work would be torture, and he couldn't stand that.

As he walked to his car, grimly keeping it together, his silenced mobile buzzed in his pocket.

'Unknown Caller' used to denote a police extension or one of his more cautious colleagues. Now it could also be the hospital with bad news. Or the Geordie, he remembered. He answered, wondering which it would be.

'Mr Cooke, that was some press conference.' The Geordie.

'What the fuck do you want?'

'Now, now. I appreciate you've had a tough morning, but there's no need to be like that, is there?'

Phil stepped behind an old maintenance shed; this was not a call for eavesdroppers.

'I'm not interested in what you are offering. I told you.'

'The whole country just saw you on Sky News. It's no secret that Superintendent Howe needs a little help. You of all people should know what she needs.'

'What the hell are you on about?'

'Don't give me that. You can't believe no one knew who you were with when your house burnt down? Did a canny job keeping it from your wife though.'

Phil slumped against the shed, no longer confident his legs would hold out.

'I don't know what you think you know, but . . .'

'Don't worry, we're all human. We can keep a secret, if it suits us. I mean, that's the last thing your wife needs to find out, the way she is just now.'

'Don't fucking threaten me. Even if it was true, who's going to believe you?' Phil was sweating now.

'You think that's a chance worth taking, do you?'

Phil's mind flashed to Ruth, tears spilling from her bloodshot eyes as she clung to Harry's picture. Could he pile even more pain on in her dying days?

'Please, don't go there.'

'That's more like it. Anyway, it seems even you agree Mrs Howe needs some help.'

Phil coughed, back on sturdier ground.

'Look, I just lost it in there. I shouldn't have said those things but it's got nothing to do with you.'

'But you did say them, Mr Cooke. And you meant them.'

'So what if I did?'

'It means you know your son's murderer will never be caught.'

'He'll be caught. I have every faith in Jo.'

'You might want to rephrase that. What about those lines of enquiry she's not following? Maybe we could help there. Let us find the killer. I promise we will and only you and we will know.'

Phil paced, head down.

'Why? What's in it for you?'

'All in good time. Sounds like you're coming round to the idea.'

'I never said that.'

'But we both know you will.'

'Then you don't know me very well, do you?'

'You're a grieving father who wants justice and a husband with a secret. What more is there to know?'

'You can't tell Ruth,' whispered Phil.

'So there is something to tell then. We don't expect all the money up front, if that's what you're worried about.'

'Money? Why would I pay you?'

'We have costs, Mr Cooke, surely you realised we're not a charity. And we guarantee results.'

'Such as?' Phil turned away from two chatting call handlers, wandering past.

'Well, we don't post testimonials on a website but, since you asked, it wasn't entirely a coincidence those two boys were found injured by Carden Park the day after that caretaker was beaten up. And their two pals? Well, those reprobates have been taken care of in a more permanent way.'

'That was you?' Phil's head was spinning.

'And that plasterer who beat his girlfriend up? You haven't found him yet, have you?'

'What are you saying?'

'Think about it, Mr Cooke. I'll call again when you've had some time to ponder.'

The phone went dead. Phil steadied himself against the shed wall, the revelations sinking in.

*

Superintendent Gary Hedges missed his mate and mentor Phil Cooke. Their contrasting skills and backgrounds were always a perfect combination.

Phil was a detective through and through. His promotion four years ago to city commander had been his first time back in uniform since he'd passed his two-year probation. In the intervening three decades there had been little in the world of serious crime he could not crack.

Gary, on the other hand, was more a 'crash, bang, wallop' type of copper. He had grown up in the back of police vans in South Wales. First, making no friends in the pit villages during the year-long miners' strike in the 1980s. Then transferring to Sussex, rising through the ranks to command hundreds of officers battling with anarchists or vicious football supporters intent on cracking skulls. He was recognised as the force's foremost public order and firearms commander, and for good reason.

Today though, he could really do with some of Phil's wiliness.

It seemed this crime wave was his, and his alone, to solve. Well, with a little help from another legend. Gary checked his watch. DI Bob Heaton had promised to be with him in five minutes. Where was he?

He was about to go and grab the ancient detective himself, when the characteristically bedraggled inspector appeared at the door.

'About time too.' Gary looked Bob up and down in dismay.

'Sorry I'm late, boss. We had something in on Operation Carbon, Harry's murder.'

'Yes, I know what Op Carbon is. Anything significant?'

'Don't know yet, but we're pissing off the phone companies with all the data we're demanding.'

Heaton frustrated the hell out of Gary. He kept everything close to his chest until he was one hundred per cent happy it was accurate, relevant and useful and that the source was adequately protected. He was just doing his job, but Gary wished he'd cut himself some slack from time to time.

'OK, sit down,' said Gary, waving Bob towards the elongated conference table that filled his office. Bob slumped in a chair halfway down and opened his investigator's notebook.

Gary sat opposite, pristine in his black short-sleeved uniform shirt and matching cargo trousers.

'Bob, I'm getting fucking worried about these attacks over the last few weeks.'

'From what I gather, they seem to be spread across the city, only really linked by the level of violence.'

'Could the attacks on the two lads at Carden Park and the caretaker be linked?'

'Not sure about the caretaker,' Bob interjected. 'I think that was Marco's crew.'

'OK, that makes sense. But apart from those biggies, we've had a nonce slashed in Moulsecoomb, a fraudster targeting old people run off the road, and a suspected rapist, a domestic abuser and two burglars who've vanished off the face of the earth.'

'Is that any great loss?'

'Not especially, it just seems strange. None of those who have been attacked or disappeared are the sort you would want to take home to meet Mum. Perhaps that's another connection.'

'What do you want me to do? I'm not exactly kicking my heels at the moment, boss.'

'I know, but we can't have people going round crippling and trying to kill folk. However obnoxious they are. It just seems bloody odd to me.'

'Boss, let me be clear. You want me to commit my scarce resources to look into something that is "bloody odd".'

Gary grinned. 'Isn't that what you suits do? Seriously, you've got to admit a spate of apparently random brutal attacks on the city's lowlife is unusual. There must be something behind it.'

'I'll get someone on to it. I can't promise anything but we'll see what we can find out. And if we discover it's just "odd" or escalates to "fucking weird", you'll be the first to know.'

'Piss off,' chuckled Gary, 'and do your bloody tie up.'

*

Tonight, of all nights, Darren Howe had to be with Jo.

Yesterday's press conference had gone viral and the debates were already raging on Twitter and phone-in radio shows. Clarissa Heard had spent the aftermath batting off requests for Jo to appear on *Newsnight*, *The Jeremy Vine Show* and even BBC Radio 4's flagship *Today* programme.

With the boys all snuggled down for the night, Darren poured two huge glasses of Pinot Grigio, took a deep breath and made his way back to the lounge which he'd only just remembered to tidy before Jo got home.

'Love, put your phone down and let's talk,' he said, passing her a glass as he settled next to her on the settee.

'Have you seen what they are saying about me? "Out of her depth", "letting the family down", "bungler".' She was close to tears.

'We both know Phil didn't say those things, but the trolls don't care about the truth. It never helps to read those saddos' comments on the websites. They are just loners sitting in their underpants munching on Wotsits in their bedrooms, while Mum and Dad are downstairs watching *Coronation Street*. You have to ignore them and have faith in yourself.'

'Why should I? He might as well have told them I'm not up to it. That's what he implied. And he's right.'

'The press are just playing the angle. It's not personal. For them it's manna from heaven that Phil turned on the politics. What's more, it's keeping the case on the front pages.'

'For what? I'm finished; a laughing stock.' She gulped her wine, and closed her eyes.

'Says who? It's Phil who's been shafted. All those who matter are right behind you.'

'You don't understand.' She shuffled away. 'My success stands or falls on my credibility among the team, not the pen-pushers in their ivory towers. If the troops don't back me, I might as well pack up and go home.'

'But surely. . .'

'No buts. They love Phil and always have. And with good reason. Right now they see a grieving dad who has lost his job for speaking up.'

'You've got to toughen up, love. I know how hard you've worked for everything, and how difficult this is. But you will get through it. Believe in yourself. Today's newspapers wrap tomorrow's fish and chips. It's not what has happened that will define you, it's how you react to it.'

He took her glass from her hand, placed it on the coffee table and held her close, stroking her shiny auburn hair, as the tears streamed down her cheeks.

11

9.00 a.m., Tuesday 8th May

Superintendent Gary Hedges' anxiety had been growing since early in the morning, but snowballed the closer he got to the Office of the Police and Crime Commissioner in Lewes.

Boasting stunning views across the River Ouse, PCC Teresa Sutton's vast offices took up most of the top floor of Sackville House, an otherwise dismal new-build plonked in the shadow of a DIY store and Tesco supermarket. It had originally housed the now defunct Sussex Police Authority, who had drawn some flack since their tenancy started just as they closed police stations and made staff redundant. An opulent two fingers to austerity.

When the dysfunctional Police Authorities were abolished, the new overseer of police, a directly elected police and crime commissioner, had taken over the premises. The swell of policy and media staff Sutton had crammed in contrasted sickeningly with the stripping out of front-line policing.

An operational cop at heart, Gary avoided coming here at all costs. But after last week's tragedy and Phil's outburst at the press conference yesterday he was, for now, in charge at Brighton and Hove. And with that came the summons to an audience with Teresa Sutton.

Despite the traffic conspiring against him, he still managed to swing through the narrow gates of the packed car park with ten minutes to spare.

Chief Constable Helen Ricks was already waiting outside, absorbed on her phone. She'd have walked the short distance down the hill from Police HQ.

Gary sauntered over, keeping a respectful distance while she finished her call, but kicking himself for not choosing his smart white shirt, black tie and tunic to match Helen, instead of the black operational uniform he so favoured.

'Hi Gary,' chirped the chief, as she pocketed her phone. 'Don't look so worried. She's all mouth. And you report to me, not her.'

'Thanks. You know, I'm quite happy to face down an angry mob intent on kicking me from here to breakfast time, but a summons to see a five-foot-four, twinset and pearls politician puts the fear of God in me.'

'I'll use that against you one day,' Helen joked. 'Seriously, she'll have a bee in her bonnet about the soaring crime, the plummeting arrests and the burgeoning violent attacks. But it's not personal. You just happened to be the one in the chair when the music stopped.'

'Talking of that, any news on Phil's replacement?'

'All in good time Gary. We'll decide today or tomorrow.' She gave him a wry smile. 'Come on, let's get this over with.'

Helen hefted open the bombproof glazed door and announced their arrival to the disinterested receptionist, who shoved the visitors' book towards her.

'Good morning to you too,' Helen said, raising an eyebrow as she filled out the register.

'You can go up,' came the monotone reply.

Helen led the way up the six flights of stairs and pressed the buzzer marked 'Police and Crime Commissioner'.

Almost immediately one of the PCC's many staff opened the door and ushered them in.

'Ah Mr Hedges, welcome,' said Teresa Sutton, far louder than was necessary, as she breezed across the open-plan office. 'Ms Ricks, I see you have come to hold the superintendent's hand. There really is no need. I'm sure you have better things to do. I mean, he looks like he can take care of himself, don't you think?'

'Just keeping the constitutional protocols in place. If you have a fight to pick, pick it with me.'

Gary winced. He knew there was no love lost between these two powerhouses, but he had no desire to be caught in the crossfire.

The PCC ushered them into a bland meeting room which boasted just a small table, a star-shaped conference telephone, half a dozen hard-backed chairs and a poorly erased whiteboard fixed to the wall. Her chief executive slipped in behind them.

Gary correctly guessed that he wasn't about to ask how he liked his coffee.

Helen Ricks sat next to Gary with the PCC and CEO facing them across the table.

'Right, we are all busy people, Mr Hedges, so I'll get straight to the point,' she pronounced, glancing at the crib sheet in front of her. 'Brighton and Hove. Overall crime up thirty-six per cent, violent crime up ninety per cent, burglary up forty-five per cent. Every day I read about some poor soul being kept alive by machines after a beating that you couldn't be bothered to get to. Not to mention the divisional commander's son being murdered. A divisional commander who, by the way, behaved appallingly in front of the cameras yesterday. What the hell's going on?'

'Just a minute,' Helen interjected before Gary could return fire. 'How often do we have this discussion? If you are going to throw statistics around then at least do us the courtesy of understanding them.'

'Ms Ricks, my question was addressed to the person who actually knows what's going on. Not to someone who barely leaves her office.'

Gary wished the ground would open and swallow him up. If these two wanted a scrap, so be it, but spare him the front-row seat. The PCC seemed to know which of the chief constable's buttons to press to spark a reaction, and Helen Ricks was renowned for detesting any form of bullying and had a look and a way that could freeze oil. Rumour had it that she'd fallen victim to a vicious campaign of intimidation while in the Metropolitan Police which had seen her sidelined for six months, then an assistant commissioner sacked. She was long past fawning over oppressive bosses.

'Well, Superintendent?' Sutton continued, stifling the seething chief.

'The situation is this, Commissioner,' Gary said. 'Crime is indeed up and I'm surprised you didn't mention that arrests are down. I accept that, but we have significantly fewer officers than we did five years ago. On top of that, we are constantly having to backfill for an underfunded mental health service. Poverty has thrown more people on the streets, and the "haves" – their sense of entitlement has mushroomed. That's before I get on to the daily protests and twice-weekly football matches we have to police.'

'That's all very well, Superintendent, but what are you doing about it?'

'My men and women are stretched to the limits.'

Teresa Sutton fixed on Gary, her silence inviting more rope to hang him with.

'One other thing,' he continued, falling into the trap. 'I believe we have a gang of vigilantes operating in the city, picking up our slack.'

'Did you know about this, Ms Ricks?'

Helen shuffled, clearly taken aback at this new information. 'No, Commissioner. I'm sure Gary was going to brief me on that today.' She threw him a fierce look.

'In fairness, it's only a theory and I have people looking at it. It's just we have a spate of random bad-on-bad attacks. Normally we would put that down to rival gangs, but these are almost too random.'

'Don't you think you need to get on to that?' Sutton demanded.

'I am on it, Commissioner, but it's early days and . . .'

'It sounds to me,' the chief interrupted, 'that there is far more work to do on this yet. Let's not get carried away with theories. And I'd prefer that the few staff we do have focus on innocent victims rather than those who have brought it upon themselves.'

'Not at all,' said Sutton, 'I'm with the superintendent on this one. I deplore people taking the law into their own hands. Mr Hedges, I want you to provide me with an update on this by the end of the week. I may well go to the press, making it clear it won't be tolerated.'

'Let's wait,' pleaded the chief. 'Let's see what, if anything, we come up with first.'

'The end of the week please, Superintendent,' said the PCC as she stood up, the mute CEO following suit. 'Ms Ricks, you'll do well to remember that while you have sole operational responsibility, with that comes accountability. To me.' She breezed out of the room.

'You ever ambush me again . . .' hissed Helen as she gathered her papers.

'What? I just wanted to show her I had my finger on the pulse,' Gary replied.

'Are you stupid? You saw how she reacted. You just loaded her gun.'

Gary saw his boss was struggling to keep her legendary cool. 'I'm sorry, I didn't realise . . .'

'Yes, well I meant what I said. Concentrate on the real victims, not the scum.' Helen flung her chair back and headed across the open-plan office, ignoring the stares she was drawing. Gary followed sheepishly.

As she stomped down the stone staircase, Gary said, 'I'll keep you updated, ma'am. I'm sorry.'

'Whatever.'

'Do you want a lift up the road?' offered Gary.

'No, I'll walk. I need to calm down,' she replied.

Gary stood, dumbfounded, trying to work out how he had ballsed up this fabulous opportunity to impress quite so spectacularly. Something told him the shortlist to replace Phil was now a little shorter.

*

The morning papers had been as brutal as their online counterparts, and try as they might, none of her team could find a morsel of hope to lighten Jo's mood. As she walked back to her office, Chief Constable Helen Ricks was heading towards her.

'Oh, morning ma'am, I wasn't expecting to see you today,' said Jo, pausing outside the door.

'Of course you weren't. I need a chat,' the chief said.

This is it then, thought Jo, as she followed the chief in. Both sat on opposite sides of the desk.

'When might you be in a position to hand the enquiry over to another SIO? I was thinking, DCI Porter?'

Jo slumped back in her chair, crestfallen.

'I understand,' she replied, voice trembling. 'Time for a new hand on the tiller.' Scott of all people, though.

Helen chuckled. 'No, you've got me all wrong. Well, you're half right. You know we've had to move Philip?'

'Yes.'

'Well, clearly we can hardly leave Brighton and Hove rudderless. We need someone strong, someone with a different style but who can hit the ground running.'

'Gary Hedges?'

'No. We think you are the right person for the job.'

Jo sat, open-mouthed.

'Are you OK? I mean, you do actually want this, don't you?'

'Yes of course, I mean . . . I'm just a little surprised.'

'Good. You have just under a week to hand Op Carbon over to Scott Porter. As of next Monday, you are the Temporary Chief Superintendent at Brighton and Hove.'

'Yes, I mean brilliant, oh, I mean thank you,' Jo blustered, her stomach cartwheeling. The only cloud being whether Scott was ready to SIO an enquiry of this magnitude.

'Many congratulations. We have every confidence in you. Mr Acers is due to be telling Philip about now, so don't waste any time in getting a handover from him.'

'Of course, ma'am. And thank you.'

'You already said that,' said the chief, smiling. 'I'm going to the incident room if that's OK. A bit of morale-boosting for your team,' she said, air-quoting the cliché. 'They must be exhausted. I'm sure seeing the chief constable is just what they need.' She winked as she glided out.

Jo sat stunned, taking in the enormity of what lay ahead.

12

Phil couldn't persuade Jo they should hand over the division somewhere more private.

He argued they may have sensitive things to discuss, when in reality he now had every reason not to be seen in public with her. But she insisted they meet at the Seven Dials Small Batch coffee shop, to save him the sideways glances a police station rendezvous would attract, apparently.

A full fifteen minutes of searching for a parking space finally bore fruit as a builder's van nipped out of a 'permit holders only' space. Phil grabbed it, wedging his police logbook in the windscreen to warn off any overzealous traffic warden.

He broke into a slow jog, clocking the name of the street he had parked in; they all looked the same around this maze.

Jo had already bagged the policeman's chair in the converted Barclays Bank – back to the wall, tucked behind the main door. Perfect for clocking the comings and goings, unseen to all but the most inquisitive.

'Grabbed my seat, I see,' he grumbled, as he perched on the wooden stool opposite, nodding at the tepid mug of coffee she'd bought for him. 'Thanks.'

'The early bird and all that. How's things?'

'So-so.' His voice cracked. 'Ruth is in the Martlets, respite they say, but I'm not so sure. Kyle's completely shut himself off. I don't know what to do about him.'

'Sorry. I can only help with preschools. Grown-up kids are way out of my league.'

'Sorry he wouldn't do the reconstruction.'

Jo shrugged. 'It was a shot in the dark anyway.'

'Listen, I owe you an apology, Jo. The press conference. I was unforgivable.'

They locked eyes for a moment too long.

Jo broke the spell first. 'What's done is done. As Darren said, it kept the investigation on the front pages for longer than might have been. I just hate the way they've twisted your words.'

'I should have seen that a mile off. Stuck to the script. Still, I paid the price, didn't I? Who's taking over Op Carbon now you've got my job?'

'The chief seemed set on Scott Porter. I didn't know she even knew him.'

'Interesting.'

'I called her earlier and persuaded her I remain in overall charge. Scott'll run it day to day, though.'

'Well, that's one good thing. Any updates? I mean, I take it you'd have told me if there was. I've been doing some digging and it seems Tyler Larbie might be out on a tag. Gave an address in Durham but it wouldn't be the first time someone's broken curfew to take revenge. Check him out, Jo. For me. I'm terrified he'll come after Ruth and Kyle.'

Jo sighed, made a show of jotting a reminder in her notebook, then looked up.

'Are you OK to do this today, Phil? Hand over the division, I mean. It can wait if you need to be with Ruth and Kyle.'

'It's fine. You're starting on Monday, after all.'

'Listen, I'm glad to be promoted, but you know I'd give it all back if Harry hadn't died and you were still in the chair.'

'God Jo, this is so hard.' He moved to take her resting hand on the table, but she gently pulled it away, a tender but emphatic 'no' in her eyes.

Phil coughed. 'Right, where do I start?' He ran through the team and key people in partner agencies, categorising everyone as either 'a complete tosser' or 'salt of the earth'. There was no middle grouping.

He saved the stripped budget for last.

*

As Phil settled into a character assassination of Stuart Acers, Jo's copper's nose twitched at a scruffy youth who slid through the door next to her. He scanned the half a dozen customers in his sight line and the two baristas, who were busily scrubbing the espresso machine. Had he craned his neck to the right, he might have walked straight out again.

A recent innovation in the fight against terrorism was the training of behaviour detection officers, deployed to scan crowds for those whose behaviour or appearance was out of place. Jo wondered, were she not so senior, whether she would have been suited to that work. Her ability to pick out a wrong'un at fifty paces was legendary.

The lad paid no attention to the chalked-up menu behind the counter. His fidgets and flicking gaze told Jo all she needed to know.

'Phil,' hissed Jo.

'What?' He boomed.

'By the counter. No, don't turn round.'

'How am I supposed to see if I don't look?'

'Well subtly then. He's up to something.'

'Like what?' said Phil, stretching and turning.

'Jesus,' sighed Jo. 'What do you reckon?'

'Let's get the little bugger,' said Phil.

'Softly softly,' she murmured. 'I've got eyeball, but be ready to go.'

'Eyeball? We're not on an operation. We're having a chat and a coffee, watching some toerag who may or may not be about to nick a flapjack.'

'Give me the money!' came the shout, louder and deeper than Jo had expected. The flash of steel waved at the terrified barista transformed the demand into a threat. The young woman, probably a student, spun round, her petrified gaze fixed on the knife. The man, maybe the manager, turned a fraction slower, then shot both hands up in surrender.

'It's OK, man. You can have it, just don't hurt us,' he pleaded; the other customers gawped on.

'Now!' the boy shouted back.

Jo and Phil sprung up – their stools clattering in their wake – and closed the ten feet between them and the robber in a second.

'Stop – police,' shouted Jo, her warrant card thrust, shield-like, towards him.

'Drop the knife, you little shit,' added Phil, grimacing as he swatted a circular table, smashing the used crockery, out of his path.

Despite having at least twenty-five years on them, the boy appeared to weigh up the odds, then bounded to the door.

*

As they burst onto the sunlit Dyke Road, Jo glimpsed the boy sprinting north past the Good Companions pub, then darting right into Russell Crescent.

'This way,' she shouted, as Phil struggled to keep pace.

'Stop him,' he shouted to the transfixed bystanders as he put a spurt on. 'Tossers,' he snarled, racing past them.

The robber spun his head round. They were gaining but he still had a good twenty yards on them.

Phil seemed to deploy his afterburners and, in a moment, had overtaken Jo and was closing in on their prey.

As she accelerated to catch up, Jo guessed that seeing a boy with a knife had ignited his smouldering rage. She knew, for the robber's sake, she had to get to him first.

The boy seemed to falter as he reached the T-junction with Prestonville Road.

Phil was now just a road's width away. He was about to launch himself when, to Jo's horror, the boy clambered up the wall ahead.

He teetered, trying to steady himself on top of the crumbling brickwork, his gaze flipping between his pursuers and the hundred-and-fifty-foot drop to the railway line.

Jo caught up. Panting, she stood next to Phil, hands outstretched.

'Get down, you'll kill yourself,' she pleaded.

The boy clung to the wire-mesh fence, his horrified expression betraying his dilemma.

Phil edged forwards. 'The game's up, mate,' he growled.

'Careful, Phil,' urged Jo, grabbing his arm.

'Get down, you fucking knob,' shouted Phil.

'Who are you calling a knob,' spat the boy as he thrust the knife towards Phil. 'I'll shank you.'

'Not from there you won't,' goaded Phil.

Jo shouldered him aside. 'Please, just drop the knife and get down.'

'Shut it, whore,' he hissed, jabbing the knife towards her.

She felt Phil move forward.

'Just get down,' she repeated, blocking Phil's way. 'We can sort this, but not if you are splattered on the tracks.'

'Put it away,' the boy shouted.

Jo glanced round and saw Phil had his phone out.

'He will,' she said, scowling at Phil.

'OK, I'm coming down, now back off,' he ordered, waving the knife between the two cops.

As the boy jumped off the wall, Phil and Jo sprung forward to grab him.

Jo made for his knife arm but he bobbed to the side, ducking her grip. She went again, but he was too swift and using her forward momentum, he spun behind her, clamping his left arm across her neck. Jo writhed, desperately trying to remember her pre-Liberia self-defence training.

She dipped her knees, kicking back, but the cold steel cutting into her neck told her it was brain, not brawn, that would win the day.

'Let her go NOW,' Phil bellowed, but she could feel from the tightening grip on her windpipe that this only riled him more.

She could barely breathe.

'Piss off, old man, or I'll fucking slice her!'

Briefly Jo felt a quiver in his grip, then suddenly he dragged her back, forcing her to reverse-pedal to stay alive.

Her vision blurred, as if she were peering through a frosted windscreen. She had to fight the fatal combination of adrenaline and asphyxiation. If she blacked out, she was finished.

Phil's and the boy's competing bellows fused as she fought to keep her footing. As she gagged for air, the hazy treetops and craning lamp posts melting into the clear blue sky, she was hoisted along. A human shield. Surely being able to feel the knife nicking her flesh was a good sign.

The cacophony of shouts grew louder and more aggressive. If only Phil could stop playing the silverback for once.

The boy tugged her down a hill. Her right shoe snagged and dislodged. Now her bare heel flayed against the coarse road surface, but her survival instinct anaesthetised the pain; all her focus was on snatching a breath.

She could make out Phil waving frantically at someone behind her, then inexplicably she was free as the boy collapsed to the floor. She stumbled back then away, throwing up over her bleeding feet. Phil was saying something, but she couldn't make out what.

She spun round. Why was her would-be killer reeling on the tarmac holding his head, his knife out of reach? She spotted a short, stocky middle-aged man in greasy blue overalls, wheel brace in hand, standing astride the stricken boy.

'That do you?' he smirked.

Jo then took in an audience of applauding oil-stained mechanics framed in the open garage doorway of Howard Motors.

'Perfect, thank you mate,' said Phil, then leapt forward to catch Jo as another wave of dizziness buckled her knees.

'Right time, right place. Are you all right?' the mechanic asked.

'Yep, fine thanks,' coughed Jo, more in hope than expectation. 'Got any cuffs, Phil?'

He gave her a look: *what do you think?* 'Are you sure you're OK?'

'Nothing a vat of Pinot Grigio won't sort. Have you got any cable ties in there?' Jo asked, turning to the mechanic.

'Sure.'

'I'm arresting you for kidnapping, attempted robbery, resisting arrest and a whole host of other things I can't quite think of just now.' She cautioned him just as the man returned with the makeshift plasticuffs. Jo knelt next to the groaning boy and strapped his hands together in the small of his back.

'Mate, get a chair for him will you,' she asked the mechanic, 'and Phil, can you call for transport?'

By the look of Phil – broken yet seething – anyone would have thought it was him who had just been strangled half to death.

*

Jo tasked Phil with guarding the boy while she scribbled down the details of the hero mechanic. It took some explaining of 'reasonable force' to convince him he wouldn't be in any trouble for his well-aimed strike.

Then a yelp jolted her. Phil's tending to the boy's head wound lacked tenderness, to say the least, so she threw him a look.

After an hour of waiting in the blazing sunshine, even the garage staff were tiring of the drama.

'Where the hell are they?' Jo asked.

'Welcome to Brighton,' Phil replied.

Her persistent calls to chase up the transport still went unmet. Even pleading with the browbeaten duty inspector brought nothing but a raft of reasons they would have to wait, peppered with a few embarrassed apologies.

Phil'd had enough.

'Watch him,' he said to Jo as he marched into Howard Motors.

A couple of minutes later a different mechanic came out, keys in hand. 'Transport's arranged,' said Phil, pointing to the breakdown truck.

'That? We can't rock up to custody in that.'

'You got a better idea? Trust me, we've had people turn up at custody in ice-cream vans before now. They'll be more shocked that two chief superintendents have made an arrest than our mode of transport.'

Jo shook her head as she dragged the subdued boy to his feet, guiding him into the rear of the cab. She slid in beside him while Phil climbed in the other side, apologising for treading on the prisoner's toes.

As the truck spluttered into life, the boy suddenly perked up.

'I know who you are,' he boasted. 'You're that bloke whose kid got killed. I saw you and her on YouTube.'

'Shut the fuck up,' hissed Phil, finding the pressure point on the boy's left elbow.

'Phil!' Jo yelled. He released the grip.

'I pissed myself laughing,' the boy mocked. 'It's happy days when a piglet gets slaughtered.'

Phil exploded with rage, grabbing the boy's head, forcing it down into the boy's own lap. He screamed.

This time Jo left Phil to it. The lad had crossed a line.

'Funny how noisy these engines are,' the driver commented. 'Can't hear a thing from up here.'

The shrieks of pain just got stronger as the truck rumbled along to Hollingbury Custody Centre, while Jo silently wondered whether there was any way back for Phil now.

13

3.00 p.m., Wednesday 9th May

Having been assured by the custody officer that taking his fingerprints by force to establish his identity would hurt – a lot – the prisoner gave his name as Oli Willis.

Once he was safely locked away, Jo grilled the weary sergeant as to why it had taken two hours to process her prisoner. His assertion that she had been fast-tracked and the average was nearer three only confirmed her view that her promotion was a poisoned chalice.

When Hollingbury Custody Centre had opened just after the turn of the millennium, its 'Starship Enterprise' bridge, behind which the custody officers ruled, its spacious cells, the pristine medical rooms and state-of-the-art interview facilities were the panacea to the damp, draughty 1960s police station cell blocks it had replaced.

Time had overtaken the dream and the demands of 24/7 policing had worn the Private Finance Initiative facility out. Cost-cutting left the centre tatty, understaffed and unloved. Jo added fixing this to her ever-growing mental to-do list.

She was about to leave when one of the civilian detention officers called over.

'Ma'am. Willis wants to speak to you.'

'Tell him to wait until someone better trained interviews him,' she replied.

'I told him that but he's insisting on talking to you. Wants to apologise,' the rotund officer replied.

'Does he want a brief?' she asked the custody sergeant, interrupting him explaining to a drunk why Donald Trump would not be the slightest bit interested in hearing of his arrest.

'He wants the duty solicitor but he's sixth in line.'

'OK,' Jo said. 'Let's go and see him in the cell.'

The detention officer pulled himself from his groaning chair, flicking the meat pie flakes from his shirtfront. He grabbed the chain of keys next to his coffin-sized lunch box and waddled towards the maze of corridors, ignoring cries for cigarettes and solicitors from behind every other green steel cell door.

The fusion of urine, body odour and feet catapulted her back to her days on Brighton CID, when a day dealing with prisoners in the old cell block was followed by three trying to wash the stench from her clothes and hair.

Outside Cell 12 the officer stopped, looked through the glass spyhole and shouted, 'Oli, stand back from the door please.' A second later he presented an access card to the lock, turned the key and hauled the solid door open.

Standing aside, he allowed Jo to step in and face the sheepish Willis sitting on the concrete bench opposite.

'You wanted to see me?' Her voice echoed off the bare walls.

'Yeah, but not here. In private,' he said, throwing a glance at the waiting detention officer.

'Don't you want to wait for your brief?' Jo asked.

'No, I've got something you might want to know. Not about this morning.'

'OK. Let's get him to an interview room, please.'

'Really?' asked the jailer. 'Are you OK on your own?'

Jo sized up the wheezing detention officer. 'I'll be fine.'

'Right lad, this way,' he sighed.

Retracing their steps around the bland corridors, they emerged into the bright, bustling reception area.

'Can you sign Mr Willis over to me for a non-evidential conversation?' Jo asked the sergeant, who offered a thumbs-up in response before returning his attention to a waxen drug addict who seemed resigned to his arrest.

She took Oli through the door that led to the interview rooms, ushering him into the first vacant one.

'Sit over there,' she told him, pointing to the furthest chair from the door.

Glancing round reminded her how long it had been since she'd last interviewed a prisoner. Nowadays the rooms resembled flight decks, crammed with cameras, microphones and digital recording equipment that she had no idea how to operate. In her day it was just a squat twin tape recorder and wall-microphone, usually swinging from its bracket.

'So, what can I do for you?' she asked, feigning disinterest.

'Look, I'm sorry for earlier,' Willis grunted.

Jo shrugged. 'And?'

'I shouldn't have done that. Any of it, but I panicked.'

'Yeah, yeah, save that for the interview. If you have mistaken me for a priest, think again.'

'Have you caught who shanked that copper's son yet?'

'What's it to you?' she replied, determined to commit his every word to memory; reaching for a pen would break the spell.

'Maybe I can help.'

'Really?'

'Do you want to know or don't you?'

'No strings.'

'Well, you could have a word with the judge. See if he could shave a couple of years off for this morning.'

'We'll see.'

'Do you know Marco?'

'Marco who?'

'Just Marco,' he shrugged. 'Works the lines. He runs north Brighton.'

'Go on.'

'Well, him and my boss, Dan, they got beef.'

'You're wasting my time. I'm not here to fight your battles.'

'No, hear me out. I'm fed up with the drug scene but I've got a habit. I have to make £200 a day. It would take me three or four shitty little robberies like this morning's to make that, so I have to sell the food too. I want out. Maybe I can get on a rehab programme in prison. Look, everyone's saying it was Marco who murked the pig— the copper's son.'

'Not to us they're not. Why him?'

''Cos he was in the area, looking for Dan. We've been trying to take over his manor and Marco's not happy. Word is he thought the dead kid was Dan. It was only when he saw the news he realised he'd got the wrong bloke. He's bricking it.'

'Harry was stabbed in the chest. How could he have thought it was this Dan fella?' said Jo.

'I'm just telling you what I heard. And it's coming from all over. Marco is running scared and his London crew have cut him off. He's fucked up big time. He's your killer, I'm telling you.'

'That it? Not much to go on.'

'It's more than you've got.'

'Anything else?' Jo said as she stood up. She would have loved to probe him further, but couldn't risk the litany of crimes he'd committed that morning being thrown out of court. Holding the door, she escorted him silently back to the reception and handed him back to the corpulent custody assistant.

* * *

106

When Jo finally blustered into her office, DCI Scott Porter and DI Bob Heaton were already waiting for her.

'Sorry I'm late, gents,' she said, dumping her bag by the desk. 'I think we might have something.'

She took them through her conversation with Willis, losing count of the number of times their eyebrows shot up. When she finished, Scott and Bob stared at her.

'Boss, you do know who Oli Willis is don't you?' asked Bob.

'I know he's a druggie and, as of this morning, an armed robber not averse to threatening to kill police officers.'

'He's Dan Jerram's right-hand man.'

Jo and Scott shared a blank look.

'You must know Dan Jerram.' Bob turned to Scott. 'Scott?'

'Not unless he's got a holiday home in Chatham,' the DCI replied, distancing himself from Bob's indignation.

'Jerram runs the drug line in the city centre. Him and Marcus – or Marco – Vaughan are forever battling over each other's patches. This is just him trying to stitch up a rival gang leader, I guarantee it.'

'But what if he's right?' Jo asked. 'What if it is Marco? We've got no motive so far, so maybe Harry was just in the wrong place at the wrong time. It's as good a theory as any.'

'Is it though?' asked Scott, fixing her with his gaze. 'Your little chat will never be admissible. No other officer. No solicitor. No appropriate adult. It'll look desperate, because that's what it is.'

'I know it's not evidential but it's a hell of a lot more than we had yesterday,' Jo replied, becoming aware how naive she had been. 'It's a start, right?'

'So, this Marco? Are you nominating him as a suspect then?' Scott asked, his pen poised for her reply.

'Not yet. But I want his phones done, his social media. I want informants leant on. I want him under surveillance. Probes in his flat. The whole nine yards.'

'You're going to authorise all this, are you?' Scott asked.

'Of course I am. For Christ's sake, we're not exactly falling over suspects, are we?'

'I thought you said he's not a suspect,' muttered Scott.

'You know what I mean.'

'Is that it?' asked Scott.

'For now,' Jo replied. 'But I want an update by 9 p.m.'

As they filed out, she was about to mention Tyler Larbie but thought better of it. After all, there was a limit to how many straws one person should clutch in one day. She'd square it with Phil later.

*

Phil could have kicked himself.

He should have been with Ruth at the hospice but, with the best part of a bottle of malt whisky inside him, he'd have to make do with a phone call.

The morning's events had hit him hard. He had chased dozens of scrotes in his time, had his family attacked, been threatened at gunpoint but, for some reason, today he'd lost it. Had it not been for Jo and the mechanic, he felt sure he would have snapped the little toerag's neck.

It was the knife that did it. That and seeing Jo in danger. Despite trying to fight it over the years, he still ached for her.

Sitting at home alone, pictures of Harry's finest moments scattered across the settee, ancient web pages about the Larbies cluttering his laptop, he was broken. The murder, his reaction, his fear. Ruth. The threats. It all coalesced into a quicksand from which there seemed no escape. He loved both his sons but his bond with Harry was the strongest.

Ruth was slipping away and he needed to make sure she did so at peace. That meant protecting her from a past that he was sure he'd buried, and the killer being caught before she died.

He was about to call Jo to tell her all when his phone rang.

'Unknown Caller'.

'Phil Cooke,' he slurred.

'Have I caught you at a bad time?' The Geordie.

'Fuck off will you?'

'Now, now. This morning must have been terrifying. That lad disturbing your cosy chat with Jo Howe. Just like old times, eh?'

'How do you know about this morning?' Phil demanded, sobriety crashing through.

'Sorry, I shouldn't tease while you're grieving and waiting for your mates to get off their arses.'

'They'll find Harry's killer.'

'Sure about that?'

'I've given them a name.' Phil kicked himself.

'So why isn't he in custody?'

'It's only a matter of time.'

'Really? Surely they'd pull out all the stops for you.'

'They need grounds to arrest. They'll be working on those.'

'One hundred thousand, Mr Cooke. That's the price to deliver the killer and keep your secret.'

'One hundred K. What planet are you actually from?'

'Do the sums. Due your pension, aren't you?'

Phil did some quick calculations. If he retired now he would receive north of £350,000 as a lump sum plus about £50,000 a year in pension. That was more than enough and, while catching Harry's killer wouldn't bring him back, at least he would get closure.

'Piss off.' Phil killed the call. Then sat. Wondering.

*

Len Bradley marked the dapper trio out as trouble the second they walked in the door.

Their chic city suits set them apart from the Ragged Smuggler's usual clientele; their brash, raucous behaviour was also in stark contrast to the regulars, who generally stared into their beers, only glancing up occasionally at the perpetually rolling sports channels Len paid an arm and a leg for.

They were pissing off the locals. Some had headed off early while others had grumbled their displeasure in Len's ear as he collected empty glasses.

His diplomatic suggestions to the unwelcome guests drew insincere apologies which were soon forgotten as their racket resumed.

They were spending well though and, in this day and age, that was not to be sniffed at. He should have ejected them sooner but as the chances of the police catching him for serving drunks hovered just above zero, the ringing tills made a refreshing change.

'Landlord,' yelled the fat one with the ridiculous red-and-blue striped braces. 'Three more pints of Krombacher on the bar, there's a good chap.'

Len sensed others watching, to see how he would react.

Len shrugged apologetically as he reluctantly drew down three more pints. 'That's £14.85,' he called back.

Braces strutted over and slapped a twenty-pound note on the bar. 'Keep the change.'

'Piss off you perv,' came a shout from near the pool table. A pretty twenty-something blonde woman wearing tight blue jeans with an off-the-shoulder floral Bardot top was squaring up to the weasel in an unbuttoned green waistcoat.

'I beg your pardon,' he slurred.

'You touched my arse, you nonce.'

'You rubbed up against my hand,' sniggered Weasel.

'Think yourself lucky,' said the third drunk.

'In your dreams,' the woman shouted, as Len stepped out from behind the bar.

'Right, settle down all of you. Lads, I think it's time you went home.'

'What, just because this little bitch doesn't like the feel of a proper man up close?' Weasel swayed and slurred.

'We've just bought three pints. We might have three more please, Mr fucking landlord,' said Braces, poking Len in the chest.

A crash of glass. Len spun round to the woman jabbing a broken Beck's beer bottle towards her harasser's exposed jugular, as one of her companions stepped forward to help out.

'Enough!' Len roared as the pub erupted into a Wild West scene. 'I'm calling the Old Bill.'

He punched out 999 and watched in horror as tables flew and punches landed. In his younger days he might have waded in and hoicked out the ringleaders, but he didn't fancy his chances with this lot.

'Send someone now,' he yelled down the phone when the call was eventually answered. 'They're smashing up my pub . . . What? Oh, the Ragged Smuggler by Preston Park Station, just come quickly . . . Half an hour? You've got to be kidding, mate, there'll be no pub left by then.'

He hung up, watching his livelihood being ripped apart in front of him. Feeling sick, he was about to put the handset down when he caught sight of the card that man had dropped in a month ago. What did he say his name was – 'Clinch', 'Crumb'? 'Rapid Response Team' it declared in crisp white font. Promising 'security solutions anywhere in the city within ten minutes'. Unlikely, Len thought, but worth a try, as a pool cue cracked through the flashing fruit-machine screen and the pool table was upended. What did he have to lose?

Len tapped out the number.

'Hello, yes I need help urgently. The Ragged Smuggler . . . No, they won't be here for at least half an hour . . . They're smashing the pub up now . . . Three blokes in suits, but some of my regulars are trying to sort them out . . . Come quick, please . . . Yes, Mr Clench explained about payment . . . Just get here . . . Thank you.'

'Pack it in!' Len yelled as Braces took a full-on headbutt from a scaffolder he recognised. The blow only fuelled his rage and Braces roared, launching himself and grabbing the scaffolder by his throat as they demolished a tableful of abandoned glasses.

Out of the corner of his eye, Len glimpsed a flying table, which he dodged in the nick of time.

Above the row, a screech of tyres came from outside the open door. Seconds later, four huge men walked in.

*

The pub had long since emptied and Len Bradley had cleared up the worst of the debris by the time the police turned up, more than an hour after his call.

He barely glanced at them as they walked in.

'All over then?' the male officer said, hoping whatever had happened was not as bad as the swept-up wreckage suggested.

'Looks like it. Is that what you've been doing? Sitting round the corner waiting for it all to die down?'

The other officer sensed the landlord's anger. 'Sorry sir, we've been at other emergencies. Can you tell us what happened?' she asked, stepping in front of her nonchalant colleague.

'Nothing to worry about,' Len lied. 'Just a group of lads getting overexcited. They've paid for the damage and they're all barred now. It's all sorted.'

'Who were they?'

'No idea.'

There was a time when the officers would have sat the landlord down and explained why he should give a statement rather than be seen as a soft touch by the local yobs. These days there was no time for that.

'Your call,' said the male officer.

The grateful officers jogged out to their waiting car, none the wiser.

'All sorted' meant different things to different people.

14

3.30 p.m., Thursday 10th May

In her short stay at the Martlets Hospice, Ruth's condition had rapidly worsened. All the old fight had gone out of her. Only Phil's and Kyle's visits kept her going.

'How are you going to cope?' she asked Phil, as he massaged aloe vera foot cream into the cracked soles of her feet.

'Let's not talk about that, darling.'

'But I need to know. We always knew I would end up like this, but now . . . well you and Kyle are going to need some help.'

'I'll be fine. Kyle will be OK too. We've just got to get on with it.'

'He's a lovely boy, Phil. Get to know him better. Spend some time together.'

Phil stopped rubbing and looked up. Quizzical.

'I mean it. It's always been you and Harry. Kyle is different but he's a gentle, funny soul. Don't think I've not noticed you two visit me separately.'

The thought had not occurred to Phil. 'I promise,' he said. If only to protect Kyle from the Larbies, he'd have to keep that vow.

Ruth perked up. 'Hey, I meant to tell you, I had a really weird dream last night.'

Phil resumed rubbing in the cream. 'Oh yes?'

'Let me try and remember. Oh yes, you and I were having a weekend break at this lovely hotel, where was it now? Cambridge? No, Norwich, that's it. We were in Norwich and who should we see at dinner but Jo Howe and her husband, only it wasn't Darren at all and they were both talking in these ridiculous Geordie accents. How daft is that?'

Phil froze.

'Everything all right, love?' she said.

'A dream you say?'

'Yes. It must be the medication playing havoc with my head.'

Phil's eyes locked on Ruth. 'Love, are you sure it was a dream?'

'Well yes,' she chuckled. 'I've not been to any swanky hotels in this state.'

'No, I mean, have you had any visitors? Anyone except Kyle and me?'

'Of course not. Why? You're scaring me.'

'Nothing. Forget I said anything.' Phil's mind raced, struggling to make sense of what Ruth had said.

'Are they ever going to catch Harry's killer?'

'It's tough for them. They really are doing all they can.'

'Is there anything you could do?'

But Phil's mind was elsewhere. Jo. Norwich. The fire. Kyle. The Geordie. The bloody Larbies – finally out now and hell-bent on paying him back for robbing them of millions and fifteen years of liberty.

'Phil. I said, is there anything you can do to find who did this?'

He looked Ruth in the eye. 'I promise you I will do whatever it takes. Whatever it bloody takes.'

*

Phil had driven home in a fury. The hospice staff couldn't be sure no one had visited Ruth and, in any case, how could he make a fuss when all she'd described was a dream? They would put it down to grief, and utter platitudes about how she was in the best place and that he needn't fuss. But they didn't know what he knew.

For once he was glad Kyle was out, as it gave him time to think, and make calls if he needed to. But that was taken out of his hands before he'd barely closed the front door.

'Unknown Caller'.

'What the hell have you done?' bellowed Phil.

'Just trying to move things along a little. It's a lovely place though, isn't it. You're so lucky to have it on your doorstep.'

'How dare you, how dare you go there. Have you no heart at all? Christ man, just let her die in peace.'

'See, we both want the same thing. There's something else too.'

'What.'

'Just sending it over.'

Phil's phone pinged with an incoming WhatsApp. He opened the app and waited for the image to download. As it sharpened, he tried to guess what it might be. It took just a couple of seconds for him to retch.

Harry, wearing just a pair of gym shorts in a changing room Phil recognised as a gym he and his son used. His muscular leg was up on a bench and he was injecting something into his thigh. Next to him was a small bottle with a white label bearing red writing. Phil expanded the image. Nandrolone.

'What the hell is this?' he said.

'What does it look like? Google Nandrolone.'

Phil clicked some keys.

Nandrolone is a banned anabolic steroid which promotes protein uptake and makes it easier for the body to build muscle. It can help athletes recover quicker and reduces tiredness, allowing them to train harder and more often.

'This is a bloody Photoshop. What the hell are you up to?'

'We can prove it's not. Your holier-than-thou son was a drugs cheat.'

'This means nothing.'

'The person who supplied the picture is one of our own. Poor Harry just happened to get caught up in one of our covert jobs. There's plenty more where this came from.'

'Even if it is true, which I'm telling you it won't be, what's this got to do with anything?'

'Just think about it. The boy whose death has broken the nation's heart exposed as a filthy druggie. A fraud. And if people believe his death was a drug deal gone wrong. Well, think what that might do to any trial.'

'You fucking dare destroy Harry's memory. He put everything into getting where he was and I'm not having you trash him. This is bollocks.'

'Really? I'll let you sleep on it. Let's hope Ruth doesn't have any more strange dreams in the meantime.'

*

Phil answered the call on the first ring. He'd had no sleep. It could come back to bite him, but he'd spent the night researching banned steroids and drug testing in football, and scouring for images of Harry that could be construed as backing up the outlandish allegations. But he came to realise there was only one way to resolve this.

The Geordie's instructions were terse. 'Good. Upper Lodges, Stanmer Park. 7.00 a.m.' Phil wasn't a man used to taking orders, but he'd asked for this. What did he have to lose? He checked his watch. One hour was plenty of time to get there but enough to plan what to say? Time would tell.

Phil could barely grip the steering wheel as he swung the car round the bends. His gaze flitted between the rear-view mirror and the road ahead, dimly aware of the stunning view across the Weald, his heart pummelling his chest.

He turned right into the car park that later would be packed with dog walkers struggling with their pay-to-park apps. He lurched his car slowly around, scanning for some clue as to who he was there to meet.

As he edged close to a thicket, far from the starburst of footpaths that spilt onto the park below, a white light flashed inside a black Range Rover.

He reversed into a parking spot, then sat and watched. The ad hoc

Morse code resumed. Phil sucked in a lungful of air and inched open the door. Careful not to look at the other car, he climbed out of the seat, stretched then eased the door shut, zapping it locked.

He ambled around the car park, feigning nonchalance. Checking for onlookers, he strolled back towards the Range Rover tucked in the corner.

As he approached, the rear nearside door opened, inviting him inside.

He stepped into the void.

'Good evening, Mr Cooke.' A deep voice. East London?

Phil's eyes took a moment to adjust. 'Where's the Geordie?' Was this a set-up?

'He is just one of our staff. I thought you'd prefer to deal with someone more – senior.'

'Who are you?' Phil asked.

'Plenty of time for that.'

Phil's eyes were acclimatising and the smartly dressed bald man came into focus. The driver sat as motionless as a mannequin.

'You know who I am,' Phil protested.

'Why did you want to meet?'

Phil was eager to get this over with and get back to Ruth. 'I want to know what the fuck this is all about.'

'I'm sorry?'

'The visit to my wife and the picture of Harry.'

'Show me.' The man clicked his fingers.

Instinctively Phil opened WhatsApp and turned the screen round.

'Oh dear, that doesn't look good.'

'Don't give me that. Your Geordie says you have more. They can't go out. I can't have Harry destroyed again.'

'So?'

'So, I've come to talk about the offer.'

'Offer?'

'That Geordie fella reckons you could find the person who killed my son.'

117

'Oh yes, tragic, truly tragic. My sincere condolences. Do you know our terms?'

'Oh, come on, you know all this. One hundred thousand. Fifty now, fifty on completion.'

'And you agree to this?'

'What choice do I have?'

'You're probably right. Doug Robinson, by the way.' He extended his hand. 'Pleasure doing business with you.'

'Fuck off. There's no pleasure in this. How do you sleep at night, exploiting grieving fathers, threatening to ruin dying women's last days and trashing naive young boys?'

'I'm not sure I'm with you. You came to me. You told me the terms. The choice was all yours.'

'You won't get away with this. If you don't do what you promised, I'll hunt you down.'

Surprise flashed across Robinson's face.

'I'll take that as an emotional outburst rather than a threat. Trust me though, I won't be so forgiving next time. We can discuss any suspects later.' The sudden ice in his voice shocked Phil.

'How do I pay?'

Robinson slipped him an envelope. 'Fifty grand in that account and then we get started. Before you ask, it's completely untraceable – even for your boffins. I think you'll be delighted with our service. We know what we are doing, which is more than can be said for Detective Superintendent Howe.'

Phil pushed a photo of Tyler Larbie to Robinson's chest. 'There's your man. Go and find him and no more visits to Ruth. And that photo of Harry goes nowhere too. Please.'

Robinson folded it and stuffed it in his pocket, without so much as a glance.

Phil was about to react when the driver mysteriously appeared at Phil's door, opening it.

'We'll be in touch,' said Robinson as the door slammed shut.

15

11.00 a.m., Friday 11th May

'Sussex by the Sea' shocked Phil from a fitful doze. The caller ID was a kick in the guts – they never phoned. He answered, full of dread.

'Mr Cooke, it's Martlets Hospice . . .' He barely heard the rest, just spluttered a 'thank you' and ran upstairs to wake Kyle.

Ten minutes later they were racing along the A27 towards Hove, with Phil illegally zapping on his blue lights and sirens whenever the need arose.

His prayer that the Geordie had not paid Ruth another visit was no less emphatic for its silence.

Faster than he thought possible, he was soon swinging the car into a bay close to the hospice entrance, then father and son sprinted into the serene building. A volunteer whisked them through a labyrinth of corridors, past Ruth's usual room, before pausing outside a door at the end of the dimly lit passageway. She tapped gently and let Phil and Kyle in.

Phil did not know what he was expecting to see, but was surprised to feel a sense of deep calm in the tranquil space, with its dimmed lights and the glimpse of a neatly trimmed garden just outside the window.

Ruth was sleeping deeply, but her breathing was laboured. Kyle slipped past Phil, straight to her side.

There was a bouquet of irises on the dresser. No machines. No monitors.

This room had just one purpose.

'She's not in any pain,' said a nurse, as if reading Phil's mind. 'Is there anyone else you'd like us to call?'

'No, it's just the two of us now,' replied Phil.

The nurse slipped back out and Phil sat next to Kyle, holding Ruth's and his hands together. Her thin chest rose and fell under the pink-and-white floral quilt. He had never seen her sleep so deeply, yet her wheezing scared him.

He looked at Kyle. His lips were still and Phil could just make out 'sorry'.

He squeezed his son's hand tighter. 'Why sorry? Just tell her you love her.'

Kyle looked up. He rubbed his eyes. 'Was I a good enough son to her, Dad?' he said with a tenderness that stung.

'We are so proud of you. What you have been through, how you have followed your heart. You are one of the bravest people I know.'

Kyle broke the grip to stroke his mum's hollowed cheek.

Phil's thoughts switched to Harry. How his future had been mapped – unlike Kyle's – how it had been snatched away, and maybe his reputation too.

'I meant what I said, darling,' he whispered to Ruth. 'We will catch him – whatever it takes.'

Kyle stopped stroking Ruth's hair and sat, almost in a trance. Phil coughed, nodding to the boy to continue.

Over the next two hours Ruth's breaths shallowed and slowed. He counted. Six per minute. Then five. Then four. The gasping was like a struggling engine on its last legs. After each, he thought she had gone.

The agony continued.

In. Out.

In . . . Out.

In . . . . Out.

After an age – Phil had no idea how long – the out-breath never came. Just a rattle.

Then, nothing.

As if on cue, the nurse returned, touched Phil's arm, and he and Kyle silently rose, pecked Ruth's cheek and slipped out. Their shattered world was crumbled, but at least she had died in ignorance.

*

Jo was becoming impatient over the progress on tracing Marco. Her main concern was that, as of next week, day-to-day control of the investigation would be down to DCI Scott Porter and, frankly, aside from his heart not being in catching the drug dealer, she worried about his overall competence.

She'd still not made the Larbies a line of enquiry. Convinced this was just Phil's paranoia, other than making an unreturned call to Probation, she'd not moved it forward.

As she regarded Scott across the conference table, next to Bob, she made a mental note to make a complete nuisance of herself to him once he was in the chair.

'Bob, where are we?' asked Jo.

'We've been watching his flat since last night, ma'am, and other than the tenant there's been no movement. Even the listening probes aren't picking anything up.'

'Tenant?' Jo enquired.

'Yes, he's dossing in a trap house with some poor special needs lad they've cuckooed. Classic county lines tactic,' said Scott.

'Have we got on to housing or social services?'

'Yes ma'am,' Bob replied. 'Not much they can do as the lad has capacity and says he's happy with the arrangements. We've served warning notices on him but, to be honest, they are just a scare tactic. In any case, it's best we don't intervene now. At least we have a place he might head for.'

'Go on,' Jo said.

'We've got all the phones linked to him on live cell site, so we know where they are whenever they're switched on. Thing is, seems they're being passed around like Smarties. It's one thing knowing where the phones are, but working out who's got them is another matter altogether.'

'But you've got surveillance responding to the phone hits?' Scott prompted.

'Yes, of course, but by the time they get to the last location, the phone's off and whoever had it has scarpered.'

'What else are you trying?'

'We're doing drive-pasts at all his usual haunts and we are monitoring calls to and from his associates' phones. That's all drawing a blank too.'

'Social media?'

'Yep, but he's hardly ever on there.'

'Christ, there must be something more we can do. Informants?'

'All tasked,' said Scott. 'But as you know, they can take ages to come back.'

'Ma'am, it would be a lot easier if we could go overt. You said you wanted to keep this quiet but, with respect, that's really tying our hands,' said Bob.

'You've changed your tune. Weren't you the ones telling me I shouldn't make him a suspect?'

'I still think we shouldn't,' said Scott. 'But we can keep the covert tactics running in the background while rattling some cages to flush him out.'

Scott and Bob watched her, used to her frozen moments of deep contemplation. After a minute, she stretched and rubbed her face.

'OK, go with it. Locate Marco. Create mayhem until you find the stone he is hiding under. Get someone to lean on Willis after he's appeared at court tomorrow, before he's shipped off to Lewes Prison. I want a witness statement from him, whether he likes it or not. Got that?'

'Loud and clear, ma'am,' replied Scott.

Both men stood and headed for the door, Scott on his phone before he reached the corridor.

* * *

Leabharlanna Fhine Gall

They drove back from the hospice in silence. Kyle flicked aimlessly on his phone, when he wasn't gazing at the passing farmland out of the window. Phil was on autopilot, his mind a whirl of uncertainty, revenge and gutter-level grief.

Since his meeting earlier and now this, he had no idea what the foggy days, weeks and months that stretched ahead would bring. Did Ruth's death change anything? Was it just one less sword hanging over him? The bombshell of Harry and the steroids was something he could never allow to get out.

Christ, what a mess.

As he pulled up outside his house, he turned to Kyle.

'You OK, mate?'

The boy shrugged, avoiding eye contact.

'Come on, let's go inside. I'll make a cup of tea.' He put his arm around Kyle but his son didn't soften. Instead, he turned, opened the car door and stepped out. Phil's heart sank. How was he going to win his remaining, enigmatic son back? How would he protect him? They say grief draws people together. When?

Inside, Phil went straight to the kitchen, filled the kettle and flicked it on. Kyle ran upstairs.

As the kettle boiled, he heard footsteps coming back down.

'Tea or coffee?' he called.

The only reply was the slam of the front door.

'Kyle?' Phil shouted, running to the door. By the time he opened it, his boy had disappeared from view.

Phil went back indoors. For the first time it dawned on him that he was truly alone. Forgetting the kettle, he drifted to the lounge, sinking into his favourite chair. He was empty. Numb. Scared.

Thumbing his phone, he found himself opening the text app. He typed.

Ruth died earlier today. K and I were with her. V peaceful. Just thought you should know. Any news BTW? Larbies? Phil xx.

Almost immediately, the phone chirped.

Oh God, I'm so sorry. Is there anything I can do? No news I'm afraid. Call you later. Jo xx

'For fuck's sake,' he yelled, hurling his phone into the corner.

Phil hoped Jo would actually call. Of the four people he'd ever loved, she was the only one left he could talk to. And talk to her he would. Demand some traction. Demand they protect his remaining flesh and blood from the Larbies.

'Oh Kyle,' he sobbed. 'I'm so sorry.'

He'd judged his eldest son so harshly.

Was Harry his favourite, after all? Maybe, maybe not, but definitely the one he understood most. The one whose dreams he could picture, he could share in. Now all that could blow up thanks to those bloody photos. What an idiot.

Ruth had been his anchor. She had been the one who kept him grounded – who was always there to rant at, laugh with, love at the end of each crazy day trying to keep Brighton and Hove from anarchy. That promise he'd made her. 'Whatever it takes.'

He re-read Jo's message. *No news I'm afraid.*

He had been a shit husband, not much better as a father. The least he could do was keep his vow. Bring some good out of this hell. 'Whatever it takes.'

16

5.00 a.m., Saturday 12th May

Phil woke at 5 a.m. in a cold sweat, trying to shake the searing images of Harry sitting in the back of a Range Rover with a needle in his leg, bleeding, but doggedly counting out piles of crisp new banknotes. Then Kyle was beside an open grave, among a clutch of mourners all dressed in football kits, throwing photographs onto Ruth's coffin. Jo was leading a chorus of 'Sussex by the Sea'. The dream seemed so real and it took him a moment to realise it was his phone ringing; then the memory of his collapsed world bombarded him.

'Phil Cooke,' he slurred.

'Mr Cooke, I'm so sorry for your loss.' That bloody Geordie. 'I hear your meeting went well yesterday though.'

'Can't you leave me alone. Let me grieve.'

'Oh, I'm afraid it doesn't work like that. Although we can't expose your shagging to your wife, exploiting the woman now leading the murder hunt wouldn't go down too well, would it? And your wonder-boy's reputation is still in our hands.'

'So what. I'll just deny it.'

'Good luck with that. Oh, there's another thing too. Listen to this.'

Phil strained to hear, but with horror could make out his own tinny voice. 'One hundred thousand. Fifty now, fifty on completion.'

'It sounds like you're conspiring to have someone murdered. That on top of your junkie son and your trouser problem, I'd say puts you on the back foot, wouldn't you?'

'You absolute bastards.'

'Let's try to keep this professional, shall we? My boss asked me to call you, as he forgot to mention a small errand for you yesterday.'

Phil sat up, rubbed his eyes, aware he needed all his wits for this. 'What sort of errand?'

'It's just a message we'd like you to pass on.'

'Message? What fucking message?'

He listened carefully, aghast at what he was being asked to do.

'And you can prove all this?'

'Of course. We think now's the time to make it public.'

'Why me?'

'You're used to talking to the press.'

'And if I refuse?'

The Geordie chuckled. 'You won't. You're in too deep. I look forward to reading all about it very soon.' The phone went dead.

Phil shuffled downstairs. His head thumped and he prayed two paracetamol and a triple espresso would at least take the edge off. He downed the painkillers, picked up his coffee and trudged through to the sitting room.

He pushed a pile of Kyle's music magazines to one side, making room for himself on the settee. He mulled over what the Geordie had told him. Surely this was one for the police, not the press.

That's what he would do; hand it over to the chief constable and be done with it. But the Geordie was right – he was in too deep. How the hell had he fallen for them recording him in the car? He was losing it. He'd given enough press interviews in the past to know how his words could be cut, pasted and used against him. What a schoolboy error, coming out with

126

the terms himself. If he didn't play along he'd be in danger of at least ten years for conspiracy to murder, and Harry's memory would be shredded.

And poor Kyle, left to pick up the pieces.

If only he had someone to talk it through with.

Ruth would have known what to do, but . . .

Kyle? He had enough pain to deal with now. He'd be way out of his depth, anyway.

Jo? Yeah right. How would he explain he'd gone behind her back?

Gary? Possibly, but he couldn't make his mate choose between friendship and career.

No, he had to decide this one alone. As the fog in his head cleared, he knew there really was no choice.

Sod it, he decided, *now or never.*

Checking his personal mobile was set to hide his caller ID, he tapped out the number which the website told him would put him through to the right person.

'*Daily Journal*, news editor,' came the frazzled voice on the other end.

'I have some information I want to give you anonymously, now, and which I will not repeat . . .'

In spite of himself, DI Bob Heaton was starting to agree with Jo.

None of the dozens of enquiries he had triggered to find the drug dealer had smoked him out. All the feedback suggested the youth had gone to ground. He was definitely hiding from something, or someone.

But that morning a glimmer of hope came from a phone tenuously linked to Marco. Most of the burners were switched on, used, then dumped, but overnight this particular one had popped up on the radar with promising regularity.

Now, phone 6298 – its last four digits – was pinging the phone masts somewhere near Sillwood Street. Either it had been foolishly left on, or someone was using it.

The analyst's charts, plotting all the people, addresses, phones and vehicles associated with Marco, had flagged up the basement flat of 103

Sillwood Street as a bolthole that Rico, one of Marco's underlings, had been chased to a few months back.

Now, Bob was watching it from a grubby Toyota Avensis, DC Donna Brand at the wheel. Both were dressed in scruffs, although in Bob's case it was hard to spot the difference.

Donna, who had an awesome reputation for spotting suspects from the most fleeting of glimpses, and in her youth had been a county sprint champion, was in her trademark blue Adidas tracksuit top, black leggings and running shoes.

Once Bob confirmed the phone was still on and in the area, they jumped out of the car and speed-walked the twenty yards to the flat.

Bob hammered on the door. Donna covered the back.

Nothing.

He knocked again. Frantic scurrying came from within.

He crouched, opened the letter box and shouted, 'Police – stay where you are.'

Then, Donna's banshee bellow: 'Stop there!'

As the shouting became more frantic, the DI was tempted to join her, but knew he would never live it down if someone escaped through the front door.

Donna called out. 'I've got him, guv. Just letting you in.'

A minute later, the bolts on the front door clattered and it opened.

Bob gagged as he took in the scene with its nauseating stench. Overflowing ashtrays, piles of putrid clothes, discarded needles and towers of crockery crusted with dried and rotting food.

'Looks like my lad's student digs,' Bob said. He looked over at the prisoner, who was wincing at Donna's overenthusiastic grip on his arm. 'What happened to you, sunshine?'

Raw – fresh – scarlet burns covered every inch of the young man's face. Bob knew acid scars when he saw them. 'Shouldn't you be in hospital?'

'I was, but I discharged myself.' His speech slurred through livid lips.

'What's your name?'

'Junior.'

'Well, you're an idiot, Junior. Anyone else in here?'

He flicked a nod. 'In the lounge.'

Bob entered and the stench of sweat, cannabis and something which he was glad he could not place, were overpowering. Piles of clothes and bedding completely shrouded the furniture. The only obvious chair was taken by a terrified boy, both legs encased in plaster.

'Dearie me, what happened to you?' Bob exclaimed.

'I fell over,' the boy mumbled.

'What, over a cliff? I reckon it's time for you both to talk. We might be your only friends, and that's not good.'

Donna brought Scarface into the lounge. Neither spoke but both looked terrified.

'Believe it or not, you're not in trouble. We just need your help,' Bob started, his tone softening.

'We don't know shit,' said the boy in plaster.

'We haven't asked you anything yet,' said Bob. 'Where's Marco?'

A telling look shot between them.

'Good, so you do know him then. He's not in trouble either, we just need to speak to him.'

'Ain't seen him for ages, bro,' said Junior, with little conviction.

'What about Rico? He crashes here, doesn't he?' said Donna, trying a fresh angle.

Bob sensed the boys' panic at the name. 'What is it? Where's Rico?'

'He's gone,' said Junior.

'With Marco?'

'No. Marco's a wuss. Rico and Benji got grabbed.'

'Grabbed?' Donna asked.

'When this happened,' said the crippled boy, ignoring Junior's eye-rolling pleas for him to shut up. 'They done this to us, then snatched Rico and Benji. Drove 'em off in a black motor. Audi, I think. We ain't heard from them or Marco since.'

The two detectives looked at each other. Sometimes you start looking for one thing only to discover another.

'I think we'd better continue this back at the police station,' said Bob, buying himself thinking time.

'Boss, how are we going to move him?' asked Donna, pointing to the plaster-clad boy.

'We'll get a van. We've got a lot to talk about and I'm not doing it in this shithole. Call up and get us some transport.'

*

Despite Doug Robinson's loathing of distractions, the vast plasma television had flickered away since the moment he'd first settled behind his pristine desk at 7 a.m.

When – not if – the news broke, he had to act fast to protect his own interests, then trigger phase two.

Phil had been told to break the story to the *Daily Journal*, but Doug knew it would look too suspicious if he was found to have constantly refreshed their site. So, he plumped for the channel that boasted being 'The First with the News that Counts', even if they did siphon it from a rival.

It was during a particularly heated phone call with Crush, who was again demanding the lorry to create some cell space, that the familiar red 'Breaking News' banner flashed across the bottom of the screen.

It wasn't the first such splash that morning. His heart had already leapt half a dozen times, only for the broadcaster to gush about some energy company issuing a profit warning or an ageing Hollywood star splitting from his wife.

But this was the one.

He ratcheted the volume up to forty.

'We are just hearing from sources that Teresa Sutton, the controversial police and crime commissioner for Sussex, is to be investigated following allegations that she was behind the exploitation of hundreds of illegal immigrants smuggled into the country to work on Sutton Farms, the multimillion-pound food supplier to the Big Four supermarkets. More on this when we get it. In sport . . .'

By the time the anchor moved on, Doug was foraging for the source of this bombshell. Only the *Journal Online* had the story in full: the unabridged version Crush had given Phil.

This was dynamite. He'd never doubted the story but had not expected the mainstream media to shore the piece up so quickly. The Independent Office of Police Conduct would be on to this in no time, leaving 'Mother Teresa' no option but to 'spend more time with her family'.

And now Cooke was on the hook, the next stage of the plan would provide a lifetime indemnity.

*

Jo showed her card to the small reader by the featureless door just yards from her SIO office. Most would assume this led to a store cupboard. Nothing gave away its true function.

The intelligence cell was the engine room of Operation Carbon. In here, snippets of gossip, fragments of data and just about anything that had come to the attention of the police was pieced together into comprehensive profiles which, with a fair wind, could catapult a bit player to major suspect in a keystroke.

Usually Jo held debriefs in her own office, but today it served her purpose to concede the territorial advantage.

When she was a rookie DC, she had once been called to the DS's office to run through a tricky investigation into allegations of physical abuse at a children's home. The case was headline news in all the local papers and even the nationals were sniffing around.

A summons to the grumpy Scotsman's lair was enough to make the hardiest detective quake. Jo's timid rap on his door had been met with a bellowed order to 'Come.' His icy stare and gruff demands, filtered through his tobacco-stained beard, had scared her witless and she'd made a complete fool of herself. She muddled up all the key details her flustered brain could recall. What should have been a simple briefing became a farce and it had taken her months to live it down. She vowed that, once she had her own staff, and when it suited her, she would put them at ease by meeting them on their ground.

Inside Room M19, Bob and Donna were both furiously tapping away at grubby keyboards. None of the screens faced the door, nor could they be seen from another desk. *Feng shui for the paranoid*, she thought.

The walls were papered with association charts and mugshots of the City's most wanted – some with prison bars crudely drawn over them.

'Hi there,' she said, grabbing an empty chair. They knew not to stand, but Donna comically sat to attention, which drew a grin between Jo and Bob.

'Ready to brief me on your two wounded warriors?' she asked rhetorically.

'How's Mr Cooke?' asked Bob, wanting to gauge when would be a good time to give his old friend a call. 'So sad about Ruth, on top of all this.'

'I've not spoken to him since she died. I'm popping up later. The two casualties?'

Bob started. 'They certainly aren't up for any Good Citizen awards. They've been bloody hard work, but we are getting there, ma'am.'

'Only getting there? Are they still here?'

'Yes. We are pretty sure they've got no more idea where Marco is than we have, but we've grabbed their phones and pumped them for as much as we can. There's a couple of new addresses for us to check but they genuinely believe he's gone to ground.'

'What are your thoughts?' asked Jo, spinning her chair to face Donna.

'Like the boss said,' she replied. 'I think they'd give him up if they knew. They're terrified.'

'Of him? Us?' probed Jo, eager to get to the bottom of this.

'Not Marco for sure. If they could get their hands on him, what happened to them would look like a playground scrap. They're not big fans of us either, but they are really scared of the blokes who attacked them.'

'Any idea who that was or where their mates went?'

'No and no,' said Bob, 'but our two are definitely the lucky ones.'

'Any connection with Harry's murder?'

Bob stretched back and rubbed his eyes, buying himself some thinking time. Donna's phone rang. She peeked at the caller display and muted it.

Finally, Bob spoke. 'I'm not sure, to be honest, ma'am. They were attacked and their mates seem to have vanished. I accept they don't know where Marco is. It's just odd that these mysterious butchers are hunting them all down just as we want to talk to Marco about a murder.'

'OK,' said Jo. 'Get them on to the Protected Persons Programme, keep at them for information, then get back out there and find Marco.'

'Is that all?' asked Bob, a hint of exasperation in his voice.

'For now.'

*

Police and Crime Commissioner Teresa Sutton cowered in the lounge of her elegant converted barn. The usual panoramic view of the South Downs was now obscured by hordes of photographers, all straining for a glimpse of the disgraced politician.

Her efforts to fob all the calls off to her press officer were short-lived, once the *Journal* reporter mentioned Sutton Farms and slavery in the same sentence. The past, which she thought was dead and buried, was back and angry.

She'd been young and in her father's thrall when she was appointed to the family business's board. Long before the recession, the unskilled jobs on their thirty-five UK farms were of no interest to a fully employed, well-paid British workforce. Who would want to toil for twelve hours a day in some swamp of a field for £5 per hour, when they could pick up cushy bar work for twice that?

Teresa soon realised she needed to break free from being Daddy's girl. So, when she was contacted by a charming gentleman with just a hint of an Eastern European accent, promising as many hard workers as she could take, at a fraction of the wage locals would demand, she jumped at the offer. And asked no questions.

Even in her naivety, she should have smelt a rat. But the farmhands came in their droves, cost next to nothing and worked like soldier ants.

How was she to know where these people lived, whether they actually received their paltry pay or whether they were free to come and go? They got the job done and Sutton Farms thrived.

Now some do-gooder had raked up the past and her solution to yesterday's problems was being judged by today's standards.

Since the call she had tried in vain to defend her position. She rolled out the usual platitudes – nothing to hide, cooperate with any enquiry, looking forward to clearing her name – but the demands for her head kept coming.

Too much to expect Conservative Central Office would back her, what with a new Modern Slavery Bill going through Parliament. The local MPs were no better and, as for the chair of the Police and Crime Panel, to whom she was notionally accountable, he was lapping it up. Bloody socialist.

Any thought of calling the chief constable, Helen Ricks, for advice was quickly dismissed; all bridges with her had long since gone up in smoke.

She wished she had listened to her election agent all those years ago. 'Make your friends in peacetime,' he had told her. Oh, how she needed some allies now.

There was no way back from this. She would have to go.

17

Arriving at Brighton Police Station bright and early on her first day, Jo stepped into the very office where she'd broken Phil's heart. The memories took her breath away.

Maybe it was too much to ask that anyone had boxed up Phil's things, but this was a shrine to his family and a bygone policing era.

She needed the space, and to make her mark, so she reluctantly started with the photos. Seeing Harry staring down at her from the incident room walls had been bad enough, but the images here of him growing into the striking young man he'd become was more than she could take.

She carefully stacked up the frames, studying each closely. She examined in awe the image of his dad directing traffic in front of the Royal Pavilion, his white police helmet crowning his authority. She welled up at Phil and Ruth's silver wedding photo, taken in Barbados if her memory served her correctly.

Phil was a clear desk wonk. A couple of trays, each containing neat green files and half a dozen memos. That would change. She'd once been offered a pitchfork to sort through her paperwork.

She pulled on the doors of the rickety double wardrobe and was met by a parade of pristine uniform tunics, coats and fleeces lined up ready for whatever role Phil would be expected to play, in any weather. Boots buffed to a mirror shine lined the cupboard floor.

As she lifted the clothing off the rail, she sensed someone watching her. Turning to dump the bundle on the conference table, she saw her deputy, Superintendent Gary Hedges, hovering in the doorway.

Jo had known Gary for the best part of ten years and had yet to warm to him. Thankfully, their paths rarely crossed. He was a 'guns and shields' man; in his element immersed in adrenaline-pumping firearms and public order operations. To him the world was black and white. She often wondered if he owned a pair of camouflaged pyjamas and war-gamed his off-duty hours away.

She, and just about everyone else, had seen Gary as Phil's natural successor. It wasn't her place to question why the chief constable had plumped for her – she hoped it wasn't just gender – but it made for a very awkward alliance.

'Want a hand with that?' he asked in his deep Welsh burr.

'Oh, morning Gary,' Jo replied. 'If you don't mind.'

'You might have let him come and clear his own stuff. God, you've even taken his pictures down.'

'Well, coming in and clearing his stuff is not going to be at the top of his to-do list, and I do have to work.'

'Suppose so,' grunted Gary, 'but have some respect.'

Jo got that Gary was hurting. He'd been a close friend of Phil's family so, as well as grieving for Harry and Ruth, he had lost his ally as well as suffered the ignominy of being passed over for promotion.

'Look, I've no idea why it's not you moving in here, but let's make this work. I'll be relying on you.'

'Will you now?' asked Gary, accusingly.

'That's not what I mean. You and Phil were a perfect match and I think we could be too.'

Gary raised an eyebrow and she regretted her words again. God, what a terrible start.

'We owe it to Phil to run this division as he would want us to. Obviously, I have some catching up to do, but I am certain we can be good together.'

'We'll see,' muttered Gary.

Before Jo could reply, Gary had stepped back to his own office opposite and shut the door.

*

At nine-thirty on the dot, Jo walked into the main conference room next door.

In her previous days at Brighton, it had been the convention that the most senior officer on duty chaired the Daily Management Meeting. Although that was now her, as it was her first day, she forgave Gary Hedges for breaking protocol.

One thing that had changed since she was last here was how sparse the meeting had become. Rather than a dozen or so senior officers jostling for space around the table, now they were joined by just two inspectors and one chief inspector. She wondered whether others would flock through the door any minute.

They didn't.

'Morning ma'am,' Hedges said grudgingly. 'I think we all know Temporary Chief Superintendent Howe. OK, let's get started.'

Following the pro forma briefing sheet in front of him, he first covered a renewed appeal for witnesses to Harry's murder, then read through the list of seven missing children – three of whom were in care. He glossed over the adult 'mispers' other than to say that Wayne Tanner and now three city-brokers had still not returned home. He mentioned, almost in passing, the twenty-three burglaries that had blighted the city since Friday – an improvement on last weekend, apparently – before ruefully listing the three protests – on student fees, fracking and cuts to council childcare – all planned for the coming day.

'Right, on to Mr Cooke's prisoner from last week, Oli Willis,' said Hedges. 'The attempted robbery at Small Batch. He got bail at a Judge in Chambers application this morning.'

Jo was aghast. 'Just a minute, Gary. On what grounds was he released?' she asked, ignoring that her arrest had somehow become Phil's.

'Search me. Must have come up with an address or a surety,' he shrugged.

'The evidence was as strong as you'd get. Two police officers witnessing the attempted robbery, chasing him, me being grabbed at knifepoint, then me arresting him. Where were the gaps?'

'The evidence was strong, that's why we charged him, but the judge must have thought the grounds to keep him weren't.'

'Why wasn't I told?' she demanded.

'You know now,' Gary replied.

'I need to call the incident room,' said Jo, springing to her feet.

'Of course. Oh, before you go, Mr Cooke formally notified the chief constable last night that he was retiring with immediate effect.'

Everyone gasped. 'He has some leave to use up, so he won't be coming back. I think you will agree with me that this has been a very sad end to an illustrious career, none of which was his doing.'

So, this was how it was going to be. Perhaps her gloves would have to come off sooner than she had planned. Whatever the rights and wrongs, he was her deputy and if he did not like that – well, there was a job working on the cuts now going begging.

18

3 p.m. Monday 14th May

Phil wasn't expecting visitors.

A few had dropped by unannounced yesterday to offer their condolences but he'd managed to fob off Jo, the family liaison officer and a few others by politely persuading them he and Kyle needed a day to themselves.

In any case, many of his colleagues struggled to find the right words. Even the chief constable had been frosty when he called to tender his retirement. In fairness though, she had enough on her plate with the PCC resigning. Luckily she had no idea who was behind that.

He had no tears left. Even registering Ruth's death at Brighton Town Hall that morning had not been as harrowing as he'd expected. Perhaps he could cruise through the rest of his life like this, once the Larbies were back behind bars or six feet under.

He had half a mind to ignore the doorbell as it chimed for the second time. Claim he had fallen asleep or some other excuse that no one would believe, but never question.

Then again, he knew what cops were like. They were hardwired to suspect the worst, and the last thing he needed was some idiot crashing through his door thinking they were on some heroic mission to save him from topping himself.

He pulled himself out of the armchair and trudged towards the front door. As he turned the key, Phil shoved the clutter of shoes to one side, the sight of a pair of Harry's trainers bringing a lump to his throat.

The chill soaking through him as he unbolted and opened the door had nothing to do with the draught coming off the downs, and everything to do with who stood waiting.

'What the hell are you doing here,' said Phil, blocking the doorway.

'Sorry to turn up unannounced, but I was just passing so I thought I'd pop in. We have things to discuss.'

Doug Robinson's type never 'just passed' anywhere.

'I don't think so. I did what you asked, now get on and find Harry's killer,' Phil replied. 'I've told you who it is and where to find them. Do what you've been paid for.'

'Shall we do this in private?' Robinson's voice took on a menacing edge as he stepped forward.

Phil grunted, turned and headed back along the hallway, leaving Robinson to follow.

Both men glared at each other in the lounge. 'Make it quick,' Phil snarled.

'May I?' replied Robinson, sitting down on the worn leather settee, not giving Phil a chance to object.

Phil opted for the armchair opposite.

'Nice place you have here,' said Robinson.

'Cut the platitudes and tell me what you want, or better still, how you're getting on.'

'Of course. I hear you've retired.'

'How the hell do you know that?' Phil clenched his fists by his side.

Robinson grinned. 'Thank you for sharing our little piece of information. A real public service, don't you agree?'

'Don't patronise me.'

'Any news on Harry's funeral yet?'

Doug's attempt at small talk was infuriating Phil, but he could not help but answer.

'No. As no one has been arrested, we have to wait at least twenty-eight days, then there will be an independent post-mortem before he is released.'

'That's a shame. Still, it will be a good turnout. Unless we are forced into releasing those pictures.' Robinson tutted and shook his head.

'Don't you dare.'

'It's in your hands, Phil. Anyway, funerals are a good place to start. You know, the killer may turn up and watch from afar?'

'You watch too much telly. The Larbies might be evil but they're not stupid.'

'You seem very certain that it's them. Why is that?'

Phil grudgingly explained the arrests, the arson, the prosecution and the threats. How it was his family and house who bore the brunt and that it was a logical step to kill his son.

'Funny how the police don't seem to share your hypothesis.'

'How the fuck do you know what the police are or are not doing.'

'Never you mind.'

'Maybe we should call this off. You return my money and I'll say no more about it.'

'Can't happen, I'm afraid. You're one of us now,' replied Robinson.

'For Christ's sake, what do you want? And hurry up. Kyle will be home soon.' A surge of terror swept over him and he checked his watch.

'The thing is, leaking the PCC's repugnant behaviour was only the start. The trigger for something bigger.'

'Why are you doing this?' ranted Phil. 'I have lost my son, my wife and my job. For all I know, my other son may be next. I can barely get out of bed in the morning. Have you any idea what that feels like? Even after the threats you made, you still come round here turning the screw, as if nothing has happened.'

Doug sat impassively, patiently waiting for Phil's composure to return.

It took a while.

'I know this is hard for you,' Robinson continued, feigning compassion. 'But we do a little more than track down those who have offended our clients, as we are for you.'

Phil went to interrupt, but Robinson's raised hand stopped him. 'We are quite a diverse operation who are seeking to fill the gap that the police no longer can. You may have spotted that certain miscreants who have previously run riot have been, shall we say, dealt with. Some have been provided with life-changing warnings, some are in our custody. The really unlucky ones will never be a problem to our hard-working communities again.'

'Vigilantes?' said Phil. 'You are running a gang of vigilantes?'

'We prefer to think of it as a highly professional and disciplined twenty-first-century security operation. Guardians, if you like.'

'How noble. That's both illegal and outrageous. Why are you telling me this? I could easily rumble you to my former colleagues.'

'But we both know you can't do that. No, you are very much part of our future plans.'

Phil put his head in his hands, rubbing his eyes. When would he wake from this nightmare? How had he gone from acclaimed divisional commander to conspiratorial widower, still waiting to bury his butchered son, all in less than a fortnight?

He looked up at his tormentor. 'What plans?'

'Now you have successfully secured the resignation of the police and crime commissioner, we see a marvellous opportunity to legitimise our enterprise. The PCC has the power to commission services to reduce crime and disorder. Of course, the lion's share will be through policing, but organisations such as ours can bid for funds to support the police's noble endeavours.'

'I don't need a bloody lecture on the role of PCCs. What has all this got to do with me?'

'Mrs Sutton made few friends in the police. She was rather traditional in her approach. Perhaps the new PCC will have a fresher style.'

'Stop talking in riddles.'

'We, or rather our boss, has decided that you should become the next PCC.'

For the first time in over a week, tears of laughter streamed down Phil's cheeks. After a moment, he gathered himself, then looked at Doug opposite. The man's dour expression revealed that this was no joke.

'Fuck right off. You want me to become the next PCC? Do you know anything about my views on PCCs? And who do you think you are, anyway? You can't just decide who the next one will be. There is a little matter of an election that might get in the way of your egotistical plans.'

'We are well aware of how a PCC is appointed; that is why you will nominate yourself as an independent candidate. We will corral a campaign team for you, behind the scenes. We have some highly respected public figures waiting to support you. Fund you. We will write your no-nonsense manifesto, drawing on all of those values you have espoused over the last thirty-odd years. All we ask, in exchange, is that when – not if – you are elected, you actively support the expansion of our security enterprise with high-value commissions and, when we need it, the turning of blind eyes.'

'Are you mad? Do I look like I'm in any state to run for public office?' Phil pleaded. 'Even if I wanted to.'

'That's why it's a perfect time. You have lost almost everything. Losing Harry and your job are a direct consequence of an overstretched and politicised police force unable to protect ordinary, decent people. Your credentials as a "say it as I see it" police commander will win over even the most cynical voter.'

'And if I say no?'

'You're in too deep. You know how unpleasant prison can be, especially for retired police officers. Think about it,' said Doug as he stood. 'You have no choice. On top of the special treatment you'll get in Belmarsh, you'll be a pariah, as will your darling Harry. And don't forget you have another son. Now none of us would want any harm to come to him, would we? And I'm not talking about the Larbies.' The threat hung there as Phil slumped back. 'Oh and, by the way, thank you for paying so quickly. Rest assured we will follow up on your paranoia. Even if it's not them, and I'm sure it's not, I'm sure we can let them experience our unique form of justice. Please, though, don't thank me.'

He smiled and held out his hand. Phil brushed it away and marched to the front door. He jerked it open and stood to the side, scowling as Robinson squeezed past.

'I'll call you tomorrow, to discuss the details.'

It took all the restraint Phil could muster not to punch that smug, smiling face. But he knew, with sickening certainty, that he was trapped. Paralysed.

If it weren't for Kyle, he would take his only way out.

19

3.30 p.m., Monday 14th May

Bob Heaton had to get out of the office. Ruth's death had hit him hard, and he needed a distraction to stop him harping back to the carefree Balearic holidays he and his ex-wife, Janet, had shared with the Cookes. He always felt the odd one out, but sun and San Miguel more than made up for his secret awkwardness.

Now, here he was being tossed around the back of a battered midnight-blue Ford Focus. The maniacal driving seemed to consist of two speeds: fifty miles per hour and dead stop. In the front, Donna hung on for dear life to the FM – fuck me – handle above her head while her right hand gripped the clipboard that listed the dozen possible addresses for Marco.

'Can't you slow down?' Bob pleaded.

'Sorry boss,' said the driver. 'You did say get to each address before word got out.'

'Yes, but in one piece would be nice.'

He grabbed the door handle as they powered away from the traffic lights at the bottom of Preston Drove. Donna spat out a chain of expletives as they overtook a bus, narrowly avoiding an oncoming Ocado van heading into town. Bob shook his head as he planned the roasting he would give the driver when they were safely back at HQ.

As the car swung right at the mini roundabout into Carden Avenue, they adopted a pace more suited to their surroundings. Rather than knock on the door of the flat Marco was said to be using, they were going to drive past then sit and watch, in case he ventured out.

As they did so, Bob called out, 'That car, get the number,' pointing at a black Audi edging out of Darcy Drive.

'Eh? Which one?'

'There. Hang back but keep eyeball.'

'What about it, boss?' asked Donna.

'Keep your eyes on it. Doesn't it ring a bell with you?'

'Oh yes,' replied Donna. 'The two from Sillwood mentioned a black Audi. There are loads about though.'

Bob ignored the comment and their driver tucked in behind a Next lorry.

'Can you still see it?'

'No. Yes, yes. Hang back a bit. You're too close to this bloody truck.'

The driver eased off, too professional to argue.

'Stand by, he's slowing down,' said Donna. 'Drive past – but don't look in, boss.' Bob forgave this egg-sucking lesson.

They cruised past while Donna kept obs through the second rear-view mirror.

'Right, right, right into County Oak Avenue. Spin round at Carden Hill and get back behind him.'

Without being asked, Bob assumed the role of log keeper, noting all he could about the car, its occupants and their actions.

They pressed on up the hill, determined not to lose the Audi before they could get back.

'Careful, he's doing a U-turn as well,' said Donna. 'Stand by, he's pulling over. Guv, we'll drive past while he's parking. Less chance of being spotted.'

They slipped into a parking space twenty yards ahead of the Audi.

'Shit, they're getting out. Three males, all IC1, all six foot plus, dressed in black,' said Donna, watching them in the wing mirror. 'They're heading to Marco's flat.'

'Are any of them Marco?' Bob asked.

'No,' said Donna. 'They've split up. My money is this is no social call. One's round the back, two at the front door. Just like we would.'

They watched in silence. One crouched to peer through a netted front window while the other walked backwards down the path, staring up at the first floor.

Bob twisted round and saw, for the first time, the state of the property, with its overgrown front garden camouflaging a kids' trampoline, the scaly paintwork at least five years overdue for a recoat and a faded 'Vote Leave' poster haphazardly taped to the inside of the semi-glazed front door.

The men seemed to be losing their patience; the one at the door hammered it with his fist then bent to the letter box, either to bellow his demands or to peer in for signs of life.

'A tenner says they're after Marco,' said Donna. 'Great spot, boss.'

'You never lose it,' chuckled Bob.

'They're coming back to the car,' said Donna, Bob scribbling the fact in the makeshift log.

'Right, I'll try to get some pics as they drive past, then we'll follow at a discreet distance.'

'Yes, boss.'

All three officers were now facing the front, relying on mirrors to see when the Audi moved.

'One, two, three targets all back in the car. Stand by, stand by,' said Donna as if providing a radio commentary. 'They are off, off, off, west Carden Avenue.'

The car inched up from behind. Bob silently thanked the wobbling cyclist who was forcing the Audi to crawl behind her.

As it drew level, taking a huge risk, Bob held his phone camera, set to 'burst', against the smoked side windows.

In seconds the Audi passed and overtook the languid cyclist. The driver pulled out and followed while Bob inspected his photos, praying at least one contained a recognisable face.

As they trailed the target, Bob's heart sank at the number of black screens he was flipping through.

Then one caught his eye. A face certainly, but too shadowed to recognise.

'Donna, how do you make these pictures lighter? I think I might have something,' Bob said, handing his phone across in defeat.

A second later it came back, the image now clear.

Bob gasped.

'You OK, boss?'

Bob did not reply.

He magnified the face, just to be sure. Despite the photo being taken of a moving car through two windows, there was no mistake. What the hell was he doing there? Of all the people. What should he do? His mind churned.

'Stand down. Take me back to HQ,' he said.

Donna spun round. 'What is it, boss? Shouldn't we follow them?'

'Back to the factory. Now,' he ordered, hoping that by the time they arrived he would have a plan.

*

Jo had planned to have this conversation with Superintendent Gary Hedges straight after yesterday's management meeting. However, she had been so cross that Oli Willis had been bailed that most of her first day was spent roasting the Crown Prosecution Service for what, according to the investigator, was a lacklustre, ill-prepared performance in front of the judge.

As she walked into her office, just before their 8 a.m. meeting, she flushed on seeing a huge bouquet splayed across her desk. The flowers were beautiful, thankfully from Darren, but not really in keeping with the hard-edged image her underlings had been used to in their chief superintendents. *Sod them*, she thought. *Why can't a gritty divisional commander also love fresh flowers.*

She'd replaced the photos of Harry with her own family, notably the four of them huddling around Chris Hughton, the former Brighton and Hove Albion manager.

She quickly caught up on overnight events, searching in particular for any update on the revelation that the police were not the only ones hunting down Marco.

Bob Heaton had done well to spot the Audi, and even better to snap its occupants. He might have been more upbeat about it, though.

'Morning Jo,' said Gary, striding brightly and breezily into her office.

'Oh, morning Gary. Coffee?'

'I'll get it. Sorry about yesterday. Very unprofessional of me,' he said.

'Forget it.' She flicked her hand. 'Hot water for me, please.'

He returned a few minutes later with two mugs bearing logos of long since defunct management consultancies. He put the drinks on the conference table and closed the door. Jo came round from her desk to take Phil's favoured seat opposite the clock. Gary sat with his back to the door.

'Before we start, Jo, can I run something past you? We've had a number of attacks on some of our scrotes over the last few weeks and I reckon we may have vigilantes operating.'

If they'd had this conversation a week ago, Jo would have dismissed it as the ramblings of a conspiracy theorist. But her chat with Oli Willis, the Sillwood Road pair and Bob Heaton's spot yesterday had got her thinking along the same lines.

'Go on.'

'You could put it down to gang feuds, but that doesn't stack up. You expect nasty assaults on drug dealers, but paedophiles with their faces slashed, fraudsters run off the road and God knows how many of our lowlifes simply vanishing? They're so random. Nothing links them, other than the victims are scum.'

'Have you got anyone looking at it? I mean as a whole rather than individually?'

'I've asked Bob Heaton to get something together, but he's being pulled from pillar to post at the moment so I'm not sure how much attention he's giving it.'

Jo nodded. 'Could they be connected to Op Carbon?'

'Shouldn't I be asking you that?'

'Sure. But we're grown-ups and you are allowed to have good ideas too, you know.'

'In that case, no. However, I do think they are after Marco, but for different reasons from you. I think the lucky ones end up crippled or scarred for life. The unlucky ones just vanish. I doubt they are being put up in a five-star hotel.'

Jo held Gary's gaze. If what he believed was true, not only did she have what was looking increasingly like an undetectable murder on her patch but also a well-organised gang literally taking the law into their own hands.

'Have you mentioned this to anyone else?' she asked, wondering why Phil had not mentioned it in his handover.

'I did touch on it when I met the PCC with the chief last week.'

'The ex-PCC you mean?'

'Yes. And I wish I hadn't. It was a case of lighting the blue touch paper but forgetting to stand back.'

'Really?'

'Oh yes.' Gary recounted how he had set the two women at each other's throats. Jo looked genuinely shocked.

'Why was the chief constable so against tackling them and the PCC all for it?'

'I think the chief felt we had enough on our plate. The PCC was always going to take the opposite stance to Ms Ricks and I was caught in the crossfire, shooting my career in the foot in the process.'

'Maybe,' said Jo pensively, refusing to take the bait of why Gary was not sitting in her chair, but she was curious. 'I'll speak to the chief. In the meantime, crack on and see what you can uncover. Keep it between us and Bob for now. I am sure if I lay the intelligence out for her, the chief will be back on board.'

Gary's look showed he didn't share her optimism.

* * *

Doug and Crush watched as the articulated lorry's tail lights faded into the darkness towards the town centre.

Neither had expected two of the city boys from the pub to put up such a fight. Even the most ferocious prisoners had all the fight knocked out of them by the time they were bundled into the old kitchens. These two had literally battled for their lives – and lost.

It had taken both Doug and Crush, and the sadistic slaughterer, to wade in to subdue them before the bolts zapped into their temples, stopping their nonsense.

It wasn't getting his hands dirty that bothered Doug so much. He rather enjoyed that from time to time – it took him back. No, it was that the cracks were beginning to show in the whole operation. He shouldn't really blame Crush but he was all too often the closest target.

'That never happens again,' he barked as he marched back into the main part of the fort.

'Aye boss,' replied Crush, 'but it's always a risk.'

'A risk we can't afford.'

His phone buzzed in his pocket, and the smile was back on his face.

'Mr Cooke, good of you to call, I was going to ring you.'

He gestured to Crush to open the door which led into the prison. He stepped just inside the dank passageway, careful not to move out of signal range.

'How can I help you?'

Doug listened intently.

'We've got some guys up north looking for them as we speak. What about our proposal?'

His smile broadened. Crush looked on. Curious.

'Thank you. I'm glad you've seen sense. We will be in touch regarding logistics, but may I be the first to wish you luck with your campaign.' Doug frowned, looked at his phone then muttered, 'How rude.'

'Good news?' Crush asked, grateful that Doug's attention had been diverted.

'Very good,' he mumbled as he thumbed through his phone. He punched the screen, held the handset to his ear and turned his back on Crush.

'It's me. I thought you'd like to know Phil Cooke has accepted.'

He listened.

'Yes, I know, but I never like to count my chickens.'

Another pause.

'Yes, it's all in place. We'll trigger it in a day or so. Put a bit of clear water between Sutton going and Phil declaring.'

He frowned.

'Oh yes, and Ruth's death,' Doug said, grimacing.

He smiled.

'You too.'

As the call ended, Crush tried to break the ice. 'Sounds promising.'

'More than that. We are about to move into the big time.'

'Eh?' asked Crush as they walked further into the fort, past the newly vacated cells.

'Let's just say, from now on, we'll have the best top-cover money can buy.'

20

Two weeks after her world had been thrown into turmoil, Jo felt she deserved some family time.

When the boys were still babies, she and Darren had promised to put them first. But as with most plans, it did not survive contact with reality, and the demands of their respective jobs put paid to their best intentions.

So, the four of them tucking into a sumptuous meze in Meraki, their favourite Greek restaurant, was a rare treat.

Costas, the owner, as ever made them feel like they were his only customers, however infrequently they now managed to enjoy his hospitality. He fussed over Ciaran and Liam in particular, mischievously slipping them extra helpings of baklava – for starters.

While the boys were laughing at Costas's dreadful magic tricks, Jo murmured to Darren.

'Bit of a shock about the PCC, wasn't it? Kent Police have been brought in to investigate.'

'Investigate what? The trafficking or the leak?'

'The trafficking primarily. The leak is unlikely to have come from us. Seems no one knew about it until it hit the headlines.'

'Well someone did, and probably someone who wanted rid of her,' suggested Darren.

'No shortage of suspects there then. I'm sure you know the hot favourites,' said Jo as she grabbed a Coke glass that Ciaran had elbowed while trying to see what was in Costas's other hand. 'Careful darling. I am sure Costas doesn't want to be mopping up after you.'

'Let them be,' said Costas. 'If they can't trash a restaurant when they are little, when can they?'

Jo shook her head in surrender.

'What do you mean, I should know?' asked Darren, returning to her accusation.

'It was the *Journal* who broke the news.'

'Have you any idea how many journalists are employed by the paper? I don't know half their names, let alone their sources.'

'No, but surely you could ask?'

'Hang on a minute. We are supposed to be out for a family meal. What's with the third degree?'

'Keep your voice down. I'm just interested that's all.'

'How would you like it if I started grilling you on why you haven't found Harry's killer yet?' he said.

'That's not fair,' she sulked. 'You know I'm burning the candle at both ends trying to solve this bloody case and run the division at the same time.'

'Now who's shouting,' Darren hissed.

Just then Costas stepped over. 'Eh, boys, you wanna see the fishies,' he chirped, taking each of them by the hand. He turned and winked at their parents in a way that said, *calm it down.*

While Ciaran and Liam were away, wonderstruck at the vibrant tropical fish gliding through the bubbling aquarium, Darren leant in to his wife, reaching for her hand.

'Sorry.'

'No, I'm sorry,' she replied.

'I do know one thing, though.'

'Just one?' she mocked.

'Just one. A little bird told me that a surprise candidate is going to enter the race tomorrow.' He winked.

'You can't leave it there,' she pleaded. 'Who?'

'Well, if I told you, it wouldn't be a surprise now would it?'

'Tell me,' she urged, squeezing his hand to press home her point.

'You're hurting me,' he chuckled. 'Come here.'

They leant together, Darren's lips almost touching her ear as he whispered a name.

'You're kidding me.'

He nodded, almost imperceptibly.

'Fucking hell,' she gasped, before a small voice, suddenly by her side, squealed, 'Mummy swore, Mummy swore.'

Only Jo did not see the funny side.

*

It had become something of a tradition for Chief Constable Helen Ricks to treat her newly appointed divisional commanders to breakfast.

Bill's Restaurant, now a national chain, had started as a small produce store serving coffee and snacks, on the bank of the River Ouse in Lewes town centre. It shared the honour, with Harvey's Brewery opposite, of being Lewes's most famous export.

Police officers stationed at the nearby headquarters regularly sneaked out for one of Bill's legendary breakfasts rather than suffer the tepid, crusted-over alternative shovelled up in the staff canteen.

Jo power-walked from the nearby pay and display car park, desperate not to be late for her boss. She had opted for uniform, minus tie and epaulettes, rather than her preferred plain clothes. A good call it turned out, as she spotted the chief ambling towards her dressed likewise.

They found a table in a corner and ordered quickly. Jo plumped for a light granola option plus toast, as she was still feeling the effect of last night's Grecian banquet. Helen chose Bill's Breakfast – a full English.

'So, how's it been so far, Joanne?' asked the chief, her lame attempt at small talk.

'Full on, would cover it. Running the murder enquiry and the division is certainly a challenge but I've had great support so far. Especially from Gary Hedges.' Jo paused, on the pretext of taking a sip from her cappuccino, seeing if Helen would take the bait.

'Yes, Gary can be very loyal. He has a lot to learn though,' replied the chief.

'You can put me in that category too,' replied Jo.

'Well, none of us know it all, but Gary needs to develop greater prudence. He tends to shoot from the hip.'

'Not unlike my predecessor then,' Jo replied, aiming to defend Gary without needling the chief.

'Quite, and talking of Philip, there's another matter,' said the chief, sliding her phone away to make room for her arriving breakfast.

Jo waited until the server had moved out of earshot. 'Yes, two deaths and a retirement. Heaven knows what he's going through.'

'I didn't mean that. My sources tell me he's going to stand to be PCC,' said Helen conspiratorially.

'So, it's true?' blurted Jo, instantly regretting it.

'You've heard?'

'Just a rumour,' mumbled Jo, hoping she was not in for a grilling on her source.

'A rumour, eh? Anyway, while it seems a bit odd, he's got to be better than the last one.'

'It's a terrible time for him to consider it though, don't you think?' Jo asked as she picked at a slice of wholemeal toast.

'Maybe he just wants to fill a void. I'm sure he's thought it through. We'll see, anyway. Now tell me what else is in your in-tray.'

'Well, apart from Harry's murder . . .'

'No. Tell me about that. Any closer to an arrest?'

'We've got an interesting lead. Some intelligence about a county lines drug dealer feuding with another gang.'

'I see. You think Harry was involved in drugs, then?' Helen asked.

'Good heavens, no. No, the angle we are working on is mistaken identity. Our source tells us that this Marco . . .'

'Marco?'

'The drug dealer. Apparently he was looking for a rival gang member, stumbled across Harry and mistook him for someone else.'

'So, who's the source?'

Jo thought about dodging the question; they shouldn't be talking about this in an open restaurant which, she noticed, had filled up since they arrived. But this was the chief constable asking and she was entitled to know everything.

She leant in.

'The chap Phil and I arrested near Seven Dials last week,' she whispered.

'OK,' replied the chief. 'Do keep me up with any developments on that. Any other leads?'

'Phil seems fixated on a gang we locked up years ago. He seems convinced they are paying him back and that Kyle – his other son – is next. They did try to burn his house down but that was years ago. I'm keeping an open mind but I'm not distracting the team with that one just yet.'

'I see.' Helen paused. 'And the division?'

'Well, Gary is looking at a string of attacks on some of our lowlifes, as well as some mysterious disappearances. He's convinced we have some vigilantes stalking the streets.' Jo sat back.

'Not that again,' said the chief, chewing on a piece of bacon. 'This is the very bombshell he landed on me when we met with Sutton. I'm all for superintendents showing initiative, but have you really got the time to be worrying what happens to people like that when there are real victims out there?'

'If people take the law into their own hands, then surely that's our business,' Jo said.

157

'Don't get me wrong, in times of plenty then yes, absolutely. But we both know that you can barely parade double figures for most shifts and the demand on them is hardly dwindling. Let's concentrate on protecting the vulnerable – the long-suffering, law-abiding residents and visitors – first, shall we?'

'But . . .'

'No buts, Joanne. It sounds harsh but we have to make choices and all the time Gary Hedges is riding this hobby horse of his, he's not doing the job I ask of him. Clear?'

'Crystal,' replied Jo, conscious that she had completely misjudged this conversation – and the woman opposite.

21

7.00 a.m., Friday 18th May

The ringing phone hauled Bob Heaton, sweating, from the depths of a nightmare. The man he thought he knew and loved had watched over two heavies as they pinned him to his desk in the MIR and poured sulphuric acid down his throat.

'DI Heaton,' he croaked, shocked at the physical effects his nightmare had brought.

He checked his watch. Seven.

'Boss, it's Donna. Are you awake?'

'Get on with it,' replied Bob, as he stepped out of the bedroom, so as not to wake Chris, or Crush as he now knew his lover's nickname to be. There was no way he could hear this conversation.

'We've got an address for Marco. He's holed up in a flat in Moulsecoomb. Have I got your permission to pay him a visit?'

'Of course, but pick me up on the way.' Bob craved the adrenaline rush of an early morning knock, and also wanted to be on hand in case Chris's mob had the same tip-off.

Once Bob was in the car, they made straight for the first-floor flat at Hawthorn Bank in Moulsecoomb Way. En route he studied the block on Google Street View. Marco would be mad to launch himself off the balcony onto the concrete terrace below, but they still planned the same approach as at Sillwood Street. Bob to the front, Donna covering the back.

As they cruised up the deserted hill, Bob kept a surreptitious eye out for any black Audis.

Secreting their car around the corner they swiftly, yet silently, took up their predetermined places.

A one-word text from Donna confirmed she was in position.

Bob gave the door the 'coppers' knock'.

No reply.

Again. This time he crouched, peering through the letter box.

No reply.

'Marco. It's the police. Open up.'

Nothing.

'We only want to talk to you. Open up before we put the door in.'

Bob was bluffing. Jo had not designated Marco a suspect and who was to say he was even in the flat? Phone companies and informants had been wrong before.

For the second time in a week, he was startled by Donna's distinctive shout. 'Stay where you are. Don't jump.'

Bob continued to shout through the letter box while Donna at the back simultaneously implored someone 'not to be so stupid'.

The crash and frantic shouts of 'Stop, stay where you are,' told Bob her advice had been rebuffed. 'Boss, we've got a runner,' panted Donna over the radio. 'Confirmed it's Marco.'

Bob took the stairs two at a time and dashed round just in time to catch Donna closing the gap across the communal garden.

He brought up the rear, realistic about his chances of catching up. He dodged round a heap of upturned wheelie bins, guessing they must have broken Marco's fall.

Donna was almost on Marco, whose terrified backward glances conveyed his realisation that the chase was nearly lost.

Bob expected him to vault the three-foot fence in one go, but he was sluggish. Marco's pitiful hurdling effort ended with him landing in a heap on an unkempt flower bed on the other side.

Donna leapt on him but he writhed and slithered beneath her, landing a well-timed headbutt square on the bridge of her nose. Stunned, she fell back. Marco sprung up and doubled back towards the flats. Bob sidestepped to block him. He drew his baton and yelled 'Stay where you are.'

'Fuck off,' Marco snarled.

Bob stood firm. Tensed. He raised his baton higher. 'Don't move.'

Suddenly Marco reached into his pocket and launched towards Bob, his features taut with rage, drawing out his hand as he lunged. Bob lashed out as Marco ducked. The impact of his steel baton connecting with his attacker's neck jolted up Bob's arm.

Marco crumpled to the ground. Bob stood stock-still, his baton hand releasing the weapon, which clanked to the floor. The next he knew, Donna was shaking him, 'Boss. What the hell was that? Boss, fucking help him.'

He came to, suddenly aware of the commotion around him. Donna was on her knees, blood dripping from her broken nose as she pumped Marco's chest in a frenzied rhythm. A small crowd was starting to build, smartphones capturing every action – and inaction.

'Boss, get a grip,' shouted Donna. 'Call a fucking ambulance, someone.' She paused. 'Shit,' she shouted. 'Marco, for fuck's sake wake up.'

No reply. The crowd pressed around. 'Get the fuck back,' she yelled. 'Boss, help me.'

Bob watched on, taking nothing in.

'I saw that. I've got all of that on camera,' came a voice somewhere over Bob's left shoulder. He snapped out of his stupefied state and paced towards a scrawny forty-something woman wearing a puce-stained candlewick dressing gown trussed around the middle. No shoes.

'That's it, have a go at me. You whacked him for no reason. This is going to the papers. They'll pay a mint for this. Love a bit of police brutality, that lot do.'

'Leave it, boss,' yelled Donna, as Bob stepped towards the iPhone-wielding woman.

A distant wail of sirens sounded.

'You called them then, boss?' wheezed Donna between puffs.

'Did he, hell,' spat the woman. 'I did. At least someone cares.'

Bob took in the carnage around him, as if for the first time.

'Right keep, er, keep that up Donna. Yes, that's it. Keep doing what you're doing.' He shuffled around as if looking for something to do, yet completely lost.

He was barged to one side and was a hair's breadth from throwing a punch before he recognised the green paramedic uniforms.

'OK, we'll take it from here.' Exhausted, Donna shuffled away on her knees to give the paramedics room.

After a minute, she stood. Resisting the urge to throttle Bob, she put a gentle arm around his shoulders and turned him away from where the medics were frantically working on Marco. Bob noticed as he was led away that the crowd's venom was rising.

'Best we get some backup,' he murmured to Donna.

'It's on its way. You need to think about what you are going to say, because this is going to take some explaining.'

Suddenly Bob felt very cold. He tried to speak but the words stuck in his throat.

'Who's in charge here?' asked the female paramedic.

'I am,' said Bob and, as if by reflex, he walked over.

'We'll take him, but he's not going to make it,' she said, in something just above a whisper.

Donna caught Bob from stumbling. 'Let's get you to the car,' she said as the stretcher was eased into the ambulance.

All Bob could hear as he was led away were the shrieks for his blood.

Part Two

22

6.00 a.m., Thursday 28th June

Stroking his smarting face as he checked for stray traces of stubble, Phil groaned at the wreck in the mirror.

Was he the first person ever to have been blackmailed into public office, he wondered? In twenty-four hours' time he would either be the newly elected police and crime commissioner or . . . or what? Would Robinson leave him alone if, God willing, he was pipped on the night?

Probably not.

There would be something else, and they'd probably out Harry as a drugs cheat just for the hell of it. He had to prevent that, at all costs. The shame would be unbearable.

He wiped away a tear then trudged back to the bedroom, aching for Ruth as he did every time he crossed that threshold, yet relieved she had never discovered his secret. Or Harry's. His elegant navy suit, crisp white double-cuffed shirt and black tie – always a black tie these days – hung from the wardrobe door. He'd bought it for the double funeral two weeks previously, as his old suits now swamped him.

Jo's team were still drawing blanks, and they seemed to be marking time since what had happened to Marco – or rather to Bob Heaton, now prisoner NJ9775. It killed him to think about his old mate banged up in that hellhole, especially when he'd been chasing the wrong rabbit anyway.

Why the hell wouldn't Jo just take a look at the Larbies? Then all this might go away. Was it pride or some kind of misplaced loyalty, that made her pretend Marco was the killer all along?

Christ, he had taught her better than that. Follow the evidence and, whilst he couldn't tell her this, who's to say that Robinson wasn't working for the Larbies? What if the blackmail and the ruse of finding Harry's killer was just them having the last laugh?

Surely not though. Planting someone in public office takes a different level of sophistication than those drug runners possessed.

Whatever, now he was trapped. By Harry, by his own stupid, stupid past, then by falling for the oldest trick in the book. At least if he won he might be able to mentor Jo a little, and guide her towards the Larbies.

Phil sprayed Lynx under his arms.

His mind turned closer to home. The promise he'd made to Ruth that he'd try harder with Kyle was coming to nothing. He was making an effort, if only to keep him safe, but every time he tried to talk, Kyle went further into himself. Little did his son know the danger he faced.

He glanced at the empty whisky glass by the bed. That had to stop. The funeral hadn't helped. It seemed like each of the four hundred mourners had thrust a dram in his hand over the course of the evening. Perhaps it was the only thing they could offer when there were simply no words.

At some point, his heartache had given way to rage and it had taken the combined might of Gary and Fiona, his formidable PA, to wrestle away his car keys and stop him from racing over to ACC Stuart Acers' house to rip the pompous twat's throat out. If he won the election, that tosser would be the first out of the door.

He'd pulled on his trousers, and buckled up the new thirty-inch-waist belt, when dread surged through him.

Where was Kyle? Christ, what if they had got to him today? What a showpiece that would be. *Grieving PCC candidate's second son found stabbed to death.* It took him four frantic unanswered calls, three texts and two WhatsApps before Kyle replied.

Dad, I'm fine. I just don't want any part of today's circus.

Phil typed a quick *I understand but please stay safe*, then threw the phone on the bed.

It buzzed again. An apology?

No, Jo.

She knew better than to give him any news on the hunt for Harry's killer by text, but you never know.

He fumbled open the message.

Hi Phil. I just wanted to say I'm thinking of you today. How you have remained so strong I'll never know but, whatever happens, it will all be done and dusted tonight. I'm not telling you who I am voting for, but these might not be the only Xs from me today! J xxx

For a second he wondered if there would be a second chance with her – after a respectable interval, that is. He dismissed the childish thought just as quickly.

He tapped out *Thanks. X.* Perhaps a little too curt, but she'd understand.

He checked his tie, slipped on his jacket and kissed Harry's Under 18s Premier League Cup winners' medal before popping it in his breast pocket: its new home.

The Uber was already parked outside, ready to whisk him around the marginal wards where his brief was to charm floating voters.

Fucking Robinson.

Clicking the front door closed, he wondered whether he was walking towards a new beginning or a cataclysmic end.

*

Jo could have throttled the supercilious jobsworth opposite.

Barely out of university, and surely without a day's life experience to call his own, he'd been stumbling through this interview for a good hour, desperately out of his depth.

He had failed the first test by agreeing to conduct this in her office. Despite her citing a jam-packed diary, he should never have fallen for that one. But he had, and Jo revelled in his discomfort.

'So, Chief Superintendent, tell me again why Mr Vaughan was arrested.'

'Look, for the umpteenth time, he wasn't. DI Heaton—'

'Former DI Heaton, I think you mean,' Toby Johnson interrupted.

'He was a DI at the time. DI Heaton was tracing him on my instructions. When he ran off from him and the DC . . . I take it I can still refer to her as a DC, as she not been sacked yet?'

'Go on.'

'When he ran off, Bob challenged him and . . . well, you know the rest.'

'But, against your orders,' suggested Toby.

'I might be in charge of the investigation, but we'd get nowhere if every decision had to be run past me. Circumstances change and I expect my officers to react, especially my senior officers. He had a knife, for God's sake. If you had the faintest clue about policing, you'd know all this.'

'So Mr Heaton said, but we've not found a knife.'

'How hard have you looked?'

'Carry on, Mrs Howe.'

'DI Heaton hasn't got a violent bone in his body. He reacted to a disgusting human being pulling a knife on him. That ever happened to you?'

'No, thank goodness.'

'You surprise me,' she replied, momentarily regretting her sarcasm. 'Look, I'm very busy and if you have all you need, I really must get on.'

Toby blanched, shuffled his papers and called the interview to a close.

Before he had managed to stuff the file and tape recorder into his tattered tan satchel, Jo was back behind her desk. Determined not to afford him the courtesy of a goodbye, she was already on the phone.

'Gary, can you come through please?' she said, deliberately ignoring Toby's insipid wave.

A moment later, Toby had been replaced by Superintendent Hedges.

'Shut the door, Gary,' she said.

'Need I ask how that went?' he said, as he perched on the conference table.

'I wouldn't employ him as a cadet,' she spat. 'Just because they've stitched Bob up so quickly, they think they can herd us all into court with him. Well they can fuck off.'

'Oh, that bad?'

'I need your advice,' she said. 'How would it look if I visited Bob?'

'In prison?' gasped Gary.

'No, round his Mum's. Of course in prison. He must feel we've all abandoned him. I owe him some support.'

'In case you've forgotten, you've just been interviewed by the IOPC for misconduct in a public office. You might walk away from that, but you can kiss your career goodbye if you sneak a visit to the prime suspect in a murder case.'

'I could make out I want to talk to him about the vigilantes. Distance my visit from the murder and Marco.'

He raised an eyebrow.

'I need to visit him. He changed over those last few days and I want to know why. He might not even agree to see me, but I couldn't live with myself if I didn't follow my gut instinct.'

'You need to think this through.'

'Ironic, isn't it. The court bangs up poor Bob but lets a scumbag like Oli Willis out.'

'You know he's on his toes? Or maybe he's another one of the mysterious missing,' Gary said.

'Bloody hell!' Another cock-up to add to the pile. 'Well, let's get on and find him. Never mind what Ricks says – catch these vigilantes before they hurt someone who really matters.'

* * *

As dawn broke, Phil eased open the door into Hove Town Hall's council chamber.

Spending the whole previous day – well, the entire three weeks – reluctantly canvassing and checking up on Kyle had wiped him out. Now it all came down to this.

Why couldn't he have his old life back? Harry, Ruth, the old Kyle. His job.

His secret.

Sure, it wasn't a complete bed of roses, but there was nothing he wouldn't give to go back in time. Everything he loved had been so brutally ripped away. And now this: cornered into running for a job he detested. The threat to Kyle, those photos and the ones of him joining Bob in HMP Bullingdon hung over him if he stepped out of line.

At least Kyle was safe; a curt 'good luck' text around 4 p.m. came as a huge relief. For now.

As he edged into the bustling counting room, he caught sight of the returning officer, Chief Executive Penny Raw, huddled in a secluded corner with her senior team, each of whom he was on first-name terms with. What did they make of all this?

An expectant hush greeted Penny as she stepped up to the podium.

'Can I see all the candidates and agents by the side of the podium, please,' boomed Penny.

He tagged behind his opponents' entourages. Penny read quietly to them from her notes and a deep dread sank into him as he accepted the grudging, congratulatory handshakes from the other candidates.

Phil followed Penny back to the podium, his dejected opponents taking up the rear.

He struggled to take in the numbers. The turnout seemed low, or so the defeated around him were crowing, but the figure that mattered, 51.3% of the vote, rang in his ears. Much lower and second-choice votes would have come into play. That might have thrown him the lifeline of coming second. All he could do now was suck it up and feign delight.

'I duly declare the Police and Crime Commissioner for Sussex to be Philip David Cooke.' The rapturous applause, stippled by a few half-hearted boos, could not drown out his inner voice shouting at him to get the hell out of there.

That was not an option, so he took to the microphone, feeling sick.

The flashbulbs flared, the cameras stared him down as he took the speech from his inner pocket.

He cleared his throat and waited for quiet.

'Ladies and gentlemen, may I take this opportunity to thank you for putting your trust in me as your next police and crime commissioner. I'd like to assure you . . .'

*

A few miles across the city in an otherwise blacked-out office block, the Boss and Doug watched on the widescreen TV in silence. They knew the speech inside out, but that was all it was – a speech.

The Boss stood. 'Right. We've heard the promises our new PCC has just made. We have work to do. Make him break every single one.'

23

2.15 p.m., Monday 2nd July

The two-and-a-half-hour drive to Her Majesty's Prison Bullingdon – not a shop or a wee stop within ten miles, it seemed – had given Jo a thumping headache. Standing in the Legal Visits queue, apparently the more dignified check-in and search area, was no remedy. All she could hope was that Bob had not changed his mind about seeing her.

Having cleared the security arch and deposited her phone and Fitbit watch in a locker, she followed the mute warder through a series of airlock doors, across a deserted yard and into the visits block. Once the drugs dog had given her the once-over, she was escorted through the domestic visits hall, where a couple of inmates' copdar triggered a chorus of 'oink oink'.

In a moment she was in the narrow corridor of glazed interview rooms, set aside for official visits.

'Name,' said the prison officer, clasping his clipboard, shield-like.

'Joanne Howe.'

'Not yours. The inmate.'

'Robert Heaton.'

The guard made a show of reading down the names, then said, 'Room two.' He opened the door to a familiarly bland room. Sea-green emulsion was slapped on wall to ceiling, with a table and two chairs – one with an orange vest slung over the back – shackled to the floor. As she stepped in, she spotted the black panic button fixed to the architrave. No need for that today.

Only the absence of recording equipment set this apart from a police interview room.

She took the seat without the tabard.

It had been a while since she had been in a prison, and this seemed almost too pristine. She was expecting more clanking, crashing and shouts. Perhaps this was deliberately soundproofed and away from the wings.

Through the toughened glass she watched a couple of prisoners – neither more than twenty-five – amble into similar rooms, greeted by people she guessed were their solicitors.

When another hobbled in, his burgundy baggy sweatshirt stained with dried vomit and blood, she was about to tell him he'd got the wrong room. Bob's strained smile failed to reach his blackened eyes, but it sparked her incredulous recognition anyway.

God, how long had he been here? A month? Five weeks at the most?

He had never had a spring in his step but his pathetic shuffle, in trainers far too big, reminded her of her father in his last days.

Aside from his black eyes, the scars on his lip had barely scabbed. As he sat, he favoured his left side, hinting at an injured right.

'Put the vest on,' the warder grunted as he stepped outside. Bob did as he was told.

'You shouldn't be here, ma'am,' mumbled Bob. 'Won't you get in trouble?'

Jo stood and stepped round to him, arms outstretched, tears unashamedly falling. 'Come here,' she murmured as she bent and hugged him, prompting a knock on the window.

'Ouch, careful,' he said, arms rigidly by his side.

'Sorry.' She sat back down. 'We are going to get you out of here. Everyone is behind you. Trust me.'

'Trust?' Bob sniffed. 'Why are you here? I take it the IOPC are on your back?'

'Sure, but they sent a boy to do a man's job. I was probably a little harsh on him – but I'm not here to talk about me. How have you been?'

'So, you've put your career on the line for some overdue welfare chat?'

'We're worried about you. In fact, truth be told, you seemed odd even before . . . well, you know.'

He sat in silence.

'Bob? What's been going on?'

He bit his raw lip. Jo left the quiet hanging.

'It's nothing,' said Bob, eventually.

Silence.

'I don't want to talk about it, OK?'

'Whatever it is, now seems like the only time to get it off your chest. I'm guessing this place isn't overrun with friendly ears.'

Bob shuffled. His eyes dodged Jo's gaze and, for a moment, she thought he would struggle to his feet and close the meeting.

Instead he looked straight at her. 'I've never told anyone this, ma'am.'

'It's Jo,' she said.

'I've kept this secret for ten years,' he continued.

She nodded, struggling to keep her dread off her face.

'I'm gay. Probably have been all my life, but for years I tried to fight it. Got married, had kids. The usual. It came to a head when Janet, my wife – well, ex-wife now – accused me of seeing another woman. I didn't mean to, but I just blurted it out. Told her she was wrong. It was a man.'

'I had no idea,' replied Jo, wondering whether her own skeleton was in the same league.

'Why would you? Straight people talk about coming out as if it's a one-off event. It's not. It's a lifelong process. The kids were next.' He choked back tears. 'That could have gone either way, but once I assured them I'd still take them to judo on Sundays and they could see me whenever they liked, they were cool about it.'

'Why not come out at work then? Surely breaking it to your family was the hardest thing,' said Jo.

'You have no idea. Remember, I joined when us queens weren't exactly shown the red carpet. Once, as a young probationer, this old-timer driving the response car ranted on about how he would never "pair up with a shirt lifter", how you "couldn't trust that lot" and if he had his way he'd "have them all castrated and their bollocks thrown off the pier".'

'But things have changed.'

'Window dressing. It would take more than a few awards and the chief constable marching on Pride to win my generation's trust.'

'So why are you telling me now?'

'I don't know. I suppose I've hit rock bottom. And it's relevant.'

'How so?'

He sniffed, then wiped his nose on his sleeve.

'Sorry. Anyway, I needed to keep who I was to myself, so I stuck to discreet, short-term relationships with men like me. Nothing serious, but we'd have an unspoken pact not to out each other. It was safe. Then it all changed. I met this guy, Chris. They say that when you find "the one", you know. I fooled myself that was Janet but when I met Chris, I was sure.'

Jo was about to speak but Bob cut her off.

'It all happened about two years ago. I was doing some groundwork for an undercover operation into a clique of door supervisors running the drug scene. Chris was the operations manager for the security company. He'd been the only one we could trust. Obliging and discreet on a professional and, eventually, personal level. To the outside world, we became pals, but really we were lovers. Chris also worked in a macho world, so he understood why I needed to keep it schtum.'

'So, what happened?'

'When I was out with Donna looking for Marco, we saw three guys banging on the same door we were watching. I didn't have a great view but after they gave up, I took a few pics of them as they drove past. I flicked through the images and, well, there was no mistake. His shaven head, Roman nose and the chunk bitten out of his left ear made him as identifiable as a fingerprint. It was Chris.'

'So, your Chris was looking for Marco too? That means . . .'

'So it seems.'

'Christ, Bob. How could you not know he was a vigilante?'

'He told me he still worked in security but at the high end. Protection to VIPs and those whose egos were only trumped by their bank balances.'

'No wonder you went all in on yourself. Why didn't you tell me?'

He locked eyes with her. 'After I saw him I did some digging, trawled a few systems – get me for that as well as withholding information, if you like.'

Jo looked around. 'That's the least of your problems.'

'Anyway, I found out what a nasty bastard he was – is. Worked for some bloke called Robbo up in London for a while. A bit of an enforcer, fists for hire. Being legit was just a front. Do you know Chris's nickname?'

'Go on.'

Bob gulped. Jo waited, willing the guard not to come through the door to declare time up.

'Crush.'

She stared at him blankly.

'Is that meant to mean something?'

'It was a name we've picked up from some of the snouts. I'd not heard of it before either, but Chris and Crush are one and the same.'

'Did you ask him?'

'What do you think? How could I tell him I'd rumbled him as a vigilante hunting down a murderer? It would all come out, at home and at work. I bottled it all up. It was driving me crazy. I didn't know which way to turn.'

'Shit, Bob. You could have just told me. It's the twenty-first century. There are plenty of out gay men in the police.'

'Doesn't make it any easier. You can't come back in again; it's a one-way street.'

'I need to speak to Gary about this. And the chief.'

'No. This is between us,' he roared.

'OK, maybe not the chief for now, but Gary needs to know. First though, we need to get you out of here. Then we need to investigate what you've seen.'

'What will people think? What if Chris finds out?' Tears streaked his cheeks.

'It'll be fine.'

Jo stood up and gently touched Bob's shoulder, as he struggled to his feet. The supercilious jailer appeared, opened the door and ushered them both out.

As he reached the door which she guessed led to the wings, Jo called out. 'Bob, next time I leave here it'll be with you.' Then to the guard. 'And you take better care of him from now, or I'm coming for you.'

24

10.00 a.m., Tuesday 3rd July

Having spent the previous day pacifying his jittery staff, many of whom were expecting redundancy notices, and being taken through the tedious bureaucracy he'd inherited, Phil was looking forward to finally talking policing.

As soon as Phil had been elected, ACC Stuart Acers found himself sidelined to the College of Policing, designing courses for direct-entry superintendents.

Since his election as PCC, to his surprise, he had been swept along by the euphoria. While his reasons for standing would remain a closely guarded secret, he quickly accepted the will of the voters and focused on his promises. The cut and thrust of the office distracted him a little from the grief and loss that were now his default emotions.

'Kate,' he called through the open door. 'Can you come through?'

His PA, in flowery top, flowing chiffon trousers and no shoes, wandered in.

'I thought I was seeing the chief constable at ten-thirty. I see a Mr Robinson is now in that slot.'

'Yeah,' she replied. 'The chief asked to be shoved back to eleven. This Mr Robinson called and asked to see you ASAP.'

Phil smarted at her indifference. Perhaps Fiona might fancy a move from Brighton.

'Did he say why?'

'No, he says you'd know and it was urgent.'

'Well, perhaps discuss requests like that with me in future?' Phil said.

'Shall I cancel then?' Was she chewing gum?

'No, not this time, but book a one-to-one for you and me. We need to set some ground rules.'

'Righto,' she replied, flouncing back to her desk.

At ten-thirty on the dot, Kate reappeared and stood aside to allow Phil's crisply dressed nemesis to march in.

'Shut the door,' said Phil.

'Nice,' said Doug, taking in the bland surroundings. 'You really should make it look like you actually want this job, though.'

'What are you doing here?'

'I'm just a concerned businessman who is looking to discuss an alliance between the police and the private sector. What's wrong with that?'

'Why the urgency?'

'I hope we can't be overheard,' Doug said, glancing out to the open-plan office. 'Wouldn't want any of your secrets to spill out, would we?'

'That useless PA of mine doesn't even listen when she's supposed to.'

'I owe you an apology,' said Doug, softer now.

'Just the one?'

Doug continued. 'We needed to have our own person in here. Teresa Sutton wasn't really interested in partnerships. Not with us, anyhow. We dangled the bait a couple of times but she didn't bite, so she had to go.'

'This is all very interesting, but I have to do what I think is right.'

'You think so? Look, you are integral to building our business and, more importantly, clearing the scum off the streets. We're creating a multimillion-pound security business here which, in time, will take over most of the police's functions, while delivering swift justice beneath the radar. It's the only way to keep crime down and that's good for you and even better for us.'

'Cut the sales pitch. I've nothing left to spend. You'll get crumbs from the table, if that.'

'I know this is all new to you, but perhaps you might feel more comfortable if you met the Boss. Then you'd appreciate how many friends you actually have around you.'

'Get him to make an appointment.'

'I can do better than that,' Doug replied. He removed his mobile phone from his top pocket, punched a couple of keys then said, 'You can come in now.'

Phil was about to protest, then his jaw dropped open.

'Helen, we aren't due to meet till eleven,' he said to the chief constable as she stepped in.

'I'm sorry for giving you that impression. Douglas and I thought it best we do it this way. Let me explain what's been going on. Mind if I sit?'

Phil's gaze flicked between Doug and Helen.

'You look a little shocked. I get that, but let me explain what's been going on.'

'If you'd be so fucking kind,' Phil replied.

'Of course. Douglas and I go way back. Believe it or not, I was once at the sharp end. Undercover. All this fuss about male UCs hiding their real selves and setting up a double life makes me die! I was working on a huge international conspiracy to import firearms into the UK; deeply embedded in the buyers' networks feeding intelligence back on a daily basis. Douglas here was in charge of enforcement – for them. Initially I steered clear of him. I'd heard what he'd do to anyone who crossed him or his paymasters. Then it dawned on me. His methods had merits. They induced total compliance. Any sniff of treachery and the suspect would disappear. We all knew that so, other than me, everyone toed the line.'

'So?'

'The Met were fighting a rising tide of crime, civil unrest, public disaffection. Whatever we did had no effect. So, I cosied up to Douglas and got chatting.' Phil grimaced at Doug's smug grin. Helen continued.

'I never revealed I was a cop, of course, but we just mused about how the police were missing a trick with pussying around as they do.'

'Get to the point.'

'In time we thought about how good it would be if the police could buy in Douglas's methods and stop crime before it erupted, as it was close to doing. It was all hypothetical and he still thought I was just a middle-ranking courier, but we threw some figures around – big money – and plotted what we could do with that. Anyway, on the day the shipment came in I was told by my controllers to disappear. I'd fallen for Douglas by now so, the night before, I made up some excuse for him to meet me for dinner in a hotel in Newcastle. Well, you know how one thing can lead to another, and there we were hundreds of miles from Harwich when the whole operation was busted. The next day I told him who I really was, how I could send him to jail in the click of a pen. I set out our future – professional and personal – together.'

'And with all my bosses locked up, it was a perfect fresh start,' added Doug.

'Trouble was we had to wait until the Coalition Government came up with police and crime commissioners, with their free-market ethos. All I needed to do was get myself appointed to a county force – it wouldn't work in London – and set up an enterprise where we could come down on crime and reap massive rewards in the process. My career and bank balance would skyrocket in parallel.'

'So, you pervert the course of justice, plot against the very profession you've sworn to serve and now blackmail me into being your puppet?'

'Mmm, theoretically I've not made any demands of you. In fact, I've kept your secrets and even promoted your girlfriend.' She smiled.

'How the hell did you know about that, anyway?'

She gave a look that said: *Really?*

'And those photos of Harry?'

'You have no idea of our reach, do you? More to the point, you have conspired to have Harry's killer hunted down and murdered, and you leaked information to the press to pave your way for becoming the PCC. Shameful behaviour. It's terrible what grief can do to people.'

'I promised Ruth Harry's killer would be caught,' Phil blurted, then immediately regretted it.

'How sweet,' Helen replied. 'Shame you couldn't promise fidelity.'

'That ship has sailed. Now she's gone, you can't hold that one over me.'

'No but your druggie son still holds the nation's hearts. You've seen how quickly the press can bring someone down. Dead or alive.'

'But . . .'

She raised her hand. 'You need to understand how things are going to work from here on in. Outwardly you will hold me to account, provide me with a budget, develop a Police and Crime Plan. All the things a PCC should do. But, in reality, you will free up funds to commission the Civil Security Group – the CSG – to develop its thriving legitimate enterprises. Event security, response patrols, provision of temporary staff, all those mundane tasks.'

'That's your company? The CSG?'

'Correct. Oh and, before you try, you'll never link it back to me, but there's enough held at Companies House for you to pretend you've carried out due diligence.' She really had worked this all out. 'You will turn a blind eye to our unique way of keeping crime down and those who commit it off the streets. We won't pay you, that would be corruption, but if you behave yourself and play the game our little secrets will stay between us and you can share the credit. And stay out of jail.'

'You are out of your mind,' Phil roared. 'How dare you come in here and lay down the law!'

'Keep your voice down. You play the game and we keep quiet about you and Dirty Harry. Oh, and we will catch his killer. For once you can keep a promise you made Ruth.'

Phil was speechless. Just as he thought his life had turned a corner, he was back down a blind alley. There must be a way out of this. He couldn't sacrifice everything he stood for just to appease these two mobsters and keep his secrets.

Before he could respond, Helen continued. 'Good. Douglas, you can leave us now. Mr Cooke and I have policing matters to discuss.' She pecked Doug on the cheek then smiled at Phil. 'I'm really looking forward to working with you. I sense great things lie ahead.'

*

'Is this about Mr Cooke being the PCC?' asked DCI Scott Porter.

'No. It's about a two-month-old unsolved murder, with not so much as a sniff of a breakthrough,' Jo replied, angrier at herself than her deputy SIO.

She couldn't shake the image of the broken man who had been, until recently, one of the force's most respected DIs. She imagined Bob quaking on his bunk, protected by a few inches of steel from the mobs whose kudos would soar if they could claim his scalp. Or something worse. The injustice raged inside her.

'How hard are you trying?'

'I can't conjure suspects out of nowhere,' Scott pleaded. 'We are going back through all the forensics. House to house has been done twice. We are even trying out something new on the phone traffic around the scene. If you can think of anything I've missed then just shout, but I've only got a sergeant and four DCs working full-time on this now.'

'Anything from Phil and Kyle?'

'I've had to pull the FLOs off.'

'Eh? You should have checked with me.'

'With respect, you've been a bit tucked up on your other job. They were getting absolutely nowhere. Phil barely gave them the time of day other than to rattle on about these Larbies. And Kyle? Well, it's like talking to a sulking statue.'

'Are you sure the Larbies are a no-no?'

'A hundred per cent. Their only opportunity was if, between being released from HMP Durham and getting his legs broken eight hours later, Tyler Larbie managed to get down here, find Harry, kill him and get himself back up to Newcastle.'

'Someone's attacked him?'

'Yep. I can't believe we hadn't found out before. Maybe if we'd asked the right questions sooner we could have appeased Phil weeks ago.'

'I was waiting for a call back from probation.'

'If you'd let me in on that, I could have chased them up for you, Jo.'

'What about their associates?'

'We've done what we can, but it's been fifteen years since the arson and no one, except Phil, has given their feud a second thought. He's just got fixated.'

'And you've explained all this to him? He understands.'

Scott shrugged. 'I called him earlier. He heard the words, but he's still sure it's them. Demanding this, that and the other. Can't you speak to him?'

'He's bound to be scared but I'll see what I can do. Oh, on another point, has the chief been popping in at all?'

'Not that I've noticed. Problem?'

'Probably not.'

Jo stared into the middle distance for a moment, mulling over whether she should say what she had rehearsed. Toby Johnson's ineptitude had first sparked the idea.

'How far have we researched Marco's boltholes?' she asked, trying to affect a casual tone – as if the thought had only just occurred.

'Marco? Why are we still interested in him? It's almost certain that he wasn't the killer, despite what your mate Oli told you.'

Jo raised an eyebrow, which was enough of a rebuke to make Scott blush.

'Almost certain,' she said, 'but not completely so. We should check CCTV, carry out house to house, do some more phone work around each of the addresses. What if he was around any of them at the relevant times? Remember, we have two missing knives.'

'Two?'

'The knife that killed Harry and the one Bob saw before he hit Marco. Or they might be one and the same.'

'Won't the IOPC have bottomed that one out? The one Bob said he saw.'

'Did see, not said he saw. I don't trust them to find their way home, let alone dig up any evidence to undermine their case.'

'Shouldn't we check with them?'

'This is our murder enquiry. We had Marco as a person of interest. We need to do all we can to find out whether he had access to a knife and, if so, whether that is still in or around Hawthorn Bank.'

'So, this isn't about Bob then? Just Harry?'

'Of course. I'd never tread on the IOPC's toes, would I now?'

10.30 a.m., Monday 9th July

It had taken less than a fortnight for Phil to seriously fall out with his chief executive, Mike Close.

He'd considered having a complete clear-out of Teresa Sutton's staff, but first he needed to understand what the hell a PCC was supposed to do and, like it or not, only people like Mike could reveal that mystery.

But Mike seemed intent on moulding him into a male version of his predecessor. He needed to nip that in the bud, now.

'Mike,' Phil bellowed, 'you got a minute?'

In an instant the trim, bespectacled chief executive appeared.

'Yes, Commissioner?'

'Come in and shut the door,' Phil commanded, flicking his hand to the vacant chair opposite. He waited until Mike sat down, pointedly taking a sip of coffee to stretch the moment out.

'What exactly is your problem?' said Phil.

'I'm not sure I follow.'

'Ever since I started you've been surly, frosty and if I hear you say "if that's what you want" one more time, I'll swing for you.' Phil flinched at his own words; he'd gone too far.

'There's no need for threats, Mr Cooke.'

'Phil.'

'There's no need for threats, Phil. I'm just here to do your bidding, so when I say "if that's what you want" I mean just that.'

'Bollocks. The scorn in your voice gives you away. What are you really thinking?'

'Honestly?'

Phil nodded.

'You're no Teresa Sutton.' Phil was about to interrupt but Mike kept going. 'But you seem to want to do it all by yourself. Take this morning for instance. I am used to joining the PCC for their one-to-ones with the chief constable, not being banished to my office to feed off the titbits you see fit to throw me afterwards.'

Phil bit his lip. Of course Mike was right, but this morning's meeting was one he couldn't have witnesses to. That said, he would need to be smarter in future or his staff would suspect something.

'That wasn't a one-to-one as such. We were just chatting.'

'Chatting?'

'About Harry's murder if you must know,' Phil lied.

'Oh, I see. I'm sorry,' muttered Mike.

'But there will be times I want to meet people on my own. I'm not shutting you out, it's just how I do business.'

'You need to be careful.'

'Careful?'

'You are the only elected person with a pan-Sussex remit. There are plenty out there, the Police and Crime Panel for starters, who will delight in you taking a fall. Part of my job is to keep everything you do squeaky clean, and that means protecting your back from all the Brutuses.'

'I'm very grateful, but I can look after myself.' Phil saw Mike's right eyebrow rise quizzically.

'Another thing?' said Mike, as if he was about to reel off a list.

'Go on.'

'These grant variations you are proposing.'

'Decided on,' Phil corrected.

'OK. These grant variations. How are you going to justify moving a million pounds from victims' services to this new "community security" priority? The Police and Crime Panel will eat you alive.'

Phil took a breath. 'I've been a victim of a crime that I wouldn't wish on anybody. I'd give anything for it not to have happened in the first place, rather than some do-gooder providing me with tea and sympathy afterwards. I want to fund ways to stop these things happening, not pick up the pieces.'

'I hope you'll put that more delicately at the Police and Crime Panel.'

'We all know the police are impotent, hence the number of victims is outstripping any budget to support them. I'm going to take the fight to the thugs who think they can run amok in this county. This money will provide extra – cheaper – manpower on the streets, who will be the eyes, ears and, if need be, the muscle to stamp down on crime before it takes hold.'

'But, have you thought . . .'

'Didn't you just say you're here to do my bidding?'

Mike stood up. 'I hope you know what you are doing.'

25

11.00 p.m., Thursday 12th July

The reaction Jo got as she walked through the door was exactly as she had predicted.

It mirrored her own on the rare occasions a fully kitted-up senior officer breezed into one of her briefings. As a PC and sergeant, she could count on the fingers of one hand how often that happened. In those days, the brass only graced the coalface to deliver bollockings or announce some shiny new initiative which was doomed to failure yet would be a rung to the next rank.

Some shuffled papers. Others sat a little straighter. Those slurping from chipped mugs with risqué slogans put their tea down. All fell silent though, their eyes somewhere between curiosity and suspicion as to why the divisional commander had joined them – at this time of night.

At first, she was surprised how few officers – she counted nine – were slouched in the dimly lit briefing room. All were diligently noting down the details of yet another familiar villain under whose mugshot was emblazoned, 'Wanted. Recall to Prison'.

'Evening everyone. Mind if I sit down?' she chirped, as she nestled herself between a rippling PC with a bewildering tattoo sleeve and a jaded-looking blonde officer.

'Carry on,' Jo told the inspector, whose frozen expression was a poor attempt at genial.

'Did you want to say anything, ma'am, before I carry on?' he asked, hoping she would say her piece and leave them to it.

'Sorry, how rude of me. No, I'm working the night shift with you. That OK?'

'Oh, I see. Perhaps you'd like to ride around with me?' the inspector said, taking one for the team.

'Good heavens, no. You're far too busy. No, I want to crew a response car and work as a PC. I even have some PC epaulettes,' she flourished them proudly, 'so the public won't know I'm usually stuck behind a desk. Wouldn't want to be picked out as the weak link, now would I?'

'Ah. I've worked out all the crewing.' A poor effort at deflection.

'Oh, come, come. You're always telling me how short-staffed you are. I'll crew a car and free someone up to deal with one of late-turn's prisoners or whatever.' She smiled, relishing his strained expression. 'In fact, could I work with PC Relf, please?' The young woman next to her tensed, while a collective sigh of relief heaved all around.

'Er yes, of course. Wendy, you are working with Chief Superintendent—'

'PC,' Jo reminded him. 'We are all constables, after all, aren't we?'

'PC Howe.'

At that moment the door crashed open and a tall, balding PC bounded in.

'Sorry I'm late, guv,' he panted. 'It was a bugger to park.'

Murmurs of 'awkward' and 'doughnuts' hummed around the room as the latecomer paused, as if expecting some quip.

He looked nonplussed for a second as the inspector fixed his gaze then flicked his head in Jo's direction. He didn't take the hint.

'I'll have a jam doughnut, if you can remember please Hedgy,' said Jo.

PC Hedgcock spun in her direction. 'You can fuck— Oh, good evening, ma'am,' he spluttered. 'Jam you say?'

The room erupted in raucous hilarity. Even Wendy was laughing as

189

Hedgy sheepishly took the vacant seat in the row in front, the tattooed colleague rubbing his knuckles onto his pate from behind.

*

As PC Wendy Relf squeezed through the red traffic lights at the logjammed Preston Circus, lights flashing and sirens wailing, Jo thought the car clock must be wrong. Surely they had not been out three hours already.

The calls were relentless. No sooner had they called in the result of their first job of the night – youths smashing up the Volk's Railway ticket office; serious damage but no trace of the offenders – than comms lined up another.

And so it went on. Pub fights in Kemptown, drug dealing in Saltdean, kids kicking off wing mirrors in Hove. There'd barely been time to draw breath. But strangely, she thought as they weaved up Viaduct Road, narrowly avoiding the ridiculous traffic-calming flower planters, no prisoners.

'Is it always like this?' Jo asked, resisting the temptation to shout for her to mind the idiot cyclist meandering in front of them.

'No, sometimes it's quite busy,' said Wendy.

'I mean getting there too late. It's not like you've been hanging around once comms give us the calls.'

'Depends how long they've been sitting on them beforehand. Suits me though. If it's all quiet on arrival that means less paperwork. Happy days.'

'But every one? How come with every job we've been to, what nine, ten, there's been no one to nick and none of the victims are that bothered about seeing us?'

'Twat,' muttered Wendy.

'I beg your pardon?' said Jo.

'Sorry, not you,' replied Wendy as she gave the finger to the driver of the taxi she'd nearly T-boned as he darted out of a filling station.

'I understand it's convenient that everything's quiet when we get there, but what I want to know is why?'

'We never ask,' said Wendy as she powered up Lewes Road, flicking off

190

the sirens as they drew close to their call: a prowler at Cockcroft Building, part of the University of Brighton. 'Look, I've never actually seen them myself, but over the last year or so we've all been hearing whispers of being beaten to half these jobs.'

'By who?'

Wendy shrugged. 'Don't know. We had one at a pub a couple of months ago. Sounded like carnage on the radio but when we got there, all quiet. Right, we're just about here. Can you get out and cover the front and I'll drive round the back?'

Jo did as she was told. Her feet had barely touched the gravel before Wendy sped away.

She found a shadow to hide in, watched and listened.

Nothing.

'CR01, we are at scene at the Cockcroft Building. PC Relf is covering the back, but seems all quiet. Can you ask the informant to meet me in the car park?'

'Roger, CR01. It's the university security. Just to warn you the job was forty-five minutes old when we assigned you. You were the first free unit.'

Jo sighed. 'Roger that.' Forty-five minutes. Of course there was no one there now. Even burglars get fed up waiting.

She stepped out into the sodium glow of the car park lights and wandered up to the building to check for damage. At that moment Wendy drove round the corner and cruised up to her, window down.

'Another no-show then, ma'am.'

'It's Jo tonight,' she replied, her mind churning. 'I want to see this security guy when he turns up. Leave him to me and, whatever you do, don't tell him I'm not a PC.'

'You're the boss,' Wendy replied, showing no intention of getting out of the car.

A moment later a white Toyota Proace with a 'University of Brighton Security' magnetic sign stuck skew-whiff to the front offside door, turned off the Lewes Road and pulled up next to Jo.

As the driver's window glided down, Jo was hit by a billow of cigarette smoke.

'Better late than never, love,' came the gruff voice from within.

'Do you mind stepping out?' asked Jo, fighting the urge to pull the man out by his collar.

'Eh? They've gone. You can bugger off now.'

'Out of the car.'

'All right love, calm down,' he said, squeezing his blubbery frame through the undersized doorway. Wendy stepped out too.

'I'm not your love,' hissed Jo, regretting immediately how close she had put her face to his halitosis. 'Now, where are these prowlers?'

'Could be anywhere by now.'

'Explain. Doesn't it say "security" on your jumper somewhere under the remains of that kebab? Didn't you stop them, find out who they were? What they were up to?'

'Do I look like I'm going to take on a group of drugged-up pissheads half my age? I called you, you didn't come, so I called the other lot.'

'What other lot?' Jo asked, fixing him with her steely stare.

'Come on, lo— er, officer. Everyone knows. We've all got their cards. We call a number, they turn up and – well, the problem goes away and the boss settles up with them in the morning.'

'How exactly does "the problem go away"?'

'Depends. A clip round the ear. Sometimes more than a clip, if I'm honest. I've even seen the problem literally disappear.'

'How?'

He shuffled.

'HOW?'

'Well, I tell myself they are giving the scrotes a lift home, but who knows? Look, you must know all this. Goes on all the time.'

Jo looked over to Wendy. The PC shrugged.

'And what do my sta— colleagues say when it does?'

'They seem quite happy. Normally shoot off. I've never had this inquisition. Look, we're all busy. If your bosses can't give you enough coppers to sort the problems out, what harm if someone else steps in?'

'Get out of my sight.' Jo turned to face her partner. 'Wendy, take me back to the police station, please. The inspector and I need to have a little chat.'

*

The following morning, DCI Scott Porter and DC Donna Brand perched on the edge of Nigel Payne's two-seater settee in his cramped, cruddy lounge. Why, however scabby the flat, was there always a fifty-two-inch state-of-the-art TV anchored to the wall? And why did they never have a volume control?

'Mr Payne, please can you turn that off or down?' Scott thundered, to make himself heard above the gunshots and galloping horses.

'If you insist, DCI Porter, but we are just getting to the best bit. Don't you like Westerns?'

'Not especially. Look, the sooner we start, the sooner you can get back to your cowboys and Indians.'

Nigel's eyes suddenly filled and he nervously twisted the hem of his tank top between his fingers.

'Please don't get upset,' said Donna, throwing Scott a glare. 'What Mr Porter meant to say was that we know you are busy, so if you can just go through again what you told the other officers earlier, we can leave you be.'

Porter took the hint. His kick-ass approach was not going to work here.

'It's very simple, officer – I'm not nosy but I am careful, so my CCTV camera is always running at the back of the flat. You see, we've had some break-ins and, well you can't be too cautious, can you? I don't need to tell you that, after all . . .'

'Yes, thank you,' interrupted Donna, 'and your disk re-records every forty-eight hours, you said.'

'That's right, unless I keep it. For example, if something interesting has happened.'

'Like when the police arrested that man from the flats in May.'

'Killed him, yes.'

Donna and Scott ignored the jibe.

'So, when the uniformed officers spoke to you today, you said you saw nothing but that you have got the arrest recorded.'

'The murder, yes.'

'Why didn't you give the recording to the people from the Office of Police Conduct when they spoke to you?'

'They asked me if I saw anything, DCI Porter. I didn't, so I said no. If they'd asked me if I'd recorded anything, I'd have told them. But they didn't ask me that. The police lady today asked me if I had any CCTV, you see.'

Donna sensed Scott's hackles rise, so she got in first. 'OK, well you've told us. Can you show us the camera and then maybe the footage, please?'

'Of course.'

Nigel led the way out of the lounge to a back bedroom. Porter was surprised at the array of recording equipment rigged up at the window.

'Are you sure this is just for home security?' he asked.

'Yes, DCI Porter,' Payne replied, the insinuation sailing over his head.

'We were just wondering if you were a professional film-maker,' interjected Donna, rescuing her boss.

'I see. Well, you can see there is an uninterrupted view of where your colleague killed that poor man, and the camera caught it all.'

'Can we see the recording, please?' Donna asked.

It took him a good ten minutes to find the relevant time but when he did, Scott and Donna were transfixed.

The whole chase and arrest played out in front of them.

'Rewind that,' said Porter.

'Please,' said Donna, 'and can you slow it down from the point Mr Vaughan trips on the fence?'

Nigel did as he was told, bringing the speed right down.

'Stop there, please,' said Donna, trying not to rile Nigel. 'Back a bit.

Stop. Forward a little. Stop there, please. There, boss. See that?'

'Where? What am I looking at?' Porter replied.

'In Marco's hand as he lunges, there,' she said, pointing with her pen at the screen.

Porter squinted at the screen. 'A knife?'

'Can you edge it forward as slowly as possible please?' Donna asked.

Nigel took it on, frame by frame. Bob seemed to glare at Marco's right hand, then struck out and Marco crumpled.

'Stop . . . please,' said Donna.

Again, she pointed to the screen – grateful that, with his back to them, Nigel couldn't see their shocked looks.

'Mr Payne, I need a copy of that recording. Can you do that for me, please?'

'Well, I'm not sure, DCI Porter. DVDs cost money you know.'

'We'll replace it, but this recording is evidence.'

'If you're sure. Would you like the knife too?'

'I beg your pardon,' spluttered Scott.

'The knife. Would you like it? I only went to the window in time to see the ambulance drive off, but then I watched the video and saw what you saw. I didn't want a child to pick it up, so I went down to find it. Look, you'll see.'

Sure enough, a short while after the paramedics had removed Marco and the crowd had dissipated, Nigel Payne ambled into shot, went straight to a bush just by where the tussle had happened and retrieved a knife.

'You still have it?' asked Donna.

'Of course. You only had to ask.'

Fifteen minutes later, Scott and Donna were back in the car heading into town, armed with a DVD, a witness statement and what could be Bob Heaton's ticket to freedom in a long plastic tube.

195

26

11.45 a.m., Friday 13th July

Jo should have known better than to expect a good day's sleep following her night shift and the revelations at the university.

After her initial outrage, she was careful not to scattergun the blame. She'd waited for Superintendent Gary Hedges to arrive for work, then made it his single priority to get to the bottom of what she described as 'police collusion in unlawful rendition'.

So, when her phone woke her at 11 a.m., after a full fifty-five minutes of fitful slumber, she promised herself not to be so hasty to work a night shift in future.

Scott Porter's news had jolted her to a state of full alert.

Now, sat opposite the chief constable at her huge smoked-glass conference table, Scott by her side, she was on fire. She insisted Scott bring the knife and the footage, to press home the enormity of what he had found.

She paused the CCTV on the money shot.

'We have to act now, ma'am. Bob Heaton told the IOPC that he saw a knife. That's why he got in first with a baton strike. This clearly shows Marco pull a knife, then it flies off into the hedge. That knife there.' She prodded the transparent tube. 'The one our Good Samaritan recovered before the IOPC rubber-heelers had so much as sharpened their pencils.'

'Could it be the knife that killed Harry Cooke?' the chief asked.

'Possibly, but even if it isn't, Bob claimed self-defence and this proves it. We need to get him out of prison.'

The chief constable looked pensive, then scribbled in her investigator's notebook.

'Scott,' said the chief, 'thoughts on Mr Payne? Is he genuine or just an attention-seeker?'

'Not at all. If pushed, I'd say he was on the spectrum. The IOPC asked him if he saw anything, so he answered that question and that question only. He didn't elaborate to say he had it on film. They didn't ask him if he went down and recovered anything, so he didn't tell them. We just asked different questions and, bingo.'

'Ma'am, you need to authorise us to go to the IOPC and the CPS. Their investigation was criminally superficial. Almost as if they didn't want to find the knife or any witnesses,' Jo insisted.

'We need to be very careful before we start accusing them, but this certainly seems to be material that will assist the defence, so they'll have to disclose it.'

'Let's do it ourselves. Today, and get Bob out of that hellhole.'

'Joanne, I share your frustration, but there is a process to follow. And you need to be ready to explain exactly what you were doing knocking on doors around their crime scene.'

'We were trying to piece together Marco Vaughan's movements around the time of Harry's murder, and this just popped up,' said Scott, unconvincingly.

'Of course you were,' replied the chief, a smirk flashing across her face. 'On that point, until you bottom out whether this knife killed Harry, I suggest that we keep that aspect between ourselves. I wouldn't want the PCC's hopes raised. Come to me with the result as soon as you have it. Now get on and write that report. I'll make some calls to smooth the way.'

Jo and Scott took their cue, gathered up their papers and the knife, and made a quick exit.

'Scott, have you got a minute?' the chief asked as they reached the door.

Jo gave him a quizzical look as he turned back.

*

Having dismissed Scott Porter, Helen moved over to her desk by the window, took her second mobile phone from her bag and dialled the only person who could sort this.

She spun her chair round, taking in the panoramic view of Malling Fields with Harvey's Brewery in the distance. After three rings her call was answered.

'Don't "darling" me, Douglas, we've got a massive problem.' She explained about the knife and the implications on their hold over the PCC, not to mention her turnover, if it turned out to be the one that killed Harry Cooke. She listened to his reply.

'No, of course I can't get rid of it. It's not a bloody TV drama, you know. You assured me it wasn't this Marco who killed him. What if this knife turns out to be the murder weapon? How do we then close the deal with Philip Cooke if it turns out Robert Heaton killed the murderer before we did?'

She frowned. 'I'm not panicking, I'm just asking the questions you should be. I need you to pull your finger out and find out once and for all who we are looking for, deal with them, then collect what we are due. Is that clear?'

She didn't wait for a reply. They both knew the question was rhetorical.

*

Oli Willis had not seen night or day for a couple of months. Banged up in that putrid cell, he'd long since lost track of time. The isolation, constant starvation, the high-pitched mechanical whining and the regular beatings eroded any remaining will to live. Only instinct was keeping him alive.

In the early days he'd dreamt of fresh air but as he stood now, or rather cowered, in the chill of the night on a clifftop gripped by the man he had come to know as Crush on one side and a brute he took to be Crush's boss on the other, he longed for his stinking dungeon.

Crush wrenched Oli's arm back and pointed to the road below. 'Watch.'

The forty-tonne, five-axle articulated lorry trundled towards the gates then stopped, its rear not fifteen yards from the entrance.

'What's happening?'

'Keep watching.'

Oli squinted, not really sure what he was supposed to be seeing.

The driver jumped from the cab and deftly untethered the tarpaulin sides. He hoisted himself into the trailer, and then a conga of forklift trucks, each stacked with long, narrow wooden pallets, emerged from the fort and served their load onto the lorry.

This went on for a good twenty minutes. Back and forth, back and forth.

At last the driver jumped down, refastened the sides, jogged to the cab and, after some expert manoeuvring, drove off the way he'd come.

'What's in those boxes?' asked Oli.

'Not what, who,' replied Crush.

Oli stared at him, confused.

'Ever noticed how the cells seem roomier from time to time?'

Oli still didn't get it.

'We don't release people from here. This is how we create space.'

'But, what? How? I mean the boxes . . .' stuttered Oli.

'Let's just say we have some very effective reducing equipment. You must have heard it.'

Oli's legs gave way. He clenched to stop his bowels voiding. Crush's grip wrenched his shoulder, just stopping Oli stumbling over the cliff edge. In a flash, he clenched his hand around Oli's mouth, choking off his screams.

'Now listen,' hissed Doug. 'Here's the deal. You were stupid to tell the police Marco stabbed Harry, but at least it threw them off the trail of the real killer. We both know it wasn't Marco, but your job now is to find out who it was. No more pissing about. We need someone the gangs will talk to. You're going to go back to Brighton and do whatever digging it takes to find out who it was.'

'You want me to grass?' winced Oli as his shoulder screamed.

'What do you think? We have been asked to find the killer. There's a lot of money at stake, so we have to get to whoever it is before the Old Bill do, and you give us that edge. We will be watching you though – any hint that you're going off-piste and you'll be back here and on that lorry before you know it.'

'But I'm wanted by the police. What if they find me?'

'Your problem. Your life literally depends on this. Any other complication is yours and yours alone.'

'What do I do when I find whoever it was?'

'That's more like it. You tell us, and then . . . well, we'll see.'

'I get to go home?' asked Oli, feeling hopeful for the first time in months.

'Let's not get ahead of ourselves. Just give us the name and we'll decide on what happens next,' said Doug, pulling on Oli's good arm. 'Right, back inside. We need to get you cleaned up to meet your public.'

They dragged Oli, hobbling, away from the cliff edge, over the ridge and through a doorway he'd never seen before.

They shoved him through another door and, to his surprise, he found himself in a sparsely furnished, but passable, bedroom. The bare light bulb threw a dim glow but he could just make out a single metal-framed bed with a grubby pillow and grey army blanket tucked under its thin mattress. A water jug and chipped white enamel mug stood on a low dresser. He spotted an opening to the right of the bed. He limped over, opened it and flicked the light switch.

As showers went it was manky as hell, but it was also the closest he'd come to any form of sanitation since he had been snatched. The toilet too was basic, but it would beat shitting in the corner.

As he returned to the bedroom, the door opened and Crush stepped in, a bundle in his arms.

'Get showered and shaved, have a good night's sleep, then in the morning put this lot on.' He nodded towards the pile of clothes. 'Then we'll take you to Brighton. Maybe you'll be able to save your miserable life. Maybe you won't.'

Oli sat on the bed.

'Any chance of something to eat?'

Crush sniggered. 'Nice try, bonny lad.'

He turned, stepped out and slammed the door – leaving Oli bewildered, frightened, yet strangely excited.

*

Despite his reservations, Phil could have kissed his chief executive, Mike Close. Not only had he made the case for moving £1 million from victim services to community security appear so compelling, but the detailed briefing he'd provided on each and every Police and Crime Panel member would have put MI5 to shame.

Phil instantly knew he'd hate this quarterly scrutiny by this hotchpotch of petty-minded councillors who knew as much about policing as he did oceanography. A few were community safety leads, but most were reluctant members who'd rather have been selected for an audit or planning committee.

At least few of them could question his policing credentials, although some tried.

'So, Commissioner, exactly how are you going to make the case to an already denuded Victim Support that you value their work while stripping their funding?' droned Michael Maylyn MBE, the insipid representative from Rother District Council.

'As someone from such a rural district, Mr Maylyn,' boomed Phil, 'I know you will appreciate the folly of closing the stable door after the horse has bolted.' A ripple of chuckles billowed around the council chamber. 'Investing in victims' services alone accepts the inevitability of rising crime. I don't. Most people would prefer not to become a victim in the first place. This is what my plans seek to do. Bolster the derisory budget handed down by the government to put more boots on the ground.' The dig at the Conservative Government was not lost on anyone, given Councillor Maylyn's allegiances.

'And why have you broken with protocol by bringing the chief constable with you today?' asked Jennifer Clayton, the Chichester member. 'Is this the tail wagging the dog?'

Phil blanched. She had no idea how true that was. He swallowed. 'I have brought Ms Ricks with me to show that she is at one with my proposal. Time and again this panel has been fobbed off by previous PCCs dodging questions because they are "operational matters for the chief constable". You must have grown tired of that, so here we are. Together and happy to reassure you on any aspect of this plan.'

'And if we are not satisfied?' Mrs Clayton replied.

'I am sure you are putting your husband's trusteeship of Victim Support to one side,' Phil growled back, 'but of course I don't need your agreement. I am bringing this as a courtesy, not for approval. I am going to do this, and it will work. I will consider any valid modifications, but I will be funding community security and I am sure your husband will welcome the drop in victims.'

The mood flipped and cries of 'shame' and 'withdraw' echoed around.

'Apologise and move on,' whispered Mike. Phil was beginning to appreciate the value of this irritating little man. If ever he needed protecting from himself, it was now.

'I apologise for that remark, but I want to emphasise the serious point that I was elected to get crime under control, and this is how I plan to do it. Judge me on my results, as I will Ms Ricks.' *Oh, how little they all know*, he thought. This was going against everything he believed in. 'Any additional comments, Chair, I would suggest be made in writing and published with the minutes – but the decision is made and it's only the detail that can now be influenced.'

'I agree,' said the chairman, his expression betraying how tedious he was finding this pointless sabre-rattling. 'Let the minutes reflect that we note the PCC's intentions. Let's move on to item 17, Working Group Appointments.'

The shuffle of papers provided cover for the chief constable to whisper, 'See, that wasn't that hard, was it?' in Phil's ear, before feigning an operational emergency necessitating her early and unexpected departure.

Phil wondered if he was the only one to spot her self-satisfied smirk as she scurried out of the council chamber.

27

8.00 a.m., Wednesday 18th July

Jo was taken aback when DCI Scott Porter said he was happy to drive the chief constable to London alone – the only time they could get in her diary. Sure, he was the deputy SIO and quite capable of briefing the boss, but there was more to Op Carbon than that and she insisted on supporting him.

She detected an edge to him as he held the front passenger door open for the chief, and had only just strapped herself in the back when Scott spun the wheels on HQ's gravel drive and headed for London.

The two women exchanged pleasantries about Jo's trials of balancing two jobs and Helen's efforts to save the new PCC from himself. As Scott cleared the Patcham roundabout and headed up the A23, they got down to the reason they were all in Helen's personal-issue BMW.

'You had some news,' said the chief, eyes fixed on the road ahead.

'Yes. Things have moved on apace since we spoke on Wednesday.'

'So I believe.'

Jo stared at the back of the chief's head. *How do you know?* she thought, then reached into her briefcase and took out a buff file which contained just one piece of paper.

'This came in late last night,' she said as she handed the CPS letter forward.

The chief glanced at the contents, then whistled.

'Scott, keep your eyes on the road,' said Jo, as he narrowly missed a white van forcing its way into their lane at Hickstead.

'Arsehole,' he muttered, as he veered into a thankfully vacant middle lane. 'Sorry,' he said, flooring the accelerator.

'So,' Jo piped up, 'because of this Bob's being released this morning. All charges dropped.'

'That's excellent,' said the chief.

'To be honest, we weren't expecting them to do anything for months,' said Scott.

'So,' Jo interjected, 'will he get his job back?'

'That's tricky,' replied the chief.

'How so?'

'Well, he resigned before he could be sacked, so it's up to him. From what I've heard, he's not our number-one fan.'

'What about the IOPC investigator?' Scott asked, still furious that the video and knife were there for the taking all along.

'Well,' said Jo, pausing to choose her words, 'you haven't heard this from me, but he might have led his last death-following-police-contact investigation.'

'Mmm,' pondered the chief, 'that might have been down to me.'

'Eh?' said Jo. 'You didn't know any of this until a moment ago.'

'Didn't I?'

Jo shook her head. You clearly didn't get to be chief constable without feline cunning and the ability to inhale information out of apparent thin air.

Despite no change in the speed limit, Scott squeezed another fifteen miles per hour out of the BMW as the A23 became the M23, almost as if it was powered by euphoria.

'Remember this is a police car, DCI Porter,' said the chief. His Pavlovian reflex saw the speedometer flick back down to seventy miles per hour.

'Joanne, get on to Professional Standards. Have them prepare a press release to be with my staff officer by 11 a.m. We're not going to gloat, but equally we are going to say what needs saying about this debacle. Now, anything about the knife itself?'

'That's the bad news. It's as clean as a whistle I'm afraid and, before you ask, the pathologist has already said it's too short and wide to be the one that killed Harry.'

'I take it you've not told Mr Cooke, as I instructed.'

'No, I'm going to tell him today. Unless you want to, Chief?' said Jo, hoping she'd relieve her of that burden.

'No, it's better coming from you. Look, we're approaching the airport and you've both got things to do. Drop me off here, I'll pick up the Gatwick Express to get into London. It'll be quicker.'

'Are you sure?' asked Jo.

'Certain. Scott, I want you to collect Robert from prison. He's going to need a friendly face after what he must have been through.'

'Yes ma'am,' said the DCI as he cruised up to the drop-off zone at the South Terminal, the overzealous traffic warden stopping in his tracks when he saw who was alighting.

As Helen Ricks shut the car door and went into the terminal building, Jo also got out. 'I'll get the train back too, Scott. You might as well carry on up to Bullingdon.'

Scott grunted something inaudible, then sped off, this time with absolutely no regard for speed limits.

*

Scott parked next to the concrete single-storey visitors' centre and sprinted in for a wee. Two hours on the M25 and M40 were enough to stretch even the strongest bladder. He made it back just in time to see half a dozen men, most draped in ill-fitting tracksuits, loll out of the prison gates opposite. He wagered that at least four of them would be back inside before the month's end.

The revolving prison doors were a fact of life for those deprived of the promised rehabilitation. Released into an alien world with no housing, no job and no family, fewer prospects and raging drug habits, they would soon be robbing and burgling their way back into C-wing.

Scott spotted the shuffling figure, dragging an HMP liveried plastic bag, bringing up the rear, and willed him to look up. The fact that he was apart from the others suggested this was Bob, but his gait and skeletal features were unrecognisable.

He had half a mind to call HMP Bullingdon reception to check Bob had actually been released, but that would take time and the last thing he wanted was for the ex-DI to take his chances on public transport, feeling forgotten and unloved by his former colleagues.

He waited for him to walk towards the minibus to Bicester Town railway station, before he silently glided up next to him.

'Bob?' he called out through the window. 'Bob,' he shouted, a little louder, unsure whether he'd been heard or had the wrong person.

The figure turned and a glimmer of recognition passed across his ghostly face.

He kept on walking.

Scott stopped the car and jumped out. Bob shrugged Scott's hand from his arm. 'What do you want?' he mumbled.

'It's me, Scott. Jump in the car, I'll give you a lift.'

'You're all right,' Bob replied, 'you don't want to be mixing with the likes of me.'

'Don't be daft,' said Scott. 'I've come all this way to take you home. We're on your side.'

By now Scott had his arm around Bob's shoulder and, this time, he didn't resist.

'Please, get in the car, mate.' He took the bag, tossed it in the back seat and held the front passenger door open.

Bob looked up, his eyes dead, and after a beat, stepped in.

Scott jogged round to the driver's side, shut the door and pulled away, vaguely conscious of the curious stares he was drawing from the other inmates temporarily at large.

As Scott accelerated down the drive and headed back to the M40, Bob still had not spoken.

'You OK?' Scott said, trying to spark a conversation.

'Mmm,' Bob grunted, staring straight ahead.

'You're going to be all right. You know that, don't you.' Scott had no idea whether that was true.

Eventually, as they merged into the motorway traffic, Bob broke his silence.

'Why did you come?'

'To take you home. Make sure you were OK.'

'You never came to visit though.'

'True,' said Scott, chastised. 'You know it's not as simple as that.'

'Mrs Howe did.'

Scott threw him a look.

'Really?'

'Yep. Don't think she liked what she saw though.'

'Eh?'

'Another time.'

'What are your plans?' asked Scott, determined to keep the conversation going.

'Plans? They're not exactly encouraged where I've been for the last eight weeks. I didn't even know I was coming out until late last night.'

'Are you rescinding your resignation? Gonna sue the IOPC?'

Scott accelerated into the fast lane, determined to make this journey no longer than necessary.

'No and no.'

'Why not? You'll need a job – although I can understand you not wanting to take on the IOPC, even though it was criminal they didn't find the evidence I did.'

'That was you?' asked Bob, genuinely surprised.

'Didn't you know?'

'No.'

'I'll tell you about it when you're ready. But why aren't you withdrawing your resignation? I mean, you wouldn't have thrown your ticket in if you'd not been stitched up, would you?'

Bob turned to Scott for the first time.

Scott glanced back. Long enough to see the anguish in his passenger's eyes.

'Prison changes you. In more ways than one. I've gone through hell in there, but others go through worse. I can't be part of a system that puts life's losers and most vulnerable into a dustbin, only for them to be preyed upon by sadistic bullies. And by that I don't just mean the inmates.'

Now it was Scott's turn to be silent.

*

Jo's head was throbbing.

Her unannounced visit to Phil Cooke could not have gone much worse. Once she had cajoled herself past his PA – not exactly difficult – and closed the door, she could see the worry in his flitting eyes.

'We could have met for a coffee. Away from here,' he said.

He was clearly struggling.

'It's fine,' she replied. 'Look, I've got some bad news.'

'Go on.'

'Scott Porter has found a witness who backs up Bob's account about Marco coming at him with a knife.'

'And?'

'Long story short, we've recovered a knife that was found close to where Bob tried to arrest Marco.'

'That's great news, surely. I mean, that exonerates Bob, doesn't it? He should be freed.'

'Already happened. Scott's driving him back as we speak.'

'And the bad news?'

'The knife wasn't the one used to kill Harry.'

'So, that means it wasn't Marco, then? Just like I've been telling you.'

'Please, keep your voice down. It means we can't prove it was him, that's all.'

'So it could be the Larbies, after all.'

'We've been through this. It wasn't. It couldn't have been. Gordon has dementia and the boys haven't even mentioned you since they were banged up. Tyler came out on a tag but was hospitalised within hours.'

'You're kidding me.' Phil seemed lost in thought.

Jo continued. 'Anyway, if it was, don't you think they'd have had a go at you and Kyle too? You've got to let that go.'

'I'm not so sure. Look, you've got two more weeks. If you haven't charged anyone by then, I'm bringing in an outside force. I don't care how it looks, I'm not waiting for ever. An outside review might just uncover what's probably been under your nose all along.'

*

When she arrived back at the police station, Superintendent Gary Hedges walked in bearing two mugs.

'You bloody hero,' she sighed as she made her way round from her desk to join him at the conference table.

'It's been said before.'

She sat opposite him and took a sip. 'Where are we on the vigilantes?'

'Overtly, I've instructed that the duty inspectors sign off any call where we appear to have been beaten to it. It's not gone down well, but putting the screws on them will push the shit down to the troops. I've asked CID to provide a DS to review every incident where we believe the offender may have been beaten up or kidnapped.'

'And covertly?'

'Well, this is where it gets interesting. I've someone from West Sussex Division looking at all the intelligence and it seems that just about every public-facing business in the city has access to the vigilante's services. Seems the only ones not using them are us.'

'Maybe we should?' Jo joked.

210

'Stop it. The problem is we have no inside information and no apparent way in. Their clients just turn a blind eye and certainly won't help us.'

'What about this Crush fellow?'

'Chris Hook? A bit of previous. Enforcing debts, that sort of thing.'

'Family?'

'Not that we've found.'

'What about the muscle? They must have histories.'

'It seems they snap up ex-cops, generally those who have left under a cloud. Squaddies too.'

'Isn't that a bit risky? I mean, how can they guarantee loyalty?'

'Easy, if they have a hold over them. Most have some secret they'd prefer to stay buried. It's amazing how pliable people become once you pick their scabs.'

Jo let the silence descend as she fiddled with her mug, an idea forming.

'What if we can get into them?'

Gary looked startled. 'Go on.'

'This goes no further.'

'Of course.'

'I mean it.'

Gary nodded then sat spellbound as Jo recounted all Bob had told her during her visit. The superintendent's face looked increasingly agog with each revelation. When she finished, he sat for a moment in silence.

'Did no one know?'

'Seems not. But Scott Porter told me on the way over that Bob's not going to ask for his job back. Seen too many horrors in prison to put any more in there.'

Jo set out the plan that was only just forming in her head as she spoke.

When she finished, Gary sat and stared. Aghast. 'Remind me never to get on the wrong side of you.'

Jo drained her mug, handed it to him and winked. 'Well, start by getting me another drink.'

28

4.00 p.m., Wednesday 18th July

Phil cursed Doug Robinson as he trudged up Cuilfail Hill towards the Martyrs Memorial, overlooking Lewes town centre. Why meet here? Once he got to the top and caught his breath, he'd make it clear to the jumped-up thug that he'd had enough of being pissed about.

As he approached the obelisk, Robinson was already there, phone fixed to his ear. Phil made towards him and, as he opened his mouth to unleash the rant, Doug turned his back.

Were it not for a couple of golfers ambling across the fairway to his right, he would have grabbed the phone and rammed it down Doug's throat. As it was, all he could do was quietly seethe.

Robinson ended the call and paced towards Phil, hand outstretched.

'I'm so sorry. Just some business I needed to sort out.'

'Don't play your mind games with me. I've had a lifetime putting scum like you in your place.'

'Yet here you are. Then you let me finish my call,' Doug smirked.

Crimson with rage, Phil spat, 'What the fuck do you want?'

'Now, now,' said Doug. 'I just wanted to update you on where we are tracing Harry's killer.'

'Go on then, humour me.'

'Have some faith. Do you want to hear or not?'

'Just tell me.'

'We've deployed a dedicated asset into the field—'

Phil cackled. 'Oh, piss off, making out this is some kind of special forces op. You're just a rabble of blackmailers exploiting my grief for your own ends. I have swallowed your trap hook, line and sinker, but as soon as this is over, I'm going to destroy you. Now cut the crap and tell me what you've actually achieved.'

'As I was saying, we have someone working on tracing Harry's killer, 24/7. We are much closer to finding whoever it was than Mrs Howe is, believe me.'

'For all you know, she might be making an arrest as we speak.'

'Trust me, we know far more than you think about her investigation. For instance, we both know the Larbies you keep banging on about are no longer of interest to her.'

Phil tried to hide his shock. 'You got me all the way up here to tell me that? I'm a busy man.' Phil made to walk off.

'There's something else. I just wanted your thoughts on this.' Robinson turned his phone to face Phil.

DRUGS CHEAT COOKE SLAIN OVER DEBT?

The curated news article, illustrated with four photos of Harry buying or injecting something, gave explicit details of how this footballing protégé – the PCC's son, no less – was far from the next David Beckham but instead nothing more than a steroid addict whose skills were only as good as his dealers could provide. Three columns which effectively trashed a boy who had no right of reply, mentioned several reliable sources and hard evidence.

'Who are these sources?' demanded Phil.

'If you ever find out, it'll be too late for you.'

'Where the hell is that posted, anyway? I've not seen that online,' said Phil, barely able to get the words out.

'Very professional, don't you think?'

'Get it down. Wherever it is, get it taken down.'

'Why would I do that?'

'Because it will destroy him. His memory. It's not even true. I'll sue.'

'Calm yourself. This is just a draft, but I only have to press the button and it'll be viral in seconds.'

'You can't make stuff like this up. I mean, even if it was true they'd have found traces of this muck at the post-mortem.'

'Only if they tested for it. And they still can. Are you prepared to take that risk?'

'You're fucking evil. You and that bloody Helen Ricks. Have you no heart?'

'Relax. Do as you're told and the story goes nowhere. In the meantime, I need to let you know that the cost of us finding the killer has gone up.'

'Take it out of the million pounds I've just granted you bunch of thugs.'

'You're not suggesting siphoning off public money, are you? That's a crime. No, the cost to you has increased. Travel, extra staff. You know how it is. It's now a hundred and fifty thousand. Twenty-five of that now, please.'

Phil erupted. 'You're having a laugh. You've done nothing so far. I'm buggered if I'm paying you a penny more.'

'Shall I press send? With your pension and a shiny new salary, this is loose change for you.'

'And if I don't pay?'

'You know exactly what will happen. Your fall from grace would be even more spectacular now you are the PCC. Your sorry arse would be at a premium amongst your fellow inmates. And poor Kyle.'

'Don't you dare threaten Kyle as well.' Phil launched at Doug but stumbled as his nemesis dodged away. 'Why are you doing this? What have I done to you?' said Phil as he regained his composure.

'It's not personal. You're just a bit-part player in our plan.'

'But why me?'

'Timing. If Harry hadn't been killed, or that incompetent Jo Howe had caught the killer quickly, we'd have left you alone. As we knew about your affair, then found out about Harry, it was perfect. We could box you into a corner, so you'd have no choice but to take our offer then be our puppet PCC.'

Doug didn't wait for a reply. He turned and walked towards the narrow lane that led to the foot of Cliffe High Street.

Phil was crushed. It all came down to that promise. *Whatever it takes.* He couldn't let Ruth down. Nor Harry.

Nor Kyle. Maybe closure would bring them closer together. Something had to.

Five minutes and a few key clicks later, he was £25,000 poorer.

*

The following lunchtime, Len Bradley sounded terrified when the call was patched through.

'You've got to come quickly. They're dealing drugs in the beer garden. I've told them to sling their hook but they won't go . . . eh? . . . no, the police say it's not an emergency. Oh, yes, it's the Ragged Smuggler at the back of Preston Park station. You came here a month or two ago. Thanks. Yes, I know how to pay.'

He ended the call, then sat back casually observing the middle-aged couple cosying up in the corner of the bar. An affair? It certainly bore all the hallmarks. He then switched his attention to the thirty-something bloke, all brick dust and tattoos, pumping pound coins into the 'Who Wants to be a Millionaire?' machine. *Bit early for a lunch break*, Len thought as he wiped down the pristine bar for the umpteenth time.

He was doing his best to keep it together, but if this went wrong he'd be finished.

Fifteen minutes later he was relieved no one else had come in. That was a huge risk, but he'd been told what to do if that happened. Easier said than done when you were doing what he was.

He saw, rather than heard, the black Lexus RX cruise up. He presumed there must have been some warning passed over the radio, but the three undercover cops in the pub showed no sign of hearing it. The couple cooed and the builder cursed, just as they had since arriving, and no doubt would throughout.

Len thought he recognised at least one of the thugs from before but, then again, one black-clad meathead looks pretty much like another.

'Mr Bradley,' said the one in front. 'You got some druggies?'

'Well, I did have but they've just left. You must have passed them as you drove up?'

'No,' said the same man, while the other turned and poked his head out of the door, presumably to check if they were still lurking. 'What did they look like?'

Len reeled off the description that the detective who called herself Donna had told him to commit to memory.

'Do you want to look in the garden?' suggested Len.

'Not especially,' said the man, who was clearly the only one briefed to speak.

'There's a back gate. In case they've come back – you know.' Len felt so awkward. Surely they'd rumble him.

Donna had asked him to get them outside so the cops in the observation posts would have their pick of photo opportunities. It also gave the mobile units time to get into position.

'OK, if you insist.'

When they came back in, the three 'customers' did not even glance – but Len guessed their covert cameras were silently rolling away, as were the invisible ones dotted about the fixtures and fittings.

'That it then?' said the thug.

'Yes, it seems so. I'm sorry to have wasted your time. What do I owe you?'

'Two hundred, bearing in mind we didn't have to actually evict anyone.'

Len opened the till and counted out the agreed fee, all in marked and recorded notes.

'Thanks fellas.'

The man pocketed the cash and bid Len goodbye, and the men walked out, got into the car and drove off. Still the couple smooched and the builder fed the flashing machine. Then, as one, the man and woman disentangled and the builder stepped back from the machine, mumbling something into an unseen microphone.

Donna materialised from behind the bar and the three 'punters' wasted no time in making their exit.

'Thank you for that. All OK?' she asked, a little too casually for Len's liking.

'What if they come back?' asked Len.

'Why should they? They must get dozens of calls like this. It's not just us who rock up late. It'll be OK.'

'That's easy for you to say.'

'Just stick to the story. We have all we need but, please, if you get trouble in future, call us, not them. Exaggerate the situation if you must, but don't phone them. We still can't find those city boys from last time.'

Len grunted.

'I need to go. Someone will be back later to take a statement from you. You've got my number if you get any problems. Like I said, night or day.'

Len held the door and muttered goodbye, then went back around the bar and poured himself a large Bell's whisky. The glass shook in his hands as he tried to settle himself down, fighting the nightmare scenarios bombarding his head.

*

Jo and Gary stood in silence, staring at the bank of CCTV screens covering the wall in front of them. The images panned and zoomed as the virtuoso operator deftly flicked switches, nudging the joystick as if it were an extension of herself.

The Airwave radio set, tuned into the surveillance channel, squawked.

Gary was used to tracking activity on CCTV and catching clipped radio updates from his years as a firearms commander. Jo, on the other hand, was playing catch-up.

'Sierra Victor 73, targets east on South Road. Held at lights, indicating left. I'll keep eyeball.'

'Sierra Victor 73, Roger that,' clipped Donna, the operational commander on the ground. She'd had to sprint from the pub to her car to pick up the follow from the Ragged Smuggler. 'Units to cover north and south of the Alpha 23 and east on Preston Drove,' she ordered and was met with brisk replies, confirming who would be going where.

'Camera 33,' said the operator without looking round.

Jo was grateful to be told which screen to watch. Gary knew instinctively. The image of a black Lexus filled the master screen a second later but was quickly masked by a furniture lorry waiting to turn right.

'Bugger,' said Jo.

'Relax,' Gary replied, 'they'll be off in a mo.'

On cue, the lorry moved just in time for them to see the Lexus complete its left turn.

'It's a left, left, left. Now offside lane, indicating right for Preston Drove. Confirmed right, right, right,' came the update from the car with eyeball.

Again, a flurry of confirmations from the others as they readjusted position so as not to lose their prey, while ensuring no one surveillance car was in sight for more than a couple of minutes.

'Where are they heading?' Jo asked, more for something to say than in expectation of an informed answer.

Gary shrugged. 'Could be anywhere from here. We'll know more when they get to Five Ways, at the top of the hill.'

The controller flipped different camera shots onto the master screen as the convoy made its way towards the chaotic interchange, a web of routes to all points in the city and beyond.

Jo was getting the hang of this, although she had given up trying to pick out the surveillance cars in the bustling traffic. The Lexus, on the other hand, was always in shot.

'What's the plan, Jo? Do you just want us to follow or are we intercepting at any point?'

'No, this is intel only for now. Just see where they go and who they are. Once we have enough to arrest them all we can strike, but that won't be today.'

They watched as the target car crossed Five Ways, heading towards Hollingdean and the Lewes Road.

The choreography of the ghost cars sounded mind-blowing and Jo hated to think how many traffic laws were being busted as they raced to get ahead, alongside and behind the Lexus, unseen.

'Stand by all units,' said Donna, 'bear in mind the logjam at the Gyratory, I want all points covered but just Sierra Victor 74 on Hollingdean Road. Keep eyeball Sierra Victor 74.'

CCTV showed a line of static traffic snaking from Lewes Road past the old abattoir, almost back to Five Ways.

The radio was silent.

The traffic inched along until the Lexus showed its hand, signalling left as it paused at the red light opposite Bear Road.

'Sierra Victor 74, it's a left, left, left on the Alpha 270 Lewes Road.'

The traffic eased and the Lexus pushed on north towards Lewes.

'They've not clocked us,' Gary noted. 'No counter-surveillance.'

Jo's brow furrowed.

'No jumped lights, recips or unsignalled turns,' Gary explained.

'Recips?'

'U-turns to you and me.'

Jo nodded.

Just then, 'Sierra Victor 71, I've taken eyeball. It's a right, right, right into The Avenue.'

'Sierra Victor 71, confirm The Avenue?' Donna checked.

'Where the hell are they going?' Jo asked, rhetorically.

The Avenue was a loop which led to the dead ends of Bevendean or fed into the warren of Moulsecoomb. Strange cars stuck out a mile on either estate; it was almost impossible to encircle the target without being spotted.

'Just Sierra Victor 71 keep eyeball. All other units cover the Lewes Road exits. If Sierra Victor 71 loses eyeball and they don't come out, we'll risk an area search.'

Donna was so good at this.

The controller sat back in her chair and relaxed for the first time.

'What is it?' Jo asked.

'No cameras up there. We'll have to wait for them to come out,' Gary replied.

Jo was about to speak but Gary placed his hand on her shoulder. 'It will be fine. It happens all the time. Just because we serve up the villains to you detectives all neat and tidy, it's not always as easy as we make it look.'

She shrugged him off.

Suddenly, 'Code Zero, Sierra Victor 71. Urgent assistance. Hyde Business Park, Auckland Drive.'

Gary and Jo threw each other a horrified glance. Code Zero translated to officers needing urgent assistance. Called rarely, it triggered a universal rush to the scene. There but for the grace of God goes every cop.

'Are you sure there are no cameras?'

'Certain. I'll alert Oscar 1.' Oscar 1, the force control inspector, would not be monitoring the surveillance channel, but one word from the CCTV room and he'd have the place flooded with officers in minutes.

Shouts filled the airwaves as the surveillance team broke cover to rush to the aid of their stricken colleagues.

Almost immediately, Jo heard the wail of sirens coming from the police station car park. The CCTV controller's message had clearly got through and officers of all ranks and roles were dashing to help.

'Sierra Victor 71,' panted a terrified voice, 'ETA for backup? Mick is down and they're coming for me.'

'We're on our way,' yelled Donna. 'How many are there? How bad is Mick?' The first question from the head, the second from the heart.

'Two, but they're fucking monsters with batons and God knows what else. Just get here . . .'

'Sierra Victor 71, come in.' Donna's car engine raced in the background of her frantic appeal.

Then, 'Sierra Victor 71, they've decamped. Heading to the Alpha 270.'

Jo and Gary took in all the frantic messages. They were both too long in the tooth to be tempted to jump in a car to help. Their place was in command.

What use is a ship's captain who spends their time tinkering in the engine room?

'Shit,' Donna shouted. 'We've been rammed. Repeat, the target vehicle has rammed me and is heading to Lewes Road. Bugger, I can't move. All units, all units, target making towards Alpha 270. He's got significant front-end damage.'

For the first time, Jo grabbed the radio handset.

'Sierra Victor units keep making for Hyde Business Park. I want a sit-rep.' She switched channels. 'Any pursuit-authorised unit in vicinity of Lewes Road to pick up the offending vehicle.'

Several units offered but all were miles away or stuck in traffic. In her heart she knew the car would get away. They could try to track it with ANPR and CCTV. Maybe even the helicopter would make it in time to help – God, how she yearned for the days when Sussex had its own – but in all likelihood the car was a goner.

Her frustration grew as Oscar 1 struggled to find a suitably trained unit closer, then switched back to the surveillance channel.

'This is Chief Superintendent Howe. Can I have an update on the crew of Sierra Victor 71 and the command car?'

'Ma'am, this is Donna, I'm with Sierra Victor 71. One uninjured, one needs an ambulance. He'll be OK, but his dancing days are over.'

'Any ID on the offenders?'

'Both believed to be the ones from the Ragged Smuggler. At least one is ex-job,' replied Donna.

'Repeat that?

'They both recognised the passenger. No names, but they are sure he used to be a PC on the Tactical Firearms Unit.'

Jo looked at Gary. With his background, if that was true, he would surely recognise whoever it was.

'Find out who they are, Gary. Whatever it takes, whatever it costs,' she roared.

She stormed out of the room, barely noticing the stunned expression fixed on the CCTV operator's face.

29

3.00 p.m., Thursday 19th July

'Did you bring me out here as some sick reminder of better days, ma'am?' said Bob Heaton as Jo returned with their drinks. She raised an eyebrow at his habitual formality.

Carat's café was nestled between Shoreham Harbour's grimy, utilitarian power station and a beach littered with obelisks that served as breakwaters against the unremitting tide and storms. Despite its surroundings, it was an oasis for locals and perhaps the only reason anyone, other than dock workers, ventured down here.

Most drove along the basin road which, with its imposing concrete and corrugated-iron warehouses, resembled a pre-apocalypse Chernobyl. Others walked across the lock gates, giving them a bird's-eye view of the viscous brine that tankers and pleasure yachts polluted as they chugged from the harbour's mouth to the quayside. Carat's, by contrast, was the transport café equivalent of a Michelin-starred restaurant. Coppers ate there and, as a general rule, any café with a regular police presence was sure to be a gem.

'When I was a DC, any prisoner who kept us from our Carat's Sunday breakfast could forget bail,' Jo replied, setting the mugs down on the sturdy table on the suntrap patio.

A nostalgic grin flashed across Bob's face. 'So why have you brought me out here?'

Jo had been deliberately coy when she invited her former DI to meet her. She wasn't playing games – it was just that she didn't trust whoever might have been eavesdropping at either end of the call.

'Well, I could say it's a "how's it going" chat or maybe a ruse to get you to think again about rescinding your resignation, but I won't insult you.'

Bob's interest piqued.

'Go on,' he urged, taking a sip of coffee.

A squabbling family bustled out of the café and, for a moment, Bob thought they would take the terrace table next to them, which would doubtlessly clam Jo up. Thankfully they scurried back up the steps to the beach.

'What are you doing with yourself? What are your plans?'

'Jo – can I call you Jo?' She smiled. 'Jo, just cut to the chase. I've had one night out of prison and, to be frank, I'm feeling pretty grim. You call me out of the blue – no thought that I might want to spend some time with Chris – so please, let's hear it.'

'OK. Sorry. You know Chris's background, right? Well, we think he is part of a gang of vigilantes who are attacking, kidnapping and probably killing criminals. More than that, businesses – pubs, even the universities – are paying them to back them up when we can't.'

'I was working on that, in case you forgot, but what can I do about that now?'

'People – maybe innocent, maybe not – are being maimed and murdered. You saw those two guys at Sillwood Road. Did they look like they'd had accidents? And they were probably the lucky ones.'

'I know, but where do I fit in? I'm just a civvy now, and an ex-con.'

Jo chose not to correct him. He'd not been convicted, thanks to Scott.

'Exactly. We need an in. This afternoon they put one of our surveillance guys in hospital and nearly killed Donna when they drove at her. And I've not even started on the list of people who seem to have just vanished.'

'God, is she OK?'

Jo nodded.

'That's all very worrying, but you still haven't explained what you want me to do.'

'You have a skill set that they would sell their grandmother for. Most of their staff are like you – ex-cops who have a reason to feel they've been shafted by the police. They'd snap you up, being so senior.'

'It was IOPC who stitched me up, not the police.'

'People will think we had a hand in that. You also happen to be living with one of their key people. Is Chris out at work? Do they know he's gay?'

Bob nodded.

'And with you?'

'Yes – look, where is this going?'

'Could Chris get you on the inside? Could you bang on about how you need to be doing something? Make it his idea to offer you a job? Then, when you are in and settled, feed us who they are and what they're up to. Help us stop the killing, Bob.'

He locked eyes with her.

'Are you kidding?' he asked.

'It makes sense. You find their methods as repulsive as I do. Just get Chris to suggest you work with him, win the others' trust – then, once you get to see exactly what's going on, tell us.'

'Simple as that, then. And all this is authorised?' he asked, knowing the hoops Jo would have to jump through to embed an undercover officer, participating informant – or whatever the hell he was – into a criminal network who would have no compunction in killing him should he be found out.

'Not your problem. We'll keep you safe. Are you up for it?'

He thought for a moment, watching Jo drain her cup.

'It's cunning, I'll give you that.'

Another pause.

'I don't know. Let me think about it.'

'I need to know today. I've put you on the spot but we can't afford to wait.'

'You really have. By the end of the day, I promise.'

'OK. Look, I need to go but, please, look after yourself. We all love you.'

She leant across the table and pecked him on the cheek.

'Speak soon,' she whispered as she stood up, picking up her keys and phone.

'Yeah, soon,' he muttered.

*

As Jo drove along the Basin Road, back to civilisation, she wondered whether she was making a big mistake. Bob was vulnerable, his loyalties were torn and she had absolutely no authority to do what she was planning. An old DS of hers had once said, 'There's doing things right and there's doing the right thing. They aren't always the same.'

She knew this was the right thing – whatever the consequences.

As she waited at the traffic lights by Hove Lagoon, she heard a WhatsApp ping on her phone. *That was quick*, she thought, hoping – praying – it was a yes from Bob.

Her heart sank a little when she saw it was Gary Hedges.

'Call ASAP. Major fire at Ragged Smuggler pub. We're in the shit.'

*

So far Oli Willis had managed to keep his head down. Looking up some carefully chosen contacts was fairly simple. Persuading them to keep his reappearance schtum was not. He'd confined himself to attempting the impossible, finding Harry Cooke's killer, so when Crush called him on the burner phone and gave him another little job, he was relieved to have something achievable to do.

He couldn't fathom why though, having been tasked to find a killer, he was told to burn down a pub. Were they testing him? Did they just see him as their bitch; there to carry out their dirty work and carry the can if it went tits up? Probably, but he could hardly hand his notice in.

He'd never liked fire. Others, he heard, could watch a burn-up and make out shapes dancing in the flames. That was bollocks, but standing here, among the gawkers, taking in the urgent scurrying of firefighters, clad head to toe in grimy Nomex, wheezing into their breathing apparatus, gave him a sense of a job well done.

He'd grabbed a spot which gave him a line of sight between two fire engines. The roar of the pumps as they spewed water through the shattered windows and the hiss as it doused the blazing roof was deafening. Every so often explosions from within triggered whistles and shouts as pairs of firefighters fled from what was rapidly becoming a smouldering shell.

He was certain that the vodka bottle, which made up the Molotov cocktail, would by now have vaporised so the chances of it being traced back to him were slim to the point of irrelevance.

The acrid smoke choked him. His eyes smarted and his skin blistered, but he was fixated. He felt like suggesting to the cops that they move the cordon back, but that would be suicide. Crush would go mad if he knew he was here, surrounded by emergency services, but he just couldn't help himself.

All of a sudden, he sensed a different kind of frenzy. A fireman sporting a white vest, with the words 'Incident Commander' picked out in the soot, was barking orders into a radio. A police officer was doing likewise.

Oli had no hope of hearing what they were saying above the thunder of engines, but all his senses told him things had just got a whole lot worse.

His head told him to run, but his legs wouldn't obey.

What was happening?

God, he hoped a firefighter had not been injured. You did hear about them falling through charred floors, or beams landing on them.

Dread engulfed him.

Pull yourself together. Stop catastrophising. Nothing's happened and, even if it had, they'd have no idea who started the fire, or even that it wasn't an accident.

He watched, searching for a glimmer that all was OK. Others were craning their necks too, but their faces were furrowed with curiosity. His wore dread.

The two things he saw, one after the other, told him he would be running and hiding for ever.

First, the enormous fireman gently hefting out a body-shaped black bag. Then, another panning the crowd with a camcorder – a sight that brought Oli's stomach contents splattering up the leggings of the horrified woman in front.

*

Jo had no idea how Helen Ricks had found out so quickly, let alone made it to Brighton from Lewes already, but the rage written across her face as she paced up and down Jo's office told the divisional commander now was not the time to ask.

'Afternoon, ma'am,' said Jo, furious with Gary for not giving her the heads-up.

'Sit down.'

Jo deliberately took her time placing her bag by her desk, and glancing at a memo marked 'urgent' that Fiona had stuck to her computer screen. Something about a custody extension for a robbery suspect. That would have to wait.

'Nice to see you, ma'am,' offered Jo, trying to buy time in the vain hope Helen might mellow. Obediently, she sat and signalled for her boss to follow suit.

Helen took the hint but not before slamming the door against eavesdroppers.

'I'll tell you how you can help,' Helen hissed. 'You can remember this is a disciplined service, I am its chief constable and when I give you an order I expect it to be obeyed.'

Jo fixed her hostile stare. She knew from her days as a negotiator that a cool head and deflection were the best ways to bring an agitated adversary down. Feigning ignorance was another.

'I'm sorry, ma'am, I am not sure I follow,' she lied.

'You know full well what I'm talking about,' replied the chief.

Well, that didn't work, Jo concluded.

'I've got the IOPC hotfooting it down here – again. At the moment, all they've got is a dubious decoy operation, a surveillance officer in hospital, a police car trashed – all culminating in another death following police contact.'

'A what?' Jo was genuinely shocked.

'Don't give me that,' said Helen. 'In the fire? The Ragged Smuggler?'

'I'm sorry, I know about the fire, but a death?'

'Mr Bradley? The landlord? The fire brigade have just pulled his body from the burning shell.'

If Jo had not been sitting, her legs would have buckled. Surely not – but the fury steaming from her boss told her there was no doubt.

'Go down to the mortuary and check if you don't believe me,' continued the chief, 'although there's not much left to recognise. "Barbecued" was the chief fire officer's rather coarse description.'

'I'm sorry, ma'am, I had no idea.' Why the hell hadn't someone updated her? Perhaps the person who'd told the chief?

'Arson, they are saying. Almost certainly as a direct result of you deliberately disobeying my specific instructions to focus on your appalling crime levels and even worse clear-up rate.'

A knock at the door gave Jo a moment to gather what she was going to say next.

'Yes?'

The door opened and a frazzled detective sergeant, whose name had escaped her, looked startled at the sight of the two most powerful women he knew.

'Er, sorry to interrupt, ma'am – er Mrs Howe, any chance of you looking at a custody extension please, only . . .'

'Sorry, I'm a little busy. Can you ask Mr Hedges or, failing that, contact Force Gold?'

'Yes, sorry to interrupt,' he muttered, backing out like an errant footman.

'I'm truly sorry about Mr Bradley, ma'am, but if this is connected to our surveillance op – and it is an "if" – then that's even more reason to go after the vigilantes.'

'The fire will be investigated – by the IOPC – but if you want to keep this command, your rank and your job, you'll start doing as you're told.'

Jo made to interrupt but Helen raised her hand and continued, 'Knuckle down, Joanne, and get a grip of this anarchic city, or I'll find someone who will. Someone who understands the rank structure.'

'But . . .'

'Enough. Just cooperate with the IOPC, albeit after your last stunt I don't fancy your chances, and do the job I pay you to do. Nothing more, nothing less. If we ever have to discuss this again, it'll be more than your job that's on the line. Do I make myself clear?' She rose from her chair, signalling that she expected nothing but compliance.

'Crystal,' muttered Jo, as Helen flung the door open and marched out.

Jo returned to her own desk, her head in turmoil about what to do next.

The vigilantes were running amok. She had a duty to hunt them down. But to defy the one person to show faith in her after Harry's death? Sure, crime was at record levels and she was being vilified in the press and council chambers for her apparent impotence but, despite what the chief said, every instinct told her that the vigilantes would stop at nothing to impose their own martial law.

Jo grabbed her phone and typed out the terse message.

You in or out?

She turned to her computer and tapped the keyboard, bringing the screen to life. She was halfway through her password when her phone beeped.

Her grin almost split her face.

In. Call me.

'Bob Heaton, you beauty,' Jo muttered, punching the desk.

30

10.00 p.m., Friday 20th July

Phil was trying to recall exactly why he had agreed to this, as the slimy floor manager signalled the countdown to 'On air'.

The studio lights glared and the red box in the corner reminded anyone who needed it that they were 'Live'.

'Good evening and welcome to *Newsnight*,' said Seb Ransom, the iron-fist, silken-glove anchor of BBC's heavyweight late-night current affairs bear pit. 'Tonight, we look at the crime explosion in the balmy south-coast city, Brighton. We look at what's gone wrong and who's to blame. To help us we have the Chief Constable, Helen Ricks, and the new Sussex Police and Crime Commissioner, Phil Cooke, live in the studio. First though, let's join our reporter Glen Windsor in the heart of this war zone.'

Seb relaxed as they 'ran VT'.

'That's a bit strong,' said Phil. 'We were told this was going to be a balanced debate.' He looked at Helen for support, but her blank look told him he might be on his own.

'I'd rather we didn't chat off air, Mr Cooke. It rather spoils the joust when we are transmitting,' said Seb, before immersing himself in whatever was scrawled on his clipboard.

When the pre-recorded video drew to a close, the floor manager's stubby fingers indicated they had 5, 4, 3, 2, 1 seconds until they were live on air again.

'Chief Constable,' said Ransom, with no preamble, 'crime up by forty-five per cent, only thirty-five per cent of 999 calls answered in time, missing people not investigated and three murders, including Mr Cooke's own son,' a sickly look to Phil, 'and another by one of your own officers. It's anarchy in Brighton, isn't it?'

So, this was how it would be, thought Phil, glad Helen had to return the first salvo.

'Firstly, it's been shown that Mr Vaughan's unfortunate death was not murder but self-defence. Returning to your broader point, Brighton is no different from elsewhere and my officers are working hard to bring down crime and catch those responsible, but there are fewer of them than ever before and demand just keeps rising. It's simple economics.'

'Mr Cooke, it sounds like the chief constable needs more money. When are you going to give her what she needs, before this once beautiful Regency city becomes a no-go area?'

Phil ran his finger along the inside of his collar, feeling strangled under the blazing lights.

'Good evening, Seb. My job is to ensure we have an effective and efficient police service and to provide the chief constable with the resources to make that happen.'

'You say that, but you've just agreed to divert one million pounds of public money into something called . . .' he glanced down, 'community security, and you've rushed to award the contract to the Civil Security Group, whoever they are. Surely that money would have been better spent on putting more bobbies on the beat.'

'The chief constable and I agree that the thirty officers a million pounds would buy would be spread so thinly as to make no difference. Investment in a more flexible, private capability will ensure the public get the help they need when they need it. The Civil Security Group persuaded me they are best placed to do this.' He was choking on his words.

'Chief Constable, the PCC says you've conspired to abandon the very ethos of a publicly accountable police service. True?'

Phil fumed, demanding this bloodhound did not twist his words, but the director had killed his microphone. Only the camera opposite Helen shone its red light.

'Of course, I would have preferred to have more money for recruitment. I've even had to cut back the team investigating Harry Cooke's murder, but the PCC persuaded me that his experiment was the way to go.'

Phil could barely contain his rage. This was a stitch-up. He'd never have agreed to hire this band of vigilantes had he not been blackmailed. He had two options. His head told him to filibuster this away, but his heart told him to blurt out the whole story, warts and all.

'That must hurt, Mr Cooke. The force, your force, cannot even afford to investigate the brutal murder of your own son. Yet you invest in this vanity project, which has no guarantee of success and must offend every fibre of your ex-police being.'

'I am confident that the investigation into Harry's killing is progressing, but as regards to growing our capability to tackle crime, with the lack of government funding and the effective freeze on raising money locally, I have no option.'

'Chief Constable, how high does the body count have to get before you shut up shop and hand the keys over to the private sector?'

'That will never happen,' she smirked. 'The public deserve a police service they can rely on and be proud of. I will watch the PCC's initiative with interest but, in the meantime, will work closely with this,' she looked at her notes, 'Civil Security Group in the interests of the hard-pressed citizens of Sussex.'

'Mr Cooke, should you really have boxed a highly experienced and respected chief constable into a corner like this? How would you have liked it when you were in the police?'

Phil could only guess that Helen had some hold over Ransom. She must have given him the bullets to fire beforehand.

'We should focus on what is going well in Sussex,' Phil tried, lamely.

'Well, I'm afraid we've run out of time. The message seems to be if you fancy a trip to the seaside, buy a one-way ticket and take your tin hat. Chief Constable, Commissioner, thank you.'

Seb Ransom swung his chair around to a different camera, allowing the studio lackeys to rush up to a smug-looking Helen and an inflamed Phil to remove their lapel microphones.

Phil stormed off set, dodging the redundant cameras and boom lights discarded across the floor – and before he crashed through a swing door, turned just in time to glimpse Helen wink at Seb Ransom as he introduced the next victim.

He found his way to the studio reception, shocking the lounging police civilian driver who had brought him and Helen up from Sussex.

'Let's go,' he said, not breaking stride.

'But what about the chief?'

'She can get the train back. Get me back to Sussex now. Any grief from her, speak to me.'

The driver hesitated, then shrugged and, in line with his army training, he obeyed the most recent order. Phil slumped in the back, ignoring the hundreds of tweets flash-lighting up his phone.

*

The next morning, as Darren Howe approached Brighton and Hove Greyhound Stadium, at the bottom of Nevill Avenue, his thoughts turned to how his two boys could be so different.

Ciaran, the more athletic, would goad Liam into playing one-on-one football on their now bald lawn, knowing he would beat his brother hands down. Then, the tables turned. Despite being younger, Liam, quite the bookworm, insisted his brother played My First Scrabble. How he kept a straight face as he insisted the ludicrous words he invented could be found in some dictionary – somewhere – was anyone's guess.

When he dropped them off at the playgroup, they were in full flow. He loved to see the other children rush over as they skipped into the hall. They would never be short of friends, which was more than many parents could say these days.

Jo was a different matter altogether. As he paused at the Old Shoreham Road traffic lights, waiting to turn left to skirt Hove Park, a police car sped by, lights flashing and sirens blaring. Of course, he was proud that whoever was in that car called his wife 'boss' or – even though she hated it – 'ma'am', but at what cost? He had predicted her promotion would engulf her, but not to this extent.

She rarely left the house later than 7 a.m. and, on a good day, would not return much before 6.30 p.m. Any notion he had of evenings being their time was well and truly snuffed out.

He swung the Nissan Qashqai into Benett Drive then onto his driveway. He sat and pondered for a second, then got out. As he clicked the key fob to lock up, a movement flickered through the lounge window. He shook his head, dismissing it as the reflection of a swaying tree opposite.

No, there it was again, but this time clearer. Had Jo popped home for something? Not without her car.

His heart raced and his legs trembled as adrenaline surged through him.

He studied the front door. It certainly looked secure, but he did not dare try it until he had figured out a plan. If there was someone in there, they'd probably got in through the back.

Fear gave way to anger. How dare someone break into his 'castle'? What if Jo had been there, or worse still the kids?

He ducked beneath the lounge window and crept to the side of the house, careful not to crunch on the pebbled path. He hoped one of his neighbours would be watching and have the presence of mind to rush to his aid.

His legs screamed as he crouched along the side wall. As he got to the back door, any doubt evaporated. It was ajar, the tool scars etched deep into the frame. He stopped, listening for any hint of movement. The distinctive grind of a drawer being wrenched open was no more than a foot or two away.

He needed to retain the element of surprise so glanced around for something, anything, that would serve as a weapon.

Typical. He had cleared the garden and path at the weekend. All he could see were bags of compost and a plastic cricket stump. That would have to do. It might not inflict much injury but it would certainly distract the bastard. Gingerly he stretched out, reaching with his left hand to grab the toy, heaving a silent sigh of relief as his fingers wrapped around it.

More shuffling from inside. He passed the makeshift weapon to his stronger right hand as he filled his lungs in preparation.

He swung round to face the buckled uPVC door and, just like he had seen on TV, booted it open with his right foot, screaming 'Stop!' Only then did it occur to him there may be more than one of them.

As he burst into the kitchen, a startled figure faced him on the other side of the island unit. His hollow cheeks, bony frame and pasty features under the blue baseball cap convinced Darren that, in a clean fight, he would have the upper hand.

Darren's banshee cry and his brandishing of the cricket stump froze the burglar, who looked more intent on flight than fight.

No way, thought Darren. *You are going to prison.*

Both knew the quickest exit route was through the back door, which Darren was blocking.

The intruder sprung into the open. Darren mirrored him, launching himself forward, thrusting his right hand to grab the man's throat, dropping the plastic stump.

The man flailed like a fish on a hook as Darren tried to propel him against the wine cooler. Both fell to the floor as he wrenched the squirming intruder away from the knife block, barely inches away. Darren used his bulk to pin the man down, but still he writhed beneath him.

'Calm down. It's over,' yelled Darren, his spittle flying into the man's face.

'Fuck off. Let me go.'

Darren was flagging. He certainly had size on his side, but this bloke must be on something to fight this hard and long.

'Pack it in,' panted Darren.

Suddenly the flash of a needle speared towards his neck. Darren grabbed the man's wrist, and wrenched the syringe away, dodging his head to one side.

The man battled beneath him with renewed vigour, thrusting the filthy sharp towards any exposed flesh.

It was like taming a thrashing cobra, the needle its poisonous fang.

With his free hand, Darren aimed a punch to the man's face. But he dodged it and Darren's fist crunched on the floor tiles. The shooting pain jarred through him, and his grip on the needle hand relaxed just enough to allow the man to punch the spike into his right arm.

Darren threw himself off his squirming opponent, who took his chance, jumped up and jabbed the syringe threateningly towards the prostrate Darren.

'Fucking stay where you are. Don't move,' he shouted as he sprinted out of the open door and down the passageway.

Darren stared in horror at the reddening puncture on his right forearm.

Snapping back to the moment, he snatched his phone from his pocket and punched in 999, running to the road as he did so.

'Shit, shit, shit,' he cursed as he bent over the garden wall, finally catching his breath. He looked left and right. No sign.

A white van pulled up as Darren straightened, still wheezing.

He felt a gentle but strong pair of hands support him, then a soothing voice. 'Is everything OK, sir?'

'That way . . . think he went that way . . . needle . . . stabbed me,' Darren wheezed.

'OK, sir, my colleague will go to find him. I'll stay here with you.'

'Careful . . . madman,' Darren spluttered as his eyes focused on the black body armour in front of him. 'Police?' he asked, more in confusion than curiosity.

'Not exactly, sir. We're from Civil Security. We work with the police now.'

'Who called you?' Darren asked.

'We just happened to be in the area. Refreshing, eh?'

31

10.45 a.m., Monday 23rd July

'Well if you didn't call them, who did?' asked Jo as she and Darren waited in the lounge for what she termed the 'real police' to arrive.

'I'm telling you, they just turned up while I was ringing 999. I didn't get through to your lot, although based on how long it's taking them to get here, maybe I should have sent them a letter instead,' he said, rubbing the puncture wound on his arm.

Darren had re-called 999 as soon as the CSG had stood down, then he'd called Jo. He had no idea where the mysterious duo had come from, how they knew he was being attacked and – come to think of it – why they had scarpered so quickly.

Jo had dropped everything and come straight away. 'You need to get to hospital. Get that checked,' she said for the umpteenth time.

'I can't be in two places at once. You said I have to wait to see the officers when they arrive.' He exaggerated looking at his watch.

'They're busy. They'll be here as soon as they can.'

'Not as soon as the other lot,' Darren muttered.

Jo didn't reply; instead she took a long draw from her water bottle and studied her phone. Darren tried to catch her eye across the table, but he'd seen her like this before. It was pointless.

'Why us? Why now?' she suddenly blurted.

'Eh?'

'How long were you gone? Half an hour?'

'Tops.'

'How many houses along here are empty all day?'

'Most of them. Certainly from nine o'clock.'

'So why did this scrote choose our place? It's a bit of a gamble if he's watching. Sees you go out with the boys, all rucksacks and mischief, obviously off to school or playgroup. What's the chances of you coming back after you dropped them off?'

'Better than evens, I'd say.'

'Precisely, especially compared to those houses with no cars on the drive, all locked up safe and sound until the 19.12 from London Victoria arrives at Hove Station.'

'I'm not with you.'

'It's a bit of a coincidence, isn't it. The one house with comings and goings happens to belong to the chief superintendent. The same chief superintendent who has declared war on the vigilantes. Every other house in the road gets ignored and he picks on ours in the half hour you're out. And steals nothing.'

'So far as we know.'

'Granted, but instead of running the second you crunch on the drive, he waits and plays rough and tumble with you. Then, out of the blue, these two knights in shining armour, who just happen to be cruising the area, rock up and save the day.'

'And?'

'Can't you see? It's a set-up. A message. Call it what you like, but they attacked you to get at me.'

'They?'

'Yes, they. The bloke you tussled with was just cannon fodder. This is a warning to show they can get to me in my own home.'

'You weren't here.'

'You know what I mean.'

'But, whatever your theory, the two chaps who turned up were from CSG. They're the outfit Phil has just awarded a million-pound contract. Surely they're legit.'

'ABC. The detectives' creed – Assume nothing, Believe no one, Check everything,' said Jo.

'They can't be?' The penny dropped for Darren.

'Why not? A vigilante mob with a squeaky-clean public façade? It wouldn't be the first time a household name has hidden organised crime.'

'But surely Phil would have carried out due diligence?'

'Phil's a good guy, but he's been through a lot. You saw him on the telly last night. He was all over the place. He's notoriously impulsive at the best of times, so may have trusted others too much. We used to play his impetuosity to our advantage and he didn't have a clue.'

'So CSG might have worked the same tactic.'

'It makes sense. He's in a job he's not suited to, after two massive and sudden bereavements. He's in an impossible position with rising crime, no money and a public baying for him to deliver on his promises. Enter CSG. They jangle a shiny new solution at him and he takes the bait.'

'Is that even allowed?'

Jo shrugged, just as the yellow-and-blue liveried police car glided to a halt outside. She sprung up and cut the PC off before he rang the bell. Darren could hear some mutterings between the two before the six-foot-two strapping officer walked demurely into the lounge.

'Mr Howe. The boss has told me what happened and that she needs to get you to the hospital.'

'The boss?' chuckled Darren. 'Yours and mine, mate. Scary, isn't she? You don't have to answer that.'

The PC stifled a grin. 'I'll just take some basic details and then you can go and get that checked out. I'll try to get Scenes of Crime here later today, or maybe tomorrow, so if you can avoid using the kitchen until then I'd be grateful.'

'He's not used it in eight years so he's not likely to start now,' said Jo. Another stifled grin.

'I'll brief Superintendent Hedges on this. There's something about it I'd like him to look at.'

'Superintendent Hedges?' replied the PC.

'Yes. Take the details, do the house to house, see if SOCO will come, then hand it all over. Clear?'

'Yes ma'am.'

*

Chris had fallen for it beautifully. Bob's three days of sulking, constant moaning about being 'scrapheaped' and being deliberately tetchy around the house flicked a switch and his boyfriend lost it and blurted, 'I can't stand this, man. I'll talk to Doug and see if we can take you on. If not, one of us will end up killing the other.'

Bob had feigned his objections, just long enough to appear none too keen, but eventually Chris made the call. Doug knew all about Bob and, as predicted, was not averse to hiring a disgruntled cop. Especially one who came with a reference from Crush – even if he did have a slightly higher profile than the norm.

Bob knew Doug had jumped at Chris's suggestion, but Doug still went through the charade of ranting at him with phrases like 'We don't normally hire killers', 'You need us more than we need you', and 'We click our fingers, you jump'. Bob sucked it up. Once he had laid down his version of the law, Doug mellowed and explained a little of what Bob would be expected to do.

The million-pound grant from the PCC had opened up huge opportunities, according to Doug. Who better to land-grab the police's business than an ex senior cop?

Jo had briefed Bob to come across sullen, let down and stitched up by the very people he'd served for nearly thirty years. Any hint of a lingering allegiance might blow his cover, the consequences of which just didn't bear thinking about.

That took no acting on Bob's part – but despite all he'd been through, his heart was still on their side, and he'd do all he could to uncover the depths of criminality running through the CSG and just who was calling the shots.

Finally, he was now out being shown the ropes by Chris – or Crush, as he insisted on being called at work.

'How was Doug?' asked Crush as he drove up Wilson Avenue, Whitehawk to his left, Woodingdean to his right.

'He's quite the piece of work,' Bob replied, gazing out of the window at the estates that he once had completely sewn up.

'His bite's worse than his bark,' said Crush, not taking his eyes off the road.

'Don't you mean . . .'

'No.'

'Hey, thanks for getting me out of the office. Who is this guy we're after?'

'He's doing some work for us. Specialist stuff. Just leave the talking to me and don't ask any questions. Then we've got a little job for you.'

'What am I, your lackey now?'

'No, it's just there are certain things that are very much need to know.'

Crush cruised to a stop, joining the line of traffic at the foot of Bear Road. For the first time, he looked across at Bob.

'This is a complex business. I didn't have to work too hard to get you in, though. They know about us and they know you're an ex-cop in need of a fresh start. Soon they'll want you to milk your old contacts, but for now they'll be watching you to see if you can be trusted.'

'They?' asked Bob.

'Doug and someone he calls "the Boss". I haven't got a scooby who that is, but that's who the orders come from.' The lights turned green and he skirted the gyratory system and headed north towards Moulsecoomb.

Bob grunted a grudging acceptance, and mulled over how he would ingratiate himself in the hierarchy without making it look deliberate.

As Crush approached Wild Park, he indicated left and crawled up the narrow road leading to the pavilion and the memorial to two girls murdered there in the mid-1980s. Bob scanned for a glimpse of the man he was to meet.

Crush stamped on the brakes and opened his window to reveal a scrawny, familiar-looking figure pacing down the hill.

'Get in,' roared Crush. Bob was taken aback at his anger. He'd never seen that side of him.

Dutifully, the boy jumped in the back. Bob, grateful for his instructions, sat silently, determined not to show his face, while desperately trying to place their new, reluctant passenger.

'Who the fuck's this, Mr Crush?' came the squeaky demand from behind.

'Never you mind. He works with us. Now, how did it go this morning?' Crush asked, as he pulled away and headed towards Lewes.

'Sweet. You'd think a copper with her money would have better locks. Shit, he could fight though. I thought he'd do me, but the twat punched their posh floor tiles so I managed to spike him. Did a runner right past the white van, just like you asked. Sweet.'

'Well done.'

'What was it all about, anyway? I thought I was just out here to find who shanked the other copper's boy.'

Bob looked down, hiding his horror and confusion from Crush. It came to him in a flash. Oli Willis. Why the hell was he working for the CSG? Or was he just working for Chris?

'We've had a few unexpected challenges. We just need you for a few extra jobs. You don't need to know more than that.'

'But you told me to keep my head down. Then you send me to torch that pub and spook the copper's husband. Not exactly incognito, is it?'

'Shut the fuck up. Tell me how you are getting on with the main job.'

'It's slow, Mr Crush. No one knows shit. No wonder the pigs can't crack it.'

'It didn't help you telling them it was Marco.'

Bob gulped at his name.

'That was the word, honest. I thought it was him. Still, the pigs sorted him out good and proper.'

Bob tensed. Chris glared at him.

'Look harder and stay in touch. There might be more errands like today.'

'Whatever,' squeaked Oli, slumping back in the seat as Crush did a 360-degree turn at the Kingston Roundabout, heading back to Brighton. 'Just don't take me back to that—'

'Shut it!' bellowed Crush, causing Bob to flinch. Crush continued, mellower. 'I want you to have some news for me by the end of the week. You're going to have to put yourself out there more.'

Crush took the left-hand lane for Falmer Station, in the shadow of the Amex Stadium. He lurched the car to a stop.

'Out.'

Oli obeyed and as he walked towards the ticket office, Bob turned his head away, sensing the little toerag might try to steal a look.

'What the fuck was all that about?' Bob asked, as they re-joined the Lewes Road, heading into Brighton.

'I said no questions.'

'No. You don't get to do that. From what I gleaned we had an arson, a burglary of a police officer's house and that little shit hunting for Harry Cooke's killer. What the hell is going on? What kind of set-up do you – we – work for?'

Chris was silent for a moment. Then as he pulled up at Coldean Lane traffic lights, he fixed Bob with a glare.

'I said, no fucking questions. Is that clear? Right, now we are off to see what you're made of,' said Crush.

'Eh?' replied Bob.

'A little test. Make sure you have what it takes to work with us. Nothing too tricky. You just need to remind a club owner, every time he looks in the mirror, to pay his debts on time.'

32

6.00 p.m., Monday 23rd July

Phil strolled towards the door, intent on asserting his authority.

He had deliberately summonsed Helen to see him; here and now – on his turf.

'Thanks for coming. Coffee? Tea?'

'Don't give me that. And don't you ever snap your fingers and expect me to jump again,' she said, as she stepped in his office.

'Yet here you are,' he said, mimicking Doug's retort on the hill.

She had already taken a seat on the visitors' side of the desk as he walked round to settle himself in his huge black-leather ergonomic chair.

'What the hell do you want?' she said.

'That press release. What the hell is that all about?'

'Just a little reminder of how easy it would be if you step out of line.'

'Then there's upping your fee by fifty per cent for the square root of bugger all. The *Newsnight* stunt. Then your thugs beating up surveillance officers, burgling Jo Howe's house, stabbing her husband and killing a pub landlord.'

'How bloody dare you. It might appear to the public that I answer to you, but never forget I hold all the cards. I put you here and I can just as easily put you in prison. And make sure you keep a close eye on Kyle. You wouldn't want anything to happen to him, now would you?'

'Don't you fucking dare. I've lost my son, my wife, my job – and although Kyle wants nothing to do with me, I'd do a ten stretch to protect him, which is why I'm in this mess.'

'Good. Just keep doing what you're doing then,' said Helen. 'We'll find the killer and you pay the money.'

'If you spent more time doing what I'm paying you for, and not torching pubs or burgling houses, maybe you'd have your money by now and I'd have the closest to justice I'm likely to see.'

'Joanne is sticking her nose in and needs warning off. I've told her to butt out but she seems intent on disobeying me.'

Phil made to interrupt but Helen raised a finger.

'I'm going to get crime under control. Why shouldn't Douglas and I build up our pension pot while we do it? Conventional policing is finished and that namby-pamby crime reduction and community reassurance shite is just window dressing. I'm going to build the same reputation as Bratton and Giuliani had in New York but without the handouts, except to me. People will remember me for halting crime in the face of austerity. That is my goal and you are now part of achieving it.'

'Sermon over?' asked Phil.

'By fair means or foul.'

'So, does "foul" include beating up detectives and stabbing the husband of one of your divisional commanders?'

'She needs to learn to back off when she's told. To fall in line and take the glory when it comes.'

'Fuck, Helen, you're sounding like a certain ex US president. You can't just run amok to serve your own career. There must be other ways.'

'Have you ever tried to be a woman making a name for yourself in this organisation? Of course not! Like you saw Joanne as a piece of meat, that's how you all see us. So, don't lecture me about what I can and can't do. I've managed to shaft one PCC and I'll do the same to you. I'm going to succeed and you're going to help me. If Joanne suffers collateral damage to make this a success, then so be it. You can flex your muscles all you like, but you're here to do what I say.'

'But what about Harry's killer? Surely you're not heartless enough to forget that's why I'm here in the first place. I need him found. Whatever it takes.'

'We'll find him, Philip. You have my word.'

*

Gary Hedges was bemused. If he'd worked with Jo for longer, he'd know that if there were two ways of doing something, she'd find a third.

'Do you know how these things work?' Jo pleaded as she punched random keys on the 'star conference phone' in the middle of the matt white Ikea table.

Renting a tiny office for an hour at the Nexus Business Centre, nestled behind the Goldstone Retail Park, was the only way Jo could keep what they were doing under wraps. However, doing so at 8 p.m. resulted in there being no tech support around. And Gary was no help.

The lights were dimmed and the blinds down, but if someone was really looking they would assume a negligent cleaner had forgotten to close up properly. They'd never guess, from this shell of an office, that an undercover operative's debriefing was about to get under way. Jo had kept all of this strictly between her and Gary.

She had told Bob to call between 8 and 8.30 p.m., but only if it was safe. If they had not heard from him by 9 p.m., Gary was to immediately trigger the extraction plan – assuming they could work out where he was.

Following a sequence Jo would have no chance of repeating, the black space-age conference phone finally lit up – just in time, as it immediately purred and its red lights blinked.

'Ripley Logistics, how can I help you?' Jo answered. You could never legislate against wrong numbers.

'It's me,' came Bob's familiar, but shaky, voice.

She and Gary nodded to each other, and hunched around the loudspeaker. Gary notched the volume down.

'How's things?' Jo asked. Time was short but if Bob was in the shit, his welfare would trump everything.

'It's worse than we thought,' muttered Bob.

'How?' asked Gary.

'Nothing I can't handle.' Bob sounded shell-shocked. 'The main man, Doug, will take some handling. I'm not sure he even trusts himself.'

'Is that a problem?' Gary asked.

'No. I'm just glad he showed his colours so soon. I'll have to be extra careful.'

'OK, what you got for us?' Jo asked.

'I take it you've told Gary about me?'

'Yes, he needed to know.'

'That's fine. I'd love to have seen his face.'

Jo chuckled as she turned to the indignant superintendent, his upturned hands protesting the unfair notion that he was not of the modern age.

'Well,' Bob continued, 'I've seen my other half's vicious streak.'

'Go on,' Jo prompted.

He told them about the short but informative drive with Oli that afternoon, and Chris's outburst when Bob tried to get him to fill in the gaps.

'Hang on a minute,' said Jo, 'so this is the same Oli Willis that Phil and I caught robbing the café? He broke into my house and attacked Darren?'

'Keep your voice down,' urged a nervy Gary.

'Yes, and what's more, he torched the Ragged Smuggler.'

Jo and Gary looked at each other, incredulous.

'So CSG and the vigilantes are one and the same, as we thought?' Jo asked.

'Most definitely, and our old boss has just given them a million quid.'

'Bob,' said Gary, 'how does Oli fit into this? I mean, we know he's a gang member and a bit of a scrote, but this is way out of his league.'

'I'm trying to work that out, but I think they got on to him after he was released for the robbery. Seems they were after Marco for drug dealing and word got out that he'd fingered him for Harry's murder. They thought he could point them in Marco's direction, so they grabbed him and—'

'Grabbed him?' said Gary.

'Yes, as we thought, they are snatching scum off the street to either get information or to just stop them doing whatever they are doing.'

'And doing what with them?'

'I'm working on that, but it seems Oli was kept somewhere. Now he's been let out, but on a very tight leash.'

'What, to burgle my house and set fire to a pub? Seems a bit of a risk.'

'No, there's more. From what I can make out, his main job is to find out who killed Harry.'

Jo was aghast.

'What the hell are they doing that for?'

'I have no idea yet. As I say, I have to play it softly-softly around this Robinson fella, and Chris just goes off on one when I ask any questions he doesn't like, so you'll need to give me a few more days.'

'But I don't understand,' said Gary. 'Vigilantism I get, but why would they be looking for a killer they know we are pouring time and money into catching?'

'Give him time,' urged Jo. 'There's more to this than we first thought and, believe me, if anyone can find out what that is, it's Bob. Bob, are you happy to carry on? It seems you're on to something but if you are in any danger, just say the word and we'll get you out of there.'

'No, I'll be OK.' He paused for a beat too long. 'Oh and Jo, just one thing.'

'Yes?'

'The needle that Oli jabbed Darren with?'

'Go on,' said Jo, her heart drum-rolling in her chest.

'Clean. That much I did get from Chris. It was a set-up job designed to scare you, but Darren's got nothing to worry about. Not that you can tell him that, of course.'

'Of course,' sighed Jo. At least that was one weight off her shoulders, but her fear was replaced by fury.

*

Hammering on Phil's front door with her bare fists half an hour later was as cathartic as it was galvanising.

It reminded Jo of when, as a young DC, she would delight at jolting some scumbag out of their stinking pit with the 'coppers' knock'. Tonight, she would not be dragging any low-lifes down to the nick, but she sure as hell was not leaving without the truth from the PCC.

A dim light strained through the mottled-glass front door and the approaching shape looked nothing like Phil.

She took a pace back, careful not to stumble on the broken pathway, as the door was jerked open.

'Oh, it's you. What do you want?'

Jo could not decide whether the reddening around Kyle's eyes was from fatigue or tears. She could tell, on the other hand, that the herbal aroma was from no deodorant Darren ever wore. He held the door so she could only see the stairs and the coats hanging on the newel post.

'Sorry to disturb you, Kyle – is your dad in?'

She knew the answer to that one. He'd never tolerate weed being smoked under his roof.

'No,' he replied. 'Why?'

'I need a word with him.'

'About Harry?' he asked. Jo saw something pass across his face.

'No, no news there. But I do need to talk to him.'

'Well, he's not here,' Kyle snapped, before slamming the door on any intention Jo may have had to continue the conversation.

Shocked, she returned to her parked car and mulled over what Bob had said.

How could all this justice be meted out right under everyone's noses, without anyone noticing? Worse – how could so many blind eyes be turned? People were being snatched, hospitalised, Christ even killed, and no one gave a damn. Why? This was more than pissed-off communities cracking a few skulls to protect their house prices. These were snatch squads.

Now it was getting close to home. Was she being warned off? From what? Who was feeding them information? And what was all this about finding Harry's killer? That was her job, for God's sake.

Just then a beam of headlights lit up the road, before being snuffed out as the BMW they belonged to drew up in front.

She got out of the car as Phil did the same.

'Jo, what are you doing here?' He sounded edgy.

'I need to talk.'

'You'd better come in,' Phil said as he glanced around.

'I tried that but Kyle had other ideas. Oh, and you might want to open a window or two.'

'Little shit,' Phil muttered as he marched towards his front gate. 'Quickly.'

Dutifully, she followed, wondering if she was going to be dragging someone off in cuffs after all.

He opened the front door and bellowed, 'Kyle! Get down here.'

No sign of movement, and Jo could see Phil was about to lose it.

'Leave it for a minute. I just need a quick chat, then I'll go and you can have it out with him.'

Phil grunted and skulked into the lounge. They sat opposite each other. No offer of a drink, which suited Jo.

'I'll get to the point. This mob you've just given a million quid to. Who are they?'

'Is that it? You've come round to my house at nearly ten o'clock in the evening just to talk through my commissioning decisions? Can't this wait?'

'I'm worried,' she continued. 'You know about the vigilantes who've been running riot across the city?'

'Running riot is a bit strong.'

'Christ, you really have swallowed the pill. I'm talking about people being maimed and murdered in the name of community security.'

'You can't go round smearing a legitimate community interest company as a gang of thugs.'

'Can't I? How much of a coincidence was it that one of those CSG vans just happened to be cruising by my house when Darren was attacked this morning?'

Phil stood up, his face flushed. He glared back at Jo, fury in his eyes.

'You should be grateful they were there. It doesn't bear thinking about what would have happened to Darren otherwise. How dare you imply they were involved.'

'I wasn't implying anything, but you have to admit it's a bit odd. I just wondered how much you knew before you bankrolled them. Other than the briefest of details at Company House, no one I know has ever heard of them. How sure are you that they are on the level?'

'I think it's time you left, Jo, before we fall out. If you concentrated on your own job, then I wouldn't have to find other ways to catch criminals.'

'Just remember who did my job before me. There is something distinctly odd about CSG and I am determined to find out what.'

'I thought you'd been told not to.'

'And that doesn't sit right either.'

'Please, just take the help you're being offered.'

Jo stood. She'd said her piece and the longer this continued, the worse it would get for both of them.

'Just be very careful,' she said as she headed for the front door, Phil on her heel.

'Just remember who I am. Get on and do what you're paid to do, and don't forget you still haven't caught Harry's killer yet either.'

'I thought they had that covered as well,' she murmured as she pulled on the front door, regretting it the moment it came out of her mouth.

'What did you say?' yelled Phil as he leant across her and shoved the door closed.

Jo felt trapped. She looked up at Phil towering above her, his face and neck taut.

'Nothing,' she countered. 'I just meant they seem to have everything sewn up.' Christ, that was lame. How could she recover this?

'Bollocks,' he hissed, grabbing her wrist. 'What did you mean about having Harry covered?'

'Phil, you're hurting me.'

She froze, hoping that Phil would come to his senses if she didn't fight back.

The tableau was broken when a door upstairs clicked shut.

Kyle. What had he heard?

Phil spun round, and Jo seized the moment and pulled the door again, just enough to squeeze through.

She darted down the unlit path, nearly tripping on a plant pot that had fallen by the gate.

'Jo,' bellowed Phil, as she clicked her car locks, wrenched the door open and flopped, momentarily relieved, into the driver's seat.

She was sure he wouldn't come running after her, but she wasn't taking any chances. She fired up the engine and spun away, going where she should have gone the moment she left the business centre – home.

Jo knew she had just made things a whole lot worse for herself, but her biggest fear was for Bob. If Phil got a hint of what she meant about Harry, her ex-DI would wish he was back behind bars.

Somehow she needed to get Phil off the scent, but with the mood she had left him in, that was going to take a miracle.

33

Oli could not have felt more out of place.

Distasteful as they were, the two previous assignments had been much more up his street than this, the main event. Sure, the old fella being frazzled was a bit of a shock at the time, but despite the camera, no one seemed to have come after him, so happy days.

Breaking into that bitch copper's house and sticking her old man must have put him on the radar though – if they could ID him.

But this? Skulking round the prawn-sandwich suburbs of Brighton looking for a killer – well, this was a first.

He literally had no idea what he was doing, but faced with the threat of a trip on that lorry, he had to agree and pretend that he had all the right contacts.

He started at the scene. That's what they did on the telly, right? It was no secret that the piglet had been shanked in the woods after strutting across Withdean Park. And that's where he was now, but why?

His torch cast a feeble beam across the undergrowth as he scanned around looking for God knows what. Ribbons of red-and-white police tape still flickered in the light, here and there. Memorials to their failed endeavours.

He wondered what else the cops might have left behind – or even missed.

Abandoning his fruitless recce, he hugged the shadows of the lanes that encircled the park, enviously spying on the well-to-do couples with their 2.4 children. Heads bowed over tablets and laptops, oblivious to each other, not to mention his watching eye just a dozen yards away.

They'd never have noticed a killer fleeing across their neatly trimmed lawns. Hell, they probably wouldn't have batted an eyelid if he had run right through their bloody lounges.

He would have liked to have done this in daylight – seen it as it was when Harry died. But that would have been madness after the last few days.

Reaching the top of Peacock Lane, he decided to call it a night. Now he knew the lie of the land, he could think about his next steps.

The trap house that Crush had made available was by Seven Dials, ironically yards from his ill-fated coffee shop raid. As he emerged on to Braybon Avenue he flagged down a passing cab – safer than dodging Old Bill through the back streets.

'Julian Road, mate,' he said as he slumped into the back seat.

'Sure, bruv. Meter or cash?'

'Cash if you like.'

'Cost you a tenner then.'

'Sweet.'

The Somalian driver's street lingo was impressive, but Oli would have bet he could switch to Oxbridge, depending on who was paying the fare.

'Where ya been den, bruv?'

Shit, why can't he just drive? 'Just milling around. Getting some air, you know.'

'You wanna be careful there, bruv,' the cabbie sniggered. 'Geezer got knifed there a few weeks ago. No safe place in Brighton no more.'

'So I hear,' said Oli, hanging on to the door handle as the driver took both their lives in his hands, darting out in front of a Tesco lorry.

'Nah, straight up. My brother, he was around here the night it happened. No one even noticed.'

'No shit,' Oli muttered.

'Yeah, he nearly wiped some guy running out the woods. Stupid twat. Lucky he's a good driver.' He chuckled again.

'What happened?'

'Nuffink. Gave the guy the bird, then fucked off.'

'Did he tell the filth?'

'What is dis man? Nah, he don't need no police digging around asking for his papers and shit.'

Oli was desperate for leads and, far-fetched as this might be, this cabbie was as close as he'd come.

'But it was when the kid got knifed, yeah?'

'Are you sure you're not Old Bill?'

'Do I look like it?' Oli sniggered. 'Nah, he was a mate of a mate of mine. Well sad.'

The driver hesitated. Then continued, 'Yeah, around that time. He says the kid was pelting it out of the woods. Looked proper scared.'

'D'ya think he'd talk to me? Just him and me. No Old Bill.'

'Why would he?'

'There's a drink in it for him.'

'You kidding me, bruv? We don't drink. Anyway, it'll take more than that.'

Oli thought. Before he'd been snatched, he had options, but now – when he was not supposed to exist – who knows where he'd get cash from, but he had to try.

'Tell him if he'll see me now, there's a pony in it for him.'

The driver pulled over, just outside the Booth Museum on Dyke Road.

As he turned round to glare at Oli, his happy-chappy demeanour had evaporated.

'Listen, you piece of shit. You get in my cab, start asking questions, strike lucky, then you insult me and my brother by dropping £25 to find out more. Shit, you could be a cop, a reporter, anyone. You could even be one of them going round lynching guys. You want to meet Ahmed, you start showing some respect.'

'How much then?'

'Depends what it means to you.'

'Every fucking thing,' Oli mumbled just a fraction too loud.

The cabbie grinned, the gap where his right upper incisor once was betraying a menace that Oli could tell was more than skin deep.

'Monkey.'

'£500? You can piss right off.' Oli pulled on the door handle but it wouldn't budge.

The cabbie tutted. 'It's rude to leave when we're talking. You stay till I say you can go. A monkey for Ahmed and the same for me. Fair?'

Oli's heart started to pound. This was a glimmer of a breakthrough, and so out of the blue. But on the other hand, it could turn out to be nothing at all. A grand down the drain. And this mad taxi driver. *Who's to say he'd take no for an answer anyway?* His mind raced; where could he get a grand from this time of night?

'You're on, but I need to make a call.'

This was going to take some doing.

*

Phil slugged down a tumbler of whisky before punching out Helen Ricks's number. He knew he should wait, but no way would he sleep with all this pent-up tension boiling inside him. He needed to sort this, and who better to go to than the one person whose problem this really was.

'Helen Ricks,' croaked the sleepy voice.

'It's Phil. We've got a problem.'

He heard a cough, then the sound of what he took to be Helen taking a sip of water. She was loading the breach.

'Philip, why are you phoning me at this time?' Placid. Measured. In charge.

'It's Jo, she's on to something. We need to put her back in her box.'

Another pause. She was draining the tension out of his rant.

'Look, if you have something to say then make an appointment, or at least phone me after my second caffeine hit.'

'She's been round here shouting the odds. Accusing me of backing criminal networks and funding vigilantism.'

'What? What did you say to her?'

Now he had her attention.

'What do you take me for? Just get her off my back, and tell her she's imagining it.'

Helen tutted, now fully awake. 'Philip, really. You're a big boy. Do you need me to fight your battles? How will that look, eh?'

He gripped the phone tighter, determined not to rise to her bait.

'I thought you'd told her to lay off, but she's like a dog with a bone. She's not going to let up, whatever you've said.'

'Leave it with me.'

'There's something else,' said Phil, mellower now. 'We got on to the subject of Harry and why she'd not made any progress.'

'And?'

'She said something like "they've got that covered too". I wasn't supposed to hear and she got all defensive when I asked her what she meant.'

'What else did she say?'

'Nothing. She clammed up as soon as she said it, but she must have got it from somewhere. Are you sure your mole on the murder team isn't playing both sides and passing information back to her?'

'Don't be ridiculous. He knows what'll happen if he does.'

'So why say it if she didn't know anything?'

'Trust me, Philip, but stop panicking. I'll sort her. Just get on with the job we agreed and stop wobbling every time someone forgets to bow and scrape.'

'Please do, Helen. This cannot get out.'

'Don't confuse the name on your office door with any notion of being in charge.' She clicked the call to an end.

Phil froze, the handset still wedged to his ear. Then, as if a director had called 'Action', he hurled the whisky glass at the wall, smashing it against his framed wedding photo.

*

Oli wondered if Crush had twigged how much he'd over-egged this eyewitness who would spill all for a grand but, nevertheless, he still handed over the money. The death threats that followed, if he failed to deliver, were coming so frequently now they barely registered.

The cabbie picked him up on the Old Shoreham Road, outside the sixth-form college, where Oli was supposed to attend but rarely did.

He got in the back, as before, but this time he wasn't alone, and the sharp jab in his right ribs reminded him of the stakes.

'You got de Ps?' hissed a voice in his ear.

'Sure,' said Oli, struggling to keep his cool – and urine.

'Show me.'

Oli reached into his left jeans pocket. The knife dug deeper.

'Mate, it's in here. How else can I show you?' As his hand touched his own blade, he decided to keep it where it was for now.

He withdrew the bundle of cash and handed it over, praying he was playing this right. The man next to him did not bother to count it; he just thrust it inside his jacket.

He noticed they were heading out of town, towards Devil's Dyke, Oli reckoned. He'd heard once of a pizza shop owner being kidnapped, robbed, beaten half to death and dumped up there to die. All for a few hundred quid. The bloke had survived but was left with crippling injuries and blind for life. Was that about to happen to him?

They had crossed the bridge over the A27 and were snaking around country lanes when, suddenly, the driver wrenched the wheel to the left and crunched to a halt in an unmade car park.

Oli was now seriously spooked.

'What's going on?' he quaked.

The man in the back hissed again. 'You wanted to talk, so talk.'

'You Ahmed?' said Oli, his head flipping between the driver and the new man.

'Sure.'

'Prove it.'

The knife prodded again and Oli dropped this line of enquiry.

'You the one who saw the boy running the day the copper's son got knifed?'

The man handed the wedge of cash to the driver, who then deftly counted it.

'All here.'

'Yeah, what of it?'

'I know Harry's best mate. I need to know what happened.'

'And you're prepared to pay a grand to find out?' the driver sniggered.

'You don't need to know any more. Tell me or give me the money back.' Oli knew the second option was never going to happen.

Ahmed paused.

'It was nothing. Just some kid ran out of the woods right in front of my cab. He had a scarf over his face. Ran like someone was chasing him or some shit. Didn't see no one else though.'

'So why didn't you tell the Old Bill?'

'You kidding, mate? Last thing I need is anyone digging about. We ain't all got National Insurance numbers, you know.'

'What'd he look like?'

The two men exchanged a glance which Oli took to be unease.

'You've got my money,' Oli reminded them.

Ahmed continued. 'It was so quick, man – he looked kind of scruffy. He had this red-and-black bandana, that's what I noticed. You get me?'

'How old?'

'Not old but not a kid. I dunno, man, I'm not good with white boys' ages.'

'Would you know him if you saw him again?'

'Maybe, but he had his mouth covered.'

'I need you to find him. Keep looking. It's important.'

'Sure, for another monkey,' Ahmed hissed.

'Nah, you've had enough. You don't want the Old Bill snooping around you, now do you? Here's what you do . . .'

Oli spelt it out. He was pushing his luck, but now he had something on this reluctant witness, it might just work.

'I'll do what I can, he's a pin in a haystack.'

Oli chuckled. 'Needle.'

Ahmed rattled off his mobile number, which Oli tapped into his phone. Then he sat back waiting for the driver to start the engine.

He didn't.

'Get out.'

'Eh?' said Oli.

'Get out and walk. We're done here.'

Oli thought for a moment.

'Suit yourself,' he said as he pulled on the door handle. This time it opened.

He stepped out into the damp air, the roar of traffic rolling over the hill from the A27, the sodium lights of Brighton and Hove glowing in the distance. Before he slammed the door, he poked his head back in.

'Start looking now, Ahmed.'

Ahmed grunted.

Like a hatched turtle, Oli headed instinctively for the brighter distance, his mind racing to make sense of the make-or-break gamble he had just taken.

34

8.30 a.m., Tuesday 24th July

Even in their most intimate moments, Doug Robinson would never admit it to Helen, but he was becoming more and more convinced they had bitten off more than they could chew looking for Harry's killer.

The whole idea, which was all Helen's, was to snare Phil Cooke into agreeing to be their plant as PCC, then blackmail him into legitimising their snatch squads. No one actually thought they'd still be looking. If only the police weren't so inept.

And now, as she ranted on all night that 'they had a fucking leak', he was at a loss. Hardly anyone knew about this, the most sensitive of their operations. His suggestion it might be Helen's own contact within the team had been swiftly quashed.

He liked Crush, his sheer brutality contrasting his Geordie charm, but shit travels downhill, so this boulder of manure was coming his way.

'Enter,' he called to the rap on the door. Robinson remained seated behind his pristine desk and glared at his number two as he walked in.

'One of your mob is a grass,' he bellowed, the lack of preamble signalling his wrath.

'Who?' replied a perplexed Crush.

'That's what you're going to find out. Seems the Old Bill, or at least one of them, has got wind of our little commission to find Harry Cooke's killer.'

'But, how . . .'

'Jo Howe told Phil Cooke last night – well, as good as. It could only have come from within, so you need to dig around and bring whoever it is to me, just before they head off on the lorry.'

'I don't know where to start. Half my lot are ex-police, then we've got Oli Willis, out there chasing his shadow. It could be from anywhere.'

'Crush,' said Doug, more gently, as he rose and walked round to where his right-hand man stood. 'You're a good man. You always deliver. Sometimes you over-deliver, but you never let me down.' Doug's arm was now round his subordinate's shoulder. 'The leak can only have come from your team, so do whatever you need to find it. Until you bring me the traitor, everyone, even you, are in the frame. Understood?'

With that he plunged his rigid fingers into Crush's brachial plexus, sinking him to his knees.

*

There were a dozen reasons why Jo might have been summoned to see the chief constable, but she guessed that this time there would be no convivial breakfast.

In fact, Jo could focus on just two possibilities. Either the chief had discovered that she was still hunting down the vigilantes and had Bob working undercover, or Phil Cooke had been on to her about last night's visit.

As she read a text from Gary about the owner of the Pink Flamingo nightclub having twenty stitches to a knife wound in his face, the huge door opened and a suspiciously cheery Helen Ricks stepped out.

'Joanne, thank you so much for coming at such short notice. I do hope it wasn't an inconvenience.'

Like you give a toss.

'No, not at all,' Jo replied, following her boss back into her capacious office.

She took the hint to sit on one of brown leather two-seater sofas, a mosaic tiled table between them.

Helen sat opposite and poured herself a coffee from the steaming cafetière. Jo's hot water was already waiting. *Is there nothing this woman doesn't know?*

'Joanne, what do you know about the Civil Security Group?'

Jo stifled a gasp, pretending she had taken too big a slurp of her drink. So, this was it. She'd been rumbled and this was the buttering up before the fall.

'CSG, ma'am? Aren't they the firm the PCC has awarded this community security contract to?'

'Yes. Well, I'm looking for a project manager to help deliver on Mr Cooke's vision to embed them into our future policing model.'

Jo looked blank.

'Sorry – we need someone to figure out how the hell we are going to work with them. Make more sense?'

'Oh, yes I see,' Jo replied, feeling a little easier.

'And, well I know you are busy with the division and Operation Carbon, but I'd like you to take it on.'

'Me? You've already said I'm barely keeping my head above water. How am I going to have time for this? With respect,' she added, as an afterthought.

'Joanne, we are all busy and, well, as your division is in more need of help than most, I thought you'd jump at the chance.'

'But you know how I feel about vigilantes.'

'These are not vigilantes. This is a legitimate private security company who the PCC has committed us to working alongside. I'm no fan of all this but, as I reminded you recently, we work in a disciplined service and this will do you the world of good.'

'Have I any choice?' asked Jo.

Helen's smile was the only answer she expected. 'I'll send you all the details. Should be interesting. Thanks for agreeing.'

Jo grunted an insincere thank you, stood up and left.

*

As she did so, Helen rifled in her bag for her other phone and tapped out a quick text.

What is it they say about keeping your enemies closer? Joanne won't have time to blink from now on, and she will be right where we need her.

Phil Cooke did not reply.

*

Oli knew it was too soon for Ahmed to come up with the goods, but if he did not keep the pressure on, he knew someone else who would. He punched the contact simply named 'A' in his phone.

'Urgh,' a weary voice croaked.

'Ahmed, it's Oli from last night. What you got for me?' he demanded, checking he could not be heard by the dozing drunks under the Palace Pier.

'I sleep, man,' Ahmed replied. 'I work night, I sleep day. That's how it is.'

'Not good enough, my friend. You weren't asleep that day you nearly wiped out my mate's killer, were you? Get up and get looking. Put the word round like I told you to.'

'Listen, I've been thinking about what you said. You know how many kids do a bunk from taxis every day? I tell the other drivers that's what he's done, and you know what they say? They say "Eh Ahmed, you and me both, bruv. It comes with the job." No one's going to look out for one white boy who bunked a ten-pound fare.'

'Ahmed, we went through this last night. It's not just the fare. He called

264

you a "stinking immigrant", promising a "holy war against you and the rest of you camel-jockey journeymen". Tell that to your mates. Make it against your people, not just you.'

'We get that shit every day. You think that makes your guy special? They blame us every time some brainwashed Muslim blows himself up. They say we send all our cash to ISIS and what they say we do to our sisters . . .'

Oli's knuckles whitened around the phone as his anger frothed. He was running out of time. 'Another half a monkey says you'll give it a shot. Put the word out, think of the worst slur against Islam and tell them he kept repeating it. Tell them where to look. Just find him.'

'Two hundred and fifty pounds. OK, I see what I can do.'

'Funny how it suddenly became so much easier, isn't it, you wanker,' Oli yelled.

Ahmed sniggered, then cut Oli off.

'What you staring at, you repulsive fraggle?' Oli shouted at the vagrant grinning at him from the archway as he strutted up the steps to Madeira Drive – hoping to lose himself, and his rage, in the crowds of day trippers.

*

Jo was still seething from yesterday's work-dump from the chief.

She paced up and down, grateful for Nexus's office allocation policy of 'you get what you're given'. How edgier would she feel if every time she met or spoke with Bob, it was in the same room, with the same neighbours and the same window for the CSG to observe her through?

It would be so simple if she could be more upfront about what she was up to, but the chief had made it pretty clear she was on the new PCC's side when it came to rooting out the vigilantes. But root them out she still would. Every fibre of her instinct told her that she was only seeing the tip of the iceberg and whatever was going on beneath the surface was significantly more pernicious.

Hard work never scared her, and this new lackey role of embedding the

CSG into the mainstream – and accountable – police was not even close to being the straw that would break her, but the quicker she could uncover exactly what atrocities Phil had actually funded, the better. Why had the chief gifted this to her, when it far better suited some doe-eyed direct-entry superintendent instead?

The door closed as quickly as it opened and there stood Bob Heaton, dishevelled, flustered, anger in his eyes.

'I can't just drop everything and come running,' Bob hissed. 'You know what a fine line I'm treading. They are watching me. This better be important.'

'Sit down,' said Jo, taken aback by his testiness. 'I know it's tough but, trust me.'

'You've no idea.'

'The chief is smelling a rat.'

'Go on.'

'After we spoke the other night, I went round to see Phil Cooke . . .'

'You did what?' Bob replied.

'Hear me out,' she replied, resisting the temptation to raise an appeasing hand. 'I went round there just to let off steam. Tell him exactly who, or rather what, he was bankrolling.'

'And?'

'Well, you can imagine how he took that. The problem is, when he touched on Harry's killer and how I should get off my butt and find him, I muttered that I thought they had that covered.'

'You said *what*?' Bob looked angrier than she'd ever seen him.

'I know, I know. I tried to cover it up but I think he heard.'

'So where does our – or should I say your – illustrious leader come into this?'

'Well, yesterday, she called me in, blithered on about the CSG–police partnership, then piled me up with the job of embedding the very firm I'm pitted against into Brighton and Hove's policing.'

'Isn't that what chiefs do? Find a busy man, or woman, to do their bidding. Why is this any different?'

'It just is, but more to the point, we need to up the ante. I need to know where they are taking the people they snatch and, above all, I need to know how and why they are trying to trace Harry's killer.'

'Jo, I'm not being funny, but that's exactly what I have been doing and as far as I can work out, other than you getting tetchy, nothing has changed.'

'Maybe not, but it seems a bit of a coincidence, don't you think?'

Bob stood up, zipped his hoodie and glared at Jo.

'Listen, I'm putting myself on the line for you. Everyone I work with knows what I used to do which, thanks to the number of retired and sacked cops on their books, doesn't make me stand out – but they don't trust me. They don't trust anyone. So, let's agree that I'll crack on, in my own way, and you try to avoid tipping the precarious equilibrium. If we both do that, we might actually come out of this with something more than granite headstones.'

He stormed out, not giving Jo the chance of a comeback.

She ran after him but he was too quick, and the fire escape door at the end of the corridor slammed shut. She sloped back to the office and gathered her bag, watching Bob scurrying across the Goldstone Retail Park loading bays. She sighed and wondered if she had been too hasty. Was she losing her nerve?

She turned for the door, just a moment too soon to spot the black Audi crawling away from behind a Furniture Village lorry.

*

Bob was ticking as he snaked his way towards Hove Railway Station. How dare she call him just because she was losing her nerve? In fairness, she had no idea what he'd had to do – and never would. He could still see the club owner's cheek gape as he pulled the knife across. Was that too high a price to pay for the access he was now granted? Whatever – he was determined to take that horror to his grave.

He preferred travelling on trains. At least you had some hope of clocking who might be trailing you, however furtive they thought they were being. Far easier than if you were on foot or in a car.

As he turned right into Hove Park Villas, his mind went back to the days when, as a young PC, he and his mates battled to keep warring football fans apart as they spilt out of the old Goldstone Ground. The absence of CCTV and camera phones was a godsend all round back then.

'Wanna lift?' He knew that Newcastle accent anywhere.

Chris's smile had not reached his eyes. He beckoned Bob over.

'Yeah, sure. What you doing over this neck of the woods?' Bob asked, battling to keep the quiver from his voice.

'Could ask you the same,' Chris replied. Glaring.

'Oh, you know. I still can't get used to freedom. It's good to get out and just walk sometimes without some screw bellowing at you.'

Chris grunted and Bob took the hint. He walked to the passenger door, climbed in and clipped on his seat belt. As Chris accelerated away the atmosphere remained thick. Bob's mind raced, his heart pounded, and it took everything not to show it.

'Doug's not happy,' muttered Chris, so quietly Bob was not sure it was meant for him.

'Is he ever?'

'Seriously this time. He's baying for blood.'

Bob knew, despite Chris's eyes being fixed to the front, that his radar was picking up every blip of tension.

'Why? What's happened?' replied Bob, deciding to speak as little as possible so as not to leak anything for his lover to latch on to.

'He reckons there is a grass among us. Stuff's getting back to him from where it shouldn't.'

'Oh?'

'Yeah, he thinks it's coming from one of my guys. What do you think of that?'

Bob gulped.

Chris continued. 'You work for someone for years, then all of a sudden they reckon you're bent.'

'Tell me about it. What's been leaked?'

'One of our jobs, that's all.'

'Which one?'

'Does it matter? After all, we wouldn't want the finger of suspicion to fall on you, now would we?' The red traffic light at the Old Shoreham Road allowed Chris a moment to blow a kiss to Bob; a kiss that came with an icy chill.

Bob just stared ahead, battling not to react to the man he was beginning to know in a wholly different way.

*

It had been bugging Ahmed. Something about that bloke he'd nearly run over had been nagging away at him. Had he been carrying something? His clothes? Hmm, was that it? A jumper? A jacket? Yes, that was it, he was wearing a jacket. Khaki, definitely khaki, but what else? What was it? Something on the front – yes – a flash of red. Maybe lettering.

With that image locked in his head, he Googled jackets for hours trying to trigger a memory. He was getting blind to it, but the extra £250 made it worth the effort. They all looked so similar, but nothing ticked all the boxes. He started to doubt himself. It was only a glimpse; how could he be sure?

Then, sitting in his cab at the bottom of West Street, he found it – or as near as damn it. Something called an Upstate Bomber Jacket on the Superdry website. Khaki with a red band, and Superdry splashed in gaudy white lettering across the front. It wouldn't be his choice.

But he had looked scruffy. Why? The jacket itself was quite trendy, so why did he look a mess? Was it because he'd been running? Ahmed studied the image on his phone, scouring his memory. What was it?

Suddenly he was startled by a bang on his window. He spun his head to see a man leering through the glass at him. He pressed the button, sliding the window down a couple of inches. A wall of alcohol fumes made him gag.

'Take me to Portsshlade, mate,' slurred the drunk as he struggled to remain vertical.

'Sorry mate, I'm booked,' lied Ahmed, as he simultaneously stabbed at the window and ignition buttons.

'Fuck you,' came the retort as the man slammed his hand down on the roof. Ahmed crunched into gear as the drunk darted to the front to block his path. Ahmed wrenched the wheel to the right and revved the engine, causing his would-be fare to dart out of the way.

Then he saw it, and the final jigsaw piece fitted.

A tear. The yob through the windscreen had a tear on the sleeve of his blue jacket, white wadding spilling out.

Just as the man in the Superdry jacket had.

That's what made him look like a tramp.

35

12.00 p.m., Saturday 28th July

Once he had an image for them to focus on, Ahmed sent a screenshot, the description and the nonsense story to his WhatsApp group of trusted drivers. He wished he hadn't. Far from the drivers being disinterested, within no time he was inundated with sightings. It seemed half of Brighton owned one of these damned jackets.

After a few hours he decided he could not race round to glimpse every one, so he asked for a photo or at least a fuller description to help triage the calls.

A few merited a closer look. If only the guy he was looking for had a swastika tattooed across his face rather than a bandana. Despite that, he reckoned he could recognise him if he saw him again. One of the more promising sightings was at Preston Park, not far from the murder scene. He prayed to Allah that finally the search would be over.

Ahmed circled the park before meandering up and down the streets off Preston Drove towards Five Ways, straining to glimpse the telltale jacket.

Suddenly, as he crawled along Balfour Road, he spotted someone in khaki walking away from him. His breathing shallowed and his heart pounded. He was used to creeping along these narrow roads, but that was usually looking for some poorly marked basement flat or a numberless house named after some tacky holiday resort.

He just needed to stay cool, cruise past and snap a pic. He had not thought the last bit through, but he'd find a way.

The figure came in and out of view as it sauntered past the row of parked cars. Ahmed was becoming more certain this was it. He was only ten yards behind and a road's width away when a bloody cyclist darted out from between two parked four-by-fours and nearly ended up splayed on his bonnet. It took every fibre of his self-control not to blast the clown off the road.

Then, just as he edged alongside the figure, a truck passed between them, totally obscuring his view.

Ahmed put his foot down, aiming for Loder Road where he would spin round and drive back, this time on the same side as his oblivious quarry.

He was lucky. There were no hazard-light-flashing vans narrowing the junction so, U-turn complete, he headed back along Balfour Road.

'You're joking, man.'

He rechecked his original WhatsApp message. Yes, he had definitely said *guy* – as in male. This 'dead cert' was the right age, right build, right hairstyle, wearing the right jacket – just the wrong bloody gender. The rip? A tissue hanging out of a pocket could indeed look like a tear to someone who struggled to tell male from female, he supposed.

*

A tedious stream of hops to and from the railway station filled the next couple of hours.

After he'd dropped off a fare at Sussex University, a WhatsApp message chirped.

Another so-called sighting. Not from the earlier joker, so at least that was something. Given he was nearby, he thought he'd take a look, so headed to the gyratory petrol station where the sighting was buying coffee.

Ahmed cruised south on the A27 to the BP garage he knew so well. He backed into the last remaining bay, seeing the familiar cabbie hotfooting it towards him.

Ahmed opened his window.

'Is he still here?' he asked.

'Sure, man. He's queuing,' the other driver said, verging on hysteria.

'Calm it, bruv,' insisted Ahmed.

'Are we gonna lynch him, man? Is we going to teach the shit infidel a lesson?'

'We're doing nuffin'. Just watching him.'

'Eh? You at least gonna get your fare back, right?'

'Look, I'll take it from here. You must have people waiting.'

'Nah . . .'

'I said I'm OK,' Ahmed replied, with menace.

The other driver shrugged, got in his cab next to Ahmed's and made a show of slamming the door and screeching off, narrowly avoiding a woman with a pram crossing the exit.

Ahmed sat in his car for a moment, contemplating how he should confirm whether or not this was the man he was after. He drew a deep breath and paced across the forecourt.

The driver had been right: he could barely get in the door, as the queue from the one cashier stretched to the back of the shop. It only took a moment, however, for him to spot his mark. Four or five back, the man – thank Allah for that – shuffled, coffee in one hand, phone in the other.

Ahmed needed to get in front to be sure. He had seen so many like him over the last few days, that he wondered if he was becoming inured and would not recognise the person after all, even if he came up and kissed him full on the lips.

He excused himself as he edged around the aisles, pretending to look for some non-existent snack. He narrowly avoided tripping over a buggy as a stressed-out mum battled to strap her two-year-old back in. 'Watch where you're going,' she grumbled as Ahmed muttered a perfunctory, 'Sorry.'

Eventually he was by the counter, opposite where the second cashier should have been. He browsed the lottery cards, ironic given gambling was *haram*. He looked up as a customer thanked the harassed cashier and left.

He was just a yard or two from the man now. All he needed was for him to glance up from his damned phone. Mustn't make eye contact though.

Suddenly, from behind him, a thwack then a piercing child's scream.

'Now bloody sit still, you little shit,' came the rebuke from the mum he'd nearly bumped into.

The whole queue spun round to where the row was coming from. Just for a second, but it was long enough.

For a moment he was rooted to the spot, then he came to his senses and made for the door. Maybe a little too quickly, as the overworked spotty youth on the till eyed him suspiciously. Ahmed brushed it off, knowing there was diddly-squat chance of him being chased.

He got in his car and in a flash was ready with his camera phone, trained on the door. He surprised himself with how sure he was. Everything, even the tear, was exactly as he remembered. Any self-respecting mother would have stitched that for him. He even had the bandana tied loose around his neck.

The door swung open and Ahmed fired off fifteen photos as the lad stepped into the daylight, waited then – shit – jumped into the passenger side of a red Seat Ibiza which drew up from nowhere.

Ahmed sparked his engine.

The Ibiza turned on to the northbound carriageway, cut across the lanes in front of Sainsbury's and turned left up Hollingdean Road. Ahmed bullied his way off the station forecourt and tried to get in sight of the car.

He glimpsed a red roof in the distance and by the time they both reached Ditchling Road there were only two cars between them. The Ibiza turned right onto the main road and headed towards Five Ways. Ahmed pushed his way out too, intent on seeing where the boy was going. He knew, if he was to stand any chance of keeping up, he would have to get through the Five Ways traffic lights on the same phase as his target or lose him for ever.

Both cars waited as the red light held them at the huge interchange. Ahmed only then spotted the L plates on the car between them.

The lights changed and Ahmed revved, ready to jump the red if needed. He watched the Ibiza clear the junction, then his collision protection system screamed at him. He stamped on the brakes as he looked up and saw, to his horror, the learner had stalled. Not only that, but they were making a right hash of restarting. Ahmed had always been patient with learners – his own son was taking lessons, after all – but now he slammed his hand on the horn, simultaneously straining to glimpse where the damned Ibiza had gone.

The learner car's passenger door opened and Godzilla stepped out.

Ahmed gulped as the bodybuilder slowly walked round to his door, watched by a transfixed crowd at the bus stop.

The door flew open and suddenly all he could see to his right was a scarred and chiselled face, snarling. Then a grip choked off his airway.

'You in some kind of fucking hurry, mate?' the monster hissed, spittle and raw onion fumes spraying over Ahmed's face.

'Sorry mate,' he croaked, before the man slammed the door, the car rocking in the aftershock.

As soon as the learner moved off, Ahmed saw the Ibiza had gone.

He pulled over, found Oli's number and dialled.

*

Unlike most undercover officers, who live two completely separate lives, Bob's lines were blurred by design. He now both worked and lived with Chris – or Crush – and he did not like what he was finding out about his lover's alter ego.

That Saturday afternoon, however, was more like the old days. Basking on the terrace of The Brasserie Fish and Grill, drooling over the million-pound yachts moored in Brighton Marina's inner basin, rigging lazily clanking on masts, was eons away from the brutal world he had reluctantly entered.

'We should do this more often,' said Bob, before swilling down the remnants of his sea bass with the last of his Chardonnay.

'We should,' agreed Chris. 'It's just so busy at work at the moment. Doug's obsession with this supposed leak, well it's more than my life's worth to skive off too often.'

'I suppose,' mused Bob, wanting to move off that particular subject as soon as he could. He closed his eyes, the sun warming his face, and wondered if this whole situation could ever end well.

Chris's ringtone jolted him from his reverie. Before Bob could urge him to let it ring out, Chris answered.

'Yes.'

Bob watched Chris's eyes widen and saw him gather his keys as he listened. Bob mouthed 'What?' but Chris blanked him.

'Right. Shut up. Send it over now and meet me in East Brighton Park. Fifteen minutes,' snarled Chris. 'Well get a cab, you twat.'

Their fellow diners glared over, so Bob put his finger to his lips in an effort to make Chris keep his voice down. But he'd morphed into Crush.

He hit the red button, then stared at the screen.

'Stick fifty quid on the table and come with me,' Crush demanded. Bob knew not to make a further scene; he'd have it out with him later. He hurried behind, hoping to catch Crush up before he reached the car.

He reached the multi-storey car park in the nick of time, jumped in the passenger seat and buckled himself in half a second before Crush wheel-span away.

'Where are we going?' he asked, more in hope than in the expectation he would get an answer.

'East Brighton Park.'

'I know that, but why?'

'What have I said about no questions?'

After five minutes of hair-raising driving, Crush ground the Lexus to a halt next to a tatty VW camper just inside the entrance to the park. He said nothing but tapped anxiously on his phone, glaring at an image.

Within five minutes, a blue-and-white Streamline taxi pulled up and Bob recognised Oli as he stepped out of the back door.

Crush flashed his headlights once and Oli ran over, about to get in the front but, seeing Bob, jumped into the back seat.

'Mr Crush, Mr Crush, I've found him. I've found him,' Oli shrilled.

'Fucking calm down, man. Where is he? Who is he?'

'I don't know?' came the sheepish reply.

'Don't know what? Where or who?'

'Either, but . . .'

'Well you've not found him then have you, you little shit?'

'But that's him in the photo. We know who he is now.'

'Right,' said Crush, making a gargantuan effort to calm down. 'Start from the beginning.'

Oli explained it all, then announced how that very afternoon Ahmed had confirmed a sighting and followed the man.

'Then lost him,' Crush seethed.

'Yes,' mumbled Oli.

Crush sat in silence. Bob knew to keep schtum.

'Bob, get a cab home. Oli, you and me are going for a little drive.'

'No, Mr Crush,' cried Oli before Bob could move. 'Don't take me back there. Please.'

Bob was intrigued. Back where? He deliberately fumbled with his seat belt.

'Shut up,' shouted Crush.

Oli was wrenching at the back door but the child locks imprisoned him. 'Don't make me go back to the for—'

'Shut it. Bob, I told you to fuck off.'

'That's the last time you talk to me like that,' Bob growled. He flung the door open, got out and slammed it closed, raging as he watched Crush wheel-spin the Lexus out of the car park. His heart hammered as he saw Oli Willis desperately banging on the window, panic in his eyes, the word 'Help' forming on his lips.

* * *

Jo's Saturday afternoon consisted of her and Darren playing football with the boys in Beech Hurst Park, with plans for an all-you-can-eat pizza dinner later on.

She had stopped to catch her breath, the boys shrieking as they scurried off, when her phone rang.

'Jo, I need to see you,' Bob insisted. 'Usual place?'

'Woah, slow down,' she said, giving Darren the shrug he'd seen all too often. He diverted the kids by kicking the ball way over their heads.

'What's up?'

Bob, panting, filled her in on Chris's phone call and the meeting with Oli. 'I need to see you. I need to know what to do next.'

'OK. OK. I'll meet you there in an hour.'

'An hour? Why so long?'

'Bob, calm down. I'm in Haywards Heath with Darren and the boys. I need to drop them off, then I'll be there. Look, if it helps, I'll see if Gary Hedges can meet you any sooner.'

'Sure, sure. I'm just really worried about that kid.'

'I know. I'll see you in a bit, just keep it together.'

*

Exactly sixty minutes later Jo pulled up outside the business centre – the boys safely at home with Darren and the promise of a lads' night in, consisting of a humongous pizza and all the Coke they could drink. Swiping herself in, she made straight for the office Gary had told her via text was theirs for the evening.

Bob looked as frazzled as he had sounded and Gary was trying his best to calm him down. Two takeaway Costa coffees sat untouched in front of them.

'Sorry I took so long. Right, fill me in.'

Bob repeated chapter and verse on his whole afternoon, dwelling on his fear for Oli Willis.

'OK, we don't know anything has happened to him though, do we?' said Gary.

'No, but you should have seen the look on his face when he realised Chris had locked the doors. He was begging me to help him.'

'And you've no idea where he was being taken?' asked Jo.

'No. I think he tried to tell me, but Chris shut him up,' said Bob.

'What did he say?'

'I'm not sure, something like "don't take me to the fo—", then Chris cut him off.'

Jo and Gary looked at each other blankly.

'I've already put ANPR markers on Chris's car and we are doing his phone, but that's off at the moment,' said Gary.

'OK so that's all we can do for now. Tell me more about the boy Oli says he's found.'

'I never saw the photo but it seems some cabbie nearly ran him over right by the woods around the time Harry was killed. I take it no one's come forward to say that was them?'

'Not at all, and it's not like we've been shy in the media. So, this jacket, did you catch the description?'

'Yes, it's a khaki Superdry bomber jacket. It's got a tear by the left pocket by all accounts.'

'How sure is he?' Jo asked.

'Seemed certain. I just wish I'd seen the photo.'

'OK,' Jo replied. 'Not much more we can do here. Bob, keep in touch. Gary and I will go back to the nick and put all this through the system. You've done well.'

'Cheers,' muttered Bob.

The two serving officers stood and made for the door, their former colleague slouching behind. Gary tapped on his phone while Jo's mind was racing. Something was falling into place but she couldn't figure quite what.

* * *

Bob stood outside and watched them drive away before reaching for his phone to call a cab. As he opened the app, a black Audi pulled up.

'Get in,' a gruff voice demanded through the open driver's window. 'Mr Robinson wants to see you.'

Bob only managed three steps in the opposite direction before the passenger, who'd slipped out of the car, seized him and bundled him in the back.

The driver eased away, melting into the traffic, but in the rear seat Bob knew the game, and probably his life, was over.

36

7.00 p.m., Saturday 28th July

If Bob thought his beating had been brutal, when Oli Willis was dragged in he realised he was the lucky one.

The young lad's face was barely recognisable from the one that had pleaded with him through Crush's car window just four hours earlier. Both his eyes were crimson, swollen slits. Where his nose once was, was just a pulp of flesh and snot and if he had any teeth left, they must have been molars. Bob thanked a god he'd not prayed to since his teens that at least he could still see, breathe and hobble.

Why had he suggested meeting Jo at the same place Chris had picked him up near a few days earlier? That appeared far too much of a coincidence, and his carelessness, and trust in the man he'd called his boyfriend, had been naive to the point of stupidity. And he knew he was about to pay the ultimate price.

The plasticuffs cut into him as he wriggled to sit up on the stone floor. He knew better than to complain. The two thugs guarding him only knew one language and that was brutally expressed in steel-baton strikes.

After a while, Bob had no idea how long, the door creaked open and another unfortunate punchbag was pushed in. In the dark, Bob struggled to be sure, but he looked African and seemed to have got off lighter than he or Oli. It was unlikely that was down to racial respect, but there must be some reason. Bob didn't have the energy to fathom what that might be.

The door remained open just long enough for Crush, who looked panic-stricken, and Doug Robinson to walk in. Crush's avoidance of eye contact was pathetic. Cowardly. The guards pulled all three prisoners into sitting positions, their screams ignored.

'Right, listen to me, you fucking scum,' said Robinson. 'Willis and Heaton, you have seriously let me, the organisation and yourselves down. Willis, while you might have taken us an inch or two forward, you have committed the cardinal sin of blabbing to outsiders.' He scowled at Crush, who'd provided the pay-off. 'Heaton, you are a fucking grass. As a result, neither of you are getting out of here alive. Mr Ahmed, or whatever your fucking name is, I haven't decided what to do with you yet, but don't be making any long-term plans.'

Ahmed groaned an appeal but the crack of the baton across his sagging shoulders replaced his supplication with a scream.

'I'm talking. Now, we have a little problem,' Robinson continued, showing them the image of the man at the petrol station on his phone. 'I'm trusting that the person in this photo might be Harry Cooke's killer. The problem is we need to find him. Any of you know him?'

Bob squinted in the hope of glimpsing the person both sides of the law seemed desperate to trace.

'Sorry Heaton, can't you see properly? Forgive me.' Doug stepped forward as the guard gripped Bob's battered arm. The man in charge thrust the phone closer.

His gasp came out before he could stop it.

'What?' Doug yelled, latching on to Bob's reaction. 'Who is it?'

'No, it's my arm. That knob is killing me,' Bob said, flicking his head to his right, grateful for the excuse to camouflage his shock.

Surely it couldn't be.

* * *

Phil Cooke was getting used to his topsy-turvy relationship with the chief constable. When he'd very reluctantly accepted the fait accompli of standing for police and crime commissioner, it was obvious he would be doing someone's bidding, but he had no idea it would be the person he was supposed to hold to account.

She had been shameless in exploiting him. Snapping her fingers each time she needed him, or keeping him in the dark over matters he should have been privy to.

Nine o'clock on a Saturday night was not a typical time for her to demand his presence, but as she refused to discuss whatever it was on the phone, he had no choice but to jump. Her choice of venue was typically oblique. The Anchor at Barcombe was so far off the beaten track that the simplest way to get there was to row up the River Ouse. He chose the cratered lane instead.

Despite playing havoc with his car's suspension, the main advantage of this place was the complete absence of CCTV and ANPR. Added to that, its garden was idyllic and large enough on a summer evening to render a middle-aged couple on a clandestine assignation invisible.

As he parked next to a classic E-Type Jag, he spotted Helen sitting at the furthest table by the footbridge, his pint of Harvey's already waiting for him. He sauntered over, doing his best to hide both his irritation and curiosity.

'Evening Philip,' Helen chirped, as if demanding his presence at the arse-end of nowhere was the most natural thing in the world.

'Cheers,' he grunted, slurping the froth of his beer. 'I hope this is as important as you seem to think. I do have an office, a diary and around fifty working hours a week you could fit into, you know.'

'What's the matter? You should be used to these surreptitious meet-ups,' replied Helen. 'Anyway, what I have to say can't be overheard by your hangers-on.'

'Go on,' he said.

'It's a good news, bad news situation.' He was about to interrupt but her hand silenced him. 'Well, actually it's fairly good news and terrible news. First the good news. There is a very good chance my boys have found Harry's killer.'

'By "my boys", do you mean your police or your thugs?'

She scowled, then carried on. 'Douglas has a photo of someone who was seen running from the scene just after Harry was killed.'

'You what?' said Phil. 'Seen by whom? When? No one's mentioned anyone running from the scene before.'

'So many questions, none of which I'm in a position to answer, I'm afraid.'

'How does this mysterious person suddenly become Harry's killer?'

'Keep your voice down. Douglas says it's more positive than that but, for very good reasons, I have not asked those questions. Neither will you.'

'Show me the photo then,' Phil demanded, fighting the urge to grab the chief constable by the throat.

'I haven't seen it. And neither will I. I don't need to remind you how important it is for me to keep a sterile corridor between the parts of my life I tell my mother about and the parts that will send me – us – to prison.'

'But what if I recognise him? I take it it's a him.'

'Keep out of it. Douglas has it in hand. We won't get to find out until the contract is complete. If then.'

'You make it sound like we're buying a fucking house,' mumbled Phil.

'Even if I did know, I wouldn't trust you not to go blabbing to Joanne Howe.'

This evil woman turned his stomach.

'So now the terrible news,' she continued. 'Despite me telling her to shelve her obsession with CSG's darker operations, Howe has carried on regardless.'

Phil felt a glow of satisfaction that at least someone was woman enough to stand up to this gangster in cop's clothing.

'That would be bad enough, but she's put an undercover officer into the organisation. My organisation,' she said, indignantly.

'Well, you do encourage innovation in your senior leaders,' Phil mocked.

'Shut up, Philip. Joanne is finished. I will bury her for this. Her UC, however, has more immediate worries, but as he's no longer a police officer, that's not my problem. Douglas's boys don't mess about once they catch a traitor.' She grinned.

'No longer a police . . . Oh my God, not Bob. Tell me it's not Bob Heaton,' Phil yelled, every face in the garden now staring at him.

Helen downed the dregs of her Diet Coke, stood up, winked and hissed, 'Breathe a word of this and you'll be arranging another funeral, and in Bullingdon Prison, before the week's out.'

*

Intelligence from undercover officers usually passed through so many filters that, by the time it surfaced, neither the UC nor their source could be identified. But this was not a normal deployment.

This had no authority, the UC had no backup, and it was against the express orders of the chief constable. The strategy was for Bob to give Jo background information so she could understand exactly what the CSG were up to and who was in charge. That was it. No one had predicted uncovering a rival murder hunt.

Jo and Gary, hot water, a coffee and a laptop between them, were racking their brains.

'I know these bloody jackets are everywhere, but there's something about that description,' said Jo.

'I'm the same,' said Gary as pulled up the Superdry website. 'What the hell is it?'

'You're crap at internet shopping, aren't you?' Jo said as the gallery of sixty-seven items revealed itself on the screen. 'Click "men's".'

He clicked. Forty-nine. He deselected some of the more tawdry styles, which reduced the net to fourteen. About half matched the description Bob had given, but that was third-hand.

'These all look so familiar,' said Gary.

'I'm surprised you know anyone so stylish.'

'Seriously.'

'Just keep thinking. It might be a coincidence but if it is, let's rule it out.'

Jo decided that, now Bob had a focus, she would leave him to beaver away and come back to her when he found something. So far as her own murder enquiry was concerned, she was worried they had dropped the ball.

First, she needed to check that this mysterious witness had not called in or appeared elsewhere in the enquiry. She had called DCI Scott Porter out as soon as she arrived back at her office, and had tasked him with trawling through HOLMES2 to double-check. He was in for a long night.

As Gary stood up from Jo's conference table, stretched and made to leave, her phone rang. She looked at the caller ID, showed it to Gary, shrugged and with a puzzled look tapped 'accept'.

'Evening Phil, everything OK?'

'Jo, thank God you're there,' said Phil. The look on her face made Gary wait in the doorway.

'What's the matter?'

'Where's Bob?'

'Bob? Bob who?' Jo replied, mouthing 'fuck' to Gary.

'Bob Heaton. Where is he?'

'How should I know? He's a free agent since he came out of prison. I have no more idea than you.' Jo battled to prevent the panic rising through her voice. She grabbed a sheet of paper and wrote *PC wants to know where Bob H is*, spun it round for Gary to see and shrugged again.

'Listen, I can't tell you why, but I need you to check he's OK.'

Gary scribbled, *don't say we saw him*. Jo flashed him a look that said, *Do I look stupid?*

'Why wouldn't he be?' she asked.

'I've heard he's in danger, and don't give me that bollocks you haven't seen him either. If anything happens to him, I'll never forgive you.'

'Hang on. Just rewind, you're not making any sense. What's happened?'

'You've had him working in CSG. Don't deny it, but right now all I care about is that he's safe. Send someone round. Go round yourself. Just check he's OK. Please Jo, I beg you.'

She wrote *he knows* on the paper. Gary mouthed 'fuck'.

'Who told you he's in trouble? What's going on, Phil?'

Gary wrote, *shall I get a car to his house?* Jo scribbled *no, could be a trap*.

'I can't say. I've done something really stupid. Just check. Please, he's a mate and after all he's been through. Do this for me,' he pleaded.

'What have you done?' Jo asked, watching Gary tapping away on his phone, probably searching incident logs and missing person reports.

'It'll all come out soon enough, but, please, just find Bob.'

'Where are you?'

'In the car. Outside Lewes. I don't want to say where.'

'Right, go home. I'll see you there in, what, half an hour?'

'Yes, but find him.'

'Don't talk to anyone, don't stop en route. Just go straight home and stay there until I arrive. I'll get someone to check on Bob. I'm sure he's fine, but you owe me an explanation and I want it tonight.'

37

9.30 p.m., Saturday 28th July

Crush was quivering. Not from seeing what had happened to Bob, nor knowing that worse was to come. That was business and, after all, hadn't the slimy ex-cop charmed himself into his bed and the company for ulterior motives anyway?

What really terrified him was that Bob being a grass and Oli going off-piste all came back to him. Doug had already made it clear he was finished. Whether that meant professionally or as a living, breathing mammal, only time would tell. His only option now was damage limitation.

Doug glared at him from across the desk.

'Have you no idea who this is?' he roared, the image now mirrored on the TV screen above them.

'None at all, boss,' Crush whimpered. 'Should I?'

'Well, if you had a molecule of investigative nous, you'd at least know how to make a start. Ever heard of a reverse Google Image search?'

Crush shook his head.

Doug muttered in despair.

A few clicks of the mouse and the screen was filled with thumbnails. Doug scrolled through, astounded how the all-seeing Google could possibly link his source image to such a mishmash of faces.

It was the fourth screen that struck him and Crush silent. Doug expanded the third image from the left and their shock simultaneously exploded.

'Holy shit,' exclaimed Doug. 'What do you reckon?' he asked Crush, showing self-doubt for the first time.

Exhilaration washed Crush's fear away. 'It's got to be, hasn't it? I mean, that's too much of a coincidence.'

Doug ignored him.

'Get a car, that fucking cabbie and meet me out the front. We're going to find this little shit and finally deliver on our promises,' Doug commanded. 'Then I'll deal with you,' he seethed, jabbing his iron-rod finger into Crush's chest.

*

As she took the stairs two at a time, Jo tapped out the familiar *Sorry. Delayed. On my way now* text she normally saved for Darren.

She had tried to leave an hour earlier, but made the mistake of catching the duty inspector's eye. Her plaintive request for Jo to authorise a domestic violence protection notice was not something she could refuse. There was no hierarchy of lives to save and the terrified woman cowering in her kids' bedroom deserved as much safeguarding from her brute of a husband as Bob did from the vigilantes.

Job done, her head was spinning. What danger had she put Bob in? Where the bloody hell had she seen a coat like that before? Why had she deliberately disobeyed the chief constable's orders? God, she could do with some top-cover now.

She got in her car and, firing up the engine, flicked on the blue lights and hit the wailer switch. Saturday night traffic in Brighton city centre competed with the Friday afternoon rush hour, and no way did she have time to amble, 'Driving Miss Daisy' style, through the gridlock.

Accelerating the Mondeo down the hill, she could already see the static taxis, buses and cars blocking her exit onto Old Steine. She swapped to a more urgent siren tone, sparking intense confusion rather than reaction from all around her. The smallest of gaps opened up and she muscled her way through, throwing an insincere salute of thanks.

Once she rounded Victoria Gardens she powered northwards, all thoughts turning to the task awaiting her.

She would have to play it cool with Phil – admit nothing while trying to squeeze whatever she could from him. Shit, he was the one who'd taught her that. How would she bullshit him of all people?

Her first priority had to be Bob, though. She'd only seen him a few hours ago. His information about a possible suspect for Harry's murder was gold dust, if a little – no, very – circumstantial. What had plunged him into jeopardy? What if someone had rumbled his meeting with her? Christ, she'd played right into their hands.

As she jumped the amber light at Preston Circus, she punched the speed dial.

'Gary, anything?'

'No, I had a drive past his house and it's in darkness.'

'You did what? I thought I said . . .'

'Don't worry, I took the surveillance van and literally did one pass-by.'

'OK. Phones? ANPR? Banking?'

'Nothing yet. I'll keep trying whatever I can think of. Can I tell anyone else? Get some help in?'

'No. Not yet. I'm heading to Phil's now. Got caught up with a DVPN.'

'OK. Give me a shout if you need me.'

'Thought any more about— shit, I've just been speed-flashed. Seventy in a thirty. That'll take some explaining. Sorry, have you thought any more about the jacket?'

'Other than Bob, I've thought of little else. Like you, I bloody know it. I just can't think where from.'

'Are you sure? I'm beginning to doubt myself. I mean, neither of us get out very much. How would we both know it?'

'I don't know, but I can picture it – and not from the website. It's driving me mad.'

'I need to call Scott to see if he's turned anything up. He knows we are up to something, so I'm surprised he hasn't asked.'

'I'm not being funny, Jo, but if there was a witness who'd reported a running man don't you think you'd know?'

'Two words, Gary: Peter Sutcliffe,' Jo said as she swung the car up Peacock Lane, now just moments from Phil's house.

'That was in the 1970s and they were overwhelmed with information and old-fashioned paperwork.'

'And a little blinkered. Right, I'm almost there. Crack on and speak soon.'

'Don't worry, he'll be fine.'

'Do you believe that, Gary?'

'Not really.'

'Well don't expect me to, then,' she replied before killing the call.

*

Crush and Doug had been on many stake-outs over the years. None compared to this in urgency and lack of manpower, though. Even on the hurry-up there was normally a couple of hours of planning before they hit the road – yet here they were, just half an hour after putting a name to the face, sat outside the target's address.

Usually there would be at least two backup cars. You could never tell when the prey might run or the front car might lose the target. So being four up in one of their ubiquitous Audis – one of those being a bloody taxi driver – with no contingencies this side of Newhaven, was verging on reckless.

Ahmed was gagged and bound on the back seat, babysat by a meathead called Ivan who did not do conversation. Doug had tucked the car behind a white BMW X5 about twenty yards from the target house. He worked on the theory that the covering car's brighter colour and more opulent appearance would distract any passers-by from the quartet crammed behind the blacked-out windows.

He positioned the mirrors to give him and Crush as close to 360-degree vision as possible. Ahmed's brief was to keep his eyes open and only speak to confirm any likely sightings. Ivan just had to keep the petrified taxi driver in situ and apply pain on demand.

'How long are we planning on keeping obs?' Crush asked.

Doug gave him a long, impatient stare. 'Why? Got somewhere else to be? We'll be here as long as it takes.'

'How can we be sure he's even at home?'

'If he isn't, then he might come home. If he is, then he'll have to leave at some point. Have you got a better plan? Maybe we could just go knock on the door?' Doug replied with more than a touch of sarcasm.

Crush's silence told Doug he got the message.

The house they were interested in had a light burning in an upstairs room and what looked like the hallway too. As far as they could make out, there was no obvious movement; certainly no floating shadows or other lights going on or off, but that meant nothing. These days people left lights on to deter burglars or just through idleness and contempt for the planet.

Despite rebuking Crush for voicing them, Doug harboured the same concerns. He'd not so much as a fag-packet strategy for this operation and he knew he'd been impulsive. In hindsight, he could have allowed himself a few more hours to get the plan and people in place to do this properly. Was he losing it? What was he trying to prove? Or was this just damage limitation? If that scrote Oli Willis had blabbed to random cabbies, who else had he told? The police? He shook his head, eager to flick these negative thoughts away.

The street was dead. It felt more like 3 a.m. than 11.40 p.m. A couple of dog walkers had broken the monotony as they dragged their mutts out for their night-time constitutional. He chuckled when one dutifully picked up his Great Dane's deposit, glanced around, then emptied the bag into his neighbour's rhododendron bush.

A few cars had inched down the road, their drivers weighing up whether their four-by-fours would fit into the Ford Fiesta-sized parking spaces. He hoped to be able to free this one up before too long.

A couple of lads of the right age passed close by, and Ivan spun Ahmed round and grunted. The shake of the head sucked any remaining optimism from the car.

After what seemed like half the night, but was actually just ninety minutes, another set of headlights bathed the street. The three employees instinctively shrugged down as it crept past; only Ahmed remained upright. The driver seemed to be yet another person searching for an elusive parking space.

Suddenly Ahmed became animated, bouncing against Ivan's clutches, excited noises battling to escape his gag. His eyes burnt with urgency.

'Take the tape off,' Doug commanded and with a rip, followed by a yelp, Ahmed sucked in a lungful of sweaty air.

'That's it,' he cried. 'That's the car I followed.'

All eyes fell on the red Seat Ibiza edging along the road.

'How sure are you?'

'One hundred per cent. I know cars. I drive for a living. I'm telling you, that's the one he got in.'

Doug looked at Crush, quite uncharacteristically, for reassurance.

'You'd better be. If you are wrong, we are blown and you are dead.'

'I'm telling you, that's the car.'

On a well-planned job, Doug would now call forward another car to intercept. But they were alone. There was no way Ivan would be allowed out of the car, not least because he was minding Ahmed – but also, Doug knew stealth and discipline didn't feature on his CV. He was more your wrecking-ball type.

With no need to say a word, Doug and Crush simultaneously eased open their doors, the interior light having already been switched firmly off, and stepped out, clicking their doors closed.

The Seat was double-parked about ten yards from the far side of the target house. They could see the silhouettes of two heads locked in a passionate goodnight kiss.

Switching to their tried and tested hand signals, they agreed where each would move to once the passenger – and experience told them it would be the passenger – stepped onto the pavement.

Doug kept his breathing silent but deep enough to fill his lungs, ready for the explosive burst that was seconds away. It would have been better for Ahmed to identify the passenger himself, but the right car in the right street outside the right house made it odds on they'd struck gold. He would confirm it later. Shame the taxi driver seemed to believe he would be free once he had made the ID.

Doug watched Crush dart across the road to make his way, unseen, past the Seat before crossing back to cut off any escape. They had not rehearsed this, but Doug was sure he knew just what to do.

He saw Crush take his position along the pavement just as the passenger door opened. Doug prayed the road would remain deserted for just a little longer.

The figure stood up, crouched back in for one last peck, then waved as the Seat roared away.

Right jacket too.

The man turned, the shock in his face clear as he found himself nose to nose with Doug.

'Excuse me, mate, have you got a light?' asked Doug. A cliché, but it served well as enough of a distraction for Crush to sprint up behind him.

Crush lived up to his nickname as he grabbed the target round his arms and chest, paralysing his lungs. Doug punched down on his shoulder, the target's collapse caught by Crush's grip. He would have splattered his nose, but he wanted Ahmed to make a definite ID.

The target writhed and tried to scream, but Doug clamped his hand over his mouth and hissed, 'Just you fucking dare.' Still the muted whimpers came and, being in a street unaccustomed to excitement, they knew they had to drag him to the car before the curtains started to twitch.

The target's legs pedalled to keep up as they propelled him towards the Audi. Crush was still wrapped around him like a bandage as Doug forced his head down. As they got to the back window, Ivan wrenched Ahmed's head round for a long hard look.

He only took a second. His frantic nods were all they needed. They dragged the man round to the boot, and Doug sprung the latch. Barely giving it enough time to open, Crush deftly bound the man's wrists with plasticuffs. Doug roughed a hood over the man's head, then tied it with twine, and in five seconds the boot was slammed shut, its cargo invisible and all but silent to any passing busybody. Both men jumped back in the car and it sped away.

38

11.45 p.m., Saturday 28th July

An hour and a half later than she had promised, Jo pulled into Phil's road and nosed into the first space she saw. She stepped out of the car and zapped it locked, her hazard lights briefly strobing the otherwise inky avenue. The council's decision to snuff out all the street lights at 11.30 p.m. might have saved them a few pence, but she was sure it was not completely unrelated to the upsurge in crime she was battling to stem.

Even being a seasoned and highly trained cop, she found the short walk to Phil's door eerie. She knew she could handle herself if some misguided mugger chanced his arm; it was just that with everything on her plate at the moment, it would be a battle she could do without.

Phil came quickly to the door, the chimes still echoing in the hallway.

'I'm so sorry I took so long,' she mumbled as he shepherded her in, poking his head out for a quick recce before he closed and deadlocked the front door.

She allowed his brief hug, then followed him as he scurried into the lounge.

He stood, agitated: face crimson, hair ruffled and beads of sweat glistening on his temples.

'Have you found him?'

'Tell me what's happened, Phil,' replied Jo, dodging the direct question.

'How could you put him in such danger?' He got up and paced the room.

'Phil, focus. Don't make this about me. Don't even make it about you, just tell me what's going on,' Jo replied, trying her level best to elicit some sense.

'All I know is that the person I was with earlier took great delight in telling me he's being sorted.'

'Exactly that: sorted?'

'Well no – "he has more immediate worries", I think were the words.'

'More immediate than what?'

'Skip the interrogation, I just need to know he's safe.'

'Gary is on it. Don't worry, I'm sure he's fine. You've got to tell me what's going on. You said it will all come out? What will?' she said.

'I can't tell you, but these people are evil.'

'These people being . . . ?'

'CSG.'

'The same CSG you have just given a million quid to?'

'I had no choice.'

Jo tutted, contemptuous for the man opposite.

'Jo, they kidnap people. Torture them. Kill them. At first it was just the dregs. Drug dealers, wife beaters, paedophiles.'

'And now?'

'Now it's anyone who gets in their way, and that includes you.'

'Me?'

'Well, you wouldn't keep your nose out, would you? Don't think just because you are in the job, you're immune. That's why you need to take this threat against Bob seriously. Get out and find him.'

'We are, but you need to give me more. I need everything, the whole story. Not just what you think I want to hear.'

Jo stood up. She needed to get to the incident room. Check how Scott was getting on with his trawl through HOLMES2. See if Gary had found Bob. But most of all she needed some serious background on the CSG, who was behind it and how she could break them. If they did have Bob, Phil was right; he was in mortal danger.

'I'm going to get back, but stay contactable. I mean it, Phil. I might need to get hold of you at the drop of a hat.'

'I will, I will,' he assured her as they reached the front door.

'How's Kyle, by the way?' Jo asked.

'As ever,' Phil replied. 'In fact, I was expecting him back by now. Treats this place like a bloody hotel.'

'You never know,' Jo replied. 'He might be tucked up in bed already.'

'No,' replied Phil, nodding at the bare newel post at the bottom of the banister. 'It's like a code. No jacket, no Kyle. He's out gallivanting.'

Jo froze. Her head began to spin.

She grabbed at the door, craving air and distance from Phil.

'Steady on,' he said, turning the key and pulling the door open.

'I've got to go,' she muttered as she bolted down the path, her fingers shaking as she searched for Gary Hedges' number.

He answered straight away.

'Gary, whatever you're doing, meet me at the major incident suite. Get there now.'

*

Even for Doug, the drive back to Newhaven had been perilous. Red lights, give-way markings, keep-left bollards, all brushed aside in his hell-bent determination to dump Harry's killer in a dungeon while he figured out what to do next.

Now, he sat in the fort's office, cradling three fingers of Jack Daniel's, waiting for Crush to return from briefing the guards.

The whiskey scorched his throat, but brought a surge of tranquillity through him, his hands steadying for the first time since the snatch. He was a master at hiding his emotions, although when he was alone things bubbled to the surface. Right now he needed to get a grip, and trusty old Jack was the sure-fire way to make that happen.

For once, he did not make Crush wait when he rapped on the door and, for once, he let him speak first.

'Holy shit, Doug, what happens now?'

At the outset, this had all seemed so simple. Well, maybe not working out who the killer was, but certainly their method of disposal. It would have been like all the others. A few days softening up in the cooler, then a short walk to the butchery, into crates and away. They had done it time and again and, other than the mammoth payday that would follow, this was no different.

'I need to talk to Helen.' He dialled the number that always nestled close to the top of his recent calls list. Crush looked startled, clearly having just worked out who the Boss was.

'What is it, love?' Helen Ricks replied, after barely one ring.

'You are going to want to be wide awake for this one,' suggested Doug.

'Go on,' she replied.

'We have Harry Cooke's killer as our guest.'

'You say "our guest" – so is he still wasting God's clean air?'

'I'm afraid so, but he's not going anywhere. I know we agreed to keep you out of the details but it's all got very tricky and, frankly, you need to decide this one.'

'Douglas, what are you on about? Just kill whoever it is and collect the money.'

'I'm not sure you will want me to do that. Not until you know who it is.'

Ricks sighed on the other end of the line and Doug turned from Crush, who seemed intent on deciphering her reaction from Doug's expressions.

'Why do I need to know? We've always agreed on my deniability. That's the key to our survival.'

Your survival, thought Doug.

'You need to know this one and you need to tell me what to do.'

'Meet me at Seaford Head. Twenty minutes. And Douglas?'

'Yes.'

'This better be good. If you're wasting my time, I've chosen a clifftop for a reason.'

* * *

Gary Hedges and Scott Porter were already in the incident room. Scott had been foraging through the HOLMES2 database for any missed witnesses, or even a snippet from the house-to-house forms, or an 'it's probably nothing but . . .' phone call – but so far, there was no mention of a running man.

Gary had no idea why he had been ordered to divert, but the tone of Jo's voice had told him not to argue.

Instinctively, they both stood as she burst in.

'Sit down, for Christ's sake,' she ordered.

'Don't keep us guessing,' braved Gary.

For Scott's sake, she recapped the significance of the khaki jacket with the red flash and lettering, and the fact that both she and Gary somehow recognised it.

'Gary, I need you to think very hard one last time before I lead you. Where have you seen that jacket before?'

'God, Jo, I've still got no idea.'

Scott's head flipped between them like a tennis fan watching a match-point rally.

'We've got no time for guessing games, but don't be biased by what I'm about to say. I've just come from Phil Cooke's and, whilst he was saying nothing about Bob other than worrying like we all are, when I was leaving I asked about Kyle. He said he had expected him home, but knew he wasn't because his jacket wasn't hanging on the banister.'

'And?' Scott asked, but Jo could see Gary's cogs whirring. She tapped into the nearest computer, bringing up the Superdry website she and Gary had pored over earlier. She selected an image, maximised it and spun the laptop round.

'Kyle's jacket. That's why I recognised it. When I went to the hospital, after Ruth was rushed in, Kyle was wearing this very jacket.'

'But . . .'

'Let me finish, Scott. I spotted the tear and had to stop myself mentioning it, in case Ruth thought I was maligning her for not fixing it.'

Gary was deep in thought. It seemed the fog was starting to clear.

'Yes!' he exclaimed. 'The day it happened. I went round to help Phil tell Ruth and Kyle and I saw the jacket. It looked new, so the tear stood out. All this white stuff hanging out. I remember thinking how angry I would be if one of mine treated his clothes like that.'

'But that's not evidence, ma'am,' Scott replied, turning to Jo.

'It's a bloody start. How closely have we looked at him? How closely have we looked at Phil, for that matter?'

'Close enough,' said Scott. Edgy. Defensive.

'Are you sure? Look. We know that CSG think they've identified the killer. We know the description they worked on. We know that Kyle Cooke has a jacket just like the one their witness has seen. We know that Kyle, and his jacket, should have been home by now but aren't.'

'How do we know all that? Anyway, what's suspicious about a young lad being late home, ma'am?'

'Jesus, Scott, prove me wrong then. I want his GPS and cell site phone data – the whole nine yards – where it is now, where it was when his brother was killed, where it's been in the meantime. Re-run all the data we've got on CSG. Everything. Let's find out where they have been over the last twenty-four hours. I want Kyle Cooke and Bob Heaton found – alive.'

Scott shuffled off.

'What do you want me to do?' Gary asked.

'Start planning the mother of all firearms raids.'

'For where?'

'We'll know soon enough,' replied Jo.

39

12.35 a.m., Sunday 29th July

Doug paced the cliff edge, tracing the lights of a fishing trawler chugging out to sea from Newhaven harbour.

The breeze was chilly, or was that the effect of Helen's threat? Weren't they partners – in every way? They'd started the CSG together. It was their retirement plan. Was she cutting him loose? Had she been playing him all along? He stepped back from the drop.

Headlights swept the grassy wasteland that separated the coast road from the precipice he was standing on. In case it was a passing police car or coastguard, Doug ambled along ready to feed them the old 'insomniac getting some air' line.

'Douglas, over here,' the distinctive voice commanded.

He did not like how close to the edge she had parked, given her threat, and he wondered whether she had free access to tasers whenever she felt it necessary.

She was in her snug green Nike sweatshirt and tight blue jeans. An unbidden lust swelled inside him. She always looked better casually dressed than in her signature blue business suit or, God forbid, uniform.

'Let's hear it,' she said once he was within earshot.

'Calm down, darling. Do you want the full story or just the highlights?'

'Don't "darling" me. I've just had an update but I need more.'

'Eh? Who from?'

'Speak.'

Doug spluttered.

'OK – as well as Bob Heaton, we've got the killer, Oli Willis and the bloke who saw the killer running off.'

'And you're sure this is the person responsible?'

'Positive, but I thought you didn't want all the details.'

Helen glared at him.

'It's Kyle Cooke,' said Doug.

'Tell me everything,' she said, her eyes burning into him.

'Sure?'

'Everything!' she bellowed.

He took her through, step by step, from the moment he'd received the call that afternoon to the point where he and Crush snatched Kyle. He assured her that by dawn the lad would have admitted everything, just before the lorry arrived.

'How long until the police work it out?'

Doug shrugged.

Helen paced a few yards away, then back.

'OK. We need to let Philip know we've completed the contract. He's going to want proof, but he can never know one son killed the other. We will lose him completely and he still serves a purpose. We need to get him to pay up and put an end to this.'

She thought for a moment. 'You go back to the fort and deal with everyone: Crush, Robert, Willis, the taxi driver, before morning. I'll decide about Kyle in due course.' She paused a moment. 'In the meantime, Ivan – or whatever his name is – will play the part of Harry's killer. Get him to confess to Harry's murder on camera – spin him some yarn about it being to get someone to pay up – then kill him, on film. I don't care how – you decide – then send the footage to Philip.'

'Are you serious?' Doug asked.

'What do you think?' she snarled as she walked away, tapping at her phone.

*

A skeleton team had answered the call, as Jo knew they would. Those who hadn't picked up their phones would be gutted they had missed out. They would trickle in shortly after dawn, but by then the sexy jobs would have been dished out to those quicker off the mark. Donna was amongst the first to arrive and was already coming up with the goods.

Jo looked up as she hovered by her doorway.

'Boss, I think you might like this.'

'Grab Mr Porter before you make my day,' said Jo. 'He was in the HOLMES suite last I saw.'

Donna went in search, returning a moment later with the DCI, whose flustered glow Jo put down to the shock of the night's revelations and the number of innocent lives hanging in the balance.

'Scott, put your phone down and listen,' said Jo.

Jo nodded to Donna.

'OK, so we've just got the data back on Kyle Cooke's phone,' she said. 'The first thing to say is that he is on it all the time. I mean, all the time. Hundreds of WhatsApp messages, Instagram posts, snapchats every day.'

Jo looked across to Scott and shrugged in bewilderment. He did not respond.

'Basically, he runs his whole life on his phone, just like every other kid his age. And he's got some very interesting numbers on there.'

'So, what does that tell us?' Jo probed.

'It's too early to go through everything, but one thing stands out. His phone is never off, except . . .'

'Except?' Jo asked, with growing impatience.

'Except fifteen minutes before Harry was murdered, until about twenty minutes after. And now. It's off now.'

Jo's mind raced. She looked over to Scott, who appeared distracted.

'Any other times over the period you've been looking at?'

'Nope, not even at night, nor during Harry and Ruth's funeral.'

'Scott, what do you reckon?' Jo asked, more to bring him back to the present.

'Err, well it could have been faulty.'

'Bullshit.' Jo was losing patience. 'Come on, it's obvious. He's a copper's son. He knows we can trace phones and he knew what he was about to do. He's turned it off deliberately. Donna, which mast did it last ping before he switched it off?'

'As far as I can tell he was in Patcham Village.'

'Yards from Withdean Park,' Jo mused under her breath.

'And when it came back on again?'

'Home, or very close.'

'And what about now? What time was it switched off and where?'

'Again, in or near his house. About 23.45 last night.'

'That's impossible. I was there shortly after and he definitely wasn't there. His dad was still waiting for him to come home.'

Jo again looked across at Scott Porter for some ideas.

'Scott, put that bloody phone down and join the party,' she yelled, not caring that Donna was cringing at this public bollocking.

'Sorry ma'am,' replied the DCI, shoving his mobile back in his pocket.

'Let's put two and two together. Gary and I recognised the jacket – not solid evidence, as you say Scott, but it's a start. The only two times his phone has been off were when his brother was killed and now.

'Go with me on this, but I reckon he's switched the phone off, killed his brother, then turned it back on again when he's safely back home. What's worrying me more is that tonight his phone goes off near his house and he's nowhere to be seen.'

Jo looked at Donna. 'Get all the CCTV and ANPR you can for all vehicles entering and leaving Phil's road between 10 p.m. and, say, 1 a.m. Spider's-web it out and see if you can account for every car, van, pedestrian.'

She turned back to Scott. 'Given we now know that CSG have been contracted to find the killer – you haven't heard that last bit, Donna – I'm certain Kyle has been snatched. Get ready, you're coming with me. We are going to pay Phil Cooke a visit.'

*

For once, Helen Ricks was petrified. Her whole plan, both her careers and her liberty hung in the balance. She never had been good at trusting others and, of all the people who could make or break her now, she wished it was anyone other than Douglas.

Back when they'd met, she'd idolised him. He was a risk-taker, someone not bound by the same rules as she was, and his ruthless enforcement with no accountability fired her up. He inspired her to use her cold-blooded intellect and position to dream big, to build an empire that sated her thirst for money and power. And he was amazing in the sack.

Now things were getting tough, she sensed a wariness in him. She had spotted it once or twice before, but the misgivings his eyes had divulged when she set out her plan made him dangerous. He'd always agreed that nothing, and no one, would get in their way, but now she suspected he was just appeasing her to keep his place by her side and in her bed.

He was a weak link and, like everyone else, dispensable.

She pulled up on her driveway and was just about to sidle out of the car when her ghost phone rang. She didn't store numbers, but committed the last four digits of them all to memory. 2801. She had to take this one.

'Yes?'

'She's rumbled it,' said the voice on the other end. Ricks got back inside the car, clicking the door gently closed.

'What do you mean?'

'Kyle turned his phone off at the time of the murder and it's off now. She's just on her way up to see Cooke. She's joining the dots.'

'How the bloody hell did she make that leap? If this is down to you . . .'

'Something to do with a jacket. She recognised it as Kyle's and she's gone off on her own tangent. I couldn't stop her. I buried as much as I could, but she was like a torpedo once she made her mind up.'

'Stop her. I'll tie up the loose ends here, but you must stop her.'

'I'll do what I can, ma'am, but with respect, if you'd kept me better informed I could have thrown her off the scent sooner.'

Helen was about to yell a reply when she heard a ruckus through the earpiece. Her heart thundered.

*

'Christ, there you are,' yelled Jo, having eventually tracked Scott down to the exhibits store. 'What the hell are you doing in here?' She spotted him trying to pocket his phone. 'Who have you been talking to?' she shouted, her eyes searching his for any hint of guilt.

'Er, just phoning the wife to tell her I'm not going to be home to take the kids swimming later.'

'At three in the morning? Give me your phone.' She closed the two paces between them as he reached into his left-hand pocket and handed her his work mobile.

'The other one,' Jo hissed.

'What other one? I haven't—'

'The other one,' she bellowed, pointing to his right pocket, 'before I rip your jacket and search it myself.' Porter, defeated, handed her a featureless black pay–as–you–go mobile. She grabbed it and flipped it open.

'PIN,' she ordered.

'I don't—'

'PIN.'

'0402,' he surrendered.

Jo tapped in the numbers and the screen flashed to life. She navigated to the recent calls list which, as she expected, contained just one number. She went to the text list. Blank.

'Whose is this number?'

'I can't tell you.' Porter quivered.

'WHO?'

Porter said nothing.

'If you've been leaking information, I'll turn the key on you myself.'

She took her own phone, whispered a command, and in seconds a DC filled the doorway.

'Wait here with DCI Porter. I'm going to get you some help but if he tries to leave, call anyone or even speak, arrest him for perverting the course of justice and use whatever force you deem necessary to keep him here.'

The DC flicked his gaze between the two senior officers, his expression suggesting he hoped this was a joke.

Jo ran out of the room, stopping briefly to hand Porter's burner phone to Donna and rattle off a list of instructions. On her sprint to the car, she called Gary Hedges. Once he was up to speed, she knew she could rely on him to put the plan in place.

*

Phil Cooke was still frantic with worry about Kyle and Bob Heaton. How had he allowed himself to get caught up in all this? Phil had thought Bob, having been released from prison, would have had the sense to disappear, maybe even try to get back together with Janet.

A text tone stirred him out of his torture. He reached for his phone by the empty whisky glass on the coffee table. He did not recognise the number and, seeing the video file attached, was tempted to delete it in case it was a virus.

It was the filename, 'Job Done', that prompted second thoughts. He tapped and watched. A grainy image of a man sat in what looked like a cell came into focus. He was wearing a drab set of matching grey sweatshirt and trousers, not unlike the ones provided to prisoners in police custody blocks. The man might have been in his mid-thirties but his patchy stubble could have disguised his true age.

The walls behind him blended with his clothing, but seemed flecked with red and glistened with damp. When the man spoke, his Eastern European accent was obvious, and his English was broken but clear.

'Mr Cooke. My name is Leonid Petrescu and I have done you a terrible wrong.' Phil froze. 'I am a good man but in May this year I did something very bad. Mr Cooke, trust me when I say I did not go out that day to hurt anyone, but I am a poor man with family in Romania I have to support. I saw your son, in all his nice designer clothes, chatting on his flashy mobile phone. I was overcome with jealousy. Why should he have these things when my children back home have no food? Mr Cooke, I followed him. I only meant to rob him. To take what he had and send it to my children, but he came at me and before I knew it my knife was in his chest. He fell to the ground and was bleeding. So much blood. I was scared, so I ran. I had been lucky. The police have not caught me, but other men have. Men who tell me you pay big money to catch me. I don't know why you did, but they have done what you asked.'

Phil was rigid. What was this? Had they really caught the killer? He wanted to call Robinson, check this was not a hoax – but he could see there were still thirty seconds of the video to play. Whoever this man was, he wanted to kill him; an eye for an eye.

The video continued. A shadow cast across the man's face, then terror flamed in his eyes. The image went briefly black as a figure moved across the lens, then alongside Petrescu. The man who had just confessed pleaded with a hooded man towering above him. All of a sudden, the newcomer grabbed Petrescu's bald head and yanked it back. Next, the glint of metal caught the arc light's beam before a knife was sliced across the man's outstretched neck, a ribbon, followed by a jet, of blood spraying from the ragged wound. A yelp, then the screen faded to black.

40

3.00 a.m., Sunday 29th July

Having narrowly avoided the wrong lane as she tore round Newhaven's one-way system, Helen Ricks cursed Douglas.

'Pick up the phone,' she yelled at the ringing handpiece. It was the third time she had called on her way to the fort. Despite bankrolling it, and providing arm's-length approval for the atrocities that took place there, this was the first time she had actually visited. And she was not happy. If her more ambitious plans were to come off, she could not be linked to the murky operations carried out in her name.

Finally, he answered.

'I'm on my way, get someone at the gate to let me in.'

'Are you sure?' Douglas replied with an insistence above his pay grade.

'Just do it,' Helen said, as she powered down Fort Road, briefly launching the car airborne over the mini roundabout.

'We've done what you asked, now we need to clear up. Can't I meet you somewhere else when we've finished?'

'Already?' said Helen, panic rising. 'I'm just by the park. Open the gates, now.'

The implications raced through her mind. Of course she should turn around, but how could she? She needed to be on the ground, cleansing any trace of herself from the fort. At whatever cost.

The huge gates laboriously swung open as she approached. Douglas hopping from foot to foot did nothing to settle her nerves. She got out of the car as he paced towards her. He was about to speak but her halting hand silenced him.

'We've got the mother of all problems. My insider has just phoned. Howe's now worked out about Kyle and knows he's missing. We need to clear out of here now. Get every prisoner away. We'll deal with the guards, but I want all trace of us gone before first light.'

'That's impossible. Have you any idea how long it will take to gather them up, kill them, then dismember the bodies? Then there's the crates, the lorry and getting the furnaces fired up. It can't be done at the snap of your fingers, you know.'

She glared at him, biting her tongue. 'Where's Kyle, Heaton and the rest of them I told you to get rid of?'

'Ivan is dead and Phil Cooke has the footage. The rest are holed up in one of the cells below ground.'

'Just kill them and get the hell out of here,' muttered Helen.

'What about the bodies?'

'Torch them. Torch everything, you useless piece of shit,' hissed Helen. 'And send that press release.'

*

This time Jo did not bother with a parking space. The house would become a crime scene soon anyway, so double-parking would just help isolate it.

She sprinted to the door and banged, not giving a toss who she woke up, so long as Phil Cooke answered pronto.

'What the hell?' he said as he opened up, but Jo was not doing this on the doorstep. She shoved him out of the way, glancing at the bare newel.

Phil followed her.

She spun round to face him, and took in his look of fear and incredulity.

'Where's Kyle?' she demanded.

'I've no idea, I told you earlier. What is this?'

'Phone him.'

'But . . .'

'Phone him,' she shouted.

Phil picked up the phone and dialled. He stared in confusion. Dialled again.

'Switched off?' Jo suggested.

'Yes, but . . . it's never off.'

'Not quite. It has been off once before, recently.'

Phil searched Jo's face for some clue as to what she was on about.

'It was switched off when Harry was murdered.'

'I don't understand . . .'

'When did his jacket get torn?'

'Jo, you're scaring me. What is this?'

'When?'

'I don't know, it's been like it for a few months. What's that got to do— How do you know it's torn?'

'Phil, you've got to come clean with me. What have you done? You said you'd done something that I'd eventually find out. I need to know now.'

Phil looked at his phone and opened up the text app. He said nothing but turned it towards Jo. He touched the thumbnail of the man in grey and let the footage run to its horrifying end. He waited until it faded before looking up at Jo. She gagged to stem the rising vomit. She was on the back foot now. Momentarily, the purpose of her visit paled.

'Who is that? It's a set-up, right? I mean, that's CGI or something?'

'I don't think so. It's what this is all about. They were going to tell Ruth about us. She was dying and I'd lied to her all those years. I couldn't let them do that to her. They said I had to pay CSG to catch Harry's killer, then they blackmailed me to be their puppet PCC. Now they have killed him, I'm trapped.' He started sobbing. Jo went to put her arm around him, then caught herself.

'Phil, it's not what it seems. I don't know if that's real or not, but he's not the killer,' she said, pointing at the phone.

'Of course he is, he's admitted it. You saw him. Oh my God, I should have left him for you.'

'Phil, you taught me everything I know about interviewing. People admit things for different reasons, even if they are innocent. That's some script. Look, I don't know who he is, whether he is dead or alive, but you need to pull yourself together. He's not the killer.' She paused. 'Kyle is.'

*

Bob Heaton knew he was breathing his last. It would be impossible for Robinson and Crush to let him escape with his life after this.

The cell walls he, Kyle Cooke and Oli Willis were shackled to were crawling with spiders and vermin. They had tried to whisper a few words to each other, but their rope gags and injuries stifled anything but frantic grunts. Kyle's eyes suggested he was more bewildered than scared, but Oli's look was of hopeless resignation.

Ivan had been relieved as their guard a couple of hours ago, or so Bob thought. The passage of time was anyone's guess. Not long after, there seemed to be a commotion further down the corridor. Shuffling. A monotone voice – Bob strained to hear what he was saying but gave up. Then a gasp followed by doors slamming. If either of them could talk, he'd ask Oli if that was normal, but that would have to wait.

Suddenly the door was flung open, its iron heft crashing against the granite wall behind. Six men marched in, two for each prisoner. Bob felt a grip on each arm. The rattle and rub of chains told him he was being moved.

From the corner of his eye, he saw Kyle and Oli being shackled too. He tried to catch Kyle's eye to send a reassuring smile, but the young lad was thrashing around – nothing but survival on his mind. Bob had worked out Kyle was the lad in the khaki coat, but was still trying to reconcile the boy he used to babysit with being a killer.

Bob was dragged out first, kicks and kidney punches propelling him forward. They pulled him to his full height when all were clear of the cell. Once he was hooded he struggled to keep his footing, but his pleas to slow down were muffled by his gag.

The guards had clearly been told not to speak – even to each other – but they didn't need to. Bob knew he would never see another sunrise.

*

'That can't be true. You're lying,' yelled Phil as he paced the lounge like a caged leopard. 'That's my only son you're accusing.'

'It all fits. The description, his movements, his phone switched off. And his bizarre behaviour. Just think about it.'

'What about DNA? Fibres? Anything. Jesus Jo, I'd have known.'

'I don't mean to be harsh, but perhaps he got lucky. It happens. The fact is that for some reason an innocent man has been duped into admitting to the murder, then probably executed, and we've no idea where Kyle and Bob are. We've got to find them. Has anyone even hinted where they keep the people they snatch?'

Phil collapsed into a leather armchair, dropped his head in his hands and wailed. 'NO.'

Jo felt her phone vibrate. Gary Hedges.

'What've you got?'

'Right.' The superintendent took a deep breath. 'The phone Porter was ringing comes down to an unregistered pay as you go, and before you ask, topped up with cash.'

'Go on.'

'Well, unlike Porter's, it's been used to call several numbers and we are running those now, but here's the interesting bit. We've got it on live cell site and GPS, and just after midnight it moved from the Kingston area—'

'Kingston, London, Jamaica or outside Lewes?'

'Lewes. Went to Seaford, probably around the Head then back to

Kingston. It takes the call from Porter then goes hell for leather back south, into Newhaven town, and now it's switched off.'

'Where? Where was it switched off, Gary?' Jo's patience was running out and even Phil, who had inadvertently sent killers on his son's trail, was showing an interest.

'It's not precise but around the football club and fort area.'

Jo's mind raced. 'What did Oli shout when he was driven off by Crush?' she said, clawing for the exact words.

'Something like "don't take me to the for . . ."'

'Don't take me to the fort. That's what he was trying to say. Shit, that's where they are taking them. Newhaven Fort.' Jo turned and saw Phil trying to knit it all together.

'We should get CCTV and ANPR results soon, but I reckon we go shit or bust to the fort,' said Gary.

'Start getting a firearms team together, but I want to know more about whoever Porter was on the phone to. Who is he? What's the connection? What's the threat?'

'I've had a chat with our DCI,' admitted Gary. 'We've not nicked him yet because, funnily enough, we can't get a car to escort him to custody, so I took the chance of asking him a few questions.'

'Be careful. There are rules about interviewing.'

'It's fine. Anyway, I wrote it all down. I asked him who he was on the phone to and what he told him.'

'And?'

'He said it was more than his life's worth and that he'd take what's coming to him. He did say something interesting though. When I asked him who he was more scared of, him or me, he replied "you don't know the half of what she's like".'

'She?' Jo replied. 'He was on the phone to a woman?'

'So it seems. Oh, and I should tell you he slipped and banged his head.'

'Call me back when you have the CCTV and ANPR,' Jo said, ignoring Gary's last remark. 'Get everything in place. I think I need to call the chief.'

315

She was about to dial again when Phil grabbed the phone.

'What are you doing? I'm trying to save your son's life here.'

'That's why I can't let you call her. You need to sit down. I have to tell you about Helen Ricks.'

41

4.00 a.m., Sunday 29th July

All the prisoners were corralled in the fort's battery: gagged, bound and blindfolded. Bob Heaton strained to hear the frantic whispering, the only sound other than the waves crashing below.

He picked up both Crush's and Robinson's voices, but the rest blurred into one. A few words, however, were repeated over again. 'Lorry', 'crates' and 'Boss' being three of them. Bob had no idea what to make of his situation, or their captors' intent. But had they also used a female pronoun? The warmth of the bodies crushed against him provided small relief from the bone-deep chill he had endured since being dumped in the smaller cell. He had no idea how many others were crammed in here with him, but the acrid suffocation gripping his lungs and his inability to move suggested, wherever they were, it was at capacity.

He had to assume the guards were armed but he had seen no weapons when he arrived, nor heard their distinctive clatter. His mind raced over whether he had given any hint to Jo and Gary that might lead them here. Hardly likely since he hadn't known this place existed, except in its previous life as a museum. He hoped they had worked out he'd been kidnapped and were planning a rescue. Did they know who else was here though, and why? That would change everything.

*

As dawn broke, Helen Ricks paced the hilltop, scouring the approach roads for any movement. Douglas had tried to coax her back inside but she was having none of it. Stopping to peer into the breaking dawn, she cursed at no one in particular.

'How would they know where we are, love?' said Doug, keeping a safe distance behind her and away from the two-hundred-foot drop.

'Are you completely stupid? Despite shagging that oaf Cooke, Joanne Howe is one of the cleverest detectives I've ever worked with. She doesn't need it all spelt out on a whiteboard. Now she knows we've got Kyle, she will have mobilised everyone and every tactic at her disposal to fathom out where he was snatched from and when. Then it's just a case of putting it all together. Where the hell is that lorry?' she said, almost as an afterthought.

'But you'll know, won't you? You'll know what she's up to? Doesn't she have to keep you updated?'

'In theory, yes, but as I have specifically ordered her to turn a blind eye to what you are up to . . .'

'We,' corrected Douglas. 'What *we* are up to.'

Helen glared at him and he visibly shrivelled.

'As I was saying, she is hardly likely to give me step-by-step updates on something she knows I'm dead against. I want these prisoners executed and out of here within the hour. I want no trace of us left here.'

'I can't promise it will be an hour. I told you what we are waiting for.'

'If it comes to it, detonate the devices and we get the hell out of here. Oh, and Douglas?'

'Yes?'

'Get me a gun.'

* * *

Phil was strapped into Jo's police car as she raced eastwards. She tried to keep an ear to her radio but Phil was finally telling all.

'Why didn't you say something when you got the first call?'

'Don't you think I've asked myself that a million times? My head was fucked. I thought I could deal with it. Tell them to piss off and they would.'

'The second call then?'

'You make it all sound so easy. They'd have told Ruth. It would have crushed her. I couldn't let that happen.'

'And this is better? What about when she died, couldn't you have pulled the plug then?'

Phil wiped his eyes.

'They had me on tape effectively asking them to kill Harry's murderer. Fuck, to kill Kyle. They made me tell the press about the Teresa Sutton business.'

'You bloody idiot.'

'I know, I know. But also, I made this promise, see.'

'Promise?'

'To Ruth, that Harry's killer would be caught whatever it takes.'

'Yes, and he would have.'

'But you weren't making any progress. You were ignoring lines of enquiry.'

'It was never the Larbies.'

'I know that now. I was an idiot, but I saw no other way of protecting Kyle and keeping my promise.'

'Bloody hell,' Jo sighed as she exited the Southerham Roundabout.

'Then they threatened to kill Kyle and leak what I'd asked them to do if I didn't stand as PCC.'

Jo glanced at him, then wrenched the steering wheel to avoid the central reservation.

'Bloody hell. I wondered why you stood for election. You were forced?'

Phil nodded. He explained how Helen Ricks had then revealed herself as being behind the CSG, all about the grant money and Bob being found out.

'I promise, if I had any idea Kyle had killed Harry, I'd never have done any of this.'

'Of course you wouldn't, but a court won't see it that way. Why Kyle though?' she chanced, risking the same illegal interview she'd warned Gary about.

'He's an enigma. He loved his mum and I think me too, but he was closer to Ruth. In hindsight I think he was jealous of mine and Harry's relationship. We were like that,' he said, crossing his fingers. 'When Ruth was given months to live, he went into himself. Stopped eating with us, was never at home. I just thought he was getting serious with his new boyfriend. I heard him and Harry arguing a week or so before . . . well, you know.'

'Why the hell didn't you tell us?' asked Jo as she turned right at Beddingham towards Newhaven.

'It was nothing? They're brothers. They argued from time to time.'

'What was this about?'

Phil said nothing.

'Phil?'

'First Kyle was shouting something about Harry having to pay.'

'Pay?'

'I've no idea but then he said, "We're all in the shit if you don't".'

'What did Harry say?'

'I didn't really hear it all, but I did hear him say "Mummy's boy".'

'For God's sake, Phil. Why didn't you tell us all this?'

Jo shook her head, then felt the buzz of a text. She chanced a glimpse.

Boss, FYI we've found a pair of jeans with what looks like spots of blood hidden under Mr Cooke's shed. Also bottles of Nandrolone. Checking what that is.

'Everything OK?' Phil ventured.

Jo didn't answer, then said, 'You just do as you're told when we get there.'

'Sure,' he mumbled.

'I mean it. You shouldn't even be here. You should be in custody,' she warned him. When he had broken the news about Helen Ricks, Jo knew she needed to go straight to the fort. She could not expect anyone more junior to confront the treacherous chief. Phil had taken the chance to leap into the car beside her before she sped off.

'Make yourself useful, dial Gary's number for me,' she told Phil. He found Gary's number in her phone and hit dial. It barely rang before he picked up.

'Jo, where are you? I've authorised firearms and deployed three specialist teams to the fort. I've got negotiators and rifle officers heading there from HQ too.'

'I'm on my way and I've got the PCC in the car, just to warn you.'

Phil went to speak but Jo's vigorous headshake persuaded him otherwise.

'Shit, OK,' replied Gary. 'Just stay out of the way, Phil.'

'We've had that discussion,' said Jo as she hurtled past the entrance to the port. 'I want sea and air covered too, Gary. Get SFOs on to a Border Force cutter and I want the helicopter up. Take no excuses but do not, repeat do not, speak to anyone above me. Is that understood?'

'Sure, but why?'

'Later, Gary. Just let me know when you have the guns in place and tell them I'm going in.'

'You're what?' Gary replied.

'You heard. Oh, and get a disaster victim identification team on standby.'

'Jo, what aren't you telling me? I'm the strategic firearms commander here. I need to know everything. Why do you want DVI mobilised?'

'I just have a feeling we are going to find a lot of bodies.'

She felt the rush of air as Phil vomited out of the window.

*

Gary Hedges was losing count of the number of pints he'd promised over the last hour. The trouble with spontaneous firearms incidents was that all the conventions and protocols dreamt up by the shiny-arsed bureaucrats relied on those very nine-to-fivers, with all their boxes of tricks, being around. So, when your boss tells you she wants you to secure, then raid a Napoleonic fort at the crack of a Sunday dawn, the old boys' network kicks in.

As he stood among his makeshift gang of radio operators and tactical advisors, scouring the incident room screens, he thanked God for infrared drones. The white blobs indicating officers multiplied across the screens: proof that the favours he had called in from other forces, most notably the Metropolitan Police, were being delivered.

He'd stripped all but the barest armed presence from Gatwick Airport, pulling some serious rank over the jobsworth duty inspector, who rattled on about national security and being the thin blue line against the international terrorist threat. Gary vowed, if he survived today with his rank and job intact, that idiot would find himself posted to custody by the summer's end.

'How are we doing with maritime support?' he asked Sergeant Sean 'Orson' Wells, his tactical advisor. He was lucky to hoist this Tactical Firearms Unit veteran from his bed. There were only a handful of tac-ads who would tell it like it was, ignoring the gulf in ranks. Most either sucked up to him or sugar-coated their guidance. If Orson thought Gary was being a dickhead, he'd tell him.

'I've just come off the phone to Steve Wharton,' replied Orson, his face foreshadowing bad news.

'What, *our* Steve Wharton?' replied Gary. Steve had been Gary's predecessor and mentor. They'd lost touch when he had retired a few years ago but, on jobs like this, he sorely missed him.

'Yes, he's Head of Maritime at the UK Border Force now,' said Orson, a wry grin on his face. Gary could only imagine how Steve's Exocet management style would be going down in the civil service. 'He says they can't help in terms of interdiction.' Gary raised an eyebrow. 'That's interception to you and me. As I say, they can't intercept vessels that might directly oppose them. That's a job for Special Forces. What he can do is move a cutter over to us to keep obs and track any suspect vessels.'

'Well, that's something,' said Gary, exasperated. 'Say yes and I'll see if I can get military support. Hopefully, we won't need it, but we have to contain the fort from the sea as well as the land.'

'Roger,' said Orson, then relayed the message to the tactical firearms commander.

More shapes were appearing on the screens. The Tactical Firearms Commander at the RV point was doing a fabulous job in deploying the borrowed armed officers as they arrived, and they were a credit to their forces in accepting the orders without question. The ring of steel was closing in.

'How long are we containing for, boss?' asked Orson, mainly to remind Gary he had to move the plan along. Sitting and waiting for ever was not an option. It wasn't like laying siege to a house where they could confidently place the target inside and, hopefully, bore him out.

The layout of the labyrinthine fort beneath the cliff was a mystery, as was the whereabouts and numbers of the hostages and hostage takers. At some point, he hoped, someone might enlighten him – but, eventually, he would just have to attack and hope for the best.

*

Jo found a spot to hide up, just behind Newhaven Football Club. In the lee of Fort Hill, it was perfect. Out of sight – she hoped – but close enough when it was time to move. She nestled the car as tight into the rise of the fort as she could, her Airwave radio chattering softly, coded confirmations that the specialist firearms officers were taking their positions. The occasional flurry followed: the rifle officers reporting movements they judged might be targets.

The sun yawned over the white of Seaford Head to their left. It had all the promise of another beautiful summer's day. Jo mused whether, soon, anyone would remember the sunshine, or just the blood that would doubtless be spilt across these chalk cliffs.

Phil was brooding. The agonies of the last few months and his own stupidity seemed to be rising to the surface. Jo struggled to keep him focused, only too aware that he should already be in a cell, not sat next to her yards from what would soon become a brutal battleground.

'Whatever I do, Phil, you stay in the car,' she stressed.

'You will save Kyle though, won't you?' Phil wept. 'He's all I've got left.'

Jo stared at her former boss. Lover. She searched for any sign of understanding.

'Phil, you do know that nothing can ever go back to normal, don't you?' she checked.

'I'll have my only son back. That's all that matters.'

She turned in her seat, open-mouthed.

'Phil, you *will* go to prison. So will Kyle. You do know that, don't you?'

He didn't reply, his stare fixed on the rusting fence and the scrub-covered hill ahead.

Jo flicked on her mobile phone and the *Breaking News* banner flashed across the screen. She tapped it and the app opened.

DRUGS CHEAT COOKE SLAIN OVER DEBT?

The pictures said it all, but she scanned the article in case – in the hope – she'd got it wrong. That word 'Nandrolone' removed any doubt.

'Phil, did you know about this?'

Phil just glanced at the screen, nodded, then sank his head in his hands.

'How much more have you held back?' Jo was raging now.

Without looking at her, he said 'Nothing. That's it. They got this from someone. God knows who, but it's definitely Harry and I recognise the gym. This was the final straw. If I was in any doubt, they'd release this and Harry's legacy would be all about steroids and cheating rather than his talents.'

'We could have fixed all this.'

'I know, I know.'

'Seems they planned to splash it over the internet anyway.'

'They really are evil, aren't they.'

'And it took this for you to realise?'

As Phil shook his head in defeat, Jo held him close.

42

As the sun broke, Helen again squinted inland from the clifftop, straining to pick out the movement she was sure she'd spotted a moment ago. She comforted herself by patting the bulge of her Beretta M9 handgun in her jacket pocket.

'Douglas,' she said, pointing up the road. 'Give me the glasses.' He handed her the black HD binoculars. She scoured the winding road leading from the police station she'd recently sold.

'Is that our lorry?' she asked, trying to hide her fear that the whole operation had been compromised. She thrust the binoculars back without daring to look away.

The few seconds it took for Douglas to be sure stretched interminably. 'Well?'

'Yep.' Douglas was suddenly triggered to action. He grabbed his radio from his belt and issued the orders, his tone leaving no doubt as to the urgency of his commands. 'Follow me,' he said to Helen, running along the cliff to the disused gun placement. She raced to keep up then threw herself behind the turret.

'Get them all bound and ready to go. Ten minutes max,' Doug shouted into the radio. 'This is a live cargo. Kill them en route. No delays. Tell the Engineerium to get the furnaces up to heat.'

'Roger,' someone squawked back through the handset.

In an instant, inaudible shouting echoed up from the parade square. The shuffle of feet was interspersed with cries of pain and profane commands in reply. The rack of automatic weapons being cocked angered Helen. How had she allowed herself to be this close to the brutality? Where would the deniability come from now?

*

'Hotel Foxtrot 74, urgent,' the rifle officer whispered over the secure radio. A key attribute of their training was the patience and discipline to remain statue-still for hours on end and then, when showtime came, to channel the adrenaline surge into controlled aggression. HF 74 would put dozens of lives at risk were she to bellow into the handset or lose her fixed focus on the approaching target.

'Hotel Foxtrot 74, go ahead,' replied the controller, equally serene.

'74, artic approaching from the white side. Looks like it's heading for us.'

'74, Roger. Description please.'

Hotel Foxtrot 74 rattled off as good a description as she could give, looking through her telescopic sight.

'Roger, keep the commentary coming. I'll get the helicopter and Coastguard to see if they can provide more.'

'74, Roger.'

Sergeant Rob Gibban, the operational firearms commander – OFC – was secreted with a team of ten in the woodland to the north-east of the fort, fifty yards from the gate. Using a series of hand signals that were a second language to his men and women, he silently relocated them close to the treeline then held them while he waited for the order to move to State Amber. Once he heard that, State Red would be his call.

The tension in the copse weighed heavily as officers noiselessly gave their weapons a final check. It was a time-filler really, as each knew that they and their Sig MCX Carbines were primed and ready to go.

Even though this was a spontaneous operation, Rob had the plan committed to memory and each of his officers knew exactly what part they'd play. As far as he knew, none had attacked a fort before, but life was for learning and they knew the basics.

'74, the artic is approx one five zero metres from the gate,' the rifle officer murmured.

'Roger, 74. Hotel Foxtrot 70, Sergeant Gibban, from TFC, State Amber, repeat, State Amber.'

'Roger. State Amber received, 70,' Gibban acknowledged; he was now poised to give State Red.

At that moment Rob heard movement from his right. Some way off, but the clank of metal followed by a dragging sound was distinctive.

'70 to Silver. I'm standing by on Red, we have movement on the white side. From the fort.'

He belly-crawled up the hill and raised his binoculars. He could not believe what he was seeing.

'70, urgent. We have in excess of two zero people being moved from the fort to the gate. All bound and hooded with armed escort.'

'Roger, 70, stand by.'

'74, can I come in? The lorry is now passing the football club.'

'Roger, 74. 70, from TFC, looks like the people you have eyeball on are being moved to the lorry. Contain the vehicle and the people in the fort. Do not, repeat do not, allow any embarkation or the lorry to decamp.'

Holy shit, thought Gibban. He only had an on-foot containment capability. Now he had God knows how many targets and an equally unknown number of innocents.

'70, did you receive that?' the controller asked, as Gibban scurried his way back to his team.

'Answer yes, give me thirty seconds to brief the new plan. Can you get that exit road blocked?'

'74, the gates are opening.'

Gibban finished whispering the new taskings into his lapel microphone. '70, stand by on State Red.' A pause, then, 'State Red. Go go go.'

*

Yells of 'Stop, armed police' bounced off the cliff face, echoing all around. The explosion of commands came close to drowning out the screech of seagulls, driven from their slumber by the raw aggression in the air.

Half of Rob's team sprinted to the gate, weapons trained on the lorry, intent on stopping its retreat. They fanned out, seeking to freeze the enemy with overwhelming threats, but just as ready to use deadly force.

The other half were instantly locked in a firefight with the guards shepherding the prisoners.

The lorry's engine roared as it thrust into reverse. The trailer jack-knifed, whipping round against the flint wall, crushing a guard. His cries went unheeded as metal screamed against stone in the driver's determination to gain control and flee.

A volley of shots peppered the lorry in vain attempts to blast out the tyres. The officers were too disciplined to fire at the driver until they saw guns. Their bellows and dancing red laser dots, however, were relentless in the effort to terrify him into submission.

With a deafening squeal, the trailer came free of the wall and the lorry roared forward then streaked away, poleaxing two more guards.

Rob burst to the gate and was horrified to see the panicked yet systematic executions playing out all around the parade square. The gunmen were dragging the hooded and wailing prisoners with them as they scurried for sanctuary. Once they reached safety, they dispatched their charges with swift headshots.

Rob squinted at his sights, desperate for a clear shot, but the target in front of him clearly knew the police rules of engagement and kept a comparatively good guy between them.

Despite the rising body count, it was impossible for all the prisoners to be culled or used as shields, and Rob spotted a group of five break away and head towards the base of the hill.

He radioed it in and, finally, fixed his sights on the nearest guard. The 5.56mm round made light work of flesh and bone and the target's head exploded, showering his prisoner with blood and grey matter.

A couple of guards had abandoned their charges and were bedding in behind cover, picking out the specialist firearms officers with volleys of fire. Rob was pinned down, unable to secure a better position, so fired bursts back, barking orders and demanding sit-reps – situation reports – down the radio.

One of his most experienced officers was just fifteen yards away and started to update, but a barrage of shots cut him off. Rob vomited as he saw his friend's peppered body fall. All his training had been about keeping focus, shutting out the horror of losing mates. It had never been tested before and now, he concluded, that was bollocks.

'Officer down,' he shouted into the radio. 'Stay behind cover until safe.' That went against all his instincts, which were to burst into the open, spraying gunfire while running to the stricken father, husband and colleague who lay dying.

The rallies and shouts to surrender persisted, but Rob was becoming increasingly convinced this was hurtling towards a bloody stalemate.

*

Doug pushed Helen's face into the concrete cannon placement. 'Keep your head down,' he ordered.

'Just tell me what's happening. You've really fucked this up.'

Doug struggled to hear the panicked radio messages over the sting of gunfire. Shit, if only he had recruited more ex-squaddies than cops. He turned to Helen.

'The lorry's done a runner and we've lost about six of ours.'

'What about the prisoners?' she hissed.

'Most neutralised but a handful unaccounted for.'

'How can we get out of here?'

'I haven't a clue. It's carnage down there.'

'Find a way. And no loose ends, Douglas.' She glared at him with that iciness that revealed her capabilities.

'Sure,' he mumbled, feeling emasculated by her sheer ruthlessness.

'Sort this here and now, and get me out before you become a problem to solve.'

He shuddered inwardly. Then it struck him. She was the chief constable, yet had not asked about police casualties.

43

4.35 a.m., Sunday 29th July

Jo was grilling Phil about how he'd been so naive and succumbed to the blackmail when a volley of shots startled them both.

Phil was the first to react, but by only milliseconds.

'What the fuck?' he said, staring at Jo as if her face would hold the answers.

'Stay put,' she said, as she jerked at the phone to call Gary, but her command fell on deaf ears. 'Phil, get back here,' she yelled as the PCC flung open the car door and dashed towards the fort's perimeter fence. 'Holy shit,' she muttered as she followed suit, just as Gary picked up.

'Jo, I can't talk, we're engaged by the gate. Officers down and targets shot.'

'OK, OK, but Phil's bolted from the car,' she panted. 'I'm after him but for Christ's sake put the warning out.'

'Will do. Get him back. He's one complication I don't need.'

She grabbed her Captor pepper spray then, for the second time in recent months, sprinted after her former boss.

'Phil, get back here,' she yelled as he reached the fence.

The thud, thud, thud of a helicopter overhead drowned out his reply but, as he cleared the barbed wire, it was obvious he had just one thing on his mind.

Jo kicked up a gear, her heart pounding in rhythm with her feet.

'Phil, get back,' she called again in vain. 'You'll get shot.'

Her words still had no effect or simply did not reach him.

She had no choice but to throw herself into the battleground.

*

Bob grabbed the straggler of his group, dragging him behind the abandoned shack. He was astounded at how many he'd managed to get away from the firefight unscathed, especially as they were all still hooded and bound. But they weren't safe yet.

They all slumped against the moss-covered wall, fear muting their protests. Bob could still not see who he had rescued or where they were, but sensed that some were fresher than others. He heard one shuffling, their strength evident in the frantic grind of their feet on shingle.

'Hey,' Bob said, as he found his potential lieutenant. 'Are you hurt?'

'No. What are we going to do?' There was a familiar ring to the voice.

'Kyle? Is that you?'

'Who the fuck are you?' came the reply.

'Kyle, it's me. Bob. Bob Heaton. I used to work with your dad.'

'Shit,' replied Kyle. 'Were you in the cell with me?'

Bob was about to answer when a crack of gunfire drowned him out. He hit the ground.

'OK, first things first, let's get each other's straps and hoods off. Then free these three, then we get the fuck out of here,' said Bob.

'Fuck off. Can't you hear the shooting? Aren't we better to stay put?' replied Kyle.

Bob sighed. Bloody millennials, questioning everything, knowing nothing. 'We'll be sitting ducks. This whole set-up has been blown open and our hosts won't want any witnesses left. If we stay here, we join the rest with bullets in their heads. We have to move.'

Bob took the grunt as acceptance. He might have couched it a little better, but his experience was that shock tactics worked well in securing instant obedience. They could chat later.

'Back to back,' Bob ordered. Kyle obeyed and they fidgeted with each other's bindings, struggling to feel the slackness that would set them free. Bob succeeded first.

'Kyle, take my hood off,' he said, suspecting the lad would focus on just the straps.

The rising sun blinded him as the putrid sacking was finally discarded. He saw Kyle was blinking too, but other than that he was not in bad shape. His hands were soon free and he made straight to the others to unveil who they were. As each hood came off, Bob became more horrified. Oli Willis's face was pulped. The other two he was fairly certain he'd not seen before but, as they had been beaten even worse than Oli and their feeble frames made them resemble prisoners of war, he'd stand to be corrected.

'OK, everybody up,' he demanded, once they had all been untied. 'We need to get you help, but first you need to work with me, so do what I say and I might be able to get you out of here.'

He could not be sure he'd been heard, but as he had managed to get Kyle to comply, he was confident he could get the others in line.

Another volley of gunfire, this time prolonged, brought startled stares from all four of Bob's charges. Their faces begged for help. The three remaining waifs stumbled to their feet. One of those whom Bob did not know dry-retched and almost choked in the coughing fit that followed.

Kyle's eyes pleaded with Bob. How the shit were they going to get out of here? Bob was as clueless as any of them, but he knew he had to try. Having escaped the carnage that was playing out in the yard, he was not throwing the towel in now.

'Right. Listen. We need to get you all to a hospital, but that is not going to happen unless you do exactly what I tell you. Working together is our only chance of survival.' Bob knew that last bit was crap. Kyle, at a stretch, might be of some use, but the others would be passengers at best.

'I need you on your hands and knees, crawling to that outcrop there,' he said, pointing twenty metres away where the cliff jutted out. 'If I shout "down", you get flat on your belly immediately. If I shout "run", you sprint like fuck for cover. We'll regroup there, find the next cover and keep doing the same.'

Kyle looked at the three injured men. 'How are they going to manage that? Look at them,' he urged as he pointed to them propping each other upright.

'They have to try. We all have to try.'

'Is it safe over there? Have you any idea what you are doing?' Kyle asked.

'Of course I do,' he lied. He was well used to feigning confidence from his days leading drug raids. It was one thing to charge into the dark, but another to seep doubt.

Bob cut off Kyle's protest. 'OK, everybody on your knees.' He waited until they were all prone. 'Ready? Go!'

*

Helen's voice still shook Doug. She had no care for anyone but herself. Everyone was expendable. He accepted that on the dark side he'd chosen, he might die by the sword, but her complete indifference to her own officers shocked him. Any hope of defying this heartless bitch vanished.

His radio was worse than useless, the gunfire obliterating any snatch of transmission that did get through. He'd seen the group break off from the main body of prisoners and felt sure they would be heading for the east wall. If they knew where they were going, and had God on their side, they stood a remote chance of reaching the road unchallenged. His life depended on them not.

No loose ends.

He belly-crawled along the clifftop, making the best of the meagre cover he could find. He was all too aware the bushes and bracken were only cover from view, not fire, but it was a risk he had to take. When the gunfire resumed below, he took the opportunity to peep over the ridge to the parade ground, assuming that the cops would be focused on where they were shooting. At first, he saw nothing other than bloodied bodies strewn like a collapsed Jenga tower. Most, he was pleased to see, were the prisoners, but he could see three in the black of his guards and at least one with Police CTSFO emblazoned on their body armour.

The shooting stopped and the offshore breeze kissed the back of his exposed neck. He turned his head to the left, for air more than a view, and caught sight of the lorry's trailer fishtailing towards the town centre. He cursed the cowardly driver.

The chop of a helicopter brought him back to the present. Not much he could do. The copse hid him for now, but their infrared would pick him up and any movement would be fatal. Still, he had to try. He was quite literally between a rock and a hard place.

He scanned for his next refuge, for when he could break cover. A bush about fifteen yards away seemed likely. He scoured the approach for any hazards that would leave him exposed, should he trip.

Then the bush moved. Shit.

He felt his shoulder holster and drew the Beretta, more for comfort than in preparation. His eyes stung as he stared into the glare.

There it was again. This time he could make out a head. Just the shape, but a human head nonetheless. He wrestled with his diminishing options. Charge the bush? Shout? Double tap? He was at a loss.

No loose ends.

Only he and she seemed to matter – to him, at least – so who cared whether this was friend or foe? It would be a loose end. He raised the gun, remaining prone like an Olympic pistol champion. He closed his left eye and the v of the sight sat plumb in the centre of the bald sphere. Doug squeezed the trigger, the pressure point just a twitch away.

The head turned and, in his shock, his focus widened from the sights.

Crush.

Jesus, what was he doing up here? Doug's mind raced. Shoot or no-shoot? Was Crush a loose end or might he still have a use? Clarity hit him in a moment. He could control Crush. Kill him later if need be, but the prisoners needed to be caught. They were the real risk, and two hunters were better than one.

'Crush,' Doug called, in a loud whisper. His second in command flicked his head round, bringing his gun up.

'It's me, Doug,' he shouted, louder to prevent the shot. The barrel of the handgun dropped. 'On me,' Doug ordered, tapping the top of his head. He had no intention of putting himself on offer quite yet.

Crush broke cover and sprinted across the clearing.

'Fuck me, Doug, what's happening?'

'What the hell are you doing up here? You should be with the prisoners.'

'I got separated when the shooting started, so I thought I'd take a recce from up here.' Both knew that was a lie and Doug resolved to deal with this coward later. For now, he would put him back in harm's way.

'I've got a job for you. Five of your charges escaped and the boss wants them found. You and me are going to do that, you understand?' Doug growled.

'And when we find them?'

'No loose ends.'

44

4.45 a.m., Sunday 29th July

Somehow Phil had raced ahead. Jo's efforts to scale the fence were hindered by her sweatshirt snagging on the wire. By the time she'd freed herself, she'd lost precious seconds.

The bursts of gunfire and shouts of 'armed police' had punctured the intermittent hush. As she stopped to get her bearings she guessed that, like Dunblane and Hungerford, Newhaven would soon become synonymous with slaughter.

Jo gave up second-guessing where Phil had gone, and headed for the brow of the cliff. Taking the high ground would provide her with the best view on what was developing. She felt an overwhelming responsibility for how all this was turning out, and needed to do all she could to save the innocent and deliver justice to the guilty.

She scrambled up the hill, grateful for the recent dry spell but conscious that stepping on just one of the desiccated branches could give her position away and spell the end. She reached a thicket and punched out a brisk text to Gary telling him she'd lost Phil and where she was heading. He'd be cursing them both, but needed to know.

Jo peered around, checking for any movement – especially if it turned out to be Phil. Why couldn't he have just stayed put?

Other than a couple of hares bolting into the undergrowth, she was alone.

She too bolted, full pelt, guessing she had another thirty yards to the gun placement at the top. Despite the battle sporadically raging below, she reckoned she was safe to close in on that.

She hoped, as she broke cover, that she was in the protective sights of the rifle officers, dug in all around, and that they were Sussex and Surrey officers – on the off-chance they'd recognise her and hold fire.

Jo looked around one more time, took a breath, then sprinted, her legs screaming with exertion.

In less than ten seconds she was back behind cover, this time the enormous barrel of the six-inch BL World War II battery gun offering protection.

She slumped against its retaining wall, sucking in oxygen, her mind racing to work out what her next move should be.

Then a familiar voice scolded her. 'Joanne, you really should have left well alone.'

She turned to find herself staring down the muzzle of a 9mm pistol.

*

Phil had no idea exactly where he should be heading, but his paternal instinct to rescue Kyle spurred him on. The rat-a-tat-tat of gunfire interspersed with the shouted demands of the specialist firearms teams acted as his beacon.

He had not hung around in the car long enough to hear exactly what was happening but he knew Kyle was in mortal danger and, whatever he was supposed to have done, he needed to get him to safety. He guessed he should head towards, rather than away from, danger. His police tactical training told him that approaching from the flanks, rather than over the top, would be preferable both for safety and to preserve the element of surprise.

Scurrying his way round the contour of the hill, he paid less attention to cover than was wise. Speed was of the essence. He thought about shouting out as he was charging into the unknown, but it would be suicide to draw attention to himself. In any case, he had no plan for what he would do when, or if, he actually found Kyle.

He reached the north-east side of the hill, still outside the fort's wall, and paused by a thicket to take stock. Keeping flat, he peered towards the harbour, straining his ears to pick up the slightest whisper of movement. Breathing shallowly, so as not to reveal his own position, he was about to press on when he heard a shuffle then a shout.

'Stay where you are,' came a gruff, vaguely familiar voice about twenty yards ahead.

Phil's heart hammered and, instinctively, he flattened even further. He craned his neck in vain to glimpse where the command had come from. He heard some muffled shouts, then, 'Stop, all of you. Stand still or I'll shoot.'

Phil instantly knew from that threat: this was not the police, and now he was trapped. Whatever was happening round the curve of the hill would come his way if he made a move.

*

'Stay where you are.'

The shout froze Bob in his tracks for a second then, regaining his purpose, he shouted to Kyle and the three casualties. 'Keep moving, head for that shack over there,' he told them, pointing to a run-down wooden shed that looked like it had once been a winch-house.

Kyle ran first, leaving Bob to gather up their injured charges.

'Stop, all of you. Stand still or I'll shoot,' came the voice again. Kyle froze in his tracks. The others followed suit.

They were trapped. Bob could make a solo bolt for freedom, or at least give it a damn good try – but how would he live with himself if, as he fled, he heard the inevitable executions that would follow?

'Hands in the air. It's over.'

The weaker two sobbed as Kyle made his way back to the group. Oli remained motionless.

Two figures scurried down the hill towards them, handguns outstretched in double grips. Bob locked eyes with the man on the right.

'Chris?' he said, a snatch of pleading intruding into his tone.

Chris faltered, looking confused.

'No loose ends, Crush,' said Doug.

Crush looked at his boss, then at his surrendering lover.

'Crush, kill them.'

'Chris, don't do this,' urged Bob, seeing him faltering.

Chris's gun dropped ever so slightly as he stood silent.

'Crush, do it.' Doug's anger was bubbling.

Chris was shaking now.

Bob could see Doug was more focused on Chris than on them. If he wasn't, he could have taken them all out.

'Chris had no idea what I was doing. He thought I just needed something after prison. All the blame is mine,' said Bob.

'You're lying. You're in this together,' said Doug, his gun now aimed at Crush.

'No,' muttered Chris.

The gunshot stunned Bob. Then he dashed forward, unsure whether to tend to Chris or floor the man who had killed him in cold blood. He chose the latter, raging at what he had just done, what he had been doing over the last few months, and what he had done to the handful of captives Bob had saved and the dozens he couldn't.

He went for the gun first, intent on depriving him of any more victims. He grabbed his right wrist and used his whole body weight and momentum to jerk it upwards.

Doug swung out a foot, catching Bob on the calf. He stumbled, dragging Doug down with him as he fell, still clamping his wrist. As they grappled together, Bob only had his feet and head to fight with. Doug managed to land an excruciating kidney punch.

Bob's reflexes let him down and he relaxed his grip enough for Doug to break his gun hand free. Registering the danger, Bob rolled away, keeping flat but moving.

Just then a female voice froze Doug. 'Stay where you are.'

His head spun round to see Helen, gun in one hand and the other rubbing her streaming eyes, chasing Jo down the hill. Poorly aimed shots rang out from Helen's pistol as Jo weaved, still gripping her pepper spray cannister. In the confusion, Bob dashed to Chris's lifeless body and grabbed his gun.

Doug glanced back, and his face turned to terror as he saw Bob approaching, arms outstretched.

Doug looked defeated as Bob closed in.

'Kyle,' came a shout from above the hill. All heads turned in horror as Phil sprinted down the hill towards his son.

'Dad, get back,' Kyle shouted, as Doug recovered and shifted his aim to the reunion happening away to his left.

Phil ignored his son's pleas, sprinting off the hill and across the road that divided them.

Doug followed, now firing indiscriminately towards Phil and Kyle.

Jo raced down towards Doug.

'Phil, Kyle. Get down!' she yelled, as she neared her target.

Bob shouted, 'Out of the way, let me get a clear shot,' but Jo lunged on. She had only yards to go but Doug was so fixed on father and son, he was unaware.

Helen had circled Jo and was charging towards her, the gun in her hands, but not firing. Had she run out of rounds or was she biding her time? Jo pressed on, her only thought to save Phil and Kyle.

Jo created a gap, allowing Bob line of sight. A perfect headshot crumpled Doug Robinson where he stood. Jo fell on his body and grabbed the gun from his twitching hands, rolling over and back to a seating position to face the advancing chief constable. A shot rang out and, in one movement, her Liberia training coming to the fore, Jo raised the pistol and fired off three perfectly grouped rounds into Helen Ricks's chest.

45

Phil and Kyle slumped against a wall, sobbing in each other's arms.

'Why, Kyle?'

'Why do you think? He was a shit, whatever you thought of him.'

'What are you on about?'

'He owed our dealer, big time.'

'You're not making any sense.'

'The same bloke who I bought my skunk off sold him his steroids. You know about them, yes?'

Phil nodded.

'He was coming on heavy, but because of the bloody football club, he couldn't get close to Harry. So he transferred the debt to me. When I told Harry he just laughed and said he wouldn't pay.'

'So?'

'I worked it out that if I killed him, his football mates would set up a fucking Just Giving page and we'd be in the money. I'd pay them from that.'

'But he's your brother. How could you? I'd have paid them off for you.'

'As if, Mr whiter-than-white divisional commander.'

Phil just stared at his son, unable to believe what he was hearing. He tried to embrace him, but Kyle shrugged him off.

'Oh, Kyle. What have you done? What have I done?'

*

The stomp of the approaching reinforcements provided Jo with some relief that Gary Hedges would now be able to regain control over this war zone. She was confident they were all safe now.

As she walked up to Phil and Kyle, she spotted three crumpled wrecks, cowering by an abandoned car. She did a double take as she recognised one.

'Oli?' she asked. 'What the hell happened to you?'

He started to cry. She knelt down beside him and took him in her arms. 'It's OK. You're safe now. Were you in there?' she asked, pointing behind him towards the fort.

He nodded, wiping tears and snot away with his rag of a sleeve.

'You've got to tell us all about it. You know that, don't you?'

He nodded again.

'And the truth this time.'

'Yep, the truth,' he sniffed.

She stepped away as two firearms medics walked up to check the three over.

'Arrest him on suspicion of murder and burglary,' she told one of the officers.

With a leaden heart she made her way over to Phil and Kyle, who were now sitting silently looking out to the harbour.

'Thank you so much, Jo. You and Bob saved our lives. How can I ever thank you? I owe you everything. How about—'

'Phil, stop talking.' She turned to Kyle. 'Kyle, I'm arresting you for the murder of Harry Cooke. You do not have to say anything, but it may harm your defence if you do not mention when questioned something which you later rely on in court. Anything you do say may be given in evidence.'

'Jo, do you have to do this now?' Phil pleaded.

Ignoring him, she turned to face him. 'Phil. I'm arresting you for conspiracy to murder Kyle Cooke. You do not have to say anything, but it may harm your defence if you do not mention when questioned something which you later rely on in court. Anything you do say may be given in evidence.'

She turned to see two firearms officers approach. She nodded to them and, wordlessly and with regret in their eyes, they handcuffed their former mentor, boss and PCC, and his son.

Jo walked away, not wanting either to see the tears in her eyes. She found Bob crouching over Chris's body. She knelt down beside him, hugged him tight then whispered, 'I'm here Bob,' as both wept helplessly, lost in their own private and shared grief.

46

Three weeks later

It had come as a shock for Jo to discover that the bodies were being incinerated just yards from her home.

As a child she had visited the British Engineerium on the west side of Hove Park on many a school trip. Engineering wasn't really her thing, but she'd marvelled how this eighteenth-century pumping station could draw up twelve million litres of clean drinking water a day from the chalk hill on which it sat and distribute it to the far corners of Brighton and Hove. It had closed in the 1950s but remained, until recently, one of the city's quirkiest museums. As a near neighbour, she was used to seeing the twenty-nine-metre chimney spew out its smoke as the boilers were brought to steam, keeping the beautifully preserved machinery working.

Little did she know that recently it had been the vapour of human beings that she saw thrown into the sky.

She arranged to meet DI Bob Heaton at her house and the two of them ambled across the Hove Park, wondering whether this visit was a good idea. It was the first time they had been allowed in following the horrific discovery of its use. Once the Yates and Thom furnaces had cooled from their 1,100-degree Celsius heat, the crime scene manager Dean Gartrell and his team had toiled for night and day in the languid heat, sifting the sooty remains.

'Have you heard Phil and Kyle are pleading guilty?' Jo asked Bob.

'I should fucking hope so,' he replied. 'What about Oli Willis for killing Len Bradley in the fire?'

'Denying it, apparently.'

'So I might have to give evidence of what he said to Chris?'

'Looks that way.'

Bob shook his head. He'd hoped he could leave all that behind him, but in his heart knew he couldn't.

'How didn't we know about this place?' asked Jo, trying not to make it sound like a slight on him.

'How would we, ma'am? No one but the boilerman comes up here these days and he certainly wasn't going to tell us. The grand-a-time arrangement he had to stuff the boxes into the fires along with the coal, no questions asked, was more than enough to buy his silence.'

Jo shrugged. The last few weeks had taught her that people would go to any lengths for their own ends. She shuddered every time she thought of what Phil and Kyle were going through in prison on remand. And for what?

She felt nothing for Helen Ricks. The helicopter footage had exonerated Bob and her quickly and, with the senior echelons of the force either dead or in jail, the acting PCC was keen to get her back to work. Thankfully she'd persuaded Bob to do the same.

'How many bodies do they think were cremated here?' she asked.

'They don't reckon they'll ever know,' replied Bob. 'Apparently it would have needed about three packing boxes per person to get them into the furnace, and the suppliers say they provided 150 over three months. So, about fifty?' Bob estimated as they stepped off the park into the Droveway.

'Jeez. That's five times the number we saved,' said Jo, aware they had only traced a dozen or so families of those likely to have been dismembered and brought here. Few were a loss to society but all were someone's brother, son, father or partner.

Wayne Tanner, the domestic bully who was snatched at Ditchling Beacon having been bailed, was one of the few to be identified by a nipple ring. Jo kicked herself that she'd not looked closer into his disappearance when the file briefly crossed her desk all those months ago. The three bankers from the Ragged Smuggler were almost certainly among the ashes too, but other than a few bone fragments and scraps of jewellery the thieving thugs at the fort had missed, there was precious little found to link to anyone.

They spotted the uniformed officer guarding the gates, and both instinctively reached for their warrant cards as they approached.

'Chief Superintendent Howe and DI Heaton to see Dean Gartrell.'

'Can you suit up while I call him please, ma'am, sir,' said the officer, as she handed them full forensic barrier suits. They did as they were told and, once clad head to toe in white, waited.

It took Dean five minutes to saunter up and another twenty to show them round. Knowing what atrocities had been inflicted here robbed Jo of her wondrous childhood memories. It was the perfect location, though. Not isolated, but that was its strength. No one batted an eyelid at articulated lorries trundling round here day and night. Not with a Waitrose supermarket and a small industrial estate yards away.

However, now she knew, she would never see those chimneys or imagine those coal holes in the same innocent light again. Dean explained to her how they thought the boxes were dropped through the trapdoors and heaved into the fires, the body parts surviving for no longer than thirty seconds in the inferno.

She had never been more grateful when her ringing phone provided her the excuse to step outside.

'Jo Howe,' she replied, with an upward inflection to the unknown caller.

'Jo, it's Stuart Acers.'

She paused.

'Used to be ACC? You remember.'

'Yes, of course.' Should she call him 'sir'? 'How can I help you?'

'You've not heard, then? I've been appointed as acting chief constable and I'd rather like you in my office, eight o'clock tomorrow morning. I take it that's convenient.'

'Of course . . . sir,' she mumbled, any notion her life was about to get easier had just blown away in the wind.

ACKNOWLEDGEMENTS

When you've been faffing around with a novel as long as I have with *Bad for Good*, the challenge is working out who hasn't helped along the way rather than who has. Honestly, what you have just read has been years in the writing, re-writing, crying over and laughing at and without all those listed here, and many I'm sure I will have forgotten, you'd never have met Jo Howe and I would never have realised my dream.

First up must be my very close friend, mentor and erstwhile co-author, Peter James. A huge thank you for having the courage to write two non-fiction books with me then to give me the confidence (and sometimes blunt feedback in the most silken of gloves) to venture alone into the world of fiction, holding my hand all the way. You're an absolute gent!

Next comes my world-class agent, David Headley. Thank you for not only believing in me as a writer but in the Jo Howe series as a concept. It's not your average crime fiction, after all. I am honoured that someone whose days clearly have twice the hours of normal mortals took me on, dealt with my many insecurities and found the perfect publishers for me.

That brings me smoothly to Susie Dunlop, Claire Browne, Lesley Crooks, Daniel Scott, Christina Griffiths and Christina Storey at Allison and Busby, my publishers. Susie's reaction when she first read the book knocked me out cold and everyone else's passion and belief at A & B since has made for one of the most humbling experiences of my life. Then there's Helen Richardson, of Helen Richardson PR, who has worked miracles at getting *Bad for Good* noticed in the congested crime fiction world. Anouche Newman and Dani Brown at Socialdaze, who I've worked with for a couple of years have been incredible at making sure my social media contains so much more than rants and breakfasts, and have brought me to new audiences.

Now all the people who have read and advised on *Bad for Good*, or just given me a kick when I needed it. As well as Peter James and Deaglan (more of whom later) Isobel Dixon, Sian Ellis-Martin and Conrad Williams were invaluable in developing the structure, characters and beats, and showed incredible patience and wisdom in reviewing the many drafts they did. Michelle Frances and Sarah Barton, who were among the first outsiders to read it, fired me up with their reaction in a way they could never have anticipated. As did Mark Billingham, who spotted some glaring plot holes and clues, Kate Bendelow, Elly Griffiths, John Parsons and Samantha Brownley who all applied their laser eye to the manuscript and helped polish it to what it's become.

I'll never forget Dorothy Koomson's advice on the writing process; 'Just write the bl#3dy thing!' That became my mantra against procrastination (which I'm rather good at.) Erin Kelly's sage advice on how to bridge time gaps and not lose pace was something I'd have paid good money for, but she's never invoiced me. The John Yorke Story course, taken about three years after I needed it, dropped the penny of structure and character for me and, whilst it created yet another re-edit, spared my blushes.

I pride myself on providing other authors with advice so their novels are as authentic as possible, so it made sense for me to seek the same. I know what it's like to be a senior police officer but not a woman in that role. So, I was delighted when, in the early days, Lisa Bell took me into her world and how she became a divisional commander, then when retired ACC Di Roskilly, provided her guidance on the manuscript. Yes I did change that character's name Di, just as I promised. I had no idea how much harder it was for you than me. Mark Streater, for the price of a Costa coffee and flapjack, helped me understand a Police and Crime Commissioner's world and Steve Voice, for nothing as I recall, put me straight on weaponry and firearms tactics. Former Chief Inspector John Rodway and John Jolly were incredibly generous in pointing out how my means of extermination wouldn't work so introduced me to the British Engineerium and the carnage I could wreak there. Thanks too to Anne Marie Chebib of Select Security and Stewarding and Matt Robinson of Beacon Security for showing me how legitimate companies work in their sector so I could work out how the naughty ones might operate.

Finally, and this is because I want these people ringing in your ears, is my family. My wife, soul mate and best friend, Julie, and my triplets Conall, Niamh and Deaglan – together with Murphy, our dog who rules the roost – have been the most incredible support I could have wished for. Each – except Murphy – have read and re-read the book (Deaglan's eye for detail is far from healthy by the way) but more so, they have given me unending support, encouragement, love and coffee to make me stick to the task, suck up the editorial notes and do something I never thought I'd be able to do; write a bl#3dy book!

I owe you all the world and am utterly blessed to have you.

Graham Bartlett
Sussex 2022

Leabharlanna Fhine Gall

GRAHAM BARTLETT was a police officer for thirty years and is now a best-selling writer. He rose to become chief superintendent and the divisional commander of Brighton and Hove police. He entered the Sunday Times Top Ten with his first non-fiction book, *Death Comes Knocking*, which he later followed with *Babes in the Wood*. Both these books he co-wrote with international bestseller, Peter James. As well as writing, Bartlett is a police procedural and crime advisor helping scores of authors and TV writers achieve authenticity in their drama.